D0755178

TRIANGLE

TRIANGLE

a novel by
TED RHODES

from the BBC-TV
series created by
TED RHODES
and BILL SELLARS

based on scripts
written by
Michael Armstrong
Luanshya Greer
Sue Lake
Leslie Elizabeth Thomas

British Broadcasting Corporation

Published by the
British Broadcasting Corporation
35 Marylebone High Street
London W1M 4AA

ISBN 0 563 17926 0

First published 1981

© British Broadcasting Corporation 1981

Printed in England
by Love & Malcomson, Redhill, Surrey

Chapter 1

Hotel Bergmann
Gothenburg
Sweden

12th September '80

Dear Mr Parker,

      Thank you so much for having such great faith in me, and in particular, for your help and encouragement before, during, and after my interview. I am extremely grateful and am delighted to have been given the contract.

I look forward to joining the ship later this month at Felixstowe. Rest assured that should I experience any difficulties due to the strangeness of my new surroundings, I will most certainly take up your kind offer of help. I'm sure though, it will not be necessary.

      Once more my thanks,
      Yours sincerely,

    (signed)
      Katherine M. Laker

P.S. I'm sorry I couldn't meet you for dinner.

Kate folded up the letter and slid it into its envelope, licking the gummed flap with a finality that would have made Arthur Parker cringe if he had seen her. The last thing she wanted at the start of a new job was a senior member of the hierarchy hounding her. He might find out after all what she had successfully concealed from him.

She placed the envelope in her bag ready for posting, and looked round the hotel room for what she hoped was the last time. It had been an interesting week in Sweden. She had combined shopping with pleasure, and business. The old saw 'Never combine business with pleasure' was dead and proven dead as far as she was concerned. Just one more day, then back to England, clear up a few irritating problems, then start the new job and put Phase One of her plan into action.

Dressing carefully in her new clothes she looked at herself in the full-length mirror. Although she was by no means vain, she was forced to admire herself, face and figure. She knew she had got 'it' and though she might never actually flaunt it, she was definitely going to use it.

'It's a new life for me from now on,' she said aloud to herself in the mirror, as she put the final touches to her make-up. 'I'm going to make life obey me, instead of me being its slave.'

Down the elevator and into the streets of Gothenburg for a quick final shopping spree to celebrate, partly her success, but mainly because she found the smartness of the shops irresistible, and her London flat was a perfect little showplace for her collection of Swedish glass. The apartment had been designed by Kate herself specifically for her collection, and as she bought a rather attractive piece, she almost instantly felt a wave of homesickness, longing to see it on one of her shelves. Only one more hour and she would be on the plane to London. She could hardly wait. Armed with the glasses, she went back to the hotel to collect her suitcases.

Kate really did seem to have the best of two worlds. She was headstrong, temperamental and beautiful, all qualities inherited from her mother, and at the same time sensible, level-headed and intelligent with good business acumen inherited from her father. At a time like this, when other people would have been rushing for taxis to take them to the airport, she thought it quite natural to go leisurely shopping. And what could be more natural than to use this time to buy something beautiful?

Back in the street with her suitcases, she posted the letter to Arthur Parker and coolly caught a taxi. She settled down in the back seat as it drove through the countryside, too rocky to grow anything but the odd tree and too familiar to her to bother watching it as it slid swiftly by. Every now and then the rocky sides of the road gave way to tantalising vistas of lakes with houses dotted around them and little pleasure boats moored or bobbing on the water. A fascinating peepshow to a visitor, but she had once lived in a house just like the ones on the lakes. A beautiful stone and timber house that her father owned. It had wide, wide views of the lake and the hills beyond and it had been like a prison to her. A prison run by her father, too busy making money to notice that her mother was steadily drinking her life away. A prison from which she simply had to escape and incur

8

the wrath, once she had made the break, of her unyielding parent. The perpetual silence between her mother and father, the gliding domestics, and the cold stretch of water on the one side, with the stark granite rock on the other, made the beautiful house a joyless and sinister place for her.

She was glad she was leaving Sweden. She had given up her job in Stockholm in spite of the management's entreaties to her to stay and in spite of the extremely generous offer they had made. No, she had to accept the job Arthur Parker had offered her with his company Triangle Lines. A shipping line in which she had more than a passing interest. If only Arthur Parker had known he wouldn't have been quite so quick off the mark with his offer of dinner. Kate had despised him. She was sick to death of handsome people who thought their attractiveness was all they needed. God, she'd really had enough of them. She'd worked hard and successfully for a very long time to get to the position she now enjoyed and with the prospect of the new job in front of her she was not, ever again, going to let any man think she was his prey.

The first thing she did to start anew was to telephone Michael, and he, typically, invited her out to dinner. They went to a small quiet restaurant that had always been a favourite with them.

Michael sensed that something momentous had either happened or was about to, but he bided his time and waited for her to tell him. Dinner was perfect as usual and the conversation was mostly small talk. At coffee however Kate drew a long breath and started, as she thought, at the deep end.

'I'm taking a new job,' she said.

Privately Michael thought 'Is that all?' but he remained attentive and silent.

'With Triangle Line.'

Now it was Michael's turn to draw a long breath. This woman really was extraordinary.

'Why Triangle? I thought you hated it.'

Kate ignored the question.

'And because I will be away most of the time, I suppose what I'm really saying is "Goodbye".' She stared at her coffee cup. This was wretched but she had to go on. 'Michael, I have never felt that we really belonged to each other, and ever since Laker and I parted — well, I've felt uncomfortable . .'

'You didn't feel uncomfortable with me before you parted from

9

Alex,' said Michael. 'I always felt, I think we both did, that I was just what you needed then.'

Kate almost blushed. He was right of course, she had needed him then. She felt callous and cold, but still she was determined nothing was going to stand in her way.

'Things have changed,' she said. 'And particularly since last week. Ever since I went for that interview with Triangle I've known exactly what I've wanted to do . . . Must do,' she added.

'And does that mean a definite break . . . Even from me?'

Kate stirred her coffee. If only she could look at him, eye to eye, with the honesty she felt she ought to be able to muster. She decided quite deliberately that she couldn't and wouldn't. This was a trait in her father's character too, but in her case it made her more attractive to men even though it exasperated them. The same trait in her father caused his business associates to quit all competition. They could both be single-minded, and that was that.

'Definite,' he said.

They sat in silence for a full minute. It was Michael who finally broke that silence.

'Why do you think that working with Triangle is going to keep us further apart than we were when you were working in Sweden?'

'I'll need to remain on the ship. I don't intend to make any more flying visits to London, and I don't intend to leave for long enough, to start with at least, for something to go wrong behind my back.'

'I repeat, why Triangle?'

'Because I hate Terson,' she said quietly.

'How can you possibly hope to get back at him, or whatever it is you want to do, by joining his shipping line?'

'I'm not exactly joining his shipping line, as you put it. I'm still a major shareholder in it, and he's getting old, and . . .' her voice tailed off.

Michael sipped his coffee and waited.

'I'm determined to make a success of it, and nothing is going to stand in my way. Nothing,' she said finally.

Michael searched for something to say, something that would hold her back in what seemed to him a headlong flight away from him. Michael loved her. He knew she had had a raw deal from life but he had hoped he would be able to shield her from more disappointments. Suddenly it all seemed as though she was determined to wreck everything, and probably go hurtling down that same path that had led her to him, unhappy all the way until they'd met. Perhaps not a path that had threaded its way through all her life, for there had been periods of happiness for her. There had been her first husband. Kate rarely discussed him. Michael guessed that his death had been a deep shock to her, one from which even now she hadn't recovered. What little she had told him about her first husband was however volumes compared to what she had said about her second. The only thing he knew for certain was that they were still married and this was a source of irritation to him. She was a very beautiful woman and he wanted her to be his wife. All right, he would be her third husband, so what? He didn't care. He knew they could be happy together and he wanted more than anything to protect her, share his life with her until they were Darby and Joan, and now it seemed all his hopes were being dashed by this crazy scheme of hers to get even with Terson somehow. It didn't make sense to him at all.

'What happens if you don't make a success of it?' he finally asked.

'Oh, but I shall,' she said, with such conviction that his blood turned to ice. He knew at that precise moment that he was going to lose her. Her ambition to succeed, as she had often proved in the past, was greater than any hold he could ever hope to have. Even love was sure to fail in the face of it.

'Your hatred of Terson is greater than your love for me then,' he said simply.

'It's not exactly hatred,' she said ignoring the second part of his statement. 'It's a chance to show him that I'm as good as he is any day.' Then with a short laugh she added, 'A chip off the old block!'

Michael had heard a good deal about her father although he had never met him. George Terson was a really big deal. Rich, successful and, Michael thought privately, for all the wealth and respect he commanded, suitably unhappy. Money and position had not bought him a happy marriage with Kate's mother, and though Michael thought Terson should be delighted with his beautiful but determined daughter, they rarely contacted each other. Whatever it was that had created the rift between them was something that Kate kept to herself. She never referred to him as her father, always as 'Terson', as though it made her able to cope with the fact that he was a stranger in her life, instead of a close relation.

'Well, then,' said Michael with a touch of finality in his voice, 'As you are determined to go ahead with it, I see no point in prolonging pain. We ought to say goodbye now.'

'You don't hate me?'

'You know I don't, nor ever could. Promise me one thing.'

'What?'

Was that a little quick and suspicious? Michael decided it probably wasn't. 'If you ever need me, I want you to know without any question of doubt, I will be here, waiting, and at your service.' Then, for the first time during the length of the meal, that had really caused him distress, he laughed easily.

Kate was very relieved. She realised that she had hurt him, and for that she was genuinely sorry, but he hadn't taken offence, for which she was grateful, and she knew that their relationship, though henceforward, distant, was actually as steady as a rock. They caught separate taxis and parted.

She made the long, dull drive to the docks alone. Ahead the road seemed interminable, like all motorways do, but at the end . . . At the end was her new life. An exciting life that she was determined she would absolutely organise. After all she had spent the best part of her life arranging other people's affairs, their business problems and their petty private problems. A hotel manageress, a tour organiser, and finally chief officer for the international chain of hotels that she had just left. Now she was definitely and deliberately on her own and determined to make a go of it. There was the new job, an exciting prospect in that it entailed largely working with men. And with men she had always had the whip hand.

She thought about Bill as she drove along. Dear kind, sweet Bill. What would her life be like now if he had lived? And she thought about Alex, her second husband. He had seemed so considerate, had taken over Bill's place in her heart, and he had been such a pig . . . .

She turned off the motorway onto the slip-road that took her to the docks. The scenery was turning industrial now; cranes and tall buildings had taken the place of fields and farmhouses.

She drove onwards to the quayside. There before her lay the Triangle Line ship. This was to be her floating hotel, her delight or otherwise, and ultimately . . .?

It was huge. Much larger than she had remembered. Cars were being loaded and passengers were milling around everywhere. Men in orange work-clothes were organising the loading of various freight. They all looked super-efficient.

She looked at the ship and tried to make out from the exterior some of the various places she had seen years before and had read about in the brochures Arthur Parker had so thoughtfully sent to her. Where would the sun-deck be? And the swimming pool? That of course would only be able to be seen from the air. The various bars and the night-club she could dimly make out as the window blinds were partly closed but . . . She stopped herself. 'Enough of this,' she told herself. 'I'm not actually here for the ride but much more important things, myself being one of them.' She tried to suppress her natural excitement at the prospect of actually setting sail within the hour. The sea was definitely in her blood, and everytime she actually embarked on a ship, was as exciting as the first time.

She parked the car and dragged out her luggage. Of course there wasn't a porter in sight. She made a mental note to do something about that as she commandeered a metal trolley and pushed her way towards the passenger check-in point. After what seemed an eternity, but really was quite short, she went to the embarkation point, presented her passport, and was on board!

Her cabin was much more glamorous than she had remembered. Obviously the whole ship must have been refurbished. It had a shower in the neat little bathroom, a bunk which folded away to make the place more roomy, and a pleasant decor with original children's paintings on the walls. The cabin could obviously be used for straight entertaining, or as a very tiny practical flat for the duration of the voyage; she found this aspect of it intriguing.

She decided it was time to explore and see just how many more changes had taken place since Triangle had converted from freight and ferry to luxury cruiser. With this in mind, she changed her clothes, dressing in something she thought, if not more comfortable, at least a little more alluring, and then set off.

Pushing her way through knots of passengers who all seemed to be stupidly lost, she made her way up onto the decks that were reserved for entertainment. To say the least they were spacious and extremely attractive. The restaurant, for example, was enormous and beautifully laid out. She hadn't expected anything like this. In fact, she didn't know quite what she had expected but the sheer luxury of the whole made her gasp. A West End hotel floating in the middle of the North Sea! She was very impressed. Terson, damn him, had done it again.

She entered the bar, a huge affair with a place for a band and a dance floor and, ordering an orange juice from the barman, moved with it to a table near a window. With only a slight shudder the ship started to move and once more she felt the thrill of that first moment of setting sail. She watched fascinated, as the coastline moved slowly and silently past the window, until the ship turned and headed for the open sea, then as thoughts of Bill, of Alex, of Michael, swam through her mind she decided to return to her cabin.

To get there she had to pass the shops. Whereas when she had boarded the ship the shops had all been closed, now they were a hive of activity. There was a cash point, where travellers' cheques could be cashed and all types of foreign money exchanged, a kiosk for small items like cigarettes and razor blades and so forth adjacent to both the main shop and boutique. She was pleased to note that the majority of goods on display were not the usual tourist gimmicks. There were, of course, liquor, sweets and tobacco in great profusion, but there were also, it seemed to her, some rather good items. Swedish glass for instance. Dutch, Danish, Norwegian and Finnish items that were not often seen in London shops. 'I suppose it's because the ship visits Scandinavia so often,' she thought.

In the boutique there was much that held her attention. French perfumes, things she had always had a weakness for, as well as gold, silver, watches, cameras, binoculars . . . How she wished she were one of those women who could tell at a glance whether or not a gold trinket on display was a bargain. No, she had always let her heart rule her head and had never considered the value of anything. Just the value she herself had put on it.

It was then that a tiny gold aeroplane caught her eye. It was a brooch, and the plane it had been modelled on was an old-fashioned wartime Hurricane.

She took a deep breath. An aeroplane! Was she absolutely mad? Every time she looked at it she would think of Bill. Still she felt that she absolutely had to buy it, wear it even. She shuddered. 'I'll pin it to something I hardly ever wear and then I won't need to look at it too often,' she thought.

At that moment she caught her expression in the mirror and was appalled. 'Is that what you've come to?' She looked again. 'Yes, you're hard. Bill wouldn't know you . . .' She studied her face for a moment.

'Perhaps it's as well.' she thought. She refused to think of the days after Bill had been killed, and she had cried as though she would never stop. Of the total horror of his death. Of her own heartbreak . . .

'I'd like the tiny gold aeroplane, please.' she said to the assistant.

She paid for the brooch and looked at it in the palm of her hand. Silly. How silly to buy something like that. She put it in her handbag and left the shop.

Kate took the lift to the top deck, sharing it with a creamy-faced youth she chose to ignore. Once on deck in the cool breeze, she looked at the brooch once more. In her hand it glinted in the sun, and against the torrent of green sea water that was pouring past in the background, her hand looked paralysed. How tiny the little aeroplane looked! Just as Bill's plane had looked after it crashed. She had always thought aeroplanes to be big things — after all you could stand under their wings and look up into the sky past the propellers, but after Bill had crashed, when she went to look at the wreckage, it all looked ridiculously small, like a child's broken toy . . . And there in the middle of it all was the place where Bill had been . . . had been . . . She threw the brooch into the sea.

'Didn't you want that, Miss?'

She looked up. The creamy-faced youth was staring at her with a blank but riveted expression.

'No I didn't,' Katherine answered, wishing he would go away.

'You could have given it to me then,' said the youth, 'I would have liked it.'

'I liked it myself,' said Kate. 'Why should I give it to you?'

'Why throw it away?' countered the youth, and with a look of accusation, he stalked off.

Kate drew a sigh of relief. If he ever came near her again she would avoid him like the plague. He looked as though he knew why she had done what she had done.

Chapter 2

The sun-deck reserved for the exclusive use of officers and crew was reached by taking the lift eight flights up. As soon as Kate stepped out she felt swamped by the sun's heat. That, at any rate, was a relief. For what she was going to do she needed all the help she could get.

She could see the bridge a little higher up, with its wide windows that looked down onto the sun-deck. Through them were clearly visible two men she recognised as the Chief Engineer and the Chief Navigation Officer. Kate slackened the hand that was holding a bath-towel loosely around her, allowing it to drop slightly open, so that the two watching officers could get their first hint of the truth — that she was wearing nothing underneath. Satisfied that she had their full, fascinated attention, she stopped in her tracks, laid the towel flat on the deck and dropped, face downwards onto it. She would have given anything to overhear the conversation of the two men; on the other hand she felt she could work most of it out for herself. She would have bet money, for instance, that one of them was saying to the other, 'Down boy!'

'Down boy!' said Charles Woodhouse, with a brief glance at Matt, sitting beside him. Chief Engineer Matt Taylor's womanising was so notorious that Charles felt sure the growl he had emitted was partly mechanical. Not that it wasn't justified, Charles conceded as he studied the beautiful naked back that had been presented for their inspection. With four years of happy marriage behind him Charles still had an eye for a good thing. In fact the only real difference between himself and Matt was that Matt, with no marriage, offered a good thing the homage of both eyes.

'Wonder what it's like topsides,' Charles mused aloud.

'I'll find out.' Matt prepared to go, but was halted by the sudden appearance of Captain John Anderson, a pleasant-faced man in his forties.

'A word, Matt,' he said.

'Wouldn't bother, John,' Charles told his Captain. 'He's on an inquiry.'

The Captain, who permitted this informal address out of hearing of the passengers, followed Charles's eye towards what could be seen of Kate. Not a flicker of expression showed on his face.

'What is the nature of your inquiry?' he demanded of Matt in what was meant to be an official-sounding voice.

'Unless you know who she is — that, sir.'

John dropped the official mask with comic abruptness. 'Can't say it's familiar, no,' he admitted, giving the matter his full attention.

'Not crew,' said Matt.

'You'd know if she was, of course.' John hoped his voice sounded more disapproving than he felt. As Captain he was compelled to take a stern view of potentially disruptive elements, and Matt's way of going through the girl crew-members like a hot knife through butter was undoubtedly that. As a man, however, Captain Anderson could not repress a slight twinge of envy. He was devoted to his beautiful Swedish wife, Maya, but he could clearly remember that in his bachelor days, when he had been about Matt's age, no-one had ever accused him of being a disruptive element; a fact which still caused him some nostalgic regret.

'I'll go and find out what she thinks she's doing there,' said Matt.

In a moment he was standing beside Kate. Unexpectedly his approach did not make her look up, so that he had a grandstand view of the superb gleaming back that swelled into firm round buttocks before tapering away into slim legs. He gulped. It wasn't fair.

'How do you do,' he said.

She looked up at him with a blank, uncomprehending smile. With one part of his mind Matt took in that her face matched the rest of her. With another part he registered that if she twisted round any more he was going to find out about the front as well. With a third part he made urgent calculations about how he wanted this situation to develop, and with the pathetic remnant that was left he tried to keep his thoughts on his job.

'Are you a passenger?' he tried again. But still there was nothing but that blank stare. 'This is a private area, you see. The crew's deck. Officers and crew . . . I'm afraid you'll have to leave . . . you are English?' he added helplessly.

Kate shook her head. To her delight Matt's face fell, and he cast a furious glance up at the bridge, where John and Charles were watching his discomfiture with unholy glee.

'Get her to stand up, you fool.' Charles muttered. In answer to

John's sharp look he added innocently, 'How else can he move her?'

Kate twisted a little further to look up at Matt. 'Svenska?' she queried.

'No.'

'Ah,' she infused a note of disappointment in her voice.

'You.'

She shook her head. Matt looked up again at the bridge. John and Charles were plainly riveted and this increased his irritation. He didn't like to be made to look a fool. After a moment he ventured to touch Kate's bare shoulder. When he had her attention he pointed to the stripes on his arm. In dumb show he tried to convey to her that his presence on the sun-deck was all right, while hers, in clothes or out of them, definitely wasn't. John and Charles enjoyed the whole performance hugely.

'She's getting the message,' said John, relieved.

'I bet she is,' Charles's eyes were glued to the sight of Kate twirling a finger to indicate for Matt to turn round as she was about to rise. In a flash John had shot out an arm and forced his Chief Navigation Officer to turn also. 'She said *him*,' Charles complained, his indignation slightly mitigated by the fact that John had also looked away.

Once on her feet, with the towel draped round her as loosely as she dared, Kate addressed Matt Taylor's back.

'What would you have done if I was Swedish, Mr Taylor?' she asked sweetly. ''Bye.'

She was gone before Matt could think of a reply, leaving him nothing to do but storm back to the bridge.

'Next time, *you* go,' he snapped to both of them equally.

'What happened?' Charles demanded, wheeling round.

'She was English. She knew my name.'

'Did you get *her* name is more to the point.'

'What would you have done if I was Swedish, Mr Taylor?' Matt mimicked savagely.

'Good point.' John was much struck.

'I felt that big.' Matt's hands indicated about a foot.

'Boasting again,' said Charles mournfully.

'How did she know my name?'

Charles stared at him and sighed. Some people never knew their luck.

The door to the Purser's Office opened onto the main deck, across which Kate had to pass on her way to the restaurant. She looked straight ahead of her, her brow furrowed with concentration for the next stage of her plan, so she never saw the young man just inside the office, nor the start he gave when he saw her, nor the hurried way he came to the door.

Peter Nuttall, the Assistant Purser, was in his middle twenties, with a handsome, sensitive face that right now was pale with shock. He stood at the office door watching the woman who had just gone by, trying to convince himself that it had been a mistake. As the tight-fitting slacks and white sweater vanished down the stairs he managed to convince himself that he'd been dreaming.

'Sorry - yes?' he said, startled suddenly.

He found himself looking directly into the eyes of Wally James, the Chief Purser, a genial-looking man of about sixty. Wally had appeared from nowhere and waved a hand in front of Peter's face.

'Where were you?' he chuckled.

'Thinking,' said Peter vaguely.

'Have you got the passenger list handy?'

'It's where it always is.' Wally stared into the young man's pale face. 'Are you sure you're all right?'

'Fine.' Peter managed to force a smile. 'Go get forty winks Grandad.'

It passed across his mind that Wally had looked poorly lately. But he supposed that was age. He stared at the passenger list, but didn't find the name he sought. The churning of his stomach eased a little. It had all been a mistake.

He'd been working mechanically for half an hour before the phone rang. It was the restaurant, urgently requiring the Purser's presence to cope with a recalcitrant passenger.

'He's resting. I'll come,' said Peter briefly.

He headed frenziedly for the door. Something was warning him that this was going to be his unlucky day after all. At the top of the stairs he almost collided with a pretty girl, dressed in the uniform of a chambermaid. He was too preoccupied to see how her face lit up at the sight of him.

'See you in a minute Sandy.'

'Peter? The flat's okay this weekend.'

He stopped and looked back at her.

'Fine,' he said, his mind elsewhere.

'Don't be so enthusiastic,' she pouted charmingly.

He managed a bright smile and a wink. 'But I'm crazy with desire. Just trying not to let it show. I've got to sort out some Egon Ronay passenger we seem to have acquired. Keep your knickers on till I get to your cabin.'

'Don't be filthy,' she giggled.

'That's what you love about me.'

He had already forgotten her by the time he reached the bottom stair. He had reached the restaurant in a moment, to be greeted by relieved waiters who pointed out to him a woman sitting at a table surrounded by plates and plates of untouched food. She seemed quite calm as she tasted first one dish then another, putting each one gently aside after the first swallow. This alone would have been bad enough. But to Peter Nuttall, the worst thing of all was that he recognised the woman as Kate Laker, a woman he had not seen for six years, and would have been quite happy never to see again.

'Oh boy, I might have known,' he muttered.

She looked up and smiled at his approach.

'Is there something wrong?' he asked politely. 'Was there nothing on the entire menu to your taste?'

'Shouldn't the Chief Purser have been sent?' she queried.

'Do you think we should have?'

'Yes.'

'Well unfortunately he doesn't walk in his sleep. But I'm sure I can help.'

She looked at him a moment before saying calmly, 'Not unless you've changed out of all recognition in the past six years.' Then she walked out of the restaurant.

He caught up with her outside.

'I'm afraid not,' he said coldly. 'Neither with nor without your help. Now, perhaps we can discuss your complaint.'

'It's nothing that can't be put right.' She walked on, but he stopped and called sharply,

'How's your father?'

She turned to him with a smile. 'How's yours?'

For a moment she thought he might lose control and hit her. But he merely said coldly, 'I imagine every member of this crew would be interested if they knew who you were.'

'I don't advise you to tell them. When the Purser has a minute I'd like to see him — in his office. Thank you for your help. Goodbye.'

Only when Kate had gone did Peter realise that Sandy had walked up beside him.

'Can't keep away from them, can you?' The words were only half a joke.

'Not as far as I'd like,' he said bitterly.

'You know her, don't you?' she detained him as he tried to brush past.

20

'Yes. But I don't believe in removing the bang from the cracker till it's pulled. Spoils the fun.'

She didn't understand him. Peter often said things she didn't understand, and that upset her because it reminded her of the unspoken barrier that was supposed to exist between officers and crew. Sometimes she felt that with Peter she could get past that barrier, and sometimes it seemed to stand as high as ever. It loomed very high now, and to cover her unease she fell back on familiar ground.

'From your past, of course. All over and done with.' She hated herself for sounding so possessive. She knew Peter disliked it, he'd told her so. But when her fear of losing him engulfed her, she couldn't help herself.

'You could say that,' he said.

'She'd better be,' she told him lamely.

Matt caught up with Kate in the ship's shopping area, not entirely by accident. She was picking up pieces of glass and putting them down again, as though unable to find anything she wanted. When she came out of the shop without having bought anything he fell into step beside her.

'Didn't you like anything?' he said.

'Not much. Lacks originality.'

'You're talking about me?' he said, rendered uncomfortable by the meaningful glance she had shot him.

'Was I?' her eyes were as innocent as a baby's.

'Were you? You like games, don't you Mrs Laker?' In answer to her raised eyebrows he went on, 'Fair's fair. You knew mine. Or is it Ms?'

'Ms?' she smiled straight into his eyes. 'I'm not a neutered bee Mr Taylor.'

'Hardly,' he agreed, running his eyes up and down her shape which managed to look almost as good fully clothed. 'Miss then?'

'A near one. But full marks for trying.' She gave him the full brilliance of her smile before turning to go. 'Since you know my name, you probably know my cabin number. 'Bye.'

He watched her retreating rear with pleasure. Honour was satisfied. The morning's by-play had merely been a move in the game. And he was always game.

Captain Anderson returned early to his quarters that night. He wasn't feeling like company. During the day the Radio Room had made repeated attempts to put a call through to his home in

England, and their failure ever to get an answer depressed him more than he felt it should. He missed Maya and he missed his two children desperately. Sometimes the need to hear one of their voices shook him in its intensity. Today had been one of those days, but he supposed he'd have to go without.

He tried to remember back to the man he'd been sixteen years ago when there had been no Maya and no children. He'd had an extended leave and had decided to use it to have a holiday in Sweden. Already he'd been doing the North Sea runs, a Navigation Officer who'd just won his master's ticket, ambitious for his own ship. He'd been day-dreaming about just that when he cannoned into a lovely young Swedish girl on an escalator in Stockholm. They had clutched each other for support, and by the time they got off the escalator it seemed only natural to invite her for a drink by way of apology.

She'd listened, wide-eyed, to his dreams and plans and afterwards he couldn't remember having told her anything. All he could remember was her curtain of golden hair that waved softly every time she turned her head towards him attentively. Three months later they had been married, Maya was installed in a small house in England, seemingly contented with the fate that had transported her to another country and married her to a man she barely ever saw, and John was blessing his luck.

In his eyes the intervening years had hardly changed her. He knew he had aged faster. The sea, and especially the North Sea, was not kind to looks. It toughened and browned them. His brown eyes were already beginning to look oddly brilliant against the tan of his skin; but his firm jaw-line, he was pleased to note, had held, and there wasn't an ounce of fat on his tall frame. That was another thing the sea did for you.

It forged friendships too. John counted himself lucky in Charles and Matt, both of whom he had found personally congenial from the start, as well as efficient at their jobs. Of the two he was slightly closer to Charles, mainly because Charles was the most like himself. Both happily married men, both slightly evangelical on the subject (to the undisguised hilarity of their randier unmarried colleagues) both yearning for the domestic hearth (and the domestic bed) when they were away from it. Both were fond of Matt; both regarded his amorous exploits with a kind of awed fascination; but they shared something in common that he lacked.

Looking at Charles, John often had an eerie feeling that he was seeing himself a few years earlier. Charles too was a Navigation

Officer in possession of a Master's Ticket, cherishing ambitious dreams. If there was a difference it lay in the happy-go-lucky streak in Charles's character that the more serious-minded John had never possessed. He did not lack a sense of humour, but the strain of flippancy that Charles could turn on at will, and which was usually brought out by Matt's presence, was not part of him.

When the knock came on his cabin door John gave a small irritated sigh as he opened his eyes, hoping his visitor would depart soon. The caller turned out to be Wally.

'It's about a passenger,' said Wally.

'They're your problem, and you can keep them.'

'A Miss Laker.'

Something Matt had said clicked in John's brain. 'Miss Laker wouldn't happen to be dark and rather —?' he made a shape with his hands.

'Yes,' said Wally at once.

'Wally, not you too.' John grinned.

'There's something about her.' Wally trailed off vaguely. He had no desire to go into details about the uncomfortable few minutes Miss Laker had given him earlier that day, when she had pointed out that there was no-one supervising the children in the play area. She had gone on to suggest that a ship that picked up passengers from Gothenburg and Amsterdam as well as Felixstowe might try a menu a little more varied than the solidly English one currently on offer.

'To be honest with you,' Wally went on, 'I think she's here to cause trouble.'

'And she's doing very well. Matt and Charles haven't been the same since they first saw her.'

'Company trouble I mean. She's wandering round the ship looking for everything she can find that's not to her liking. If they really do intend carrying out their plans to cut this as a passenger run, they've sent her to gain the ammunition.'

John stared at him. It was some time now since Triangle Lines' Head Office had been making noises about freight being more profitable than passengers.

'Then perhaps we should ask a few questions,' he said at last.

'You'll get nothing out of her.'

'I will out of Head Office. And I will out of her passport — which you're going to get me.'

From that point events moved in a way no-one had expected. Coward-like Wally delegated the task of 'borrowing' Kate's passport to his young assistant. There the buck stopped, as Peter Nuttall made it plain beyond a shadow of doubt that he wasn't going to appropriate the passport of George Terson's daughter.

Wally stared at him, thunderstruck. 'How do you know her?' he managed to say at last.

Peter's face closed tight. 'Sorry Wally, that's my business and not your problem.'

'That's a right turn up for the books. At least now we know what we're up against. The big chief sure dredges deep to get his own way.' He meant Terson.

'And she's just like him,' said Peter bitterly. 'Watch it - or they'll be dredging for you and all.'

He didn't see the look Wally gave him before turning away to the phone.

John, receiving Wally's call in his cabin, refused to believe his ears. When he was finally convinced that the bad news was true he gave a small, grim smile.

'Well,' he said, 'Arthur Parker really will get a nasty shock when they tell him she's overboard.'

Alone in her cabin Kate sat on the edge of her bed and reviewed the evening. It had been instructive in many ways, having been spent in the ship's night-club, where she'd made the acquaintance of one person she instinctively liked and one she didn't.

Not that she could have put her finger on anything specifically unlikeable about Tony Grant, the croupier. On the contrary, he had the full measure of smooth charm that his job demanded. Perhaps that was it. The measure was too full. It made you wonder what lay behind that good-looking face with the edges only just beginning to blur, and the tightly clad figure that was still successfully fighting the flab of the late thirties, but wouldn't for much longer.

He'd been all deference when Kate had won a large sum of money at the wheel, and walked off with it. But she'd turned her head just in time to catch a disgusted look on his face. Anyone would have thought it was his own money he was giving away.

Mentally Kate wrote off Tony Grant as a flash boy, too typical of his kind to be really interesting. She had more time to spare for Jo Bailey, the night-club singer, a professionally sultry, late-thirties blonde, who sang extremely well, if in a somewhat derivative manner. She had a good deal more talent than this job demanded, and Kate made a mental note to ask her some questions later. Her efforts to get Jo talking that night had met with no success. Jo had politely declined a drink with Kate in favour of taking one with Tony. The angle of her gleaming head as she leaned close to him had told its own story. Kate had made a mental note of that too.

Her eyes flickered towards the photograph beside the bed. It showed a pretty, eager-faced little girl, of about five, whose features clearly proclaimed her to be Kate's daughter. It had been taken a month before she died.

Kate wondered if she should put the picture out of sight for the coming encounter. It didn't accord with the image she'd been at pains to present to the man who ought to be knocking at her cabin door any time now — the image of a randy divorcee panting for anything in uniform. Everything else about her looked the part, right down to the glittering evening-style jump suit with the zip down the front that came open at a touch.

Kate decided to leave the picture where it was. Matt probably wouldn't see it. He'd arrive pleased with himself and ready for an easy conquest. Kate, a just woman, conceded that he probably had cause for his attitude. There couldn't be many women who wouldn't respond to the frank, genially careless sexuality that he carried with him like an aura. It had nothing to do with looks, although he had the looks as well of the classic dark, bron∕ed-skin variety that fitted his uniform so well it was almost a parody.

Kate had felt her own powerful flicker of electrified response the moment she'd looked up at him on the sun-deck that morning. Her mind had juggled with two thoughts at once - 'He oughtn't to be allowed out' and 'My God, if I wasn't naked already his eyes would have had it all off me by now.'

She had firmly suppressed her own reaction, although under other circumstances she would have enjoyed it. Instinct had told her that she could have Matt Taylor whenever she wanted, but then so could any woman. And one place Kate Laker didn't intend to stand in was a queue.

She knew who it was as soon as she heard the knock at the door, but still she called, 'Who is it?'

'Opportunity,' came Matt's voice from the other side.

She pulled it open and looked him up and down. 'Yours or mine I wonder?' she said.

It was there again, the pleasurable stirring deep down inside her, intensified by the look in his eyes that told her he was reacting the same way. This was going to be harder than she'd thought.

She stood back for him to come in, and closed the door.

'Do sit down,' she said.

He seated himself, watching a little puzzled as she sat opposite him and fixed him with a calm level gaze.

'You did expect?' he said at last. 'To?'

She nodded. He nodded back.

Unexpectedly he swivelled his eyes so that they fell on the picture of the little girl.

'Your daughter?'

'Yes.'

'She's pretty.'

'She's dead,' said Kate abruptly.

With a swift movement she seized the front zip of her jump suit and whipped it down. Matt was caught off guard, both by her abrupt announcement and the sudden revelation that she was naked beneath the suit. For a moment his mind balanced the two situations as he tried to decide which one to react to.

'I'm sorry,' he said at last. 'I didn't know.'

Somewhere far back Kate's mind registered a mark in his favour. The insensitive oaf that he might have been would never have bothered to say that with her breasts staring him in the face. But she allowed none of this approval to show.

'How could you?' she said. 'But you do know I am in the process of undressing. You can see that?'

'Yes.'

'And?'

'What do you expect me to say?'

'I don't know you well enough,'

'I like it?' he said hopefully.

'I'm glad one of us does.'

He stared at her blankly. He had not the slightest idea where he was in this conversation. He remembered having had the feeling before — that morning on the sun-deck.

'Do you want me to go?' he said at last.

'I would have preferred it if you'd never arrived. Shall I keep going?'

'With what?'

Kate shoved the shoulder of her jump suit down. The movement was so at variance with the cool look on her face that Matt could only scratch his head.

'What is this?' he said.

'It's called "difficult circumstances for an officer to explain away".'

A little snake of alarm began too crawl up his spine. 'Wait a minute — you asked me here.'

'Wrong,' her face was hard.

'You said you presumed I had your cabin number.'

'Right.'

'That was an invitation.'

'The Queen lives in Buckingham Palace. Do you drop in on her too?'

'Not my type.' he quipped lamely.

'All I have to do now is scream rape.'

'Then scream away,' he said, getting up and moving to the door. 'I've no intention of fulfilling your rape fantasies.'

'At this point the lady would scream louder.'

He stopped with his hand on the doorknob.

'What lady?'

'The one that could have been me. The one you've just rejected.' As he stared at her she zipped up the front of her suit and faced him.

'Do you always fall into traps so easily?'

'Traps?'

'A crook of the little finger isn't always a promise of happy times. Women don't like being rejected.'

'Now hang about. I didn't . . .'

'*She* thinks you did. She says you raped her.' Kate's eyes were relentless. 'So how do you intend to explain away your presence in my cabin to the captain?'

'You asked me.'

'I deny it.'

'Then you tried to seduce me — *she* did . . .'

'*She* denies it.'

'John will reckon that bit of zipping was seductive.'

'But I didn't unzip anything. You did.'

'You're crazy,' he said slowly.

'Aren't most women whose reason for taking a cruise is a bit of uniform?'

'I think I'll leave before the lady rips my uniform off.'

'That was next on the agenda.' As he turned an amazed stare on her she added, 'You don't usually keep it on, do you?'

'The million dollar question — do you want me to stay — uniform on or off?'

'I want you to go — uniform on, and a little wiser.'

He looked back as he opened the door. His gaze had something of the horror of a rabbit frozen by a snake.

'What do you do for the second house?' he managed to say.

She smiled. 'Strictly once nightly.'

He managed to smile back, although the muscles of his face felt petrified. Despite himself she had managed to convey a real sense of his danger to him.

'Would you mind closing the door behind you?' she asked sweetly.

'After you've saved me from a fate worse than death? But of course.'

He left Kate staring at the closed door, not sure whether to be glad or sorry.

In the Radio Room John Anderson was awaiting the results of his summons to Arthur Parker, Chief Personnel Officer for Triangle Lines. The news that Parker was on his way to the company's head office in Felixstowe drew from him a grunt of satisfaction.

'If I'd known the identity of that backside I'd have closed my eyes,' said Charles faintly.

'In reverence?' John asked.

'In terror. Where's Matt?' Charles gave a sudden laugh. 'You wait till he finds out who he was playing charades in the nuddy with.'

Suddenly the line crackled and Arthur Parker's voice came on, relayed over the speaker for the benefit of Charles and Wally.

'John, old boy, I hear you've got a problem . . .'

The voice was just too hearty. As John had suspected the big hard-faced man at the other end of the line had not believed the 'overboard' story. But he had still been worried enough to get out of his bed in the small hours and come pounding down to Head Office.

A terse conversation culminated in Parker saying lamely, 'I'd no idea she was on the ship yet, old boy.'

'Yet?' John snapped. 'Well you know now, and I want to know why.'

'They're talking about your girlfriend,' Charles muttered to Matt who had just come in and was giving them all a curious glance.

'She's there without my knowledge.' Parker was huffing and puffing over the speaker. 'She's not due to join the ship till next week.'

'That doesn't get you any further out of it Parker,' John roared. 'Or the lady's father - Mr God Almighty Terson.'

'*Terson!*' Matt rapped out the word but his voice was lost in John's bellow.

'I don't care if he owns every ship in the North Sea. You will repeat to Terson himself that I will not have the morale of my crew members undermined by him or by his bloody daughter.'

'She's Terson's daughter?' Matt whispered palely, his mind occupied by just how his confidence had been undermined that night.

'Did you say Katherine Laker was Terson's daughter?' Parker sounded as though he'd just had a nasty shock.

'And heir,' said Charles, answering Matt. 'To throne — or bridge.'

He grinned as Matt hit his forehead with his hand and turned away.

'John —' Parker's voice had become urgent. 'She's not there for any of the reasons you imagine. I can swear to that. I didn't know she was Terson's daughter.'

'Pull the other one Arthur. Don't bother swearing. Just tell me what the lady's doing here.'

'I told you, I have no idea. She's not due to be with you till next week. I was going to tell you when you docked.'

'Tell us what?'

'Katherine Laker, whom you now tell me is Terson's daughter, will be taking over the job of Chief Purser as from next week. She got the post purely on merit and . . .'

His voice vanished as Stephen threw a switch. 'We're into radio silence.'

One thought possessed his listeners. The three minutes' radio silence would give them just time to demand of Wally, the Chief Purser, if *he* knew what the hell was going on. They turned on him in a body.

But Wally had gone.

Chapter 3

John pushed open the door to his cabin.

'Do come in Miss Laker. I'm sure you have a great deal to tell me about my ship.'

He'd been looking forward to this meeting all morning, ever since he'd heard that Kate Laker was looking for him. He knew that the grapevine had already told her she'd been rumbled. Now he wanted to know a few other things that only she could tell him.

'If you could hold on a minute or two . . .' he said when he had closed the door behind him. He moved into the bedroom section of his cabin and lifted the phone. 'Stephen — try my home again will you? Thanks.'

He returned to her and they sat down, facing each other.

'How did you find out?' she demanded.

'It's our business to check on suspicious passengers. They can be a risk. Especially when they travel under assumed names.'

The phone rang. Excusing himself he moved into the bedroom, and Kate heard his voice change tone abruptly.

'Emily? It's Daddy. How are you darling? — who was it answered the phone? I see — no, nothing's the matter darling. I was just worried when I couldn't get an answer last night . . . oh, Mummy sent you to stay with Granny. How's school? Good . . . . Emily, I've got a surprise for you. That's right. The next trip — it's your holiday anyway and — no, I'd rather you didn't go to Granny. — Mummy? — well, that doesn't matter, does it? — Emily? — I love you little one — take care.'

He had not quite managed to wipe the look from his face when he returned to Kate and she averted her head out of respect for his feelings. She had no desire to intrude on the naked love and pain that was written there.

'Sorry about that,' he said, forcibly recovering himself. 'We were talking about your name.'

'*You* were talking about my name.'

'Yes, well — as you can imagine, it's come as quite a surprise to find ourselves with the new Chief Purser on board, who just happens to be Terson's daughter, who also just happens to be the owner of this happy little fishing fleet.'

That wasn't the only surprise, he reflected. There had also been Wally's terse insistence that morning that he had asked to be retired early so that he could retire to Devon and grow vegetables — Wally, who had no family beyond the crew of the ship and wouldn't know one end of a carrot from the other.

'We don't choose our parents,' said Kate levelly, 'and I got this post on my own merit. My father knows nothing about it and Arthur Parker doesn't know who I am. I've had several years experience in hotel management . . .'

'I find all this secrecy hard to believe,' said John, although a small voice was telling him that Parker's outrage of the night before had been genuine.

'On the phone just now — was that your daughter you were talking to?' Kate asked.

'Emily — yes.'

'Then perhaps if I told you that my father has never spoken to me in that way — on or off the phone — you might understand. The reason he doesn't know I've got this job is that he doesn't know much about me at all. Or want to. Fortunately the feeling is mutual.'

'He's about to find out though,' said John, and told her about the events of the previous night. She gave a cool smile when she heard about Parker's reaction.

'Yes, he'll rush to tell my father. He'll imagine that Terson will be tickled pink when he finds out.'

'But he doesn't know . . .'

'Exactly. You've heard there's a battle going on about this line at board room level.'

'Rumours, yes.'

'I presume that's what concerns the crew at the moment. The possibility of its being chopped.'

'Are they right to worry?'

'It's not clear cut yet. There's a certain faction on the board who feel it would be more profitable carrying freight.'

'And Parker's one of them?'

'Oh no. Parker's an ambitious man. He won't decide till he knows who's winning.'

'And your father?'

'I don't know. But I imagine he'd accept the board's decision. If this ship could be proved to be running at a loss, then it would be in my father's best interests to go for freight.'

'It is running at a loss,' said John simply.

'It needn't. Passengers can make for good balance sheets provided you give them what they want.'

'And you intend to?'

'Yes.'

'Even if it might be against your father's wishes?'

'That doesn't come into it. We never see each other and I owe him nothing, and that's about as much as he cares for people, friends, staff, anyone. He makes money, and a lot of it, by having his finger on the pulse of all his companies. The profit margin is all he cares about.'

'And you don't?' he tilted his head cynically.

'Oh I understand balance sheets Captain. I inherited that much.'

They looked at one another in silence for a moment.

'So why?' said John at last.

'Why what?'

'Why look for a fight with him. Wouldn't want my girl trying to sort me out when she's your age. I love her.'

'Perhaps that's it.'

'What happened?'

Before his eyes her face became shut away, secretive, hard. He gave up. He was going to get nothing today.

'Okay' he said. 'But it's not going to be easy to convince the others to accept you "on merit".' He gave the last words a satirical edge.

'Let's wait and see.'

'They'll give you a rough ride.'

'Yes.' She was smiling again.

'If you like, I'll show you around,' he offered. 'Officially.'

'Thank you. I'd like that.'

'But I want to know why you came on board as a passenger.'

'Seemed logical. The Purser looks after the passengers. So I wanted to look at the job from the passengers' point of view. At least, that's what I intended.'

'What about our point of view — from the bridge? And I'm not complaining — just asking.'

'I'm sure I'm not the first or last female to appear scantily clad on this ship. I wanted to see how the crew would react. After all — I'll be responsible for passengers' complaints.'

'And did she? The passenger in question?'

She gave that smile again. 'Let's say they simply underestimate the devious nature of the female. My job's to protect them from the passengers too.'

By this time they were heading towards the crew's cabins. Kate took only the briefest look inside Wally's, which would soon be hers. Time enough for a real look when he'd gone. On the way out they met Matt.

'Does the lady purser wish to inspect my cabin too?' he asked icily.

Oh-oh! thought John. I wonder what really *did* happen last night.

Matt had pushed open the door. 'Go ahead love. You'll find pot in the lavatory cistern and the heroin under the mattress.'

'Could be true with him,' said John. 'Check.'

'Not funny,' Matt snapped.

'That's what I thought,' John assured him.

Matt turned to him. 'By the way, you're wasting fuel according to my calculations. Either put the stabilisers in and make Amsterdam on time, or keep the passengers from throwing up and arrive behind schedule. And I'd rather you didn't impress Miss Laker, as vast fuel costs will go down on my budget. If there's nothing else.'

Without waiting to hear if there was or not he went inside and shut the door.

'There's no love lost Captain,' said Kate, unperturbed.

John shrugged. 'With three feet of corridor between you, I'd be happier if it was the other way around.'

'If you don't mind, I'd rather not oblige.'

'Someone at home?'

'Not any more. You're one of the few lucky ones.'

'We'll be coming into Amsterdam soon,' he said quickly. 'Not a bad view. Perhaps you'd like to see it from the bridge?'

Kate didn't waste time berating Peter Nuttall for revealing her identity. After all, he'd never promised to keep it a secret.

'I'm surprised you've stuck this job so long,' she said to him when they encountered each other as she was on her way back to her cabin to get ready for going ashore.

'How could I let you down?' he asked with a slight sneer. 'It still didn't work out for you though, did it?'

'No.'

'Do you ever see him?'

She shook her head: 'Do you?'

'What for?'

She shrugged, unable to think of an answer.

'You never knew what you were doing, did you?' he went on. 'Or did you?'

'I don't know what you're talking about.'

'I used to listen through the keyhole.'

'I'm surprised you didn't look through it.'

'It was bad enough to listen,' he said, his face darkening. 'I imagined the rest.'

'Your girlfriend's looking for you,' Kate's sharp eyes had picked up Sandy approaching them.

'She always is,' he said carelessly. 'Keeps her slim.'

'You shouldn't fool around with people's feelings Peter,' Kate spoke very seriously.

'You did. Maybe it's your fault.'

'Of course,' she nodded. 'If it makes it easier for you.'

'You'd never kiss it better,' he said with a touch of petulance. He caught Kate's steely eyes on him and reddened, 'I'm sorry.' He watched her walk off. 'Kate.' He hurried after her till she stopped and looked back. 'I was very sorry to hear about Emma. I mean it.'

She gave him a brief nod and moved away again without speaking. Peter found himself confronting Sandy.

'I'd steer clear of her if I was you . . .' she said.

'Aren't you glad you're not me then. 'Cos I can't steer clear of her — not yet.'

Kate had recognised her father's limousine as she stood waiting to leave the ship. She could see nothing through the darkened windows, but she knew George Terson would be sitting in the back. She knew, too, the expression that would be on his face — harsh, impatient, furious at having his busy schedule interrupted by Arthur Parker's unwelcome news.

It was like him to have turned up without warning her in advance, taking it for granted that she would simply get into the car at his bidding. In fact she did just that, reasoning that they might as well have the row now as later.

As the car glided through the streets of Amsterdam, George Terson explained his position in the voice of a man who was used to having to speak his mind only once, and then have his wishes acted on. There was a note of finality in his voice when he said,

'Therefore I'd be obliged if you'd resign the post immediately.'

'You talk like a telex father. Do you know that?' Kate spoke without looking at him.

'You'll leave the ship today and fly back to London. I'll take care of everything.'

'I've paid my fare. I'm a passenger.'

'I'll reimburse your fare.'

'But I don't want it reimbursed. I also don't want to resign. Sorry about that.'

'We can't all have what we want in life, Katherine.'

Without warning she turned her head and looked him full in the face. 'Just you?'

They continued the fight over lunch in a floating, glass-roofed restaurant on a canal. Kate was beginning to enjoy herself slightly. Hate, she had discovered, could be very pleasurable. She knew she had disconcerted her father with her last remark in the car for he had said nothing after that till they reached the restaurant. She also knew that she was one of the few people who could disconcert him because she was unimpressed by the aura of wealth and power this man carried with him. She of all people knew how useless his wealth and power could turn out to be, and the way she had discovered this lay like a poison between them.

'Do you remember that ship you had in a bottle?' she said as she began to eat. 'I must have been about five. I loved that ship. I wanted it so much. But you said it wouldn't come out of the bottle.'

'No, I don't recall it,' he grunted.

'I do.' She smiled, knowing she had confused him. 'It did come out.'

He lost his temper suddenly. 'I have damn good reasons for not wanting you in this job without having to put up with this — nonsense.'

'But it isn't nonsense. Anything but.'

'There are company matters about which you know nothing . . .'

'You're sure of that, are you?' she shot at him.

She refused to elaborate. This was not the time to let on to George Terson about the bright young man on his ship — the one Kate had become friendly with. Being a woman had its advantages — even if one was a woman who had never been forgiven for not being a son.

'This is a lovely lunch,' she assured him.

He tried a different tack. 'If you'd had the courtesy to ask me before you applied for the post . . .'

Her eyes were hard. 'I asked you for something once in my life. Never again. I'll take it, but I'll never ask for it.'

'You never had to ask,' he blustered. 'I've denied you nothing.'

Her voice was low with hate. 'Where were you when the only

chance my child had was an operation I couldn't afford but you could? Tell me father — where were you when I tried to break through the red tape of your company to find you? When I tried to track you down in every country, every city, every hotel and every whorehouse in the world? I telephoned. I cabled. I telexed. But *you* were not to be found. *You* were not available. *You* killed my child.'

She knew she had delivered a savage blow below the belt, and she was glad. There was a bleak hell on his face which slightly eased the pain in her heart. The matter was not referred to again until his car drew up at the docks and she turned to him before getting out.

'You shouldn't have come here today. I was beginning to forget why I hated you so much, *father*.'

'I shall quite simply have you removed.' Terson's voice had a thin quality, as though he had only just recovered the use of it.

'Really? But you never did like bad publicity, did you? I think it would make quite a spread.' She was half out of the car. The ship loomed above them. 'I like your ship by the way. It reminds me of the one in the bottle.'

She slammed the door behind her and walked away.

John Anderson had paused to finish a letter before going ashore. He looked up, irritated, when there was a knock on his door. Matt came in.

'How is she?' said Matt, eyeing the letter. 'Your wife.'

'Fine. Yes Matt. She's very well.' John spoke heartily.

'I'll buy you a beer.'

'I'd rather finish this.'

'John — it wasn't my place to go on at you about Terson's daughter. I'd like to apologise.'

'No need for that. Seems you were right. After all, we all saw whose car she got into a few minutes ago, didn't we?'

'And you said "Trust her. Give her a chance. Her father doesn't even know she's on the ship".' Matt spoke not maliciously but in a tone of wonder.

'I remember what I said.'

'And once inside the safety of the limousine the big chief divulged the second phase of his dastardly plan to his beautiful daughter,' Matt went on theatrically.

'I think I'll take you up on that beer,' said John. 'Do us good to get away.' He screwed up his letter and tossed the ball into the waste bin.

They collected Charles on the way and were gone long enough to return more or less cheerful. At the top of the gangway they all turned and looked down on the docks, where Terson's car had just drawn up again, disgorging Kate from the back.

'I reckon we'll give her a run for her money,' mused Matt. 'She'll be begging old Terson to get her out of it. Help! Daddy! Save me from those terrible sailors!'

Charles had grown philosophical. 'We're pawns in life's game, Matt. You'll never change that. Just lie back and enjoy it.'

'No thanks. Two can play the same game, Charlie boy, and I've just learned the rules.'

'Tell me, tell me.' Charles begged.

'There aren't any.'

Chapter 4

Arthur Parker was having a terrible day. It had begun with the visit to his office that Kate Laker had made as soon as the ship docked at Felixstowe. She had refused to be intimidated, pointing out that she had a contract for her job, and daring him to dismiss her. Parker had tried what bluster could do, promising to be rid of her for the first tiny mistake. She had seemed unimpressed.

His second bad moment had come when his sharp-eyed secretary, Sophie, had pointed out something that he should have noticed, and hadn't; Kate Laker couldn't possibly be playing a lone hand. She was being backed, possibly be someone on the board. Otherwise, how had she known that the Purser's job was going vacant?

His third depressing experience was about to happen, he reflected as he got out of his car at Felixstowe and went looking for John Anderson.

'Was Wally forcibly retired from his job?' John demanded as soon as they were alone.

'No.' said Parker.

'Then why?'

'The reason is in confidence John.'

'Confidence be damned!' John snapped. 'There's enough going on in this company that spills over onto my ship without keeping me in the dark as to why one of my crew members is being retired early.'

'We had no choice. It's his health John.'

'If Wally James is ill the rest of us are already dead, Parker. Now come on, tell me the truth.'

'I can only tell you what I've been told,' said Parker, losing patience. 'Wally says it's terminal.'

He looked the Captain in the eyes. He was getting a certain satisfaction from having reduced him to shattered silence.

'There is something you could do for me, John. Miss Laker — if you could keep an eye out. If you know what I mean.' He shifted a little under John's curious eye. 'I'm afraid I have to find just cause to dismiss her.'

'Dismiss Terson's daughter?' John doubted he'd heard correctly.

'Those are my orders. I'd be obliged, John.'

'Don't be. I have no intention of doing your dirty work for you. Or Terson's.' John began to walk away, then turned back. 'The day she affects my crew, that will be my business.'

He wondered if the world had gone mad or he had. Was Terson in cahoots with his daughter or wasn't he? If he wasn't, why did he pick her up for conspiratorial lunches in Amsterdam? If he was, why did he want her fired?

He came across Kate in the Reception Area. She was not yet in the uniform she would wear, but from the way she was consulting notes she was wasting no time getting the hang of the job.

'Wally's moved out of his cabin already,' she told him, looking troubled.

'If that's what he wants, Miss Laker . . .'

'I hope you've been told officially that Wally was not retired to make way for me.'

He nodded. 'Wally knows that too, does he?'

'I suspect he does,' said John evasively. He was still to upset to want to discuss Wally with her. 'If you'll excuse me, Miss Laker . . .'

'I'd feel less of an intruder if you called me Kate.'

He looked back and nodded. 'In time.'

It was later that evening, when the ship was well on its way to Gothenburg, that Matt knocked at the Chief Purser's cabin, and discovered something he didn't like.

'You really can't wait, can you?' he said, eyeing Kate who had opened the door.

'It was Wally's idea.'

'Thumbscrews give us all great ideas.'

'Then perhaps you should ask *him* why,' said Kate, losing patience. 'I wouldn't mind knowing myself.'

'You're joking,' he jeered.

'Hardly.'

'It's the gentleman in him. He'd step off the pavement for a lady and get hit by a ten-ton truck. Don't expect that from me.'

'Not in my wildest dreams,' she assured him fervently.

'By the way,' he added as he turned to go. 'You do know there's nothing in the book about labour relations — or relationships — in these quarters, don't you?'

'How interesting,' she said, keeping her face carefully blank.

'It is. Very interesting little neighbourhood we've got here. Don't be shocked at the off-duty activity. Wally, John and I pass them around like a parlour game. Maybe you'd care to join in.'

'As what?'

'A parcel.'

He'd thought it might make a good exit line, but she looked through him.

'It's true,' John confirmed when Matt faced him on the bridge. 'Wally asked her to move in.'

'Then he's a fool,' declared Matt.

'Maybe not. By the way, he wants to buy us a drink tonight.'

'Wally?' Charles looked up from some charts he was studying. 'He gave up the booze.'

'It's for Miss Laker's benefit. Wally feels she'd been given a hard time and he's trying to ease things for her.'

'What yarn did Parker spin you this time, John?' Matt demanded.

'Give it a rest Matt. The way you're carrying on, Wally's quite right. At least she deserves a fair crack of the whip.'

'Hand it me,' Matt pleaded.

The phone began to shrill. He seized it and exchanged a few words with the Engine Room.

'The boiler's playing dixie again,' he sighed when he had put the receiver back. 'I'll have to go down there. And I'm busy tonight. Give my excuses to Wally will you?'

'You'll be there Matt,' said John quietly. 'Eleven thirty in the pub.'

'Is that an order?'

'Only if you don't give a damn about Wally's feelings.'

'You know where to put the knife in,' said Matt, and departed quickly before he said something worse.

'What's that saying about the lady protesting too loudly?' said Charles. 'Matt's protesting pretty loud it seems to me.'

John didn't seem to have heard him. 'Would you say I was difficult?' he demanded. 'Hard to talk to?'

'Who said that?'

'I mean personally. About things that matter. Would you confide in me?'

'I use you like a confessional. You could have me keelhauled for half the things you know about me.'

John nodded and looked away. He was not comforted. 'You haven't got any real problems,' he said. It lay heavily on him that Wally, who had real problems, had kept them to himself.

Down in the Engine Room Matt, swathed in overalls, was wrestling with the problem of the boiler. Finally he and Joe Francis, the burly young engineer assisting him, got it into a state where it would just about hold till Gothenburg. After that it would need proper repairs.

As they entered the lift and removed the ear-muffs that the hideous noise down there made necessary, Joe said edgily, 'I was going to have a word with Wally about this, but I'll try it on you.'

'What's that?'

'Young Peter Nuttall, We don't like him carrying on with that bird Sandy.'

Matt gave the young man an amused glance. 'Jealous?'

'That's not the point Matt. He's an officer, she's crew.'

'She's pretty.'

'Makes no odds. She shouldn't mix with officers.' The slight righteousness on Joe's face would have fooled nobody, Matt thought. Joe had never been known to bother about the ship's caste system before.

'Okay Joe, leave it to me.'

'Don't mind what they do in private, you get me?' Joe added unconvincingly.

Matt gave an inward grin. On the contrary, mate, he thought. It's *exactly* what they may be doing in private that's eating you.

But all he said was, 'I get you Joe.'

Joe Francis would have been even more troubled had he been able to see Sandy that minute. She was standing behind the bar pouring a gin for Peter who was sitting on one of the bar stools, a depressed expression on his face.

'You haven't mentioned Miss Laker to me all day,' Sandy said lightly. 'Am I winning?'

'Hands down.'

She leaned across the bar and gave him a swift kiss. Her eyes were shining. 'Sorry, I was jealous.' She watched him as he swallowed his gin. 'You know Wally's buying us all drinks tonight. He asked me to serve here from eleven thirty.' Suddenly she tilted her head to one side and gave him a curious look. 'Is that what it is, Peter?'

'What?'

'I'm not good enough for you? Not in your class. Just a servant?'

'Don't be daft. If that's what I thought I'd hardly be seen publicly with you, would I?'

'No. I suppose not,' she said in a dubious voice. 'It's odd though. You seem to make more fuss of me in public than at any other time.'

'Does it embarrass you?'

'No.'

He drained his glass. 'See you at half eleven.'

'I'll be here.'

The one person who seemed genuinely delighted to see Kate installed in Wally's cabin was Wally.

'I knew it would be right,' he beamed as he looked at her sitting in his old chair. 'Looks like it was designed for you.'

Her glance took in the whole cabin. 'It's lovely.'

'You are coming to the pub?'

'Of course.'

He got up and headed automatically for the bedroom shower area, stopping himself at the door with an embarrassed smile.

'Sorry, I forgot. Would you mind if I got myself a glass of water?'

'Would you rather have drink?'

'I don't. Thanks a lot. Won't be a minute.'

He went into the shower-room, but left the door open. He had plainly forgotten the mirror that stood at a slight angle to the door, and, glancing in it, Kate was startled to see him take a pill from a small bottle which he took from his pocket. He then ran the tap, filled a glass with water, stood thinking for a moment, and took another pill.

'Have you always been teetotal?' she asked him when he reappeared.

'Certainly not,' he chuckled. 'Used to be a great one for the booze. Used to drink your father under the table. Doubt if he'd remember that though. Those were the days, before it got so impersonal. He was a seaman first and foremost, your father you know. Now I reckon it's about all he can do to remember the names of his ships.'

'And hotels and factories,' Kate finished. 'But maybe you're right. He is a seaman at heart.'

'It's in your blood too,' he said, looking at her kindly.

'I suppose it must be. But times have changed. My father won't change.'

After staying to chat a few moments more he left her, but returned later that night to escort her to the pub. A shout went up as they appeared together.

'At last Wally,' Charles called. 'We're all dying of thirst. Come on Sandy — pour them out.'

Wally held up his hand. 'I'd just like to say — before you all pass out —' he had to raise his voice above the roar of laughter, 'I'd just like you to know this is really a small get-together I've arranged for

Miss Laker. As we're all going to be working together I thought we should say hello first.'

Charles moved up to Kate, smiling and holding out his hand. 'Hello. I mean it. Come on everybody — let's hear it. One, two, three . . .'

In the bellow of *'Hello'* that went up, only Matt and Peter kept rigid silence. Kate's own answering 'Hello' sounded feeble in comparison.

At Wally's orders Sandy began pouring drinks, the atmosphere dissolved into general goodwill. Kate looked around her and found little groups within groups standing out as clearly as if her eyes had thrown a spotlight onto them. She was particularly aware of Peter sitting at the same table as Tony Grant, who was apparently showing him card tricks, and Jo, standing by the bar, her eyes fixed on Tony with a gaze that was both possessive and frightened.

Jo became aware of Kate's gaze flickering back and forth between herself and Tony, and her alarm increased. There had always been fear, she now realised, in her relations with Tony. Sometimes she could pin it to certain things, like his habit of depositing mysterious little bundles of money in her possession and ordering her to keep them hidden in her cabin. He'd never say where that money came from but she supposed she could guess. Who was to say how much had been won and lost on a roulette wheel?

He'd kept her quiet with the promise that this was to pay for their future, for his divorce — just as soon as he could get one. But Tony had no wife. Jo had ascertained that a few days ago when the ship docked in England and she had dashed off to an address she'd found in his cabin. Oh there was a Mrs Grant living there all right, and a sweet old thing she was. Only she was Tony's mother.

She'd faced him with it that very afternoon, and he'd got out of it with his usual skill.

'I always say I have a wife when I first meet a woman. That way no-one gets hurt if it doesn't work out. But you're different Jo . . .'

That was when she'd looked him in the eye and told him that all his money was in a safety deposit box, with a letter, explaining how it was come by.

'Sounds like blackmail,' he'd said when he recovered himself.

She shook her head. 'You haven't got anything I want,' she assured him.

If only it were true, she thought now. But the truth was that she was as big a sucker for him as ever. Even now, when she knew how he'd lied to her and made use of her, he'd only have to turn and give her that certain smile of his, and her heart would turn over inside her. She'd never give him away. It was all bluff. Oh God, let him not find that out! Let him be nice to her, even if it was only because she'd got him scared now . . .

Jo came out of her unhappy reverie to realise that Kate and Wally were approaching the table where Tony was showing card tricks to Peter. Like a mother tigress Joe moved in protectively.

'I've got your drink over here Tony,' she called.

For a moment she feared he wouldn't come, but her eyes managed to convey that he'd better. While she waited by the bar she heard Matt say to Sandy,

'Give me a scotch for Wally.'

'He doesn't drink any more,' Sandy protested.

'Just tonight. He deserves one. Come on.'

Jo pulled Tony to one side as soon as he neared her.

'Forget the tricks,' she urged him. 'Kate Laker is too clever to show off in front of.'

'Don't be daft.'

'I'm warning you.'

'What have I got to lose unless you marry me?' She stared at him in amazement. 'I mean it.'

She pulled away from him, confused to the point of speechlessness, and went to the microphone to sing a song for Wally. Vaguely she heard Matt pressing the scotch on Wally.

'Tonight's special Wally. Come on. Just the one.'

Wally looked up at Jo who had started to sing directly at him. A beaming smile broke over his face.

'Yes, it is special,' he agreed. He turned to Kate, then to Matt, 'To all of us.' Then he threw the whisky back in one gulp.

Charles had moved up to Matt's side, his eyes on Kate who was just out of earshot.

'She really is a cracker, isn't she?' he muttered beneath Jo's song.

'If you like that type,' said Matt.

'That's one great thing about it John. I can see her and say — yes — that's nice. But that's all. I'd never have believed that before I married Jenny.'

'I don't believe it now,' said Matt regarding him cynically.

'You will when it happens.'

'Matt's face hardened abruptly. 'No way. I enjoy them all too much to single one out.'

At that moment Kate turned back and their eyes met. Charles watched, delighted.

'You've met your match there, I reckon.

'Give me odds,' Matt laughed.

Protesting again, thought Charles, life was going to be interesting from now on.

At that moment when he thought no-one was watching, Wally slipped quietly away from the pub. He was pleased with the success of his evening. The ice had been broken and he reckoned he'd persuaded them to give Kate a fair chance. But now it was done and he knew he had no-one else to think of but himself. And he knew that if he didn't escape soon the pain that was gnawing his guts would make him betray himself.

He went out onto the deck and stood by the rail, staring out over the ocean, seeing nothing. He gripped the rail, hunched against the pain. He felt a hundred years old.

He became aware of footsteps that stopped abruptly close to him. He looked up and saw a woman of about forty with a sad, plain face. She was staring at him as if he was an unwelcome intrusion.

'Are you all right madam?' he forced himself to say.

'Fine,' she too seemed to speak with an effort. 'Just getting some air.'

She hurried on, leaving him alone. He forgot her almost at once, staring down into the water that churned away from the ship's bows. He found that if he concentrated on it very hard he could forget the pain — forget everything —

By the time the evening was over, and he was relaxing for a nightcap in John's cabin, Charles was in a mood of total euphoria.

'You know something,' he said as John poured. 'I've been thinking about that place Wally's going to retire to in Devon. I've often thought I'd like to settle down somewhere like that with Jenny one day.'

John remembered some of the hairier stories that had gone around about Charles in his pre-Jenny days, and his eyebrows raised a little.

'Not your scene, is it?'

'I can see Jenny now — collecting the eggs and catching the pigs to fry the bacon . . .'

'Not everyone's got a Jenny,' John put in.

'You have. And two kids,' he considered a moment. 'Six. That's what I'm planning on.'

John leaned back in his chair. 'Six eggs or pigs, or acres?' he enquired politely.

'Kids you fool.'

'I hope you've warned Jenny.'

'We'll have Matt in the net as well, you see. For all his talk he ended up escorting Miss Laker to her cabin door. I wonder how much further he escorted her.'

'They were walking in the same direction,' John corrected him gravely. 'Since their cabins are a mere three feet apart they could hardly have done anything else. I don't think there was any escorting about it. My guess is that right now he's in his bed and she's in hers.'

This was shrewd of John because the dispositions were exactly as he had predicted. What the Captain's crystal ball had not shown him was the sight of Matt staring at the phone by his bed for five minutes before picking it up and dialling a number.

'I just wanted to say goodnight,' he said when Kate answered.

'Goodnight,' she said politely.

'Wally asked us to be nice to you,' he paused for her reaction, but there was only silence reaching him through the receiver. 'I can be. Very nice to you.'

'Can you?'

'Yes. Would you like me to be?' he listened to the silence again. 'If you'd rather, I'll tell you now how nice I can be, then you can decide.'

After a moment he snatched the receiver from his ear and stared at it, as though it had scalded him. He put it back and listened again. But his ears had not deceived him. Incredibly, through the ear-piece came the unmistakable sound of a snore.

'Goodnight Miss Laker,' he snapped. 'Sweet dreams.'

Kate heard the receiver being slammed down the other end. It was as well, she thought, that he couldn't see the grin on her face.

In the Captain's cabin, Charles was just thinking it would soon be time to go. One more little drink.

The phone rang. John picked it up lazily, but as he listened the sleepy expression was wiped from his face to be replaced by fear and horror.

'What is it?' demanded Charles.

'A passenger has just reported seeing someone fall overboard,' said John, scarcely able to speak, 'from the deck near the pub.'

After two hours searching in the North Sea you were supposed to give up. There was simply no point in going on any longer. Anyone you found after that would be frozen dead long ago. But John, driven by old friendship and dreadful guilt was still circling four hours later when Kate appeared on the bridge to say that the passengers were complaining of the delay.

'So the lady knows my job better than I do,' John raged. 'The same way she thinks she knows Wally James's job, and now by God she's got it. Do you want mine too?'

Kate faced him, unafraid. 'Fact Captain. Wally is dead, and no matter how long we circle we can't help him now.'

'Does anything enter your head other than what you're after? Have you ever wondered *why* he killed himself Miss Laker?'

'You should know that, since he'd been with you long enough.'

John went white. 'I'll be damned if I'll take this, no matter whose daughter you are. Get off my bridge or . . .'

'John . . .' said Charles warningly.

'If you're blaming me, Captain Anderson, I want to know why,' Kate told him firmly.

He had turned away and now stood in silence, looking out of the window at the darkness. When she realised he had no intention of answering her Kate turned to go.

'Miss Laker —' John's voice stopped her, 'you can tell the passengers we'll be getting underway now.'

Matt, who had just appeared, shook his head regretfully, 'Afraid not John. We'll need a couple of hours.'

Kate looked at him. He had in his hand the ear-muffs and greasy overall he had just removed after two hot hours in the engine room wrestling with a boiler that had decided to play up again as soon as he had got to sleep.

'Surely you can contain your problem till we reach Gothenburg,' she said.

In another moment she found herself holding the dirty overall that Matt had thrust at her in his fury.

'It's a bit hot and greasy down there in the engine room Miss Laker. My men are tired and edgy but I'm sure they'll welcome your engineering know-how with open arms.'

'I asked you a simple question Mr Taylor.'

'To which there's a simple answer. *No.*' Matt grabbed the overall back and turned away. 'You've stepped into a dead man's shoes. If they don't fit, that's your problem.'

Kate stared at him as he went, stunned by the ocean of hostility that had washed over her from two directions. John kept his back turned and Charles, plainly embarrassed by the scene, made a sign for her to go. Tight-lipped, she did so.

'You were a bit harsh on her John,' said Charles.

'Who asked you?'

'She was right, Captain.' Charles emphasised the last word slightly.

'I'll be in my quarters,' said John heading for the door. 'Call me when Matt's ready,'

When he had gone Charles exchanged a look with Thomas Kelly, a thin-faced man of forty who as first mate was also responsible for coping with the ship's medical problems, and who had been holding himself ready on the bridge in case Wally should be recovered and need his help.

'That was really rough,' said Kelly.

'He was very close to Wally.'

'Blames himself doesn't he?' said Kelly shrewdly. 'It wasn't Miss Laker he was attacking. It was himself.'

Kate was not pleased to see Peter step out of his cabin into the corridor ahead of her.

'I told you to stay in the office,' she said sharply.

'Having abandoned Wally to his watery grave, you've now licked Captain Anderson into shape, have you?'

Something inside Kate snapped. Hardly aware of what she was doing she drew back her hand and slapped him across the face with all her strength.

'I should have done that years ago,' she said.

He recovered from his shock sufficiently to speak. 'Do you think that would have made any difference?'

'It might have helped *me*,' she moved past him. 'Wash your face and be in the office in five minutes.'

Peter retreated into his cabin quickly, not in obedience to her order but because out of the corner of his eye he had just made out Sandy, watching the whole scene, and he didn't feel up to explanation. When he looked out a moment later she had gone and he hurried to the Purser's Office.

Kate was there ahead of him, already going through the Purser's mail. A letter she held in her hand seemed to hold her riveted.

'Give me the passenger list', she commanded in a tense voice.

She ran her finger down the list till she came to a name which she checked with the one on the letter.

'What is it?' said Peter.

48

But she ignored him and dashed out of the cabin as if the hounds of hell were at her heels. A moment later she had reached the passenger cabins and was running past the doors till she found the one she wanted. As she had half expected it was unlocked and totally empty. There was no suitcase, no clothes, nor any sign that this room was inhabited by a human being. Yet the passenger list said it had been allocated to Mrs Mary Gordon. Kate began to run again, this time in search of the Captain.

'I thought you should see this immediately Captain,' she said when he opened his cabin door to her. She held up Mary Gordon's letter to him. 'It was in the post box. Her cabin's totally empty. Cleaned out.'

He glanced at the letter. 'That's the way they do it if they're determined enough.'

'You mean she took the ship for the sole purpose of jumping overboard?'

'I'm glad something surprises you, Miss Laker,' John said coolly. He looked back at the letter, then up at her suddenly. There was a tense pause as their eyes met. The same thought had dawned on both of them. 'Did anybody check Wally's cabin?' he said sharply.

Wally's cabin was empty of Wally, although all his clothes and possessions were still there. It looked as Mary Gordon's had not looked — as though its owner had expected to come back.

While Kate was checking the bathroom John picked up an empty bottle from the dressing table and slipped it into his pocket. His eyes were troubled.

'There could be one simple way of finding him,' he said. 'Why didn't we think of it before?'

The harsh sound of the loudspeaker requesting Wally James to go to the Captain's quarters stunned every member of the crew. Wherever they were they turned and stared up at the nearest speaker, as though demanding that it explain itself for the sick joke.

Matt, who had been sitting in the pub listening to Joe Francis give a graphic account of how he'd overheard someone groaning away a hangover in the brig, tore off to the Radio Office and almost collided with John who was coming out.

'What's going on?' he demanded.

'It looks as if there's been a mistake,' said John.

'That announcement was no mistake.' said Matt furiously. 'I want to get hold of the joker who . . .'

'It was a passenger who went over the side,' John cut him short. He handed Matt the letter.

49

Matt looked up after a moment, and gave a curious glance at Joe who had joined them.

'Was anyone tossed in the brig last night?' he said.

'No,' John looked blank.

'You said there was someone in there,' Matt said to Joe.

'I heard them.'

John was already running towards the brig. 'Send Kelly down,' he called over his shoulder.

Wally was curled up on the floor of the brig, shivering and mumbling in delirium. John knelt beside him and hauled him up a little so that he could support him in his arms. Matt, chasing after John, stopped in the doorway, taken aback by what he could hear. John was talking quietly to Wally, who plainly could not hear him.

'It's all right Wally, I'm here now. You're not going to let a damn fool disease kill you. That's an order, you hear me Wally.'

Matt turned away. He could see Kelly running towards him, and it was obvious he wasn't needed here. He went to the Radio Office, where another surprise awaited him. Kate was standing there, speaking into the telephone.

'There's no passport here,' she said, 'but you must have her address on the booking form. Mrs Mary Gordon. Right. I'll read it to you.' She picked up the letter, and read from it, 'Please tell my children it was the only way. I can't live without their father. Ask them to give their stepmother a chance. They love each other.' Kate's voice shook slightly, but she recovered herself and read on to the end. 'Tell them I loved them. Goodbye.'

She replaced the phone and stood still for a moment before turning and walking blindly into Matt.

'We've found him,' he said quietly.

'Where?' she moved past him as she spoke, trying to keep her face averted.

'The brig,' Matt followed her outside. 'It looks as if he put himself there. Are you okay?'

'Yes.'

'You reacted to that letter as if you knew the woman.'

'I did,' she said briefly, and left him.

He decided to pay a visit to the sick-bay. By now the Medical Officer had had time to find out how Wally was.

He arrived to find Wally lying on the examination couch, frighteningly still, while Kelly listened to his heart.

'He's in a coma,' said Kelly at last. 'We've got to get him to hospital immediately.'

50

He began to undo Wally's clothes, and stopped, with a wary look on his face, as his hand encountered a small bump in the inner jacket pocket. He pulled out a small bottle and read the label.

'Did he drink last night?' he said quietly.

John reached inside his own jacket and handed Kelly the bottle he had taken from Wally's room. It was identical.

'What's drink got to do with it?' he said.

Kelly looked at the two bottles. 'If he'd taken an overdose of this to keep himself cheerful, and then had a drink, I'd understand it. The mixture could be fatal.'

'He did,' said Matt, white in the face. 'I gave him a drink last night.'

'I'll have him picked up straightaway,' said John moving to the door. 'The sooner he's in hospital the better.'

Kelly looked up from feeling Wally's pulse to see Matt staring at him, totally stunned.

'You didn't know he was on that drug any more than I did,' he said. 'You can't blame yourself.'

'Did John know?'

'Evidently yes.'

It took Matt some time to get John to himself. The Captain had gone personally to the Radio Room to call up the Royal Navy for the helicopter that would take Wally to a hospital in Gothenburg. But finally Matt managed to pin him down in his own quarters.

'When did he tell you?' he demanded.

John turned away in an evasive manner. The question seemed to upset him.

'He didn't,' he said at last. 'I got it out of Parker.'

'Wally didn't tell you himself?'

'No,' John turned back and smiled painfully. 'Says a lot for me, doesn't it?'

A phone call from Sweden prevented the conversation from going further. When it was plain that John was talking to his wife Matt turned and left. Whatever John was hearing down that line was obviously delighting him, and it seemed to Matt that the subject of Wally had been dropped with relief.

The Casino was empty. Just half an hour ago it had been full of vaguely irritable passengers, having their nerves soothed by an impromptu performance by Jo. But now they were on the move again towards Gothenburg Jo had felt free to leave off. There was only herself, packing up her things, and Tony, fiddling with the chips, checking figures on a sheet of paper in his hand.

'All tallies does it?'

Tony jumped slightly at the voice over his shoulder. It belonged to Peter Nuttall who was looking at the croupier with a smile that was just too innocent to be true.

'Never was much good at maths myself,' Peter went on jovially.

'Are you trying to be smart?' Tony snapped.

'I don't have to,' Peter stretched his mouth again. 'You do.'

As he walked off he had an uncomfortable feeling. He had begun by making a remark to pass the time of day, but the smouldering look in Tony's eyes had been a warning. It was worth considering. Tony wouldn't be the first croupier with sticky fingers — if that was what it was.

The uncomfortable feeling persisted, giving him the sensation of being followed. By the time he had reached the men's washroom he knew it was not just a sensation. Tony faced him, his face black with fury, and told him just what he thought of jumped up little kids who made uncalled for remarks.

'It's a warning mate, that's all,' he finished.

'Sounds like a threat,' Peter tried to keep the fear out of his voice, but it was thundering inside him. Tony must have twice his strength.

'As you like.' Tony half agreed. He stepped away and moved to the door. 'Just think about it.'

When he was gone Peter gave himself a moment to calm down before following. He went straight to the Purser's Office, dismayed to find Kate there. He could have done with a little longer on his own. He tried desperately to keep his manner normal.

Kate was already making plans for the trip from Gothenburg to Amsterdam. She handed him a list.

'You see to this and I'll check the dining room,' she said.

'Be done in two ticks.'

Something ultra-willing in his voice made her shoot him a suspicious look. 'What are you after?' she demanded.

'You'll find out,' he smiled. 'Oh, Mrs Maya Anderson joins the ship at Gothenburg. She's the Captain's wife. He's got the cleaners doing a job on his quarters right now. Clean sheets on the bed — the lot.'

'What was it you were after?' said Kate repressively.

'I'd like time off in Gothenburg.'

'That's not possible. We're late, and without Wally we . . .'

'Time enough for what I want.'

Kate's patience was running thin. 'You can't always have what you want. We've got hours to make up.'

52

'I said I need time off,' Peter said in a low bitter voice.

'If you step off this ship you'll be fired,' said Kate flatly.

Peter paused as he pulled the door open. 'But you'd have to admit you were a failure as a mother to do that.' he said. He blew her a kiss. 'See you later, mummy.'

Kate hardly heard his last words. Her attention was riveted by the sight of Sandy McCormack, standing in the corridor just outside, plainly having heard the last few minutes. Sandy's face was aghast, and she made no effort to stop Peter going. She just stared and stared at Kate, until Kate moved over and shut the door firmly between them.

Chapter 5

In the quick turn-around at Gothenburg there were a million and one things to be done as Kate took over Wally's job at a moment's notice. It irked her to have to waste valuable time arguing with the restaurant manageress.

Susan Porter was in her mid-twenties which meant, Kate thought, that she must be very good to have reached her present position. What was more, Miss Porter knew her own strengths, and had no inhibitions about arguing with the new Chief Purser.

'I refuse to be ordered around by a new chef who knows nothing about the running of this ship,' she was saying, her pretty face contracted with annoyance.

'He's preparing the food, not paddling the canoe,' said Kate mildly. She wanted to see how far into deep water Susan Porter could be lured.

'There's a difference between catering for a city restaurant and one at sea. He's extravagant.'

'You'd hand the passengers a fishing rod and tell them to catch their own, would you?' Kate gave a faint grin.

'I don't think this is a matter you can dismiss so flippantly, Miss Laker. He wants the entire dining room rearranged. I simply can't cope with the extra work entailed.'

Miss Porter had finally ventured to a point where she could no longer touch bottom.

'You're not offering your resignation, are you?' said Kate. 'I always thought you were a good restaurant manageress.'

'I'm not offering my resignation. But I am pointing out that the restaurant and kitchen staff might refuse to work under him.'

'You wouldn't allow that to happen, would you?'

'I can't control their action.'

'But that's your job,' said Kate pointedly.

There was a pause in which Susan Porter seemed to be measuring the strength of the opposition.

'Miss Laker, you hired a new chef without consulting me or anyone else. If you have the right to hire and fire people at will . . .'

'If they can't cope with the changes — yes.' Kate smiled. 'I'm sure you'll manage, Susan. If not, let me know before we're under way.'

She was gone without giving Susan a chance to reply. The interview had left her feeling both pleased and dissatisfied. On the one hand it was good to have established her position without doubt. The more people who knew how firmly she meant to be in charge, the better. On the other hand, she now had one more person seething with resentment against her; and on the whole she felt she had enough already.

In the Reception Area she encountered Captain Anderson with a statuesque blonde who could only be Maya. The introductions were made, and the Captain's wife said 'Please, call me Maya.' in what Kate felt was probably a good imitation of a friendly manner. She had a strong sensation of having been coolly appraised in a way that was more calculating than personal, and when she turned in the corridor and saw Maya giving her a slightly satisfied look, she was sure of it. It was puzzling, but she was too busy to give it further thought.

'Vaga vara dig sjalv,' Maya murmured as Kate disappeared.

'Pardon?' John looked at his wife.

'Dare to be yourself,' she translated.

'I don't follow it in English, let alone Swedish,' he said with a shrug.

'There's no need to call her Miss Laker for my benefit.' Before he could reply she added, 'Which way?'

He led her to his quarters, feeling suddenly irrationally nervous. His meetings with Maya often did have this effect on him, possibly because they had to spend so much time apart. But this time he sensed that something was different. Her last-minute decision to leave Emily behind at her grandmother's home in Sweden and visit him alone had sounded romantic when she explained it on the phone, but since she came on board he had sensed a hard brightness about her that did not accord with the 'second honeymoon' atmosphere he had been expecting.

She looked round his quarters as politely as a stranger.

'It's very nice,' she said. Her eyes fell on the flowers. 'For me?'

'Yes.'

She moved into the bedroom and pulled back the covers, revealing the fresh white sheets.

'For me too?'

'Of course,' he said, puzzled.

She gave him an enigmatic smile. 'You didn't have to change your sheets for me.'

There was no time to ask her questions. He had work to do before the ship got under way.

'I'll be back soon,' he said, collecting up his papers. 'Just make yourself at home.'

When he had gone Maya drifted round, looking at everything but touching very little. She stopped before the picture of herself and the children, picked it up, studied it and replaced it. Her face was calm.

'Come in,' she called at a knock on the door.

It was Kate who came inside.

'John isn't here,' said Maya.

'No. I'm sorry I troubled you. I'll find him.'

'You know where he'll be, do you?'

'Yes. Excuse me.'

'No please,' Maya smiled. 'I'd like to talk to you a moment.'

'I'm very busy Mrs Anderson. Perhaps later on.'

'In private,' Maya insisted. 'Your cabin perhaps.'

'I don't spend much time in my cabin.'

'No. How silly of me.'

Kate was beginning to feel irritated. If Mrs Anderson wanted to be enigmatic and significant she could try it on someone else.

'Excuse me . . .' Kate was backing out of the door as she spoke.

In the corridor she found herself facing Matt.

'I've been looking for you,' he said.

'Why? What's wrong?'

He ignored the unflattering implication. 'Nothing yet. Just wanted to book ten minutes of your time.'

'I haven't got any,' she tried to edge past.

'How about lunch time?'

'I'll be very busy.'

'Dinner time.'

'I'll still be busy.'

'Bedtime.'

He was grinning at her. Unwillingly she grinned back. You had to award him a medal for cheek — even if you weren't prepared to award him anything else — yet.

'Some time,' she said, and slipped away.

She had something far more important on her mind than either Matt or Maya. When she tracked John down on the bridge she came straight to the point.

'I asked Peter not to leave the ship at Gothenburg because of the quick turnaround but . . .' she shrugged.

'He went regardless?'

'Yes.'

'And he's late,' supplied Charles.

'Yes.'

'Always is,' John's voice was casual.

'Leaps on at the last minute,' said Charles.

'Do you mean he's always doing this? Hasn't he ever been reprimanded?'

'Yes,' said John as his phone rang. 'That's probably him now.'

But the call was to say that someone was asking to see Kate at the Terminal Office.

'Who is it?' said Kate.

'I'll find out. Who is it Lars?' John looked back at Kate. 'Jeremy Gates. Lars seems to think it's important.'

'I'll be as quick as I can,' Kate brushed past Matt who had appeared in the door in time to hear the last part of the conversation. He turned and fell into step beside her.

'Looks as if Peter's missed the boat this time,' he said.

'For the last time.' Kate's face was grim.

'You can't be that tough on the kid.'

'Life is.'

They were approaching the restaurant now, and had to slow their steps behind Susan Porter who was descending the staircase immediately ahead of them.

'By the way, who's Jeremy Gates?' said Matt.

'A friend.'

'A good one?'

'Yes. Are you interested?'

'Just don't want to step on anybody's toes.'

'He wears jackboots,' said Kate with a little smile.

'Then I'll put on some armour,' he winked. 'You won't forget our date?'

She smiled but made no reply. Matt looked at his watch. There was just fifteen minutes left before the ship sailed. She was going to have to move fast to talk to Mr Gates, whoever he was, and get back on board.

Two hours out of Gothenburg, Matt was sitting in his office thinking longingly of his approaching lunch, when Joe Francis came in. There was something oddly furtive about him that looked strange alongside his burly no-nonsense appearance.

'I think you'd better come down Matt,' he said awkwardly.

'Have we sprung a leak?'

'Just come, will you? I want you to see something.'

As soon as Matt reached the distant corner of the engine room where Joe took him, he understood why the business had to be kept secret.

'Stay here,' he said tensely. 'I'm going to find Miss Laker.'

'You sent for me Miss Laker?' Sandy tried not to sound too sullen, but she was sick with apprehension over Peter, and she had answered Kate's summons unwillingly.

'Yes Sandy. I wondered if you could help me out. You know Peter hasn't rejoined the ship?'

'You fired him didn't you?'

'No.'

'You did.' Sandy's efforts at control fell away from her as her eyes filled with tears. 'If you think you can push people around and expect me to help you . . .'

'Sandy please, calm down . . .'

'In case people see what kind of woman you are? Let them see you — see how much you hate your own son?'

Her sobs choked her, and she turned and fled from the Purser's Office. After standing tight-lipped for a moment, Kate followed. She went straight to Sandy's cabin and found the girl leaning on the wall in the corridor outside. Her shoulders were shaking convulsively.

'When you've calmed down, Sandy, I'll try to explain.'

'I know what you've done to him. I know the moment he saw you Peter changed. I suppose you're proud of that too.'

'No. Because it's not the way it is.'

'Then where is he now?' Sandy flashed at her. 'If you didn't fire him, where is he?'

'I presume he's in Gothenburg.'

'And that suits you just fine, doesn't it? You've got rid of Peter because you couldn't stand him being on the same ship with you in case we found out. But I know and now everybody's going to know. You're not just Peter's mother, you're a bitch. *A bitch of a mother*.'

'Sandy,' said Matt's voice quietly.

Neither of them had noticed Matt's approach down the corridor, until he was standing beside them. After one look at his face Sandy gave another sob and vanished into her cabin. Matt touched Kate's arm.

'You'd better come with me,' he said quietly.

'I don't need your protection Mr Taylor.'

'I've found Peter. He's in the engine room. Someone's beaten him unconscious.'

When Matt and Joe Francis had deposited Peter on Kate's bed Matt stood back and looked at her, unsatisfied.

'Wouldn't it be better if he was in his own cabin?' he said.

'I'd rather he stayed here,' she said firmly. She was leaning over Peter, wiping his face as she spoke, and did not look up at Matt.

'Do you want me to report it to John, or will you?' he said.

'I don't want it reported to anyone.'

'It has to be. If one of my men did this to Peter I have to know about it.'

'There's no need,' she looked at him. 'Please.'

Matt threw a brief glance at Joe. 'Are you sure you didn't see who did this?' he demanded.

Joe shook his head. His eyes were perfectly expressionless.

'Thanks Joe. That's all. You can go now.'

When Joe had gone and closed the door behind him Matt looked back at Kate, baffled.

'What are you afraid of?' he demanded.

'Destroying him,' she said simply. She halted in the doorway, her face troubled. 'I daren't be away too long. Someone could be looking for me now . . .'

'I'll stay,' he offered at once. 'Joe knows where I am if I'm needed.'

When Peter began to come round half an hour later it was Matt he found leaning over him, telling him to lie still.

'God — my head —'

'What happened Peter? Who attacked you?' Peter closed his eyes but Matt persisted. 'I want to hear it from you. Tell me what happened.'

Peter opened his eyes wide, staring at Matt belligerently. 'What for? She told you enough, didn't she? I bet she didn't leave anything out, either.'

'She's told me nothing,' said Matt deliberately. 'She won't even let me report it.'

'Why?'

'You must know the answer to that.'

'Why the hell should I know why she does anything?'

'I think you do.'

'To get what she wants,' said Peter with startling venom. 'She's got me. The same way she got my father. Then killed him.'

Kate, who had entered her cabin seconds earlier, halted before entering the bedroom area, turned and departed without either of them having been aware of her.

In the restaurant the new Swedish cook's smörgasbord was receiving its first airing. Only Susan Porter did not seem to approve.

'Are there any fish left in the sea I ask myself?' she muttered as she surveyed the lavish arrangement.

With the customers there could be no doubt the new menu was a success. Maya Anderson in particular was enjoying her meal. But the Captain had eaten only a few mouthfuls before his food turned to ashes in his mouth. All his wife's mysterious and unreasonable hints about his supposed relationship with Kate (a woman he had known barely a few weeks) had suddenly explained themselves.

Almost as soon as lunch began Maya calmly outlined her reasons for taking the children on an unexpected visit to Sweden — and leaving them there.

'Emily will go to the local school and Teddy will be old enough to go to the gymnasium. Eat John, it's delicious.'

'When?' he demanded blankly.

'As soon as possible. I can't see any point in putting it off. At least your children will grow up bilingual.'

'Are you mad?' he demanded. 'You walk onto the ship, clap your eyes on Miss Laker, and suddenly you want a divorce.'

'No, no, no,' she said soothingly. 'It's not sudden at all.'

'No. *You* want a divorce and you're looking for an easy way out. Who is it? The man. Who is it?'

'Don't try that, John. I'm not a fool. You see, *I* am divorcing *you*.'

She looked up at him and smiled, her face almost as smooth and perfectly beautiful as the day he had married her. It was the face he had dreamed of for over a thousand lonely nights at sea, had longed to get back to. And now here it was, sitting across the table from him, calmly informing him that his life was about to be smashed up for her convenience.

'Never,' he said at last. 'If you want a divorce you're going to have to get it the hard way.'

'But why?' she asked, eyebrows raised in pained, reasonable surprise.

'Because I refuse to be used any longer,' he snapped. 'Do you think I haven't known what's been going on? Do you think I'm some kind of a raving idiot? Whoever and whatever your fancy man is, if you want him you'll have to get him crawling through the mud — and *without* the kids.'

'But I told you — the children want to be with me.'

'If you think I'll let you take my children to live with you and your bloody lover, you're wrong.'

'Then I must take it you refuse to give me a divorce?'

'That's right.'

There was a long silence. During it Maya gave the slightest little shrug. It was as though all that had gone before had been merely the first move in a game, a hopeful throw, but not seriously expected to produce a result, and therefore no cause for despair in a player who had come well prepared.

'This is your life, isn't it?' she said at last.

'My job.'

'Your *life*,' she corrected.

He refused to be drawn into her implications. He felt the ground becoming unsafe beneath his feet.

'Is it too much to ask who he is?' he said bitterly.

This time she did not bother to deny it. 'He's Swedish.'

'Back to your own kind?'

'You could put it that way. Or — you could say I've discovered it's only possible really to make love in your own language.'

He was glad they were in a public place. Otherwise he might have hit her for the brazen way she looked him in the eyes and said that.

'What will I tell the children?' she went on. 'About why you don't want to come home any more? You won't be, will you?'

'Try stopping me.'

'You'll confuse them. Is that what you call being a good father? It's too late to change the way they feel, John. Who's always been there when they needed help while their father roamed the high seas? No words can undo that.'

He stared at her.

The disruptions that were making Arthur Parker's life a misery showed no signs of ending. First there had been the urgent call from Miss Laker from the ship instructing him to contact her father and tell him — *tell* him mark you — to go and visit Wally James in hospital. How Arthur Parker had chuckled at that one. Miss Laker had played right into his hands. Ordering George Terson to go and visit a humble crew member could be turned into a firing matter in moments.

Only it hadn't turned out like that. George Terson, when his daughter's message was relayed to him, merely demanded to know which hospital exactly, when was the next flight to Gothenburg, and why hadn't he been informed sooner?

Arthur Parker would have got an even bigger shock if he could have seen Terson now, sitting by Wally's bed, talking to his old friend, an anxious expression in his eyes.

'Terminal cancer?' Wally was exclaiming in amazement.

'That's what everyone on the ship thinks.' Terson told him. 'Also, they think that's why you resigned.'

'Why?'

'Arthur Parker told John.'

'But it was only an ulcer. It perforated,' said Wally, bewildered.

'Why do you suppose Parker thought you had cancer?'

'Can't think — except that I handed in my resignation round about the time I told him I was ill. I didn't want to be fired — so I resigned.'

'Was Parker trying to get rid of you?' said Terson in a voice that boded no good for Parker.

'I don't know,' said Wally. 'But he told me that Head Office had lists of complaints about me. They were trying to stitch me up — force me into an early retirement.'

'Why didn't you talk to someone about it?'

'Who?'

'We've spent enough time in the past with no-one but each other to trust — against the *sea*, let alone *men*,' Terson reminded him.

'That was a lifetime ago.'

'It makes no difference.'

'You're the skipper now,' said Wally.

'Them and us.' Terson sighed, as if by sighing he could bring back the good old days.

When the ship finally docked at Amsterdam, Arthur Parker's life took a sharp turn for the better. For it was at Amsterdam that Susan Porter put through a call to Felixstowe, where she found herself talking to his secretary, Sophie. In a brief conversation a name was exchanged, after which Sophie did some quick checking, and took the results in to her boss.

'Jeremy Gates,' she said. 'He does control forty-nine per cent of the voting shares in this company, doesn't he?'

'By proxy,' said Parker. 'And he uses them. What about it?'

'One jumped-up accountant who was called in seven years ago to solve a financial crisis and is now the power behind the move to oust Terson, go public and carry freight.' Sophie paused for emphasis. 'He's Miss Laker's other half.'

Parker sat up sharply. 'How did you find that out?'

'Let's just say I've got a mole who's willing to pass on information damaging to Miss Laker. And she says Miss Laker met Jeremy Gates just before the ship sailed at Gothenburg.'

'That would be dynamite if it's true,' Sophie smiled.

In Kate's cabin Peter was preparing to depart and face the world.

'I'll say I fell downstairs,' he mumbled sulkily in answer to her concern.

'It would be better if you stayed here.'

'Whatever your reasons for "protecting" me I won't bother thanking you till I get your bill,' he said nastily.

'Peter — I heard what you said to Matt — about what you think I did to your father.'

'Not think.'

'What about yourself?'

'I was just the pawn in the game.'

'And you loved every minute of it,' she said impatiently. 'I didn't steal your father from your mother. She gave him to me. Because she didn't want him. But more than that, she didn't want anyone else to have him. It was as simple as that. The only thing you were good for as far as she was concerned was to use you to try and destroy the happiness he found with me.'

He was standing by the door, itching to go. 'I haven't got my violin,' he said icily.

She sighed, exasperated. 'Playing both ends against the middle was fine when you were a child. I could even understand that you blamed me then too. But you're not a child any more, and you just have to accept that she used you like a pistol at your father's head.'

Peter gave a sarcastic laugh, but Kate persevered.

'And when that didn't work — or he screams "look what you've done to me" — she ditched you.'

She knew from the sudden change in his face that she had struck home.

'The blame isn't your father's, mine or anyone else's.'

He looked her up and down, 'If you hated me so much, why did you take me on with you?'

'If you've listened I don't have to answer that,' she said patiently.

'To save me,' he was sarcastic again. 'Ah! And now you've done it again.'

He pulled open the door. 'Hallelujah!' He turned back suddenly, his eyes alight with unpleasant mischief. 'You can put up your hand when the Captain asks if there's any reason why these two people shouldn't be joined in holy matrimony. You will be there, I hope? When the Captain marries Sandy and me on board.'

She gazed at him aghast.

It was strange, Jo thought, how badly something could hurt, even when you had thought yourself well prepared for it. She had been waiting for Tony's retaliation ever since the moment she had rejected his offer of marriage, making it insultingly plain that she knew why it had been made. Jo could be taken for a ride just so far and no further, and that point had been reached. There was also the additional problem of Peter Nuttall who had made his suspicions obvious. Jo had witnessed the conversation in the casino, and the determined way Tony had walked out after Peter.

'What are you going to do about Peter?' she had demanded when she told Tony what he could do with his suggestion of marriage. 'You can hardly marry him too.'

Tony had stormed off without a word, but his livid eyes had told her that he would make her sorry. And now he had.

'It had to be one way or another,' he told her. He had come to find her in the empty night-club where she was putting together her music sheets for the performance. 'You've left me no choice. I don't take kindly to being held over a barrel by anyone.'

'I'm holding onto that money to protect you,' she told her. 'From yourself.'

'There's only one way to do that now.'

'By *dismissing* me?'

'Replacing you with a fresh entertainer. I want you off this ship the minute we get back to England.'

Kate had seen the name Marion Carter on the passenger list before they left Gothenburg, so it was no real surprise to receive an urgent message to come and sort out some trouble in the restaurant. She had been waiting for something of the kind.

The restaurant was empty save for a well-preserved, attractive woman in her fifties whom Kate recognised as her father's 'girlfriend' of many years. She was eating in leisurely fashion, oblivious to the fact that the rest of the place had closed around her, and Susan Porter was fuming. Kate advanced on the table without hesitation. Might as well have the confrontation now.

'Well Marion,' she said as she sat down. 'I knew you were on board of course. I was just waiting for you to show your hand. However, even I could hardly imagine you'd have the gall to try to disrupt the workings of the ship. This restaurant is closed.'

Marion smiled. 'There's no point in owning a restaurant if you don't use it,' she said. 'A bit of fish and a spot of wine isn't stretching anyone I hope.'

'Owning it?'

'In a manner of speaking,' Marion looked directly into Kate's eyes.

'Then I hardly need to tell you that the kitchen runs to a tight schedule, and if is disturbed so are the customers. And the customers are your money, Marion.'

Marion leaned back and regarded Kate with sardonic amusement. 'You know, I picked you up from school one Christmas and you gave me a lecture just like that — about a lazy art mistress. Do you remember?'

'The end of my childhood, and *you*, are two things I have made a point of forgetting and ignoring,' said Kate emphatically. 'Just as you and my father forgot and ignored me by filing me away in finishing schools.'

Marion refilled her glass. 'Your father tried to talk to you some little while ago and it ended as all your conversations ended. That's why I'm here.'

'The day you walked into my father's life and took him over, every day since then you've been nothing but trouble for me.'

'Nonsense! No-one takes anyone over unless they want to be taken over. George wanted me — and I love him.'

'So did my mother.'

'It's a bit late in the day to be getting into disturbed childhoods.'

'So you're going to try and disturb me *now?*'

'I hope not. Unless, that is, you're disturbed by twenty thousand pounds a year.'

'Tell me the rest.'

'What George was trying to do in Amsterdam was to make you an offer. And I think it's a good one. We both know what's going on behind Triangle's closed doors . . .'

'Do we?'

'I think so. And it suits George — and me — not to have you in the way. So — twenty thousand pounds a year, a mews cottage in Knightsbridge, and capital funds of up to £100,000 to start up whatever takes your fancy.'

'My God, I have got him worried.'

'I admit he's showing signs of concern — as far as he ever does.'

'I'm glad he's worried, because that's my intention. And when you get off this ship you can tell him that — *and* you can tell him that the stakes I'm playing for are a good deal higher than anything he's offering. Now, please finish your lunch as quickly as possible, so that we can all get back to normal.'

As she walked out she hoped it wasn't obvious that she was shaking all over.

In the hour it had been in Amsterdam docks, the ship had contrived to turn itself from one world into another one; from a thrumming hive into a ghost ship. Maya had departed, leaving John to make whatever excuses he could think up. Some crew members had slipped ashore for a few hours' leave.

Among those who remained on board was Linda Kennedy, who was not entitled to time off ashore, having only just rejoined the ship at Gothenburg after a brief holiday. She had now been on board for little more than twenty-four hours, yet her presence was felt. She had never yet left and rejoined without providing a topic of conversation on the bridge. As Charles said, she was like the weather. One way or another you ended up talking about it.

At the moment, however, the eyes of the three men on the bridge were fixed on George Terson's limousine, clearly recognisable on the docks, waiting for someone.

'What does he want this time?' Matt demanded.

'He wants to see me.' John told him.

'Good. 'Cos *she's* seeing *me*.' Matt did not have to spell out that he meant Kate. 'By the way,' he added as he turned to go. 'Just to warn you — *she's* back.' Again, no-one needed to ask which 'she' was meant.

'I know,' said Charles.

'You too already?' Matt grinned.

'The buttons one. I found all my buttons sewn onto the inside of my shirt.'

'So Lind's back, is she?' said John.

''Fraid so,' Matt told him. 'I had no middle to my towel. Try drying yourself with two inches of border some time.'

'Wonder what she's got in mind for Miss Laker?' said Charles.

'She wouldn't dare,' said Matt in an awed voice.

'Why not? She's the only one who doesn't know who she is yet.'

Matt grinned and left. Charles turned to John.

'Don't let Terson take up your time John. It's your wife's.'

'She has to fly home from here.' John had his eyes fixed on some dials.

'But she's only just joined you.'

66

'One of the kids is ill. Nothing serious. But you know what women are like where kids are concerned.'

'Ah well,' Charles shrugged. 'Now she's finally made the trip she'll come again.'

'Unfortunately, she has to stay at home where she's needed,' said John, realising even as he spoke that he was falling into the trap of doing exactly what Maya wanted him to do. But what else could he say? He was beginning to understand just how clever Maya had been and how little he had to fight with.

Walking towards his own cabin a few minutes later Charles found Linda heading in the other direction. Confronted with that pretty cheeky face he instinctively put his hands across the corridor, barring her way.

'Caving in are they?' she enquired.

'What?'

'The walls?'

'Not unless you've seen to them, Linda,' he was grinning. Everyone liked Linda. 'How are you?'

'Keeping well ta. And you?'

'Just a little trouble with my shirt.'

'*No,*' Her voice was a perfect mixture of outrage and disbelief. He tried to stop his grin from growing.

'Yes,' he assured her.

'Good thing I'm back then, isn't it sir. Get a bit of Law-rrr-and Order back on board.'

'Law and order?' he said, scarcely able to believe he'd heard right.

'Glad you agree sir,'

She made to go, but he kept his arm across her path. Quick as a flash she looked down at his flies, then up again, her eyes wide with horror. By the time his frantically groping hand had told him it was a false alarm she had slipped past him.

'Law-rrrr-and-Order at the ready sir,' she assured him as she vanished.

He was grinning as he went into his cabin.

When he received no answer to his knock, Matt pushed open the door to Kate's cabin and stepped inside. The door to the bedroom was open just far enough for him to see something that might have been Kate lying on the floor. But when he hurried inside he found only her uniform dropped in a crumpled heap. Kate herself was stretched face downwards on the bed. She had obviously thrown herself down in weariness after stripping off all her clothes, and was now sleeping heavily.

Noiselessly Matt picked up the uniform and hung it over a chair. Then he reached over Kate and began to pull the cover up over her naked back, just as he might have done with a small child. After which he returned to the lounge area and sat down to wait for her to wake up.

It was about an hour before she appeared in the doorway swathed in a bathrobe.

'Thank you,' she said simply. 'I lay down to close my eyes before I changed, and that was it.'

He shrugged. 'You're obviously worn out. We'll forget about going ashore, shall we? Just pass the time here.' At once her eyes hardened into a look that said 'Not again'. Matt slammed down the magazine he had been reading, '*Jeez!*' he said in disgust.

'It is what you have in mind, isn't it?'

'No.'

'You don't often seem to have much else planned.'

'It's what everyone expects, isn't it?' he said, growing angry.

'It's the way you behave.' To Kate's annoyance she felt herself growing defensive.

'The way people expect me to, you mean.'

'Then why always do what they expect?'

'I'm not, dammit. I thought we could talk quietly, have some food, maybe even a drink! Because you are tired. But now. That's not what you expect. You expect me to pounce on you in an upsurge of animal passion. Look at you — in a judo position already, and I haven't made a move except to tuck you into bed.'

'Sorry,' she smiled. 'You've surprised me.'

'Would you like a drink?'

'Please.'

In getting it he turned his back to her and said over his shoulder, 'Which doesn't mean I don't want you.' He turned and gave her a brief look. 'Get dressed.'

While he waited for her to be finished in the shower he leaned back and thought about some of the people who might be surprised if they could see him now. The Schofields for instance, whom he still thought of as his family, although he hadn't seen them for years.

Somewhere he had a real family, a mother and father who had made his childhood a living hell with their fights and bickering, and constant attempts to use him as a weapon against each other. He had parted from them when he was sixteen, running away with his birth certificate that he had found at the bottom of a drawer, and joining the Navy.

Thereafter he had spent his leaves at the Schofields' house and they had treated him as a son, because everyone knew that when Matt had got his itchy feet out of his system he was going to marry Betty and settle down. Even then he wanted to marry her, although he wasn't sure about the settling down part. Betty was his girl, had been since they'd been at school together, and he wanted no-one else. He knew she was troubled about his wandering life, but then what woman wouldn't be? Other sailors got over the problem, and there was no need to think of it for a while.

He was a good engineer and he knew it. His colleagues said the machines talked to him. By the time he was twenty-two and ready to leave the Royal Navy to seek for more exciting assignments he was loaded down with qualifications and commendations. Life stretched ahead of him, it looked totally happy and filled with possibilities. He'd see some of the world then marry Betty. Perhaps he could get a job on a passenger ship and she could work on it too; the details could be worked out later.

He signed on for an assignment with a tanker owned by an Australian company. For two years he was unable to get home, but when he did the Schofields welcomed him with open arms. He waited for Betty to press for the marriage they had often discussed, and was slightly relieved when she said nothing, although he loved her as much as ever and still meant to marry her — soon.

But sometimes he thought he caught her giving him a strange sad look. He would have liked to ask her about it, if he'd known what to say. He thought he knew the answer one night when he'd been staying with the family for a week, when she called him in a soft voice just as he was passing her open bedroom door. After that they were lovers, and when her returned to sea three months later the pain of leaving her was so great that he almost offered to give it all up and stay with her.

Now he wondered — as he had often wondered these last few years — what would have happened had he done so. For when he had been gone a month he received the letter that shattered him. Betty wrote to say that she was sorry, but the last three months had convinced her that she could not cope with the misery of loving a man who was always away. So she had married — not a man that she loved as she did Matt, but a man who was always there, who would give her the home and security she longed for, and who would be a good father to the child Matt had given her.

This was the first he'd heard of a child, and the knowledge came in a letter that brutally smashed the dreams that had sustained him through the long hours of loneliness. It was the finality of it that had shocked him. There was no offer to let him put matters right, just a swift decision taken when he was not there, and a *fait accompli* that he could either take or leave, but could do nothing about.

At the first stop he'd gone on a pub crawl that had landed him in the brig. That had been his first anaesthetic — booze. Then he switched to women. They were more fun and didn't leave you feeling too sick to work afterwards. Not that he'd always been totally faithful to Betty. In the circumstances that was hardly to be expected. But there was a big difference between the odd fling to make you forget your loneliness for the girl you really loved and the career of determined womanising that he had subsequently embarked on, and which had made him something of a legend.

He knew that new girls who came to work on the ship were warned about him on the day they arrived, and the knowledge had so far given him nothing but pleasure. He had no regrets about his way of life. It had been too much fun. He did not pine for Betty, or for the child he had never seen, and who must be about eight years old now. But he did just occasionally wonder how he might have turned out had things been different, and whether it might have been pleasant to be able to confront a woman like Kate Laker without having to explain to her in words of one syllable that he wasn't Casanova and Don Juan rolled into one, and that his whole personality wasn't concentrated below the belt.

Chapter 6

Linda Kennedy's reaction, when Sandy showed her the sparkling ring on her left hand, was definitely unflattering.

'Where d'you nick that?' she demanded at once.

'Peter gave it to me,' said Sandy, who knew Linda too well to be offended.

'Where did *he* nick it?'

'You know what it is, don't you?'

'Hot.'

'It's an engagement ring. Peter's asked me to marry him.' Sandy's eyes were shining with joy, but they soon clouded over as Linda began to chuckle. 'What's so funny about it'

'You're Peter's *fiancée?*'

'Yes.'

'I didn't know fiancées happened any more. Haven't met one in years.'

'You promise you won't tell anyone just yet. Some people might be a bit . . .'

'Yeah — crew and officers, I know.' Linda gave the ring the admiring attention that was clearly expected of her before saying, 'Hey, what's going on with Matt and that new Purser?'

'In case you've got any plans Linda you should know she's Terson's daughter,' said Sandy warningly. 'Just don't try any of your tricks on her.'

'Me? Never?' said Linda in her most innocent voice.

But as soon as she'd got rid of Sandy she stopped in the corridor outside Matt's cabin. After listening at the door for a moment she produced her set of master keys and slipped inside. When she came out again she had one of Matt's jackets tucked under her arm.

As soon as the ship was under way Kate answered the summons to John's quarters. He told her everything he had learned about Wally's condition during his talk with her father, and finished up,

'I don't believe your father is the man you seem to think he is. We've all got him wrong.'

'I know my own father,' she said, tight-lipped.

'He's basically a simple seaman. He cares about his men. He's shown that over Wally.'

'He asked you to tell me this, did he?'

'As a matter of fact he didn't mention you at all.'

'As usual. Perhaps if he'd shown the same care he's shown you and Wally to his family at home, I'd feel differently.'

John looked at her for a long moment before saying quietly, 'A father who gets his living from the sea can't give the time he might want to. It doesn't mean he cares about his children any the less.'

Kate met his eyes. 'Yes — your wife told me before she left the ship. She said she asked me to help "make you see sense" as she put it.' She considered a moment before adding, 'Be careful.'

'It would seem to be too late for that.' John got up and moved about restlessly. 'It's the children, Emily. She needs the care.'

'Then take care for her sake.'

'I intend to fight for just that.'

'It's never a fair one.' Kate mused. 'You never know what weapon she'll pick up next.'

He answered her with a slight shrug and she left him. It troubled her that a man she basically liked and respected had been won over to her father's side, although she realised his own situation was partly the cause of that.

She forced the subject from her mind. She had too many other things to think of. She felt pleasantly on top of her job. The quiet afternoon spent with Matt had left her feeling relaxed and refreshed. They had talked companionably and he had done nothing more than take her hand on the way back to her cabin. She grinned slightly, wondering how many years it could be since Matt Taylor had held a girl's hand, and let matters go at that.

She made a mental note to drop into the Casino that night and keep an eye on Tony. Two of the passengers had been unable to disembark at Amsterdam because they'd lost all their money after drinking too much. It was the kind of thing that gave Triangle a bad name, although Tony had been unable to see matters in that light when she put it to him. He'd as good as told her to mind her own business, but that she had no intention of doing.

She realised the evening was already fairly well advanced. Half an hour in her cabin to freshen up, and she'd be ready. But when she had brushed her hair and applied new make-up, there came a knock on her cabin door. She opened it wide, to reveal what could only be called an apparition.

Linda stood there wearing Matt's large uniform jacket, and nothing else. She was looking up at Kate pathetically.

'Sorry to trouble you — but have you seen Matt?' she begged.

'No,' Kate surveyed the girl, refusing to allow any expression on her face. 'Is there something I can do?'

'Get my clothes out of his cabin. You've got a key, haven't you?'

'Yes.'

'Pushed me out like this and rushed off when the Captain called, didn't he? Not gentlemanly to my way of thinking. Oh — my name's Lindall by the way. Nice to meet you.'

'Lindall?' Kate ignored the outstretched hand.

'Linda'll do this, Linda'll do that. Linda'll do. Get me?'

'Yes,' said Kate grimly. 'I think I do.'

'What's yours? Might as well be on first name terms seeing as we share the same — well — you know what I mean?'

'Of course.' Kate smiled. 'My first name's Miss Laker. Shall we use your key or mine to open his door?'

She was pleased to notice that the girl's mouth dropped slightly at this evidence that Kate wasn't fooled. She opened Matt's door with her own master key without looking at Linda again, then returned to her own cabin without a word. She shut her door behind her with slightly more force than was necessary, and stood for a moment, her eyes glinting.

So much for holding hands.

At about that same moment Matt, happily unaware how a promising relationship with Kate was being shredded, was joining Charles and John on the bridge. The talk was all of Peter Nuttall, whose bruised face had attracted attention despite Matt's not having reported the incident. It was John who dropped the bombshell.

'Matt, I'm well aware certain members of the crew resent Peter's relationship with Sandy.'

'Especially Joe Francis.' Charles put in. 'You know how he feels about her.'

'Do you think there might have been a punch-up?' said Matt.

'Just leave it alone, both of you,' said John, who felt he'd said enough.

Matt grinned. 'Somebody's bound to suggest our lovely Miss Laker engineered the whole thing anyway. You know — gave him a little push? She's behind just about everything else.'

'Well she's certainly up to something.' Charles agreed. 'I don't know what, but something; why else have a private lunch with Tony Grant?'

Matt stared: 'How do you know?'

'Susan told me. They've booked a private room for tomorrow.'

He kept the rest of the conversation to himself. Susan's frank invitation to him to have 'a little private lunch' with her had embarrassed him slightly. Not that she wasn't a looker, and had he been a bachelor he'd have jumped at the chance. But Charles wanted no-one but his Jenny. He was also vaguely embarrassed by his own fidelity. Considering his randy youth, it had its funny side. But he had no desire to change anything.

From the disgusted look on Matt's face, Miss Laker was giving him a hard time. That had its funny side too when you thought of it.

Matt might have been happier if he could have seen Kate sitting opposite Tony in the small private room next day. The private lunch had all the trimmings, including champagne, and Tony was putting out all his charm to impress her — and getting nowhere.

'I thought it was a way of getting to know each other a bit better,' he oozed. 'Can I level with you Miss Laker? I mean — rumours do tend to get around about people and I wouldn't want you thinking — well — in case somebody might have said something?'

'Who? Jo Bailey?'

Tony took a deep breath. This lady was always one jump ahead of him, and he didn't like it.

'I've known her — worked with her a long time. It's not secret that sometimes she has one too many and — well, she says things. If you know what I mean?' He was sweating slightly.

'Is that why she's leaving?'

'No, no — another engagement came up. It was a better offer. I didn't want to stand in the way of her career.'

'Very generous of you,' said Kate politely. 'So what is there she could possibly have told me that I don't already know?'

'Nothing — I mean, I just wondered.'

'I know she's in love with you — which gives you a hold on her,' said Kate. 'And may explain why she's never exposed some of the little tricks you get up to. Like occasionally dipping your hand in the till.' She paused to allow Tony to defend himself, but he seemed transfixed. Kate gave him a cool smile. 'Would you say we're getting to know each other a little better now?'

At the first chance Matt waylaid Linda in the corridor. He had a bone to pick.

'How was I to know we'd got a new Purser?' she defended herself, wide-eyed. 'Got the shock of my life I did.'

'Well it didn't go down so well, did it?' said Matt exasperated. 'Apart from blowing my chances.'

'Do you good to go to bed on your own. You get more sleep that way you know.'

'Just be warned. She's a tough lady.'

'Wouldn't have thought she was your type?' She cocked her head on one side, hopefully, but Matt didn't rise to the bait.

'Shouldn't you be working?' he asked.

He made his way to the Purser's Office where he found Kate deep in paperwork.

'Just to say we might have a slight hold-up,' he said. 'The boiler-room fan's playing up again.'

'How long a delay?'

'Half an hour maybe. Joe's working on it now.'

'You'll let me know —' Kate spoke without looking up.

'Had a nice lunch did you?'

Now she looked up. 'Was there anything else?'

'Tony Grant — I never figured he'd be your type.'

'Close the door behind you. It's hard to concentrate with all that noise outside.'

He thought that if Miss Laker was getting her revenge for Linda she was doing it in fine style.

The first thing Gary Rae did when he boarded at Felixstowe clutching his luggage in one hand and his guitar in the other, was to search for Tony. It wasn't just that Tony had hired him for the night-club and was therefore his boss. Gary wanted to know just what the hell Tony was up to.

'I needed a quick replacement. You're just somebody who sprang to mind,' said Tony lamely.

'After all this time?' Gary jeered. 'Come on.'

'You know showbusiness.'

'I know *you*. Or had you forgotten?'

'It's a professional engagement like any other.'

Gary gave him a cynical look and followed Tony through into the crews quarters.

'For what it's worth,' he said, 'Granger's still looking for you.'

He was just close enough to see the sudden fear on Tony's face, quickly followed by a look of bravado.

'So who cares?' Tony said at last.

'I would if I owed him money.'

A door ahead of them opened and Peter stepped out directly into their path. Gary's eyebrows flew up.

'Peter!' he exclaimed.

Peter turned pale. He looked at Gary as a man might look at a ghost.

'Er — hello,' he managed to say, then pushed past them down the corridor without another word.

'You know each other?' said Tony, who had watched both their reactions with interest. 'Where from?'

'Oh — around,' said Gary evasively. 'What happened to his face?'

'He had an accident. Fell down some stairs.'

When they had reached Gary's cabin and he was unpacking he reverted to his original theme.

'So you thought of me — after all this time? I'm very touched.'

'If you'd only listen to me —'

'I did once. Remember? Boy, was I naïve in those days. You know, my career was actually going right till I met you! Personal Manager! That was a joke. What kind of lies did you tell Jo Bailey about what you were going to do for her? The same ones you told me?'

'Okay.' Tony sighed. 'So I gave you a rough deal. That's the way it goes sometimes. But the past's the past isn't it?'

Gary answered him with a cynical look and Tony quickly changed the subject.

'So how come you know Peter Nuttall?'

For a brief but perceptible second Gary tensed. Then he relaxed with an effort, and laughed.

'Through a mutual friend, that's all,' he said.

Tony reckoned he'd have to let it go at that. But he hadn't finished with the subject. Not by a long chalk.

The atmosphere on the bridge was definitely domestic. Charles was making himself a coffee and occasionally consulting a sheet of paper containing a scrawled list.

'Hey, what's this then?' Matt read from the list. 'Corner table-lamp, dinner-set, shower-unit —?'

'Thank you.' Charles snatched the list and thrust a coffee into Matt's hand.

'Choose something from it please,' groaned John. 'He's been driving me mad, keeps asking my advice.'

'It's Jenny's wedding annniversary present.' Charles explained.

Matt gave him a pained look. 'That's one of the best reasons for not getting married I've ever heard — a wedding anniversary.'

'I'm telling you that's what you need,' said Charles piously. 'A good woman to take you in hand.'

'I'd rather have a bad one — more fun.'

'Talking about Miss Laker then?' Charles ribbed him.

'You're joking.'

'Take a leaf out of Tony Grant's book. Set up a private lunch.'

'You mean it wasn't —?' Matt gaped. 'He invited her?'

'So I gather.' Charles gave him a wink.

'Excuse me.' Matt vanished without drinking his coffee.

Charles grinned. He felt as if he'd done his good deed for the day.

'How is Jenny?' John spoke without looking up from a chart he was studying.

'Terrific. Looking forward to my leave naturally.'

'Naturally.'

Something in John's tone made Charles look at him sharply.

'Matt told me about Maya,' he said awkwardly. 'Not in gossip mind, genuine concern.'

'Thanks. Yes it's Maya. I'm thinking of quitting.' John spoke heavily.

'You can't be serious!'

'When things were running smoothly for Maya and me, everything was — well — smooth. Okay, Maya always wanted me to give up the sea and become somebody with a garden. I resisted. The rift became serious and widened. You — with Jenny — you can hardly understand. But for me — well, my kids need a father . . .'

'Won't they still have one?'

'Yes. Me. I've no intention of abdicating responsibility. Certainly not to someone else.'

Charles gave an involuntary shiver. 'I hope I never have to go through anything like a separation. I can't imagine what I'd do. Life without Jenny is — well, it's unthinkable.'

'Then don't think about it.' said John.

When the knock came on Peter's door he looked up quickly expecting to see Kate, who knew he was looking for her. After fleeing Gary Rae he had gone searching, and finally run her to earth outside the restaurant. All he had got for his pains was a sharp reminder that she didn't want the passengers to see his bruised face, and a command to get back to his cabin until she could find time for him. It had actually been a relief for him to go and hide himself away again.

He was afraid that anyone meeting him could see the terror that was flooding through him.

His visitor turned out to be Sandy with clean sheets for his bed.

'It seemed as good an excuse as any to see how you were,' she said, giving him a nervous smile. Instinct told her that something else had gone wrong with him, but as always with Peter she was baffled.

'I'm okay,' he said.

'Everyone seems to think it was because of me — what happened?' she said, looking at his face.

'No. Anyway, does it matter what people think?'

'It matters to me — and you, the way you behave sometimes.'

'Sandy —' he pulled her into his arms and held her reassuringly.

'There's so much I don't understand about you,' she whispered. 'I want to but —'

'I love you. Isn't that enough?'

'I don't know what to think any more.'

His voice became urgent. 'Sandy, I need you. I really do need you — more than ever now.'

She was reaching up for his kiss when the door opened and Kate stood on the threshold. She would have backed out but Sandy pulled away and dashed past her. Kate stepped into the cabin and closed the door behind her.

'What was it you wanted to see me about?' she said.

'Bringing Gary Rae on board,' he said bitterly. 'You couldn't resist it, could you?'

'Don't be ridiculous. I don't book the entertainers on this ship. You know that.'

'Oh really? That's what your lunch with Tony Grant was about, was it?'

Kate sighed. 'If you don't think I've got better things to do than —'

'I thought I'd got away from you. Now here you are trying to mess up my life again.'

'The only person who's ever messed up your life is yourself.'

'You mean *you* had no part in it — *mother?*'

'Stop calling me that.'

'You asked me to, once — or have you forgotten?'

'Stop it Peter. Just stop it.' The authority in her voice seemed to have the effect of quietening him, because he relapsed into sulky silence.

'I've never wanted you to hate me.' Kate went on.

He turned away helplessly. 'I don't hate you . . .'

'When I married Bill — the last thing I ever wanted to do was come between you both. You know that.'

'Yes, I know . . .'

'And when he was killed — what was I supposed to do? You were under age — I thought when I met Alex —' she gave a shrug. It was old history. 'Peter — I care —'

'Is that through guilt or a misplaced sense of responsibility?'

But now Kate had had enough. She turned to go, to stop herself saying something unforgivable to this petulant child.

'Did you bring Gary Rae on board?' His voice stopped her at the door.

'No, I did not. I don't even know him.'

'He knows me,' Peter said quietly.

Suddenly understanding his meaning she stared at him, horrified.

When Kate went into the bar a few minutes later, Gary Rae was so firmly on her mind that when she saw him there she half thought he must be an hallucination. Then she realised that she was really seeing him, and seated next to him was Susan Porter. They appeared to be deep in conversation. She surveyed them for a minute, too disturbed by what Peter had just told her to know what to do next.

'Hey!'

She turned with a start to find Matt standing there.

'I've been looking for you,' he said.

'I'm flattered,' she said absently.

'To say I'm sorry,' Matt persisted, conscious that he did not have her attention.

'For what?'

'Well — I found out who took who to lunch.'

'Tony Grant,' she said, light dawning.

'Yes.'

'A lady never refuses an offer of lunch — or dinner.' She smiled at him. It was some hours now since she had recovered her sense of humour about Linda Kennedy.

'Is that an invitation?' Matt asked tentatively.

'Depends . . .'

'Lunch?'

'Tomorrow'd be fine.'

'Dinner tonight would be even better.'

She smiled at him. 'I'll look forward to it.'

'Eight o'clock?'

'That'll be lovely.'

Before leaving the bar she took another glance at the table where Gary Rae and Susan had been sitting. But it was deserted.

At lunchtime Matt made straight for Susan Porter. He had a favour to ask.

'One of your specials,' he begged. 'A nice intimate dinner for two — in my cabin.'

'And who's holding the lucky ticket number this time?' she queried ironically. 'Not another student from economy class?'

'No way. This is the big time. Katherine Laker, no less.'

It pleased him to know that he'd left her staring.

The crew restaurant was two decks below, and was self-service. Linda and Sandy, who often lunched together, saw Joe Francis as soon as he came in and joined the queue.

'Why don't you just ask him direct?' urged Linda. 'I would. It's better than keeping on wondering. He'd probably tell you.' As Joe reached the end of the queue Linda hailed him.

He needed no second invitation, and his eyes lit up with pleasure when he saw Sandy. As he settled himself beside them Linda launched straight into the attack.

'Joe, Sandy's got something she wants to ask you,' she glared at Sandy who had been frantically shaking her head, and now sat there covered in embarrassment. 'Go on,' said Linda. 'If you don't, I will.' She turned to Joe. 'It's about Peter Nuttall. No-one believes it was an accident, what happened. Everyone thinks you and he had a fight.'

'I can't help what people think, can I?' he said evasively. He gave Sandy a tentative look. 'Is that what *you* think?'

'I don't know,' she said miserably.

'I'm asking you.'

'It's just —'

'All I did was find him. Why's everyone making such a fuss?' His voice had risen belligerently.

'You'll have to excuse me,' Linda said suddenly. 'I can't miss this.'

She darted across to the service hatch where she had spotted Gary Rae. Joe and Sandy couldn't hear what was said, but they saw Linda grab a serviette and Gary write something on it, looking flattered. After a minute the two of them sat down at a table together.

'I'd better be getting back to work,' said Sandy, rising hurriedly.

'Sandy —' Joe's hand on her wrist stopped her. 'He's not right for you.'

'Joe, I love him.'

'You know I'm fond of you. I'd hate to see you get hurt.'

'Yes I know. I appreciate it.'

His voice became significant. 'You should listen to me when I say I'd hate to see you get hurt *as well*.'

She stared at him for a moment, then left the restaurant at a run.

Tony Grant was sitting in his cabin humming softly to himself. Suddenly it was Christmas again. Just when things had looked black he'd had another stroke of good luck.

It had been pure chance that he'd been in the Radio Room this morning when Susan Porter was putting that call through to Arthur Parker in Felixstowe; pure chance that he'd happened to be alone; and pure chance that a switch had been left on that caused her call to be amplified into the Radio Room.

So Susan Porter was Arthur Parker's spy, was she? That meant Susan Porter could be a very useful ally to him — as he'd told her when he caught up with her immediately afterwards. Not that he was asking for something for nothing. In return for her help he wouldn't tell anyone what she was up to.

A sharp knock on his door made him seize the pocket calculator he had been holding, and the little book in which he had been entering figures, and shove them both under his pillow.

His visitor was Susan.

'Thought you might like to hear what I managed to find out,' she said.

'If it's going to help get that interfering bitch off my back — even better, off the ship — yes.'

'Well, if it helps any, you were right about one thing. Your singer's covering up for something in Peter Nuttall's past.'

'So's Miss Laker,' Tony mused.

'I get the impression Peter's her Achilles heel.'

Susan was both worried and cheered when she left Tony's cabin. On the one hand it was good to have an ally. On the other hand Tony made her nervous, the more so since he now had a kind of power over her. There were too many people who had power over her. Arthur Parker was another. Two days ago in Felixstowe she had made a brief visit to his office, during which he had made it plain he would not hesitate to use a certain fact he knew about her — if she made it necessary.

All these thoughts were driven abruptly from her head by the sight of Charles Woodhouse just ahead of her, entering his cabin.

After pausing a moment she plucked up the courage to knock.

'I just thought as I was in the vicinity . . .' she said when he opened the door.

'Come on in,' he said cheerfully. He seemed to have forgotten their last meeting. He was scrubbing at his hand with a handkerchief.

'I've cut my hand,' he said. 'Don't ask me how.'

'Let me see . . .' Before he could say anything she had taken hold of his hand to look at it. Something in the way she held it reminded Charles sharply that this was a woman to be wary of, and when she looked up and their eyes met he was certain of it. He pulled away and hurried into the bathroom.

'Can't think what I was doing . . .' he called over his shoulder as he put his hand under the tap.

When he returned she was looking at the photo of Jenny that he kept by his bed. He was glad she'd noticed it.

'You need someone to look after you,' she mused.

'Well I've got Jenny.' She said nothing, and he floundered on. 'I'm still trying to work out what the hell I should get for our wedding anniversary. Trouble is, it's next Tuesday.'

'I've never known such a devoted husband.' She looked up at him.

'I'm a one-woman man, you see,' he said apologetically.

She gave a rueful half smile. 'Maybe that's the main reason you're so attractive.'

'Who, me?' he said in alarm. 'You're kidding. According to Jenny I snore. Call that very romantic?'

'If that's all you base love on . . .' she shrugged. Suddenly she blurted out, 'I wish you weren't married.'

He took a deep breath. 'I am. And I do love her — really.'

'I know that.'

'It wouldn't work,' he said gently. 'Jenny or no Jenny. I'm sorry.'

When she had departed in tears he breathed a sigh of relief. He had no nostalgic yearnings for the days when he would have responded differently. He was conscious only of a longing to get off the ship and back to Jenny as quickly as possible. He changed his shirt and got out of his cabin quickly in case she came back.

Barely had he joined John on the bridge when Matt came bounding up the stairs like an exultant schoolboy.

'Howzat!' he demanded of them both. 'Ten o'clock tonight, the indestructible Miss Laker finally succumbs to the indefatigable charms of one Matt Taylor.'

'Congratulations!' said Charles. 'Everyone seems to be getting their end away tonight. I was having my ear bent by Gary Rae not so long ago about the bird he's got lined up.'

'Who is it?' said Matt. 'Anyone I know?'

Charles shrugged. 'Search me. He didn't say a name and I didn't ask.'

John turned and faced Matt. 'You know I don't normally interfere but . . .' he hesitated in front of Matt's stare. 'Matt, it's not a good idea. She's not just another . . .'

'Listen — I know what I'm doing. Okay?'

'What you do in your private life's one thing, but anything that's likely to affect the running of this ship . . .'

'Just stuff it will you,' said Matt furiously.

Charles, looking, horrified from one to the other, sensed that there was something dangerous in the silence that fell between them. This was no ordinary row.

'Hey, come on, you two . . .' he said lamely, and fell silent because nobody was listening to him.

'As long as I'm Captain of this ship it'll be run to my specifications. Is that clear?'

'Perfectly,' said Matt, tight-lipped. 'As long as it's to do with the ship.'

'That includes the behaviour of everybody in it?'

'What's the matter? Jealous?'

In the pause that followed Matt could see John trying to control himself. At last John said,

'You're good at your job. I consider you a personal friend. Just don't force me into doing something we could both regret.' .

'Then don't push it,' said Matt coldy. 'Or we will regret it.'

Just for tonight, Gary thought, he could forget that he was forty and feeling it. That little raver he'd met in the restaurant today had looked at him as though he was Elvis Presley and she'd jumped at the chance of another meeting tonight. And now it was nine-thirty in the evening, and here she was, bang on the dot.

'Not bad,' he said as Linda appeared, in the bar.

'Well it's not every day I get asked for a drink by a celebrity, you know.'

'A has-been,' he said, fishing.

'I wouldn't say that,' she responded on cue. 'I mean, I knew who you were, recognised you straight off.'

He tried his favourite opening gambit. 'Tell me about yourself.'

'Oh there's nothing to tell,' she shrugged.

'Family?'

'Not really,' she looked away evasively.

'But your brother — the one you got me to sign that serviette for?'

'Oh yes — well there's him of course.'

'What does he do?' Gary persevered.

'Look, let's drop the subject shall we? I thought you asked me for a drink? Not a bleedin' inquisition.'

'Okay, okay. Let's go. Where is it?'

'What?' Linda stared at him as he rose from the table.

'Your cabin,' he said patiently.

'What?'

'Well, you're a groupie, aren't you? All this — "Not every day I get asked for a drink by a celebrity" —'

She jumped to her feet. ''Ere, I'm off.'

'Right. I take it it's your place then.'

She gave him a glare. 'Nobody comes to my cabin. *Nobody*. Is that clear? You come after me and I warn you —'

'What?' he sneered.

'I'll just yell for help. I've got friends on board this ship you know. You haven't. And they can really hurt you.'

'Yes, I've seen at least one of the results.'

Linda did not tie this remark up with Peter. She was too busy pursuing her own line.

'I wouldn't invest in a mirror if you try anything,' she finished.

When she had stormed out Gary stood rubbing his chin ruefully. He'd miscalculated there and no mistake. And yet he could have sworn that she was a groupie. It was odd the way she'd got edgy as soon as he began asking about her brother . . .

He looked round the bar to see if anyone had witnessed the scene. He could see Joe Francis sitting alone, looking as if he were rapidly getting drunk. At a corner table John, Charles, Susan and Kate were deep in conversation and had no eyes for him. Gary wandered over to the bar where he could see Peter, who also looked as if he'd had one too many. Sandy was watching him with nervous, possessive eyes.

'Well, been avoiding me?' Gary eased himself onto the stool beside Peter.

'Who's been avoiding you?' Peter gave him a bleary stare.

'I just thought . . .'

'Stop thinking. I haven't been avoiding you. Why should I?'

'I was just going to say it's nice seeing you again,' said Gary soothingly.

'You don't have to be so bloody polite, you know,' Peter snapped.

Sandy set drinks down in front of both of them. While Gary fumbled for money Peter seemed to tense his shoulders as if preparing to leap at something. Suddenly he turned on Gary,

'I've got something to tell you though . . .'

'Peter, you're drunk.' Sandy whispered frantically.

'Of course I'm drunk. I don't need you telling me. I want to say something.'

'Look,' said Gary hurriedly, 'Let's leave it till tomorrow.'

'I just want to say —' Peter struggled off his stool and stood there unsteadily, '*Everybody!* I want you all to know — Sandy and me — we're engaged. We're engaged to be married — so cheers.'

In the stunned silence that followed Peter downed his drink in one swallow, while Sandy, looking anything but a delighted newly-engaged girl, burst into tears of embarrassment and fled from the bar. She got as far as the desk outside, then stopped, leaning on the rail, shaken by sobs. When she felt the looming presence of Joe Francis beside her she turned, without thinking, and went into his arms for comfort.

'Oh Joe - why? Why did he have to? And like that? It made me feel so cheap.'

'You're all right. I'm here. What do you want with people like him anyhow? You've got me. I won't hurt *you* . . . I'll take care of you . . . Sandy . . . Sandy . . .'

She became aware that his tone had changed from soothing to urgent, that his arms had become a prison from which she could not escape as he tried to kiss her.

'Joe — please — Joe . . . don't — I —'

'Don't leave me Sandy . . . don't leave me . . . I'll take care of you . . .'

She managed to fight him off at last, and fled, leaving him standing there. He was too unsteady to follow her, and by now some of his fragile control was returning. After a moment the bar door opened and Peter came out, propelled by Kate who was whispering something urgent and furious into his ear. Joe watched them wearily. Then he went back into the bar, determined to spend the rest of the evening getting even drunker than he was.

When Kate had seen Peter to his cabin and uttered a few well-chosen words of wrath at his uncouth behaviour, she went and knocked on Gary Rae's door. It seemed a good moment to tell him of some plans she had made on his behalf over the ship's radio that afternoon.

'I want to talk to you about Peter,' she told him.

'Everyone on this ship seems interested in Peter. You're not the first enquiry I've had.'

'I've made my own enquiries and I understand you're not a bad entertainer. Too good to be messing around with Tony Grant.'

'Really?' he said in a cautious tone.

'Peter Nuttall is a relative of mine. Naturally I wouldn't want him to suffer any . . . pain. Your presence on this ship could cause him pain.'

'Well I can't exactly jump off can I?'

'No but we don't remain at sea for ever.'

Silently she handed him a sheet of paper. His eyes widened as he read it. It contained details of an engagement with a very wealthy chain of hotels in Holland — at a very generous price.

'This shipping line has a lot of clout with that particular hotel chain, and they own a good number of clubs too. Europe and Scandinavia will love you. As you can see the money's excellent — and it's not a dead-end job.'

'And what if I refuse?'

'You won't,' she smiled at him. 'You're a chancer.'

They talked about it for a few minutes but they both knew this was a formality. He was going to do what Kate wanted, and the rest was just talk. When she rose to leave they were in perfect accord with each other.

As she opened his door and stepped out into the corridor Kate gave him her warmest smile. After all, she had nothing personally against him, and she wanted to keep him sweet until she'd got rid of him.

'Goodnight,' she told him warmly. 'And — thank you.'

She closed the door and turned to find herself face to face with a furious Matt. One glance at his expression was enough to tell her that it was way past the time she should have presented herself at his cabin for an intimate little dinner. In the troubles of the evening she had forgotten all about it, and now Matt's grim eyes told the whole tale of the hour he'd spent waiting alone in his cabin while the dinner spoiled. Something deep inside Kate wanted to enjoy a good chuckle at his expense, but she suppressed it. He was quite angry enough.

'Doing the rounds are you?' he demanded. 'Leaving me sitting there like a —'

'I'm sorry —'

'Hadn't even the decency to tell me,' Matt's head jerked towards Gary's door. 'I see now who his pick-up for the night was . . .'

He was silenced by the force of Kate's hand across his face. It was an action of blind instinct, and one she immediately regretted, but she knew at once that she would be wasting her time apologising. Matt's eyes were hard and unforgiving as he said, 'John was right, telling me to stay clear of you . . .'

Chapter 7

Charles paused in his packing to give an amused glance at the sight of Matt slouched in a chair, smoking a cigarette and looking thoroughly discontented. His left hand clutched a glass of Charles's whisky, and his face bore the look of a man who could get through the whole bottle without any encouragement.

'Hey!' Charles hit him gently on the side of the head. 'You never listen to me. Get married.' Matt squinted cynically up at him. 'If you were married you wouldn't have to think of this as having been stood up.'

'How else could I think of it?' said Matt, rubbing his cheek slightly.

'You'd just think your wife missed dinner because of her work. And you'd be very relaxed because you'd know she'd be there tomorrow.'

Matt snorted into his whiskey. Miss Laker *was* going to be there tomorrow. Miss Laker was there every damn day. And a fat lot of good it did him. It was all very well for Charles, packing to go home for his wedding anniversary with his beloved Jenny, to peddle platitudes.

Matt drained his glass and got up to leave.

'Think I'll hunt up that brunette who was making eyes at me in the dining room this afternoon,' he said.

Charles followed him to the door. 'Hair of the dog that bit you, eh?'

'Exactly.'

'Passenger?'

'First class. My love to Jenny if I don't see you before you go.'

'Will do. Have fun.'

'Will do,' Matt smiled wickedly and left.

He felt slightly better now that he had reminded himself that there were always other fish in the sea. Also, he had the feeling that his final jibe to Kate had gone right home.

In fact it had stung her even more strongly than he had suspected, strongly enough to send her storming off to find John and demand an explanation. She caught up with him just outside the Radio Room. He was staring numbly at a cable in his hand, but she paid no attention to this.

'How dare you try interfering in my private life,' she raged at him. 'If you've any complaints, kindly restrict them to my work.'

John looked up from the cable, anger suddenly erupting from him.

'All right. You want complaints — here's one. Leave my crew alone, do you hear? Stick to the job you're paid for instead of disrupting my ship with your adolescent flirtations.'

'How dare you!'

'Get your father to fire me if you want to,' he shouted. 'But until he does, remember, I'm still the Captain of this ship.'

'The prerogatives of a ship's Captain do not include managing the other officers' social lives. So with all due respect, Captain, I'd like to know what the hell's the matter with you.'

John sighed, and his shoulders sagged slightly. 'I'm sorry. It's this,' he waved the cable slightly. Kate took it and read it, her eyes widening with horror.

'Oh God,' John muttered. 'I don't know how to tell him.'

'Would you like me to do it?'

'No thanks. It comes with the job.'

'Right.' Kate thought for a moment. 'I'll arrange to have him taken off by helicopter.'

'You know,' said John slowly, 'I worked all my life to be a Captain. Sometimes I wish I were a cabin boy — or a cook.' He sighed heavily and went off towards Charles Woodhouse's cabin.

Charles welcomed him cheerfully. 'What brings you here in the middle of the night?'

'Why don't you sit down?' said John lamely.

Charles caught sight of the cable in John's hands. It seemed to send out warning signals to him.

'What's that?' he demanded in a sharp voice. 'What's going on?'

'Why don't . . .?'

'Is it Jenny?' Charles interrupted him harshly.

'There's been an accident . . .'

'It is Jenny.'

'She's still alive.'

'Still alive!' Charles was white to the lips. 'What do you mean — still alive?'

'Her condition's critical . . . Kate's radioing for a helicopter now to take you ashore.'

Charles began to dress frantically. His hands were shaking.

'I feel like a rat in a trap. Stuck on this ship in the middle of the sea and my wife alone in some hospital.'

'She's not alone. Her mother's with her.'

'*But I'm not with her.*'

Charles snatched the cable and read it thoroughly.

'The car,' he said bitterly. 'I *told* her about the brakes John. I *told* her to take the car to the garage. She wasn't paying any attention. Wasn't listening to a word I said.'

He stopped at a knock at the door. John opened to find Kate.

'I can't get the helicopter till morning,' she said quietly. Unseen by Charles she handed John another cable that she held in her hand.

'Terrific.' Charles was ranting. 'Just terrific. Look, are you sure. Can't the Navy send one out?'

He seemed to realise that John was staring at him. For the first time Charles saw the new cable in John's hands, and his eyes met the Captain's.

'What is it?' he whispered frozenly.

There was a long silence before John could get the words out. 'She's dead Charles.'

Charles stood immobile, wide-eyed, silent. He looked from John to Kate and back to John again, his eyes desperately pleading. When finally he spoke, his voice was barely audible.

'She's not,' he said.

'Kate's had it confirmed.' John said quietly.

He gave Kate a look as he spoke, and a brief jerk of the head. She understood. Whatever needed to be done for Charles, only an old friend, and another man, could do. She left the cabin and returned to the Radio Office. There were more arrangements to be made for Charles now, and on the whole she felt it was she who had the easier job.

The tall and extremely beautiful blonde who was trying to write something outside the closed door of the Purser's Office next morning seemed to be having trouble with her pen.

'Can I help you?' Peter Nuttall offered, coming up behind her.

'I don't know,' she said in a low, attractive voice. 'Something terrible's happened.'

He unlocked the office door and showed her inside.

'Have a seat,' he said.

'I've been waiting for ten minutes,' she fretted. 'Why isn't someone on duty?'

'I am. What has happened Miss . . .'

'Gibson. Rachel Gibson. I've been robbed. It was a red leather wallet, with a two-hundred-year-old diamond ring in with the change.'

Peter made a brave effort to cover his alarm.

'It's worth over £5,000,' Miss Gibson continued. 'Don't you think I should be making a proper report to the Purser?'

'I'll see that she gets this information immediately,' Peter promised. 'Now when was the last time you remember seeing your wallet?'

'When I went to bed — well, no. I don't suppose I remember having it after I put it back in my bag in the Casino last night. Yes. I was having a drink with the croupier.'

'Tony Grant?' said Peter involuntarily.

'That's right,' she beamed. 'I had my wallet then.'

'I think you're right,' Peter confirmed. 'This is a situation for the Chief Purser.'

There was a turn-up for the books, he thought. Who'd ever have believed that he'd be anxious to see Kate? And actually worried when phone call after phone call failed to find her.

The news of Charles's tragedy had swept through the ship like wildfire. Matt, sitting with him, was continually anwering the door to solicitous callers. To all of them he returned the same answer. Charles was sleeping under the influence of a heavy pill that the Medical Officer had given him, and thank you for asking.

One who was not so easily put off was Susan Porter, who appeared bearing a tray covered with a large napkin.

'I've brought some food. I thought Charles might want to eat,' she whispered.

'No, I don't think so.'

'He might. You never know. You ought to have something here.'

While he hesitated she slipped deftly past him and headed for the bedroom.

'I'll leave it, just in case,' she insisted.

Charles opened his eyes and stared at her blearily as she entered.

'I've brought you some food Charles,' she said tentatively. 'Shall I put it down here?'

'Food?' he was looking at her with the unfocused gaze of a confused child.

'Let me have it,' said Matt. He reached for the tray but Susan held it out of his reach.

'Why are you bringing me food?' Charles demanded.

'I thought you might be hungry.'

He frowned as though trying to concentrate on something. 'No you didn't. You thought you'd get your hooks into me now Jenny's dead.'

Even Matt was horrified, pitying Susan for her deep blush and her gasp of 'Oh no —'

'Come on, Susan,' he said, taking her arm. 'Get out of here.'

'What are you?' said Charles his voice rising. 'A bloody vulture?'

'Charles —' Susan spoke frantically as Matt was pulling her out of the room. 'I just thought you might . . .'

'Might be interested in seeing you? Ha! Just because my wife's lying on a cold slab in some morgue you think I want to see you?' He banged his head back against the wall as Matt and Susan disappeared. He remained as he was, staring at the far wall seeing against its blankness the smiling face of Jenny, whom he would see no more. And slowly he began to cry.

Matt remained discreetly in the outer room after Susan's departure. When he heard another knock at the door he heaved a sigh of exasperation. When he opened the door he and Kate were equally startled to see each other. Despite the present situation the events of last night hung heavy between them.

'I thought John was here,' she said.

'I think he's in his cabin,' Matt told her quietly.

'I came to see how Charles was doing.'

Matt stepped out into the corridor and closed the door behind him. His tone was polite, but no friendlier than it had to be.

'Not very well, really,' he said. 'He's asleep.'

'Well . . .' Kate did not know what else to say. She rustled the papers in her hand.

'I've almost finished making the necessary arrangements,' she said.

'Good.'

There was an uncomfortable silence. She could feel his determination to do nothing to help her.

'Look Matt, I'm sorry about last night. It couldn't be helped.'

'Forget it.'

'Really.'

'Really. Forget it.'

She frowned at him, realising from his tone that she was still being shut out. 'All right.' she said. 'If you will,'

'Consider it forgotten,' he said lightly.

She knew she hadn't been forgiven.

Later that afternoon Kate returned to her own cabin stripped off for a shower. She felt exhausted. She'd been up since five that morning coping with the paperwork connected with Charles' arrangements. Then she had had to listen to Peter becoming voluble and excited over his failure to find her to deal with a theft from a passenger who apparently *had* to talk to the Chief Purser and no-one else. When Kate heard the value of Miss Gibson's loss she could understand Peter's concern, but she felt irritated that he couldn't have put himself out to convince Miss Gibson that his own attention would be adequate.

Then, when Kate had the time to deal with the passenger, Miss Gibson was nowhere to be found, something which threw Peter into another tizzy. Thoroughly exasperated Kate had told him, 'If she does come back, do you think you could get her to wait, while I shower and change?'

And now here she was, sitting in her own cabin, wrapped in a bath-robe, and feeling fresh for the first time that day. She made a face of annoyance when she heard someone at her door. That would be a message to say Miss Gibson had been found, and Kate could have done with another half an hour to herself.

But her visitor was Linda Kennedy, looking visibly agitated, and when Kate heard the story she had to tell she understood why. It didn't surprise her in the slightest to discover that Linda went in for a little eavesdropping, but on this occasion she felt she had to allow the ethics of it to pass. Linda had been listening to some purpose, and what she had discovered made the hairs rise slightly on the back of Kate's neck.

'I don't know what Tony Grant and Miss Porter have got against you,' Linda said when she was comfortably ensconced, 'but they're doing their level best to get that Miss Gibson to lay a complaint against you with Head Office. They practically had it all written out for her — negligence, ignoring a passenger's complaint — that sort of thing.'

She paused and studied Kate's thoughtful face.

'Has she made a complaint, Miss Laker?' she asked after a moment.

'Yes,' said Kate thoughtfully. 'She's had something quite valuable stolen.'

"I thought it must be something like that. I heard Tony Grant say

'Mr Parker will catch your thief.' He also said she'd be doing a lot of people a big favour if she telexed a complaint to the General Manager, because you were incompetent and there'd been any number of complaints against you. I expect he made that up,' Linda finished quickly.

Kate permitted herself a small smile. It was obvious that Linda had had time to discover that she was George Terson's daughter. Kate wondered if that was her sole reason for coming here, and doubted it. Whatever her faults Linda was plainly a plucky girl, not lacking in spirit. Without having a chance to know her well, Kate sensed instinctively that 'sucking up to the boss's daughter' just wasn't in character for Linda. There had to be some other reason, but there was no time for her to go into it now.

'I deeply appreciate your coming to tell me this,' she told Linda.

'Well, I've had people out to get me before, and when I happened to overhear it — it didn't seem like fair play to me.'

'Yes, well . . .' Kate was trying to think.

'I knew you'd be well caught with your pants down if she'd called the General Manager and he had the ship crawling with coppers before you even got a chance to solve the crime yourself,' Linda interrupted.

'Yes, well . . .'

'You *can* solve it without bringing in a million coppers, can't you?' An impartial observer might have thought Linda's tone a little more anxious than the situation warranted, but Kate was too preoccupied to notice.

'I'd be really disappointed if you couldn't after all I've heard of you and how marvellous you are.'

'I'll take care of it. I'm grateful to you Linda. I've often found the best method of defence is attack.'

Linda beamed. Positively, Kate thought, there was something here she didn't understand. But there was no time to worry about it now. She had to get dressed and send off some cables.

'There's something funny going on,' said Sophie, waving a telex at Arthur Parker. 'About twenty minutes ago this came in from Miss Laker reporting a theft on the ship, and asking us to do everything short of involve the Home Office. She wants us to run the passenger list past the English, Swedish and Dutch police, every insurance company in the book, and all the other passenger carriers — land, sea and air.'

'Five minutes later, this —' she held up another telex, '— came in from the passenger who's been robbed, complaining that the Purser on duty — Miss Laker — failed to respond to the theft. What do you make of it?'

'Are the receiving times on the telexes?'

'Yes. It seems to me that we came within five minutes of separating Miss Laker from her job.'

To Kate it was a positive pleasure to confront Rachel Gibson in her cabin and outline everything she had done to track down the thief.

'Swedish plainclothes men will be looking over disembarking passengers when we dock in Gothenburg in a half an hour to see if there are any familiar criminal faces in the crowd,' she said reassuringly. 'We're doing everything in our power.'

She supposed it was slightly mean of her to enjoy Miss Gibson's obvious discomfiture, but in the circumstances she felt she was entitled to.

'I'm so sorry I sent that telex Miss Laker. I can't explain — I was so upset —'

'Perfectly understandable.' Kate soothed her. 'I'm terribly sorry I wasn't available, but an officer's wife was killed in a car crash and I was busy making the necessary arrangements.'

'If there's any way I can undo what I've done . . .'

'Please don't worry. Now — did you discuss the theft with any of the ship's crew other than Peter Nuttall?'

There was a long pause before Rachel Gibson answered. 'No,' she said at last. 'I hope I haven't jeopardised your position . . .'

'You haven't,' said Kate, rising and smiling to herself. 'I've taken care of *everything*.'

As she covered the last few feet to her office she realised the door was open and through it she could hear Sandy's voice saying coaxingly. 'They'll give us a hotel room for a couple of hours. Shall I book —?'

Peter's mumbled reply was inaudible to Kate, but the next moment Sandy was standing at the door, calling back into the room,

'*I'm* the one who's supposed to plead a headache. I don't understand you.'

Kate just stepped aside in time to avoid Sandy who was obviously too annoyed to look where she was going. Peter looked up as she came in and began rummaging among papers on her desk.

'Have you calmed Rachel Gibson down?'

'Yes.'

'How? Barbiturates?'

'Creative grovelling.'

'Don't think I've ever seen you grovel,' he said, fascinated. 'Wish I'd been there.'

She straightened up and looked at him. 'There's not a thing wrong with grovelling Peter, as long as it's the means to a desirable end.'

When the ship docked at Gothenburg Kate stayed aboard. The call she had to make to Arthur Parker in Felixstowe could be made from where she was. She was looking forward to it.

'Did you get my telex?' she asked him without preamble. 'Good. You're acting on it? Very good. As long as you understand the importance of taking every measure to catch Miss Gibson's thief I'll be happy.'

'If you're happy I'm happy,' he assured her.

'I wouldn't be too happy if I were you Arthur,' she said sweetly.

'Oh? Why?' She could hear him trying to keep the note of alarm out of his voice.

'Well, it seems only fair to tell you that since my father's encouraged you to try to hang me with my first mistake, I've decided to hang you with the same rope.'

'I beg your pardon?' The alarm was unmistakable now..

'Your first mistake Arthur,' she spelled out for him.

When she had put down the phone Kate leaned back in her chair and smiled contentedly to herself.

Someone who was feeling less content was Susan Porter, who had left the ship to make her call to Arthur Parker. Once before she had disobeyed instructions about not calling from the ship, and look where that had landed her — straight into Tony Grant's hands, that's where. Now there was worse to come. Briefly Sophie put her in the picture about how Miss Gibson's telex had arrived a tantalising five minutes after Kate's.

'Damn!' said Susan. 'She knew. She knew Miss Gibson was going to complain. Someone must have tipped her off. And she probably knows that Tony and I put her up to it. Oh God!'

'Well I don't envy you if you're right,' said Sophie with relish. 'I wouldn't want to be that far on the wrong side of Katherine Laker.'

'She can't possibly know that *we* were behind that complaint,' said Tony when Susan told him. 'Did *you* tell her? Did *I* tell her? Why would Miss Gibson tell her?'

'How do you explain her telex getting there five minutes before Miss Gibson?' said Susan pacing agitatedly up and down her office.

'Our rotten luck.'

'Somebody *told* her.'

'Who? Anyway, as far as I'm concerned Miss Gibson and I never talked about anything but the weather.'

He sauntered out, leaving Susan alone with her worry. He wasn't too worried. If the worst came to the worst he could always see that Susan alone carried the can. It was marvellous what a bit of determined denial could do. He was still confident that he could ultimately deal with Kate Laker.

The first twinge of doubt assailed him when he passed the entrance to the night-club. Coming faintly through it was a sound he'd thought never to hear again. Pushing open the door he crept in far enough to ascertain that it wasn't a bad dream. Jo Bailey really was sitting alone at the piano in the empty room, playing and singing quietly to herself.

She looked up when he was half way down the long room, moving towards her. She gave him a smile and a wink, but continued singing. Tony stopped, stared at her as though unable to believe his eyes, then turned on his heels and stalked out. Jo watched as the swing doors flapped behind him, and went on crooning sadly to herself.

Tony covered the distance to Kate's office at top speed, and stormed in without knocking.

'What the hell is she doing here?' he yelled.

'Who?' Kate looked up from where she was working at her desk.

'You know bloody well who. Jo Bailey.'

'I booked her.' Kate said, unruffled.

'It's *my* job to book entertainment.' Tony raged. 'My job, not yours.'

'Had you booked a replacement for Gary Rae?'

'No, but . . .'

'Then I've done you a favour, haven't I? If we'd sailed without an entertainer, Tony, you could have been accused of dereliction of duty, couldn't you? You might have been sacked for that.'

The frustrated way he slammed the door behind him had a satisfying sound to Kate's ears. She had a feeling she was getting on top of things.

The door opened again almost at once to admit Matt, who stepped inside and leaned against the doorframe.

'Trouble with Tony?' he asked lightly.

'Nothing worth talking about.'

'There's a rumour floating round the ship that we've had a major theft. What are you going to do if you find the guy?'

97

'Follow standard procedure,' she said formally.

There was a hint of a jeer in his smile. 'That so? You're going to arrest him, are you?'

Kate sighed. 'I don't mean to be rude, but I do have work to do.'

'Think you can do it by yourself, do you?'

'If I need help I'll call for it,' she said, straining to be cordial. 'Now, if you'll excuse me I must get through these papers.'

'Well, best of luck to you.' Matt began to ease out of the door. 'Hope he's not too big or too strong.' As he said the last words he gave a brief rub to the cheek she had slapped the night before, and was gone.

He joined John on the bridge. John was staring out over the water. An hour out of Gothenburg they were already far from visible land.

'Beautiful today, isn't it?' Matt said.

'Always.' John muttered. 'Always.'

'How did it go with Maya?' Matt ventured. He knew John had been going to meet his wife in Gothenburg.

John shrugged but made no answer. There was no way he could have spoken about his talk with Maya which had been both brief and disastrous. She had informed him flatly that affairs were already in the hands of lawyers. After sixteen years of marriage she was beginning a new life — and he had no place in it. He could still see her face as she said the words. The pain was intolerable and he could not make himself speak of it, even to so good a friend as Matt.

After a moment Matt clapped him on the shoulder and said uncomfortably, 'Well, I'll leave you to your work.' He headed for the stairs.

When he was sure he was alone John pulled a small flask out of his hip pocket and took a long swallow. Then he stared out blindly onto the comfortless sea.

On the deck immediately outside the restaurant Matt came across a sight that held him spellbound. Susan Porter was hurrying along, trying to keep up with another woman who seemed anxious to get away from her. Matt couldn't make out Susan's words but she seemed to be trying to persuade the woman of something in a tone that was a cross between an argument and a plea.

But it was the woman who held Matt's attention. She was young, slim, blonde and quite stunning. It took him only a few steps to catch up with them.

'How's it going Susan?' he asked casually.

'No complaints.' Susan said brightly.

He could see that she was trying to conceal a violent agitation.

Well she needn't worry for his benefit. All his attention was for her companion. He smiled and held out his hand.

'Hello,' he said, looking directly into the woman's eyes and putting out all the force of his charm.

'Oh —' Susan made flustered introductions. 'Rachel Gibson, Matt Taylor — Chief Engineer.'

Matt showed off his even white teeth in a smile. 'Are you enjoying our ship?'

She smiled and made the polite response, showing off her own teeth in turn. Each seemed to find in the other something to approve of, for after a moment Matt detached Rachel Gibson from Susan and took her away. Susan watched them go, totally exasperated. She had seen Matt go through his performance with lady passengers a hundred times before, and at any other time but now she would have found the clockwork perfection of it amusing. But now she was too full of dread to find anything funny.

After a while she went back into the restaurant and tried to concentrate on her job. There was nothing else to do.

Tony's knock on the door was a mere formality, as he entered without waiting.

'Did I say "Come in"?' said Jo, who was taking clothes from her suitcase and hanging them up.

'Did I ask?' Tony slammed her cabin door shut behind him. In one movement he had reached across to the wardrobe and begun hauling Jo's clothes out again.

'Just go to hell and get off this ship,' he stormed.

He knew at once that something had changed. It was nothing you could put your finger on, merely that Jo, instead of being intimidated as she would once have been, merely began to collect up her clothes and replace them in the wardrobe.

'Where to darling?' she asked him coolly. 'Out there?' She nodded in the direction of the porthole, and laughed. 'I'm a good entertainer, but I can't walk on water.'

Tony stood back and regarded her. He was panting with effort and temper.

'Don't you get it? I'm finished with you. I don't want you here.'

She gave him another smile, almost pitying this time. 'Tell me some news, Tony.'

He was almost speechless with rage and the frustration of not being able to scare her. 'Listen . . .' he managed to say.

'No. You listen.' Her voice was quiet, but it had a razor-edge that he had never heard before. 'I've had a few days to get my head screwed back on straight. I saw something in you. Can't imagine what it was, but there's no fool like an old fool, is there? Anyway, I don't see it any more.'

'You old . . .'

'Don't interrupt me,' she ordered him calmly. 'I need this job. I have bills to pay and a roof to keep over my head and *I* don't steal for a living.' She took a slight breath as Tony grabbed her wrist hard, but managed to say lightly, 'Still violent I see.'

'What do you mean?'

'Forget it. Anyway, if you don't cross my path, I won't cross yours. But if you do — watch out.'

When he had gone Jo sat on her bed, lighting a cigarette. It was difficult because her hands were shaking as they hadn't been while Tony was there. But now he was gone she was suffering a reaction.

She knew that it was a good thing for her that she had finally seen through him, and was on the way to getting over him — but there was one part of her that persisted in being sad and sorry. She had really loved Tony, and she knew that now she was in her late thirties her chance of loving another man as much were decreasing every day. Looking at her future with dry, realistic eyes, she knew that she had probably said goodbye to the last real love of her life, and it hurt to have to send him off like this.

She tried to look on the bright side. Miss Laker for one. When Jo had given that impromptu performance to keep the customers happy while the ship circled for Wally, Kate had thanked her and promised to repay the favour one day. Well, now she had repaid it. She had not merely got Jo her job back, but she had tacitly offered Jo her friendship and support should any difficult situations arise. For almost the first time in her life, Jo Bailey experienced the pleasures of friendship with another woman who was powerful enough in her own right to give that friendship some real clout. It wasn't to be sneezed at.

Just the same, as Jo sat there in her cabin, staring at her face in the mirror through a haze of cigarette smoke, her heart ached, and she felt old.

Kate was chipping away at a mound of paperwork in her office when Rachel Gibson put her head in, seeking news.

'Not yet,' said Kate. 'I'm due a report on headquarters police work in about two hours. Why don't you meet me here about nine this evening and I'll tell you whatever there is to be told.'

Miss Gibson shook her head regretfully. 'Nine wouldn't be good actually. I'm having dinner then. With a member of your crew. Matt Taylor? The Chief Engineer?' She smiled as Kate's eyes widened. 'Lovely guy, isn't he?'

'Quite,' said Kate politely. 'Perhaps we can meet in the morning then.'

It was dark when Sophie entered Arthur Parker's office. She was holding something in her hand and looked excited.

'This just came in on the telex from London,' she said. She stood watching him as he read it. 'It's one for the books, isn't it?'

He handed her back the cable and smiled grimly. 'Send the information to Miss Laker.'

'I wonder how she's going to cope without Jeremy Gates to hold her hand.' Sophie mused.

'Time will tell. The ball's in her court now.'

As soon as Kate received the telex from Head Office she went dashing off in search of Rachel Gibson. There was no sign of her or Matt in the restaurant.

'I'm looking for a passenger —' she told Susan hurriedly. 'Rachel Gibson . . .'

If she'd ever doubted Linda's story those doubts were cleared up the minute she saw Susan blanch. Just in time Kate remembered that neither of them could afford to seem aware of how much the other knew.

'You wouldn't know her,' she said quickly. 'She had dinner with Matt.'

'Yes, of course,' said Susan with relief. 'A pretty blonde girl.'

'Right. Do you know where they went?'

Susan was recovering her composure. 'It's hardly my business to keep tabs on passengers and crew, is it?'

Before she could stop herself Kate had yielded to the temptation to say, 'I wouldn't have *thought* so, no.'

It might have been unwise, but it had also been irresistible.

Matt reckoned everything was going just about perfectly. Over the romantic dinner (with champagne) they had gazed into each other's eyes and exchanged the meaningless conversation that would turn into the prelude to a walk to somebody's cabin. Now they were dancing closely together in the half-light of the night-club, and his hand could feel that beneath the thin fabric of her evening dress she was wearing precious little.

He reached up and pushed back a stray wisp of the incredible blonde hair.

'You have beautiful hair,' he murmured. 'Did anyone ever tell you that?'

She gave a deep throaty chuckle that had him holding onto his self-control. 'My hairdresser,' she crooned.

'Nobody else?'

'Wouldn't you rather think you were the first?' she whispered in his ear.

'Every time.'

As he led her back to their table he thought, there was no doubt about it! She was a stunner, first-class, diamond studded and all the trimmings. Every man in the place was giving him envious looks. In fact all that was needed to make his joy complete would be for Miss Toffee-Nosed Laker to see him now, and find out for herself that there were plenty of other fish in the sea since she'd passed up her chance.

And there, like an answer to prayer, was Miss Laker herself, who had loomed up beside them like a genie from a trap-door. Only she didn't look dismayed, or regretful, or any other of the things she had looked in Matt's vengeful fantasy. She looked prim and official and very much in command of the situation.

'I'm terribly sorry to interrupt,' she said, addressing Rachel. 'Do you think you could come with me for just a minute? I have some news.'

'Have you got —?'

'Wait, wait,' Matt interrupted, glaring at Kate. 'Miss Laker, this lady and I are speaking privately . . .'

'I think it would be better if Miss Gibson and I spoke privately,' said Kate.

'Are you kidding?' he demanded.

Kate spoke to Rachel as if Matt wasn't there. 'Can we talk outside?'

Rachel looked at Matt. 'I'll be back.' And followed Kate out of the club.

On the deck outside Rachel said, 'Have you found the thief?'

Kate took a long, hard look at her. 'You're really very good,' she said.

'What do you mean?'

'But you're not a professional.' She waited to see what Rachel would say, but the other woman was looking blankly at her through a cloud of cigarette smoke. 'I'm going to have to put you under arrest.'

At once Rachel's veneer began to crack. 'Are you kidding?' she demanded.

'No.'

'Who do you think you are?' Already her voice had coarsened slightly.

'The person who's charged with controlling crime on this ship,' said Kate coolly.

Matt emerged from the night-club in time to hear Rachel say furiously, 'I'll have you fired. I've never been so insulted in my life.'

'What's going on?' Matt demanded.

'This isn't going to help,' Kate told Rachel.

At once the blonde clutched Matt's arm, her eyes wide and appealing.

'First she ignored me, now she's talking about arresting me.'

'Have you lost your mind?' Matt demanded furiously of Kate.

'Hardly. I've never set foot in the Engine Room and I have no intention of doing so. I don't interfere with your work. Don't interfere with mine.' In the silence between them it was his eyes that moved first, towards Rachel, then back to Kate. He was beginning to look uncertain.

'This woman has insured and then "lost" the same diamond ring three times,' Kate continued.

'That's a lie,' Rachel burst in, but neither of them heeded her.

'Three different companies have paid her claims over the past two years. At the moment she's working on number four.'

'She's crazy,' Rachel's hand clutched Matt even more firmly.

'But since you never bothered to use a different name and address, a quick check with the major insurance companies soon found you out.' Kate told her.

Slowly, firmly, Matt began to peel Rachel's hand from his arm.

'Oh please don't let her do this,' she begged. 'I didn't mean anything wrong!'

'You'd better go,' said Matt.

He stood looking after the two women as they walked away, just in case Rachel decided to give any trouble and Kate needed his help. But no help from him was needed, and on the whole he decided he wasn't surprised about that. He headed back into the night-club with the fixed intention of getting drunk. Everything else had failed him this last couple of nights.

About an hour later Sandy, serving in the staff pub, looked up to see Linda perched on a stool in front of her.

'Did you hear what Miss Laker did?' Sandy demanded.

'I don't care what that old witch does,' Linda sulked. She was feeling disillusioned with Miss Laker, who had not apparently solved the crime with one hand while running her office with the other.

'But this is really good —' Sandy paused for effect. 'She arrested a passenger. A woman. A jewel thief or something. Threw her right in the brig.'

'No,' Linda's eyes widened.

'Yeah. That's what all the security was for.'

Linda picked up a spoon that someone had left on the bar, looked at it, then dropped it into her bag. Sandy stared at her. Her private opinion was that Linda was going potty. Look at what she'd done. And she was always doing things like that. Not to mention the extra food she kept swiping. The peanuts were always vanishing.

'Well isn't that Miss Laker something,' Linda said brightly. 'Didn't even bring any coppers on board,' she said these last words with relish.

'Did it all by herself she did.'

'Yeah. I told you that Miss Laker was all right.'

Sandy stared at her. 'I thought . . .'

'Best purser we've ever had on this ship I say,' Linda beamed.

When getting drunk on his own got boring Matt decided to go and drink with his Captain. It was soothing to have a male ear into which to pour out his wrongs.

'Nothing any woman does will ever surprise me again,' said John when he had heard the tale.

Matt discovered that his sense of humour was beginning to return. 'Yeah. I thought she gave a jolt to my social life when she stood me up. But throwing my date in the brig —' he found he could actually laugh, 'Whew! No mercy!'

John took a long drink of whisky. When he spoke it was with dreadful bitterness.

'Women are a different species Matt. Not to be trusted under any circumstances. Nothing is too low for a woman. You can never tell what they're going to do next.'

Chapter 8

Jeremy Gates was at the meeting place first. He was an ultra-punctual man, and when Kate had sent ahead the message that asked him to meet her in the most expensive restaurant in Amsterdam, she had known he would go there promptly and without quibble.

He looked what he was, she thought as she approached his table — a man who had gained great success in a financial world, and acquired a certain smoothness of aspect to fit his smoothness of character. He was in his late thirties, handsome in a chiselled, classic way enhanced by the horn-rimmed half spectacles he wore. His air of authority looked as though he had been born with it. Kate knew better. She had seen it grow over him as he had increased and consolidated his power on the board of Triangle Lines. He was a strong ally, and he would be a strong enemy if they fell out. But Kate too could be strong. She knew how his power had been created — and how it could be defeated. She knew him for a superficially attractive but ruthless man, but she knew that she too could be ruthless.

Right now, though, she was not playing power games. She wanted a friendly chat with Jeremy to boost her morale for the battle she was fighting on board.

She did not talk immediately of business, but spent the first part of the meal entertaining him with tales of ship life. Their last meeting on the docks at Gothenburg had been an affair of ten minutes, giving her no time to do more than make a brief progress report. This time there was an excellent lunch to look forward to, and time to enjoy his company.

'You're as tough as old boots,' he said admiringly when he had heard her story.

'If I had to do it over again I wouldn't start with that sun-bathing stunt,' she said between bites of salad.

'Why? It made them sit up and take notice, didn't it?'

'Mmmm. Created certain authority problems though.' She

thought for a moment, 'You know Jeremy, if I had even one ally, I wouldn't need to be talking to you.'

'But you haven't.'

'My father's seen to that. Right now my biggest problems are Tony Grant and Susan Porter. But for Miss Porter I think I have a plan . . .'

Briefly she outlined what she had in mind, and he nodded approvingly.

'Yes. That sounds like a reasonable way to deal with her. Tony Grant is tougher. Unless you catch him red-handed . . . the independent contract, you know.'

'Can you get me a copy of his contract?'

'Certainly. You're a determined woman Kate.'

'No more than I have to be.'

Later they strolled together along a path beside one of Amsterdam's canals.

'I suppose we look like lovers,' said Kate, raising an eyebrow. 'The gruesome twosome.'

'You wouldn't want to change your mind about that?' he enquired with deceptive casualness. 'Give the world some of what they already think they're getting?'

For a moment she almost seemed to be weighing up the idea seriously.

'No,' she said at last with a half-smile.

'Well,' he said ruefully, 'I'd feel a bit strange anyway. So long as you insist on thinking of me as the helpful father you never had.'

'So to speak.'

'Beg pardon?'

'Never had you.'

'Mmmm. Most unfortunate.'

They walked on a moment in silence. Jeremy seemed to be choosing his words carefully.

'Not personally Kate, but professionally, you owe me something.'

'Do I?'

'Yes,' he said firmly.

She smiled up at him. 'I'll tell you what. I'm due back at the ship. Why don't we shelve the discussion of who owes what to whom until we meet again.'

For a moment a look of anger crossed his face, but he controlled it.

'All right,' he said.

'You'll still get me that contract?'

'I'm good for my word.'

106

'So am I.'

After that she managed to keep the conversation on indifferent subjects until she got into her taxi to return to the ship.

Susan Porter was one of the first to return aboard. She hadn't really wanted to leave the ship in the first place, but Tony Grant had insisted that they do some sleuthing together to find out who Kate Laker was meeting. After the fright she'd had over Rachel Gibson, Susan would have given anything she possessed to get out of spying on Miss Laker, but Tony had made it brutally plain that there was no question of that — not unless she wanted the Captain to be put in possession of a little secret about herself that Arthur Parker had happened to let slip. She was caught like a rat in a trap.

So they had followed Kate, and Susan had dutifully identified Jeremy Gates, and Tony had put through a call to Felixstowe. By now the information was probably already on its way to George Terson. Whatever ructions that produced Susan reckoned she was bound to come out the loser. She was sinking in deeper and deeper.

And as if to add the final straw the salad she had prepared for herself and left for a moment had simply vanished off the face of the earth. It was a trivial thing to be getting worked up about, but it was when trivial things started to get on top of her that she knew she had to get worried. She didn't want anyone saying she was imagining things.

'Problems?'

Susan jumped violently at the sound of Kate's voice right beside her. She had not seen her approach, she had been so preoccupied in staring at the place where her plate should have been.

'Not really,' she said uneasily. 'I just put my lunch down here . . . never mind.'

'No problems then?'

Something was beginning to warn Susan of approaching danger, but all she could think of to say was, 'No, none.'

'Good. Then you won't mind if I give you a few.' Kate had taken out a small notebook. She proceeded to go throug' a lengthy check-list of minor faults she had found in the restaurant, and which she wanted put right immediately. Some of them, Susan thought, were trivial beyond belief. The napkins for instance . . .

'I want them all refolded before dinner.' Kate told her. 'Four folds, not two.'

'You're joking?'

'And I'm telling the chef to take the sole off the menu.'

'But it's already prepared,' said Susan, outraged.

'I've had several complaints about the Bloody Marys,' Kate continued, not heeding her. 'I want them more American: tabasco and Worcester Sauce, lemon and pepper.'

'Miss Laker . . .'

'Shouldn't you be writing these things down?'

'Who do you think . . .?'

'The Purser on this ship.' Kate interrupted, one step ahead of her. 'Your immediate supervisor.'

'I don't believe this.'

'*Believe it!* Now I've also had complaints about dirty glasses.' Kate peered at Susan's shirt. 'There's a spot on your shirt. When I come back I don't want to see any spots. None. Do you understand?'

'I think I do. Yes,' said Susan bitterly.

'Good. You'd better get your people working. I'll be back in three-quarters of an hour.'

Kate left the restaurant without bothering to look back. That, she thought, would give Miss Porter something else to think about rather than spying into what was none of her business.

Linda, coming quietly up behind Sandy who was leaning on the rail staring out to sea, touched her on the shoulder and got the shock of her life. Only a few hours ago the two girls had been shopping together in Amsterdam. Sandy had bought a bridal veil which Linda had duly admired, and when Linda had last seen her she had been standing on a corner, waiting for Peter to arrive. Now she turned round to reveal a face that was red and blotchy with weeping.

'He never turned up, that's all,' Sandy sobbed. 'I waited more than an hour.'

'Are you sure you were in the right place?' said Linda.

'Yes.'

Linda put an arm round her friend and patted her consolingly on the shoulder.

'Oh come on now, don't cry. He's not worth it. Creep.'

'Joe was right.' Sandy sniffed, wiping away some of her tears. 'I'm not one of them. That's why he treats me like this.' Then her misery broke out in a fresh burst of tears. 'But he's going to be sorry. He's going to be so sorry.'

It occurred to Linda that Sandy was over-reacting. Peter was bound to be on board and Sandy could see him at any time to sort out whatever misunderstanding there had been. And a more level-headed girl would have seen it like that.

But, Linda realised, Sandy was far from level-headed. She was an emotional impulsive girl who waded into even the smallest crisis with all her feelings firing away on four cylinders. Linda was too fond of her friend mentally to accuse her of being hysterical, but she did silently concede that Sandy would be easier to live with if she didn't get carried away so easily.

She soothed her as best she could, but Sandy was still weeping as she made her way back to her own cabin. At the door she encountered Peter who was just raising his hand to knock. He gave her an irritated look.

'Sandy, where were you?'

'Where was *I*? I was in the usual place.' She pushed past him into her cabin and he followed.

'But we changed it — didn't we?'

'That's not true Peter and you know it. You knew where we were supposed to meet — where we always meet.'

He sat on her bunk and put his head tiredly in his hands. 'Can't I make one mistake?'

'*One mistake*? What about the way you annouced our engagement?'

'I said I was sorry.' This time the irritation was in his voice.

'Sorry's just a word,' she flashed. 'Words are cheap. The truth is you just don't care about me.' She struggled with her tears, because Peter hated weeping females. But why couldn't he do something to make her feel better? Just take her in his arms? Or anything, rather than just sit there. A little hard stone of desolation seemed to be sitting in her chest about where her heart should have been.

'You know what I did this morning?' she went on. 'I called my Mum and told her I was engaged to a wonderful man. You know what she did? She cried. Because she was happy. She'd have cried even more if she knew how you treated me.'

'I don't see what's being gained by all this emotion,' he said sullenly.

'Just because you don't have any emotions . . .'

'Can't we pretend — just for a minute — that we're civilised human beings?'

'Don't get sarcastic with me Peter Nuttall,' she yelled. 'I'm not an idiot.'

He stood up and reached out for her but she pushed him away. He looked at her in silence for a moment.

'I love you,' he said quietly.

She almost hissed back at him, 'So you say.' She looked directly into his eyes. 'But you don't mean it. You're going to be sorry that you treated me like this.'

Repelled by her uncontrolled temper, he reverted to sarcasm, 'I thought sorry was just a word.'

'The way *you* use it. Not the way I'm going to use it. Now get out of my cabin.'

She held the door open for him, and without even looking at her he went. When he was safely out of sight she threw herself on the bunk and burst into another storm of tears.

Kate, responding to a summons to the bridge, discovered that Tony Grant had lost no time in striking back at her.

'I don't recall having had any problems with the croupier when Wally James was Purser.' John said, pacing fretfully.

'Perhaps that says more about Wally than me,' Kate ventured. In truth she was somewhat stunned by John's abrupt attack.

'Miss Laker, booking entertainment is part of Tony Grant's job. It's in his contract.'

'If I hadn't rebooked Jo Bailey we'd have sailed with no entertainer at all — and a shipload of unhappy passengers.'

Neither of them noticed Matt who appeared in the doorway wearing dirty overalls, and drew back slightly when he saw that a conflict was in progress. He did not, however, go away.

'Not according to Tony,' John went on. 'He says he had another singer lined up and had to send her away.'

'That's simply not true,' said Kate hotly.

'You're accusing him of lying?'

'If I could think of something nicer to call it, I would. Look, as I see it . . .'

John interrupted her angrily. 'As I see it, we'd all be better off if you performed more efficiently in your own job and let other people get on with theirs.'

Kate took a deep breath before saying quietly, 'Thank you. I appreciate the advice. In the future I'll be much more careful.'

Matt just managed to make himself scarce before she turned to leave the bridge. He made it back to his own quarters at top speed and had rid himself of the dirty overalls by the time he heard the unmistakable sound of Kate's furious footsteps coming down the corridor. There was a slam, which was presumably her door, then silence. Matt gave her a few minutes for angry pacing up and down before he went across and knocked.

Kate was less than pleased to open her door on the sight of Matt wearing no shirt or shoes. If he wanted to flash his bare torso around he'd come to the wrong lady. But before she could say anything he gave her a friendly grin and said, 'I haven't had a chance to congratulate you on making your first arrest.' (The luckless Miss Gibson had been taken off the ship into police custody in Amsterdam.) 'May I come in?'

He was in before she could stop him, sitting comfortably on her couch while she continued to pace.

'You know,' he said conversationally, 'the Captain's been giving me a hard time lately.'

'Has he?' she said, not much interested.

'Yeah. Calling up the Engine Room and demanding twenty-five knots when I know full well that twenty would do. He knows it too. He's just got to take it out on someone. I don't feel too bad about it though. His personal life's intruding on everything.'

Kate stopped pacing and faced him. 'Are you trying to tell me something?'

'Only if it applies.'

She sat down facing him. 'It applies,' she confessed.

'I thought it might. Don't let it get you down.'

She cocked a cynical eyebrow at him. 'Since when have you been concerned about my moods?'

'Don't know really. I suppose since I accepted the idea that you're really a member of the crew. Which I suppose I had to, to let you arrest my companion the other night, didn't I?'

She shrugged vaguely to indicate assent.

'You really did do it very well you know,' Matt added. 'Wally couldn't have done it better.'

'So I'm *Which* magazine's Best Buy am I?' she said. Her tone was wary but not unfriendly, and she could sense much the same feeling in Matt. The electric spark that had flashed between them from the first moment was still there, but now they were each wearing protective gloves to handle it.

'I'm making a case for mutual professional respect, Kate.' She said nothing, but kept on looking at him, forcing him to continue. 'This is a small community. The same way I'm sensitive to John's moods, I have to be sensitive to yours. And I'd expect you to be sensitive to mine.'

She continued to regard him carefully. She'd have felt happier if she could have worked out just where the worm was in this apple.

'If I didn't know you were an Engineer, I might take you for a diplomat,' she said at last.

Matt looked down at his bare chest and feet, as if noticing them for the first time.

'Na,' he said deprecatingly. 'The clothes are wrong.' He was glad of her smile, but added more seriously, 'Look, I'm extending the olive branch. Are you going to take it?'

'Any strings attached?'

'None.'

The phone rang and she answered it, keeping her eyes on Matt as she talked.

'All right — thank you. 'Bye,' she said at last. 'I have a passenger complaint to attend to. A Mr Smith. I wonder how many Mr Smiths we've had aboard at one time or another.'

'Can we continue this civilised line of conversation another time?' he said, following her to the door.

'Certainly.'

In the corridor outside she looked him up and down. 'Did I say I liked your outfit?'

He looked down at himself. 'Rather like it myself,' he admitted. 'Of course, it's better without the trousers.'

She smiled at him. 'I bet it is. Good day Mr Taylor.'

She departed, leaving him well-satisfied with himself. It was just as he'd thought. He'd just needed a new approach.

Absorbed in their conversation neither Sandy nor Linda noticed Tony getting into the lift with them. The tears had dried on Sandy's face but she still looked upset.

' . . .'cause nobody believes that story about him falling down the stairs,' Linda was confiding.

'I don't care if someone did beat him up, and I don't care who it was because I don't care about him any more,' said Sandy defiantly.

'Oh come on,' Linda jeered. 'You still care.'

'Really, I don't. I'm not kidding.'

'Well the rumour's all over the ship,' said Linda tantalisingly.

Sandy tapped her foot and put on a brave show of not being interested. Tony, with his back to the two girls, felt as though his ears were coming out on stalks.

'What rumour?' said Sandy at last.

The lift stopped and the doors opened. As the girls got out Tony heard Linda's fading voice saying,

112

'Well, it's interesting. The story is that Joe saw the whole thing, but won't tell who it was.'

The lift doors closed on Tony, just in time to shut out the sound of Sandy asking, 'Joe Francis or Jo Bailey?' and Linda replying, 'Joe Francis of course.'

A few moments later Tony had cornered Susan on the sundeck behind the restaurant and was giving her instructions.

'I want you to get Jo Bailey to tell you what she knows about who beat up Peter Nuttall.'

'Why?'

'Because I'm telling you to.'

'You're crazy.'

'No, luv. You're the crazy one, remember?'

She went white with shock. For a moment it was as though someone had struck her a blow. Then she forced herself to say, 'I'm telling you — no.'

'This is getting tedious Susan. You'll do exactly what I tell you to and you won't ask any questions. When I say "jump" you'll jump. Do you understand?' Tony's voice had risen till he was shouting.

'You — pig!' she spat at him

'Music to my ears, sweetheart Music to my ears,' he grinned at her.

They were both too absorbed in their private row to fear being seen or overheard. Neither realised that they were clearly visible through the window into the restaurant, and that they had one very interested spectator. Kate, coming to pay a visit of inspection before moving on to deal with Mr Smith's complaint, paused inside the restaurant, riveted by the sight of her two enemies having apparently fallen out. She couldn't hear them but from their faces and the gestures they were making it was plain that some sort of altercation was in progress. That was all to the good. Kate was about to make Miss Porter's life more interesting yet.

She picked up one of the refolded napkins and beckoned a waiter across.

'This won't do,' she said. 'Put them all back the way they were.' In answer to his confused look she added, 'It's all right. When Miss Porter comes in, tell her I told you to do it.'

She hurried out of the restaurant before Susan could return, but by the time she had reached the corridor that led to Mr Smith's cabin she could hear the sound of agitated footsteps chasing her.

'Miss Laker —' Susan shouted down the corridor. 'Just what do you think you're playing at?'

Kate paused just long enough to glance over her shoulder and say, 'Susan — just don't get yourself in a mix-up like that again.'

She knew she had left Susan Porter fuming and totally confused — which was just how she wanted her. But in another moment she had forgotten Susan's existence. At the end of the corridor she found Mr Smith's door and knocked. The door opened and a gracious voice from inside said, 'Katherine, come in.'

After a long moment Kate found her voice. '*Father!*' she said.

George Terson stood back to allow his daughter to enter. There was a smile on his face but his eyes were cold. Kate frantically tried to recover her composure. Terson had gained a big advantage by taking her by surprise, but she would do anything not to let this show.

'To what do I owe the pleasure, father?' she said coolly, when he had closed the door.

'I have business in London.'

'You haven't set foot on one of your ships in twenty years,' she eyed him. 'I suspect you've come especially to see me.'

'I think we have things to talk about, yes.'

'And travelling under an assumed name. How very clever,' she said sarcastically.

'Not unlike a new Purser booking as a passenger,' he countered.

'I'm flattered to think I could teach you something useful.'

'My dear, if I ever stopped learning new tricks I'd be dead.' He gave her that cold smile again. 'Did you enjoy your lunch with Jeremy Gates? And did you hatch any good plots?'

She supposed she didn't need to ask how he'd got his information. Somehow Tony Grant and Susan Porter would be behind it.

'If I lunch with Jeremy Gates it means I'm plotting against you, does it? That sounds suspiciously like paranoia to me,' she told him.

'Oh?'

'I'm a shareholder, father. If you'd been more attentive you'd have noticed I've been on speaking terms with Mr Gates and everyone else in the company.'

'You haven't an ounce of loyalty, have you?' he said tightly.

'To you?' Kate laughed. 'You've never been loyal to me.'

A look of uncertainty crossed his face and he reverted quickly to his original theme.

'Of course, the idea that you and Gates were discussing the way you got this job is equally unappealing.'

'I don't know what you mean.'

'I mean Gates falsified a dossier of complaints against Wally James to open up this position for you.'

114

Kate gave an exasperated sigh. 'It's not even conceivable to you that the complaints were legitimate, is it?'

'Well hardly. Wally's been . . .'

'What Wally's been is willing to call you "sir" and flatter your ego,' she interrupted him. 'Wally had been letting both passenger services and profits slide for years. But you wouldn't know anything about that. Because you can put on your duffle coat and go to the odd seaman's bar when it suits you to think of yourself as a man of the sea, but you've been in the boardroom for almost a quarter of a century and you haven't given a damn about things as unimportant as the day-to-day workings of your ships. And because you haven't cared you haven't the foggiest notion what's really happening out here on the water.'

'You don't know the first thing about Wally James you little —'

'Purser, father, Purser,' she put in. 'You may own the ship but I work on it.'

'You sleep with Gates then, do you?' he sneered.

Kate suppressed a smile of satisfaction. If he had to fall back on vulgar abuse then she had him on the run. But all she said was, 'You just can't accept what's really going on, can you?'

'*Your* version of what's going on.'

'Let me ask you one question. What's the real reason you don't want me to have this job?'

'I think I've made myself amply clear.'

'No, you haven't. Is it the bleeding heart response to Wally James's situation? Did you give a damn about him for twenty years? *That's* not what's got you bothered. Although I imagine it does make you feel good to think of yourself as the soul of human kindness from time to time.'

'Oh the little wheels are turning, aren't they?' he jeered.

'Always,' she informed him flatly. 'And as for your fear of my being in collusion with Jeremy Gates . . .' she shrugged. 'Other people in the company have far more power than I. Even if I did decide to throw my weight behind Jeremy's plan to turn the line over to freight, I'm not nearly as dangerous as some.' She crossed to the door. 'Frankly father, I don't see why you're here.'

He gazed at her thoughtfully. 'They used to say that women on board ship brought bad luck.'

'You still believe that, don't you?'

'The world hasn't changed so much. I don't like to see you wearing a uniform meant for a man.' His eyes raked her neat white blouse. 'Probably drinking, swearing and sleeping around like a man too . . .' He noted with pleasure the slight tightening of her lips. 'It's still bad luck.'

She did not answer him directly, but instead took a calculated risk.

'Mother used to say that before you met her you were very much in love with an independent, self-interested woman. In fact, she used to say I was just like her.'

'You bitch,' said George Terson softly, and hit her.

She would not give him the satisfaction of seeing her rub her face. She looked at him unforgivingly for a moment before saying, 'I consider myself fortunate to be protected from you by a contract.'

She knew that he was almost as shocked by his own action as she was, but she hurried out before he could say anything. She went straight to the nearest deck and stood there, staring out over the sea. She hated him. It was so typical of him to have used brute force when he could no longer cope with the words. Most of her life Kate had been able to worst him in argument, but he had always been able to fight her off with his power.

She touched her cheek which still hurt, and looked down into the water, which was beginning to darken as the light failed. An hour later she was still there.

As far as Joe Francis was concerned it was Christmas and his birthday rolled into one. He'd been sitting at a table in the staff pub, minding his own business and staring gloomily into a pint, when Sandy had appeared beside him and calmly dropped her engagement ring into his beer. She'd retrieved it, of course, but she'd said enough to make it plain that this was no empty gesture. The engagement was off.

What was more she was actually flirting with him, making remarks with double meanings and laughing loudly at all his jokes. If only he could have got her out of here everything would be perfect.

'Let's go where we can be alone,' he said, glancing over his shoulder to where Peter Nuttall and Jo Bailey were sitting at the bar together.

She followed his gaze, and seemed to become aware of Peter for the first time.

'Just because Peter's here?' she said. 'Let him leave.' She raised her voice on the last words and from Peter's slight stiffening it was plain that he had heard.

'I don't like him looking over my shoulder,' Joe muttered. 'Come on.'

116

'No,' she said firmly. 'Let's stay.' She smiled at Joe coyly. 'Please?'

Reluctantly he agreed and concentrated some more on making her laugh. But after a while he dropped his voice and said, 'My friend Terry's got a little cottage in Wales.'

'Mmmmm,' he had the feeling that she was feigning interest.

'I'd like to take you there.'

'That'd be nice,' she said vaguely.

Out of the corner of his eye Joe could see Peter say goodbye to Jo and leave the pub.

'You like the country, do you?' he said desperately.

'Excuse me,' Sandy had jumped to her feet. 'Have to go to the loo.'

Without a backward glance she was off towards the door. Joe watched her, then took a long swallow of his beer. It tasted sour suddenly.

Peter, ascending the stairwell leading up from the pub, found himself pushed aside by Sandy in her dash past.

'Sandy — wait a minute.'

She stopped and looked back at him. 'What?'

'What are you doing?'

'What business is it of yours?'

'What business is it of mine?' he echoed, amazed. 'You're engaged to me. Everything you do is my business.'

'I'm going to get some cassettes, actually,' she told him. 'Joe and I are going to play them. Together.' She looked at him fixedly to make sure he'd got the message.

'I mean — what are you doing with Joe Francis at all?'

'What does it look like I'm doing?'

'Making an ass of yourself,' he said frankly.

'Making an ass of you is more likely.' She turned to go.

'Sandy — wait.'

'For what? For you to decide I'm worth treating like a decent human being? I'd be an old woman by then. No thanks. Here —' she had reached into her pocket and now thrust something into his hand. It was her engagement ring. 'Give it to somebody who enjoys being treated like a dog.'

'Oh come on.'

'You come on. Know where I'm going to be tonight? In bed. With a man who thinks I'm the best thing God ever put on this earth.' She gave him a level gaze and added slowly, 'And I'm going to do my best not to disappoint him.'

She ran up the rest of the stairs, leaving him standing alone. He looked at the ring in his hand, then pressed his fingers urgently to his temples, as though the sight of the ring had given him a headache.

Matt, turning the corner of the corridor that went through the staff quarters, nearly collided with Linda who was backing out of her cabin, and apparently talking to someone inside.

'Ta ta — see you soon,' she whispered.

'Got company?' Matt asked pleasantly.

She jumped and slammed the door quickly. 'Oh blimey!' she breathed theatrically. 'You scared me.'

'Sorry.'

She gave a laugh that sounded nervous. 'Company? Who'd want to visit me?'

'Well, I don't know . . .' said Matt cautiously, wishing he'd never started on the subject. After all, Linda's love-life was her own concern.

'Na. I'm just saying goodbye to my little cabin,' Linda went on confidingly. She took Matt by the arm and led him firmly away down the corridor. 'A woman's cabin is her castle I always say, and I do everything I can to stay on the best of terms with mine. I bring it flowers, I keep it tidy . . . I talk to it. You don't talk to your cabin?' Matt shook his head and smiled. 'Really should, you know.'

'You're too young to be so eccentric,' he said, laughing.

'Runs in the family,' she assured him. 'Runs in the family.'

They had reached the intersection of the port/starboard corridor.

'Going that way?' she said, nodding towards it.

'Yes.'

'See ya then. Give my best to your cabin.'

'Will do,' he assured her, diverted.

Just before turning the corner he looked back, to find her still there, watching him. If it hadn't been ridiculous he'd have thought she was waiting to be sure he'd gone. Then he put it out of his head. He had serious problems to concern him. His Captain for one. Matt knew for a fact that John's intake of whiskey had increased over the last week; not on the bridge — nothing as serious as that. But if you dropped in on John in his own quarters there'd like as not be a glass on the desk.

More worrying was a faint but perceptible apathy in the Captain's manner. Only that morning Matt had had to call him up from the Engine Room to report that there was no reading on the fuel intake gauge, and to check with John's gauge. It had been hard to interest the Captain in the problem at all, and when Matt had put the phone down he had been conscious of a nagging worry over the fact that John was on the bridge alone. At one time it would never have troubled him, but now he found himself longing for Charles's speedy return.

His next concern was to haul Joe out of the staff pub and get him down to the engine room to work on the gauge. Which reminded him of another problem.

'Anything that affects the ship is my business,' he said as he watched Joe tinkering with the wiring. 'Two things. One, I hear you've been putting down quite a few in the pub. When I took you back on I told you — you've got to watch the booze. It affects you. And two: You're asking for trouble with Sandy. She's engaged to Peter Nuttall.'

'Not any more,' said Joe, his eyes on his work.

'Oh?'

'Yeah. She's my girl now. I'm seeing her tonight and . . .' Joe shrugged lamely. He still found it hard to put his good fortune into words, partly because he still found it hard to believe it. But it was true that Sandy had promised to meet him at ten-thirty that night. He held onto that.

Linda, returning to her cabin for something she'd forgotten, had another encounter just as she was leaving. This time it was Sandy, who would have eased her way into the cabin had not Linda stepped firmly into the corridor and closed the door behind her.

'It's a mess,' she said, jerking her head at the cabin by way of explanation.

'So?' said Sandy puzzled. Everyone's cabin was a mess, wasn't it?

'I'm embarrassed. You know how neat I usually am.'

'Well, clean it up.' Sandy hissed. 'I may want to stay with you tonight.'

'*Why?*' Linda's eyes widened with what might have been horror.

'I — implied to Joe — I might spend the night with him.'

'So why do you need my cabin?'

'Because I told Peter I was staying with Joe.'

Linda's brow furrowed. For some reason this seemed a less than adequate explanation.

'I don't want to be in my cabin if Peter decides to check up on me.' Sandy spelled out.

'Oh . . .' Linda was still baffled.

'So I'll stay with you if I decide not to stay with Joe. It's a back-up. All right?'

'Isn't it a little cruel? I mean, to Joe.'

Sandy's shrug dismissed Joe to his fate. 'After all the things I've done for you . . .' she pouted.

'I'm sorry, I'm sorry,' said Linda hastily. 'Okay I'll clean it all up.'

'Good. Thanks.' Sandy hurried away, leaving Linda to clutch her churning stomach and wonder how she was going to get out of the mess she was in now.

Susan Porter was on the telephone just outside the Radio Room. Contrary to her instructions she was calling Arthur Parker in Felixstowe, from the ship. And for the last time. The worm had finally turned.

'I know what you told me Mr Parker and I don't care,' she fumed. 'I'd like you to tell me why you've unleashed Tony Grant on me. Why did you tell him about me? I thought it was confidential — just between you and me.' She listened to Parker spluttering on the other end of the line, then drove on, 'No quick answer, is that it? Did it just slip out?'

'All right, so you had no idea he'd use it against me. Well, he has . . . No, I don't care what you're holding over my head any more. I'm not going to jump every time a cheap gambler like him says so . . . Two can play at your game, Mr Parker. You've had me spying on the boss's daughter. I could make things very hard for you by sharing that information with the right people, couldn't I? . . . Yes, I'm sure you're sorry. Well I'm not having any more to do with him.'

She slammed the phone down, then went off in the direction of the Casino. Tony was there alone, idly restacking his counters.

'Tony — I have something to say to you.' She waited until he had looked up and she had his full attention. Then, slowly and deliberately, she said, *'Drop dead!'*

She turned on her heel and left before he had a chance to recover from his amazement. She hadn't felt so good in weeks.

It was incredible, Sandy thought, as she sat brushing her hair in front of the mirror that night, how you could have everything you'd told yourself you wanted, and still go on being miserable.

She'd achieved exactly what she'd set out to achieve that morning. She'd told Peter exactly what she thought of him and had the satisfaction of seeing his face pale with shock when she gave him back his ring. She'd had the even greater satisfaction of seeing his expression when she said she was going to sleep with Joe that night. So now he knew that he couldn't push her around, and that was splendid.

Joe had obligingly taken the bait she offered him. After giving Peter his ring she'd returned to the pub and asked Joe if he'd care to see her that night, and he'd jumped at it. Just what she was going to do with him later she wasn't sure. But she'd sort that out when she came to it. But whether she slept with him or not Peter would think she had, and be upset about it, and that was what mattered. In short, everything was going just as she'd planned. So why was she so wretched?

Her brush strokes slowed as she stared at herself in the mirror and realised that she could scarcely ever remember a time when loving Peter hadn't made her wretched. She'd loved him from the first day she'd arrived on board, full of excitement at the 'glamorous' life ahead of her. To her the whole ship was redolent of glamour. Just having her own cabin was exciting after forever sharing a room with her sister at home. Of course it wasn't Mum and Dad's fault that they lived in a council house, or that the house was too small, or that Dad was so often out of work. But she had longed to get far away, and now here she was — away.

She'd discovered soon enough that the hours were long, the work was hard and mostly menial, and if you were one of the humbler crew girls you were expected to keep your eyes — and your hands — off the officers. But to her the officers were the most glamorous of all. They were so different from the men she had known in her previous life. They dressed neatly and spoke in educated voices, and seemed to occupy their minds with other things than horseracing and football.

Despite the unspoken barrier that was supposed to exist between officers and crew-members she found that most of them considered it legitimate to 'try their luck' with her. She didn't mind that. She knew how to say no, and on the whole they took it graciously, which made a nice change from some of the boys back home. There were no hard feelings, even from Matt, whose reputation she gathered she had somewhat dented by her persistent lack of interest. But from the first day Sandy had eyes only for Peter and she wanted no-one else.

He was different from the others. He'd made no attempt to try his luck until she encouraged him a little, and even then his initial advances were tentative, as though he were nervous about something. His aloofness, the difficulty of catching his attention, only made him more desirable in her eyes. Her sense of gratification, when he finally showed some interest in her as a woman, was enormous.

There was no calculation in her. She loved him honestly and with her whole heart. But there was always at the back of her mind a secret sense of jubilation that she was loved by a man who was out of the common run of what she'd been used to. And with that jubilation came fear; fear that he looked down on her and was looking for an excuse to leap back across the barrier, and leave her. It was a fear that had always made her over-sensitive where he was concerned, and she knew in her honester moments, that it was she herself who provoked most of their quarrels by driving him too far in her demand for reassurance.

Her insecurity was like a worm, gnawing away at the very heart of her love. And now it seemed to have gnawed right through and destroyed it.

The knock at her door made her flinch. It wasn't quite ten-thirty, the time she had appointed to meet Joe. But probably he'd arrived early to make sure of her. What little willingness she had ever had for him began to drain out of the soles of her feet.

There was no-one in the corridor when she opened the door, but when she looked down a large bunch of white flowers lay on on the floor, and beside it was a small wrapped package. She picked it up, and turned it over and over, frowning.

'Open it,' said Peter's voice.

Where had he appeared from? She would have sworn he had been nowhere in the corridor before. But here he was, smiling at her in that mischievous way she had never been able to resist, and saying, 'Go on, open it.'

Her eyes shining, she drew him into the cabin, remembering to scoop up the flowers from the floor first. Her heart was thumping. It had worked. She'd got him back. The package turned out to contain a bottle of the most expensive perfume to be bought in the shop, and a delicate gold chain. It was Peter who sprayed the perfume behind her ears, and Peter who fixed the chain gently on her wrist.

'Oh Peter,' she whispered, 'it's beautiful. Really beautiful.'

He leaned over and sniffed the nape of her neck.

'So are you,' he said. 'And you smell good. Where'd you get that terrific perfume?' Gently he took her hand and kissed the palm. 'Am I forgiven?'

'You're forgiven, you horrible thing,' she murmured.

The sound of footsteps stopping outside her door made them both start and look up. There came a knock, then another one. Sandy froze. She knew Joe was standing out there, waiting for her, and she knew she had treated him badly. But she couldn't help that. She couldn't think of anything now except Peter, that he still loved her, and she was going to be sure never to quarrel with him again. She felt his arms go round her and she forgot everything as she turned to kiss him. She did not even hear the sound of Joe's footsteps as they went away.

'Excuse me Captain, have you seen the Chief?'

'No. Sorry.' John turned as he spoke and looked at the apparition that had confronted him on the bridge. 'Apparition' was the only word for it he thought. He'd never seen Joe Francis dressed up like that before. Like a shiny apple, John thought. Somehow it didn't suit him. And what on earth was that white flower he was clutching in his hand?

'Is there anything wrong?' John asked sympathetically.

'No.' Joe was turning to go, despondently.

'All dressed up with nowhere to go, is it?' said John. 'In that case, I have a wonderful idea. Join me for a drink.'

'I couldn't do that, sir,' said Joe, aghast.

'Nonsense.'

'Really Captain . . .'

'Please — don't make me insist.'

For the first time Joe realised there was something odd in his Captain's manner. He shrugged. Why not? He didn't need any encouragement to drink. And drink might help to blot out the pain of the way he'd been made use of that evening. He could still hear the faint murmur of voices from within Sandy's cabin, one of which he was sure was Peter Nuttall's, and then there'd been the flower on the ground outside the door. He'd picked it up to take with him, hoping that by looking at it he could work out what it meant.

An hour later he found himself leaning on the rail of the deck outside the Radio Room, not quite sure how he got there, but knowing that he was very drunk. He was accompanied by the Captain, also very drunk. And reciting Shakespeare.

'The wills above be done,' he intoned, leaning on the rail. 'But I would fain die a dry death. Know what that is?' he turned to Joe.

'Nope.'

'Shakespeare. *The Tempest*.' John spoke as though he were proud of himself for remembering it. Then his shoulders sagged and he became despondent. 'Yes — I want to die.'

'Stop.' Joe commanded imperiously. 'We swore. No more suffering over women.'

'You're right.' John agreed. 'Cows. They're not worth it.'

'Right.' Joe began to sing tunelessly, and after a minute John joined in.

Neither of them saw Matt slip out of the Radio Room behind them, standing listening for a moment with a look of horror on his face, and move away quietly.

He came across Kate a few minutes later, also leaning on the rail, looking out to sea. Although she, he was glad to notice, appeared sober.

'Penny for your thoughts,' he offered.

'Oh —' she shrugged. 'I wasn't thinking really, just drifting.'

'What's come over you — coming out here at this time of night.'

'I couldn't sleep. Had a nightmare.'

Matt leaned on the rail beside her. 'Yes,' he said heavily. 'I know the feeling.'

Chapter 9

Kate presumed that her father left the ship at Felixstowe since she did not see him again. Neither of them made any effort to say goodbye to the other. She used the few hours in dock to do a small but vital piece of shopping. On her return to the ship she went along to the Captain's quarters, clutching her purchase.

'What is it?' said John when she handed him the wrapped package. He opened it to reveal two steel marbles, and looked up at her, puzzled.

She put the marbles into his hand. 'You roll them together,' she said. 'That way we'll know when to mutiny. Humphrey Bogart. *The Caine Mutiny*? Get it?'

If she had any hopes that he'd see the funny side they were disappointed.

'Very amusing,' he said sourly. 'And what precisely are you trying to say, Miss Laker?'

'That your behaviour is upsetting the crew.' She ignored the cold look he gave her. 'You've locked yourself up in a world of your own, cut yourself off from the rest of us. All right, your wife has left you. Are we to blame? Or your children?'

'Who the hell do you think you are, woman?' he demanded, livid with rage.

'Someone who's trying to help.'

'The day I need your help, I'll ask for it.'

'Not you. I don't give a damn about helping you Captain. I'm thinking about your children. They're in it up to their necks, and you owe it to them to stop hiding. *I* can understand why you're behaving like this, but other people might draw conclusions. The wrong ones.'

She dared give a slight flick of her eyes to the empty glass that stood on his desk. It was the faintest movement but she knew he'd got her message. Then she left him, quickly. She knew she'd driven him as far as she dared. As she closed the door she could have sworn she heard the click of steel against steel.

Someone else who came aboard at Felixstowe was Charles Wood-house. The company had offered him longer leave if he wanted it, but he had chosen to return at the earliest possible moment. There was nothing to keep him at home now, and the ship drew him back as though only there could he find what it was he now wanted.

Those who saw him stalk aboard in his heavy duffle coat remarked how much older and heavier he now looked, but added that it wasn't surprising in a man who'd lost his wife in that shocking way. But anyone who got close enough to observe his eyes might if they were perceptive enough, have noticed another change. There was more there than the deadness of anaesthetised grief. There was a coldness there, a habit of looking straight ahead, as though nothing on either side of him could be of any interest.

There was something purposeful about the way he went straight to the bridge. Apart from one duty navigator who sat with his head bent over his desk, it was deserted. Charles moved at once to the computer panel, and pulled out a half bottle of whiskey from the depths of his coat. This he deposited within the computer panel, making sure that it was concealed. Then he left the bridge.

He returned in the evening to find Matt and Thomas Kelly up there, but still no sign of John. To Matt's friendly, 'Hullo Charles, how are you mate?' he gave a brief nod.

'Things seem to have changed in my absence,' he said coldly.

Matt tried to smile, but the change in Charles had hit him like a blast of freezing air, and it dismayed him.

'And you're going to put us back in order?' he said genially.

'I'm talking about areas of responsibility. Has John opted out?'

'Of course not,' said Matt, still trying to sound friendly. 'He just doesn't happen to be here at the moment, and there's no decisions that we can't take.'

When Matt had gone Charles said to Kelly, 'Has John been ill?'

'No. Why?'

'I just wondered why he didn't come in for dinner.'

'You don't need to stay up here,' said Kelly, unwilling to prolong this conversation. 'If you'd like to go for a drink — relax —'

'I don't plan on relaxing,' said Charles, still in that same detached manner. 'And if I wanted a drink I wouldn't have to go far.' He moved to the computer panel and shifted the bottle into sight. 'Not far at all,' he said, smiling.

In the night-club Jo Bailey was just finishing her first stint. She accepted Kate's offer of a drink with relief.

'I wondered if everything's okay with Tony?' said Kate when they were seated together at a small table.

'Who?' Jo turned blank innocent eyes on her.

Kate smiled and nodded. 'Obviously it is,' she said approvingly. 'What about you and — everybody?'

'I just never look down, Jo.' Kate smiled.

'Sometimes I wish I'd never looked up.' said Jo ruefully. 'It all seemed so glamorous then.'

'Life at sea?'

'Under the spotlight. I thought the world was my oyster at seventeen. I never realised it would be limited to working men's clubs in Huddersfield — and this.'

'We're all the same at seventeen.'

'What did you want?' said Jo curiously.

'Everything I couldn't have.'

'That can't have left a lot.'

'I never got it.' Kate's voice seemed to close the subject and abruptly she rose and went to the bar for more drinks. When she returned she said, 'We were talking about you — your dreams.'

'I made it once you know. Topped the charts for a week. I guess that's the problem. Just a taste of success and you keep plugging away regardless of the price.'

'What price?'

'A husband, children, a happy family life.'

'They don't go hand in hand.'

'No. But maybe now it's too late I realise it's what I wanted after all. I've got no-one now that I can call my own.'

'I know what you mean,' said Kate simply.

'Do you?' Jo gave George Terson's daughter a faintly cynical look.

Kate smiled at her, perfectly understanding the look. 'Why do you think I won't look down?'

'In case you see what you really want?' said Jo.

Kate nodded and smiled. 'I'm damn sure it's there.'

After that the conversation turned to other channels and by tacit consent all further personal references were avoided.

In another part of the ship Linda Kennedy was coping with her own problems. The first one was a frazzled telephone conversation with her mother which, she confided to Sandy, had left her feeling more worn out than a day's work.

'Cluck, cluck, cluck,' she muttered furiously. 'You'd think he was two years old.'

'Who?' said Sandy.

'My brother. He's taken off. Left home — and Mum's got her knickers in a twist! Funny isn't it? Parents can up and walk out at any time. It's called divorce. They even get a bloomin' certificate to prove they done it. But kids — if one of the kids walks out — he's a delinquent.'

She ran her hands through her hair, rumpling it still more. Tidiness was never Linda's strong point. She meant to go to her cabin at some point in the evening and straighten herself up, but somehow there never seemed to be time. Not that the passenger in No. 87 objected to her appearance. He was feeling under the weather, and when she brought him some pills from Thomas Kelly to make his stomach settle he was too full of gratitude to care what she looked like.

'If you need anything else sir, just ask,' she said as she closed his door.

She turned to walk away, and bumped straight into Charles.

'Hello love, all right are you?' she asked kindly. She made her voice as deliberately friendly as possible, for she knew that many of the crew members had been too embarrassed to speak to him.

Charles stopped and looked at her untidy clothing. 'Have you been in there with a passenger?' he demanded.

'He's gorgeous,' Linda clowned. 'Didn't you reckon I was capable of pulling a good 'un?'

'There's no need to look the part,' he said cuttingly. 'This isn't a tramp steamer.'

It took her a moment to realise that he had actually said this. By the time she called 'Hey' he was walking away. He looked back and his face was that of a stranger.

'I don't reckon that was called for, mate,' she said.

'Mr Woodhouse,' he said, deliberately.

Linda sighed. It was obvious to her what had brought about this change in Charles, and her kindly heart was touched. She moved towards him, talking gently.

'It won't help taking it out on me. Or anyone else. Won't help no-one,' she said. 'I think I know what it's like for you, but you can't feed on the hurt. Know what I mean? Sir?' She gave the last word a slightly satirical lift, inviting him to laugh at his newly-pompous self.

Charles looked at her silently for a long moment. Then he spoke.

'The next time I see you, I'll expect you to be tidy.'

He left her standing there, amazed, and gave her not another thought as he strode on towards the bridge. He dismissed Kelly, who was on duty, and perched himself on one of the high stools. He sat there alone for half an hour, staring into the darkness, until footsteps on the stairs announced John's arrival.

'Charles. How goes it?'

'Fine.'

John moved to the window and stood there, looking out.

'I thought Kelly was on.'

'I sent him off.'

'I'll leave it to you then,' John turned to go.

'It's still there,' said Charles quietly.

'What's that?'

'What you came for.' Charles reached out and took the whiskey from the computer panel. 'Don't worry. I'll keep it confidential.'

'What are you trying to tell me Charles?' said John in an odd voice.

'Well, there had to be an explanation. You've kept yourself to yourself from what I've heard. Don't blame you. It'll stay between us.'

John eyed him curiously for a moment. He seemed to be trying to decide something. At last he held out his hand for the bottle. Charles gave it to him.

'I want the name of every officer on watch and every look-out over the past two days.' John said firmly.

'What for?'

'You know what I have to do now. I'm responsible for the safety of this ship and everyone on board, and that begins with ensuring I have a crew which is capable of carrying out their duties twenty-four hours a day. There's no margin for error in an emergency.'

Charles nodded like a bored child. His smile seemed to say that John was going through the prescribed ritual but neither of them was fooled.

'I will of course need you to back me up in my enquiries,' John added.

'I hardly think you need me.'

John held up the bottle. 'You found it. You're prepared to stand by that, are you?'

After a second's hesitation Charles nodded.

'You're playing with dynamite Charles,' said John quietly. 'It has a nasty way of backfiring.'

'It does, doesn't it?' said Charles with a slight sneer. 'Especially in your position.'

John handed him back the bottle. 'Then perhaps you'd better think again about where you found this. I don't have to spell out why.' He headed for the stairs, but before he reached them Charles had recovered himself.

'To protect who, Captain Anderson?'

'I think you know the answer to that better than I,' said John, and was gone.

Tony Grant, who once felt he had all the answers, now felt as though the whole world were shifting under his feet. Susan had recovered her courage enough to tell him to drop dead, and now, when he had come looking for her to give her a firm talking to, she was reacting in an alarming way. Oh, she was showing fear all right. But it wasn't the kind of fear he wanted to instil into her. It wasn't fear that he could control, and therefore it was no use to him.

She had begun by running away, and when he'd come after her she fled still faster until she reached the rail. Her eyes were wild and he felt it would take very little to make her jump over.

'Don't touch me,' she screamed.

'What's got into you Susan? I just want to talk to you.'

She pressed herself back against the rail. 'You're one of *them*. You can't fool me. I know they're after me — *they* sent you —'

As she made a movement he jumped forward and seized her arms. The last thing he wanted was the silly cow jumping overboard and creating a scandal with him in the centre of it.

'Calm down Susan,' he tried to soothe her. 'Just calm down.' She seemed to relax and he turned her to look at him. 'That's better. You've got to trust me. *Jeez!*'

This last exclamation was jerked from him by the force of her thrust that sent him reeling back against the rail. She darted away from him before he could recover. He began to run after her, seriously alarmed. In this mood she might do or say anything, and who knew what damage that might cause him?

He followed her almost to her own cabin, but at the corner he stopped. Susan had brushed violently past Jo Bailey, thrusting aside Jo's attempt to hold onto her. Jo stared at Susan's cabin door for a moment, then looked up the corridor to where Tony was beating a retreat. Then she went into her own cabin and picked up the phone to call Kate.

Kate was there in five minutes, slightly puzzled. Jo had said that Susan was hysterical, but to Kate's eyes Susan looked totally calm and in command of herself.

'I think you should tell me what happened, Susan.'

'Nothing,' said Susan coolly.

130

'Do you make a habit of behaving like that then?'

'He needed a fright. He didn't tell me to jump this time.' Susan gave a small satisfied smile. 'He thinks I'm crazy.' She looked up suddenly and stared Kate directly in the eyes. 'I was. A long time ago.'

'You were what?' said Kate, not certain she'd heard correctly.

'Can I trust you to tell them? It's in the interests of this ship.'

'Tell who?' said Kate, thoroughly confused. 'Tell them what?'

'Arthur Parker. I want you to tell Arthur Parker the truth about my past. I was ill once — a mental breakdown. It's a long story, if you've got time.'

'You want to tell me —?'

'The skeleton in my cupboard.'

'Who's rattling it?'

'Me. But I need you to tell Arthur Parker.'

'Tell me everything,' said Kate, and leaned back to listen.

Before disembarking in Gothenburg the following day Kate put out a call for Tony Grant over the Tannoy, asking him to go to the Purser's Office. There was a message waiting for him, but she entrusted the delivery of it to Peter.

'I'll enjoy giving it to him,' said Peter, with a meaning she did not stop to query. 'Have fun.'

'We will,' said Matt, who was waiting to collect Kate.

When Tony arrived Peter opened up a note to read to him.

'I can read,' said Tony, snatching it.

'So can I,' said Peter with a smile. 'Mr Collier-Brown. Quite a name to conjure with.' He was enjoying the shock and horror on Tony's face, and the nervous way the croupier glanced at the exit. 'And don't keep him waiting. You might have paid off Grainger, but this one's flown all the way from London to see you. Mr Collier-Brown doesn't forget.'

It had been Matt's idea to go swimming in Gothenburg, and when they were floating in the large warm pool Kate conceded that it had been a good one. Her cares seemed to float away from her, leaving her mind as light and easy as the water made her body.

She gasped as Matt picked her up suddenly, holding her high in the air and letting her slide slowly down him till their faces were even.

'Let's throw caution to the wind, shall we?' he murmured.

'Why not?'

131

It might not be the way she'd imagined it, but the contact with his near-naked body had excited her, and she suddenly had no desire to put him off any longer. Her eyes held his as he moved forward slowly to kiss her.

Then, suddenly, he had vanished and she was facing only empty air.

'Where've you gone?' she laughed, feeling him moving around beneath the water, near her ankles.

'Katherine.'

The hated voice made her jump and twist round. It was Marion Carter who had spoken. She stood there on the side of the pool, complacent, waiting for Kate to come out and join her. It was obvious that Matt had seen her first and dived beneath the water to escape her attention. Kate wished she could do the same. Instead she pulled herself out and collected a towel that was lying at Marion's feet.

'I don't like being spied on,' she said furiously, 'and whatever had to be said was said on the ship.'

'I don't give a damn about the boat,' said Marion. 'George is my concern, that's why I'm here. Sorry I broke up your party.'

'Don't apologise Marion. I've as much concern for my father as he showed for my daughter.' Kate moved to the side and sat down, towelling her hair to avoid looking Marion in the face. Marion came after her. Fully dressed as she was she felt uncomfortable and out of place surrounded by water and semi-naked swimmers, but she sat down determinedly on the same bench as Kate.

'I've lived with George's guilt too long,' she said firmly. 'Your daughter's death nearly destroyed him.'

'Her name was Emma.'

'Emma.' Marion conceded. 'We were in Switzerland when it happened, and believe me Kate, we didn't know. George always refused to allow business to interfere with the few days we get alone together. The man in London was stupid. He didn't use his head.'

'He didn't dare.' Kate snapped. 'It wasn't *money!* I don't care about your days together. Emma died during your days together.'

'Kate —' Marion was pleading. 'George fired the man. All right — that means nothing, I know. And he knew, and couldn't face up to you. What could he do?'

Kate stared at her, unforgiving. 'And so your consciences are clean.'

'How can they be?'

'You didn't come here to talk about my father's conscience. And you're wasting my time Marion. What exactly do you want?'

'To know what you want.'

'I didn't tell *him*, and you can follow me all round the North Sea and get the same answer.'

'I love George, and I don't like what you're doing. The pressure's showing.'

'Good,' said Kate calmly.

'I'd hoped to call you off —' said Marion slowly, '— somehow — but I'll look after what's mine. George is mine . . .'

'And Emma was mine.'

Marion stared at her with something like hate. 'How long are you going to make him pay for one mistake? A lifetime?'

'Yes,' said Kate with soft venom.

Marion stood up. 'All right. You're not fighting my man any longer. You're fighting me.'

She turned on her heel and walked off, leaving Kate there. Kate watched her go until she disappeared. She had an odd sensation that the battlelines had been drawn up — and they weren't where she had expected them to be.

Chapter 10

Three hours out of Gothenburg they ran into a pea-souper. It was the kind of weather that brought a captain out in a cold sweat; but not because of any danger to his ship. John knew that the ship was bigger than anything he was likely to encounter, and in any collision it would be the other vessel that went to the bottom. That was just where the nightmare lay. No captain wanted to figure as the Goliath that had sent a fragile, helpless David to its end. And the trouble with the little Davids was that they were often manned by amateurs — at least, they were amateurs by John's standards. Too often the boats were made of wood, and hadn't got their metal reflectors properly fixed. And without metal there was no way they could be picked up by radar. So you collided with them in the fog, and the public mourned the little vessel and said you'd been careless, and a black mark went on your record.

The bridge was crowded when John took up his position. Charles and Kelly were there, and several other members of the crew, silently watching dials, their brows furrowed with concentration. They all knew the danger. John had a cold feeling going up and down his spine. Years of experience had developed his nose for this kind of situation. He knew when a small boat was heading for him even when the machines didn't.

'I'm *sure* there's something there,' he muttered for the hundredth time.

'Nothing on radar?' said Kelly.

'Nope.' John went hurriedly outside.

Kelly looked to where Charles was standing to one side, arms folded, the picture of indifference.

'I'm just letting him do his job,' said Charles in answer to Kelly's raised eyebrows.

'You could give a hand.'

'I'm here to take orders. So are you.' Charles gave a cynical smile as Kelly turned away in disgust. 'Complying with the rules, Kelly.

John's Captain. John's responsible.' Charles made a gesture indicating the fog. 'Just him.'

He jumped suddenly as John reappeared in the door, moving as though the hounds of hell were at his heels, leaping across to the wheel, seizing it from Kelly and yelling frantically,

'Full astern and blast her.'

In a reflex action Kelly pushed two buttons, raising the appalling clamour of the warning sirens. Over the deafening noise John roared,

'Damn wooden barges!'

Kelly had moved outside and stood there, peering into the fog.

'Are they okay?' John yelled.

'I can't see them,' Kelly called back. 'Why the hell can't they keep their eyes skinned?'

At that moment the phone rang. John seized it, and relaxed visibly when a voice from the Radio Room said, 'I've picked them up, sir.'

'Then ask them where the hell their regulation metal reflector is.'

'They said it fell off, sir.'

'I've heard that one before.'

'They said, thank you for avoiding them, sir.'

'Sure.' John snapped. He slammed the receiver down, realising that sweat was pouring down his face. Relief was making him weak at the knees.

'I hope it frightened them out of their wits,' said Kelly, reappearing.

'That's hardly the point of the exercise, is it?' said Charles.

John seemed to become aware of Charles, standing aloof and detached in the corner.

'Give her ten knots Kelly,' he said briefly, and went up to face Charles.

'No Charles,' he said in a quiet voice, that only the two of them could hear. 'The point of the exercise is to get through this fog without damaging this ship, or any other ship — even a damned wooden fishing vessel; all without endangering the passengers' lives. What's the point of *your* exercise?'

Their eyes met, held, then Charles's fell. He moved backwards a step and returned to the navigation table without looking at John again. John knew that he had won a small but significant victory — not merely over Charles but over himself. The adrenalin that had coursed through his veins in the crisis had, for the moment, washed away the apathy that had been threatening to destroy him. But he felt no sense of victory. On the contrary. When he looked at Charles he felt sick at heart.

Kate allowed Susan Porter to be present when she telephoned Arthur Parker and to hear the conversation amplified from the other end. She felt it might help to bind Susan more closely on her side, and it was also a chance to impress her with her own style of dealing with people — just in case Susan ever felt like trying anything again.

'Don't worry about it Arthur,' she soothed him when she had repeated to him the story of Susan's breakdown as relayed to her. 'You couldn't possibly have known Susan had suffered a severe mental breakdown when you engaged her.'

She gave Susan a wink when she said this. She was in possession of the full story, not only of Susan's illness, but of how Parker had held it over her head as a way of controlling her. It was a pleasure to cut the ground from under Mr Parker's feet. Also, Kate fully appreciated the shrewdness with which Susan had insisted on Parker's being told. It was a masterstroke.

'Have you any idea why she had a breakdown?' Parker's voice sounded tense on the phone.

'A man. Usually is. But rely on me. I'll do my very best to keep your hands clean. You didn't know about it and that's an end to it. I'll back you up all the way, and I'm very happy to keep her on. In the meantime — is there anything you wanted to tell me?'

'No Miss Laker, I don't believe there is.'

Kate put the phone down feeling fully satisfied that Parker had got the message. He was only one step away from a great deal of trouble.

'That should settle it,' she told Susan.

'Thank you.'

'There's still Tony Grant of course.'

'Forget him,' said Susan. 'He really thinks I've flipped now.'

'I wonder if that's why he took his annual leave so suddenly,' Kate mused. 'He left a message to that effect in Gothenburg.'

Or was it, she wondered, anything to do with the mysterious Mr Collier-Brown whose message to Tony had been so urgent? But she did not share this thought with Susan. She was a long way from trusting her.

'Miss Laker — I'll never let myself be used again,' Susan assured her.

Kate looked at her hard. 'You've only seen the tip of this particular iceberg,' she said, and left her.

'Go away.'

Matt, lying on his sofa with a cushion over his face, did not bother to look up when his door opened. Nor did he remove the cushion until he felt an envelope drop onto his stomach. Then he looked up to find John sitting down beside him. When he opened the envelope a gold stripe fell out. It was Matt's fourth stripe, to which he had become entitled on his promotion to Chief Engineer a couple of months earlier, but which had not become available until the ship had last docked at Felixstowe, a couple of days ago. John had been waiting for the right moment to give it to him.

'What did you expect?' said John, grinning. 'A ceremony?'

'Needle and thread maybe,' said Matt, struggling to wake up.

On the word John took a packet of needles and a reel of cotton out of his pocket.

'Give me your jacket,' he said.

'*You're* going to do it?'

'Safer than Linda. So long as I can thread the damn needle.' He was concentrating ferociously. When he had the needle threaded and had taken up the jacket, he said, 'Thanks for the work you put in down there during the fog, Matt.'

'My job,' said Matt briefly. He watched as John sewed away. A warm and pleasant feeling was creeping over him. This was the old John Anderson. 'I'd have had you down for knitting,' he said at last.

'Crochet actually,' John assured him.

He looked up to meet Matt's eyes, and they both smiled companionably.

'Hi,' Matt greeted him.

He knew enough had been said.

That left him with the problem of Charles, whose intentions were getting plainer by the minute, although Matt had no way of knowing whether John had seen the danger.

He tried it out on Joe the next time he saw him.

'But Charles isn't the only one with a master's ticket.' Joe objected. 'There are several other officers on this ship who could take over from the Captain if — well, if anything happened. They're not all snapping at his heels.'

'They've got something else in life.' Matt pointed out. 'Ambition sometimes takes a woman's place, you know.'

As soon as the words were out he regretted them. It was common knowledge on board that Sandy's engagement to Peter Nuttall had been resumed. Joe had never spoken of the subject, but Matt clearly recalled his confidence that 'She's mine now.' And the sight of Joe, dressed up and drunk in the Captain's company, had told its own story of rejection. Matt wondered if Sandy had the slightest idea of what she was doing.

'I haven't lost her yet.' Joe told him brightly. 'And there's no way I will.'

'You have,' said Matt gently. 'She's marrying Peter.'

'Just engaged.'

'They're all users Joe. Forget her,' Matt turned off into the corridor that led to his own cabin, waved a brief farewell and was gone.

'He really is quite something that guy,' said Joe, to Linda who had appeared carrying a pile of linen.

'Talking 'bout yourself again?' She ribbed him.

He fell into step beside her. 'Do you know what it takes to make Chief Engineer at Matt's age?'

'I think you're going to tell me.'

'Genius. Not to mention that he saved the last ship he was on from blowing itself sky high when his Number One was overcome by fumes. That's how. Got the Chief out and saved his life, then risked his own and saved the lot by going straight back down and taking over himself.'

Linda considered for a moment. 'Strikes me he'd have made Chief a darn sight easier if he hadn't bothered saving his Chief in the first place,' she said.

After her last contact with the Captain, Kate's surprise was considerable when she received a summons to his quarters to learn that he wanted her advice.

'I thought you'd had enough of that,' she said with a wry smile.

'Sit down.'

She sat opposite him, realising that this was a different John Anderson. He looked as sad and weary as ever, but a certain tension had gone out of him, and his eyes no longer had the same tendency to slide off into a distant stare.

'I saw my wife in Gothenburg yesterday,' he said.

'And the children?' she asked at once.

'No. But she's got them there. And that's where she intends keeping them. They are now Swedish citizens.'

'But they can't be. You're their father . . .'

'Since the first of July 1979 that is apparently irrelevant.' Kate stared at him in dismay. 'They decided then that all children of a Swedish mother could automatically become Swedish citizens. My wife made the application then.'

'That long ago?' said Kate, appalled.

He nodded and looked away. 'I'm so darn confused Kate. It happened all at once. Well, for me — not for her obviously. For all I know, there wasn't even another man then. Does that surprise you?'

'Not really.'

'You seem to know exactly what women do, and why.'

'That's almost inevitable, isn't it? What does surprise me though is you with your head in the sand. You must have known it was going bad for years.'

Their eyes met. 'Do you expect me to comment?' said John..

Kate shook her head. 'You asked for my advice. All right, get yourself the dirtiest lawyer in London. The dirtiest woman lawyer.'

'No.'

'*Yes.* You'll never get your children away from her now; but visiting rights — staying rights — that's what you must get.' As he looked down she drove her point home. 'That is what you want?'

He looked up and nodded. 'You know a lawyer who lives up to your standards?'

'I use male lawyers.' She rose and prepared to go. 'But they know each other. I'll ask around.' As she moved to the door her eyes fell on the photograph of his family that John always kept by him. Despite what they had been saying she was slightly shocked to note that Maya's face had been neatly cut out, leaving a hole where her head had been. Then she noticed the nautical maps spread over John's desk.

'Are you planning a trip?' she asked.

'Maybe.'

A photograph of a small boat lay on top of the maps.

'In that?'

He nodded. 'She's called Em.'

Kate flinched slightly. 'Short for Emily?'

'Yes.'

'And Emma,' she said, half to herself. 'Don't do anything silly.'

'Such as?'

She gave a significant glance at the maps with their expanse of ocean where a man could get lost.

'Use the law,' she said. 'It's a double-edged weapon.'

At Amsterdam, Jeremy Gates was waiting for her and they drove away together. He had been looking at the results of her work and wanted to express his displeasure. To a man hoping to convert the line to freight Kate's success had a sour taste.

'It's just that from the receipts you seem to be *improving* the passenger side,' he said fretfully.

'To safeguard our investment,' she told him.

'Of course.' He did not look at her but kept his eyes on the road. But she could hear the faint hostility in his voice and decided that the time had come to show Jeremy Gates that she wasn't to be intimidated.

'Come to think of it,' she said in a casual voice, 'I wanted to talk about investments. Those you made on the company's behalf eight years ago, which resulted in my father promoting you so rapidly. That is how it happened, isn't it?'

'Common knowledge.'

'Clever too, using idle company funds, investing them in gold, silver etc. Result: the company makes four million pounds.'

'Three-point-seven-five,' he corrected.

'Correct. You put it in a Swiss bank account in the company's name, then went to my father and said, "There you are sir. That's how to handle idle money." '

'Not quite so heartily,' he put in.

'Of course not. After all, you had embezzled the money in order to invest it. Albeit in the company's name.' She kept her eyes on the road ahead, but she knew the moment he threw her a quick frowning glance before giving his attention back to the car. She smiled. 'All I need to know is the date you transferred that Swiss bank account from your name to the company's name.'

The car gave a jerk as he made a convulsive movement. But he recovered himself quickly. 'No surprise, love,' he said smoothly. 'I am aware of your "research" into my affairs. But be careful!' Behind the suave voice the implicit threat was unmistakable.

'Always,' she promised him. 'Now where is this restaurant we're going to? I'm very hungry.'

It was a beautiful car, a turquoise blue Saab 900. It had been delivered onto the car deck early that afternoon, ticketed 'Miss K. Laker', in whose name it was also registered. By the time the ship left Amsterdam its presence was common knowledge and providing a talking point on the bridge.

'It's quite something,' said Kelly, who had seen the car's arrival.

'I'm sure it is,' said Charles.

'Wouldn't mind one myself,' mourned Kelly.

'Crew don't qualify,' Charles told him with a smile. He was, Kelly was relieved to note, smiling slightly more now, and seemed closer to the Charles they all remembered.

140

'Just her, it seems.' Charles continued, raising his voice for the benefit of John who had just appeared on the bridge. 'Not even the Captain.'

'What's that?' said John.

'Just talking about Miss Laker's new company car.' Charles told him.

'What company car?'

'It seems she's getting precedence. Of course, there's a chance they plan to give us all one. If we're good boys. What kind are you going to pick? Can't be over two litres, of course.'

'What?' said Matt who had just appeared and caught the last few words.

'You haven't heard?' said Charles coolly. 'Well ask Miss Laker. She knows all about it.'

When the situation was explained to him, Matt made Kelly take him down to the car deck for a visit of inspection. He wondered just what new turn his relationship with Kate Laker was going to take now. He knew he'd nearly had it made when they went swimming, but then Marion Carter had shown up, and by the time Kate came back to him it was too late. They'd spent a pleasant afternoon together, but the moment had passed and they both knew it. Also Matt had been able to sense that she was slightly upset, and it had been consideration as much as anything that had made him keep his distance for the rest of the time. They had finished their swim, he'd taken her for a drink, they'd talked about nothing, and then returned to the ship, without so much as holding hands. They might have been brother and sister.

In Amsterdam he had seen her drive off with Jeremy Gates. Not that he had asked her about that, and she had certainly volunteered nothing. Since then there had been no moves on either side. Now there was this to be considered.

'It might be a two-litre,' he said when he had looked it over, 'but that turbo charger makes it three.'

'Then it can't be a company car,' said Kelly.

'Never a company car,' Matt confirmed. 'What's Charles trying to stir?'

'Anything to cause trouble,' Kelly ventured.

As they went back up in the lift Matt said, 'All I've got of theirs is an alarm system.' He thought for a moment. 'It even matches her eyes.'

'Does it?' said Kelly with meaning.

Matt grinned. He was saying nothing. Let them think what they liked.

As a result of the car Kate found herself an object of interest, from Peter, who remarked snidely that he imagined it was bullet-proof, to John, who called her into his quarters and said, 'In a friendly way I'm turning the tables. I've decided it was time you accepted a little advice from me.' He handed her a scotch. 'That car you've bought. I don't think you should talk about it too much.'

'I haven't.'

'Then let's say it is being talked about and causing a certain amount of jealousy which could lead to friction.'

'I didn't buy it.' Kate explained.

His eyebrows rose. 'Company car?'

'No,' she smiled. 'It appears to be a present.'

When she left the Captain she found herself hailed by Matt who ran a few steps to catch up with her and dropped her cabin keys into her hand.

'Where did you get them?' she demanded.

'You left them in your office. Peter gave them to me.'

'He's not supposed to give them to anybody except me.'

'You've got them,' he grinned. 'Stop complaining. I don't know what you need them for anyway. You never lock your door.'

They had reached her cabin now. 'Only when I'm in here with these,' she said lightly, and slipped inside, closing the door in his face. He knocked at once.

'Yes?' she said, opening up.

'Would you lock it if I was in there with you?' he demanded.

'No.'

'I think it might be a good idea if I was.'

'Why?'

'Well, we could discuss Freud's theories on women who lock themselves in to protect their keys. And then how she gets out when she's locked in with the only keys there are.'

He cocked an eyebrow quizzically at her. Kate couldn't help laughing.

'All right. She sends for the engineer.' She stood back to let him in.

Over a drink she told him all she knew about the car — which was very little.

'A Swedish car, delivered in Amsterdam, with English number plates,' she said. 'Gets curiouser and curiouser, doesn't it?'

'And you're still taking the car?'

'Of course.'

'Even though you have no idea who gave it to you?' She nodded and he leaned back to regard her. 'Very cool.'

'I'll say thank you,' she added.

'Just like that.'

'How many ways can a person say thank you?'

'I can think of a few,' he muttered. 'What are you mixed up in Kate?'

'Only what's mine.'

'And Jeremy Gates? Where does he come in?'

'That's business.'

'No pleasure?'

'Sometimes they're one and the same thing.'

'I see.'

'I thought you were talking about that car.'

'Maybe I am.'

'I never take payment.'

'Just pleasure?'

'Yes,' she met his eyes steadily, seeing a kindling in their depths that answered her own. 'Don't you?'

Before he could answer, her phone rang. After a moment she held it out to Matt.

'The Captain. For you.'

He took the phone but covered the mouthpiece to speak to her again. 'You know why he's called me here, don't you?'

'Because you weren't in your cabin?'

'Think about it,' he spoke into the phone. 'John, what can I do for you?' There was a silence, in which his face darkened with concern. 'I'll be right there,' he snapped.

He almost leaped out of the cabin in his urgency. Kate did not follow him because she had been suddenly struck by the meaning of his final words to her — that of all the cabins on the ship John had known to look for Matt in this one.

Peter had said it would be two hours before he could get away, but Sandy reckoned those two hours would be just enough time to get herself ready for him. The nightdress and the negligée she had bought for the occasion were laid out on the bed so that she could give them a fond look now and then as she got on with her preparations. She showered and towelled herself, regarding her slim young body in the mirror, trying to see it through Peter's eyes. She wanted so desperately to be desirable to him.

She applied her make-up carefully, then slipped on her night-

143

clothes. Last thing of all was a liberal dab of the perfume he had given her. It had an expensive, luxurious smell that pleased her. She gave her hair a flick with the brush. It wasn't necessary, but it was something to do until he came, which should be any moment now.

When the knock came at the door she smiled to herself and called, 'You can come in now.'

But it was not Peter who opened the door and came inside, but Joe Francis. He stood there swaying until he leaned back against the door for support. It slammed shut, trapping her there inside her cabin with a man who she could see was very drunk.

'What are you doing here?' she demanded, outraged.

'You asked me to . . .' he said blearily.

'I didn't — Joe that was ages ago — please go away —' she said frantically.

'Sandy — please —'

He tottered towards her and in another moment he had her down on the bunk, his huge weight pressing her beneath him.

'Let me go Joe — please —' she was struggling beneath him but it was useless. He was far too heavy for her. Vaguely she could sense that he was fumbling at her clothes, but details were blotted out in a rising surge of fear and disgust.

Then the door opened again and she went weak with relief.

'Peter —' she called.

But Peter made no move towards her. Instead he stood quite still in the doorway, his eyes fixed on the struggling pair on the bunk. He seemed to be in a state of shock.

'Peter —' she screamed, '— please — Peter —'

Joe turned his head and leered drunkenly. 'Come on, lover boy. You want another beating up? Come on — she's calling you . . .' He grabbed Sandy, pulling her head up so that he could kiss her more easily. She twisted away from him, and through disbelieving eyes saw Peter turn and walk away, leaving her alone with Joe.

Almost at the same moment she felt Joe go limp on top of her. The amount of drink he'd taken on board that night had finally become too much for him. With a mighty heave she managed to send him slithering to the floor, where he lay, motionless, while she fled the cabin.

Matt listened to Sandy's story in dismay, his mind half refusing to believe it. She was crouched in a chair in John's cabin, her face buried in her hands, her shoulders shaken by sobs. John had stood on one side the whole time.

'Wouldn't it be better if Miss Laker took care of her?' Matt said at last. 'It's what she's here for.'

'Is it?' said John in a cold voice. He moved over to Sandy and spoke to her gently. 'I think it might be easier for you if you left it to us now. Why don't you go . . .'

She gave him an angry look. 'So you can sweep it under the carpet you mean?'

'That's not my intention.'

She looked from John to Matt, her tear-stained face distorted. 'You're all going to stick together, aren't you? All of you officers, the lot of you.'

She jumped up and ran from the cabin. John made a movement as if to follow her, but Matt stopped him.

'Let her go, John.'

John turned on him in a fury. 'That girl has been raped by one of your men, Mr Taylor.'

'I'll know that when I've got the facts from Joe Francis.'

'What facts? You know damn well what's happened. A girl gets raped — your department. Nuttall gets beaten up — your department. There's no discipline down there Matt because you're so busy organising your social life — they know it — I know it and that's fact.'

Matt stared at him. The charge was so idiotic that he knew he had to face the almost unbelievable fact that had previously only been a suspicion — John was jealous of himself and Kate. It was incredible, but there was no other explanation for this unreasonable outburst.

'Are we arguing because I was in Miss Laker's cabin?' he challenged.

'Because what —?' John recovered quickly and shouted, 'I don't give a damn where you were or why.'

So he'd been right, Matt thought.

'Then as one of *my* men is involved, please allow me to handle it in my way. I presume you're going to have the girl medically examined.'

'There's no need for that.'

'That girl's accused Joe Francis of rape, I want evidence.'

John gave him a hard look. 'There was a witness.'

'Where is Joe now?'

'Still in Sandy's cabin I imagine.'

Without another word Matt left the Captain and made his way to Sandy's cabin. He found Joe lying on the floor, breathing heavily and dead to the world. After slapping his face a few times Matt gave up trying to rouse him, and hauled the inert weight back to Joe's own cabin. Then he returned to John.

'What did he have to say.' John demanded.

'Nothing. He's in his own cabin now, sleeping it off.'

'He should be in the brig.'

'No sir. Do you want it straight? Witness or no witness?' John waited in silence, his face angry. 'Besides a skinful that would make anything impossible, Joe Francis was fully clothed. Unless you have that girl medically checked you'll take this matter further *after* I've handed in my resignation.' He turned to go, but looked back a moment. 'Perhaps that's what you want. You can tell me in the morning before we dock.'

Sometimes Jo Bailey wondered how it was that she became involved in other people's troubles. She didn't exactly see herself as the Universal Aunty, but that's what seemed to happen. She'd known that some kind of crisis was going on when first Peter and then Sandy had collided with her in the corridor, both of them obviously upset.

She hadn't followed Sandy because she was fairly sure the girl wouldn't confide in her. Sandy distrusted Jo ever since she'd seen her having a friendly chat with Peter who was playing the night-club piano. It would have been ridiculous if it hadn't been sad, but poor Sandy was jealous of everyone. Jo knew that Peter felt at ease with her because her twelve years' seniority gave her a safety factor that younger women didn't possess. But there was something more. Jo's greater experience had enabled her to divine something about Peter that she knew Sandy didn't suspect. She had never dared broach the subject with him, but she could see the time coming when it could no longer be kept a secret. The evening's events left her with the feeling that that time was almost here. So it was to Peter's cabin that she went.

'What was I supposed to do?' he asked sullenly, when he had told her what happened.

'I can't tell you that Peter.'

He turned from where he had been tracing patterns on the window with his finger. 'It was disgusting,' he said.

She sighed. So she had been right. Poor Sandy.

'Because of Sandy?' she asked gently. He didn't answer, but turned away again. 'You're going to have to face the facts.'

'I have. If that's what she wants she can have it.'

'Peter,' Jo spoke sharply. 'You know that isn't what she wants.

And I think you know what you've got to do.' He was silent, holding her eyes. 'It's truth time Peter. I understand. So will she.'

He did not ask what she meant. It was written all over her face that she had discovered his secret.

'I don't need it,' he said sullenly. 'Hers or anybody's. You want me to understand that animal I saw in there with her — that's normal?'

She didn't answer. There was no answer she could have given that would have averted this tragedy.

'Do you want me to talk to her?' she said at last.

'No — I will,' he sighed. 'But not just yet.'

It was about ten the following morning when the ship reached Felixstowe. Before getting ready to leave it Matt went to find John on the bridge.

'Have you arranged for a doctor to see Sandy?' he demanded.

'No.'

'You're dropping it then?'

'Keeping it on the ship.'

Matt reckoned he'd have to leave it at that for the moment. He had the feeling that matters had improved slightly for Joe in a way he would have found hard to define, but he was as determined as ever to resign if he saw Joe being victimised. In the meantime there was nothing to do but play a waiting game.

Before leaving the ship he went to see Joe, whom he found sitting on the edge of his bunk, holding his head.

'I didn't know what I was doing Matt . . .'

'I told you to stay clear of the booze. You went directly against my orders, and this is the last time.'

'I didn't hurt her. I swear Matt. I just wanted to show her. He's not good enough for her. Officer or no bloody officer, he's not good enough.'

'From now on,' said Matt quietly, 'you're confined to your quarters unless you're on duty.'

Joe looked up sharply, and blinked with pain. 'You can't do that,' he mumbled.

'Can't I?' Matt demanded cuttingly.

'I'll go over your head damn you — I'll go to Anderson . . .'

At once Matt stepped aside and indicated the door, 'Go ahead,' he said. 'Go to Captain Anderson.' He began to yell. 'Go on. What's keeping you? *She* also went to Captain Anderson — *she* accused you of rape to Captain Anderson.' He watched as Joe sank back against the wall. 'Now, would you rather we kept this between you and me?'

147

Joe nodded despairingly. Matt felt safe enough in leaving him then. It was plain Joe had had the stuffing knocked out of him, and he was unlikely to give any trouble.

Felixstowe promised to be interesting. Kate, who had received a message from her father to meet him there had asked Matt to take her new car and go in her place. For some reason that he still hadn't fathomed, he had agreed to her outrageous request.

'This way you just might discover exactly what kind of man my father is,' she had said, handing him the keys.

'Do you really think he gave you the car?'

'Yes.'

'To bribe you off the ship?'

'To establish my price. The car is probably just the beginning.'

'Tell you what — let's take it all and run away to land,' he clowned.

She refused to respond to the joke. 'Matt, will you say thank you to him for me? I'd like you to.'

'Why me?'

'Perhaps because I'm beginning to care what you think of me,' she said quietly.

He gave her a gentle smile. 'One question ma'am. Are you sure your father won't look on me as a prospective son-in-law. Another way to buy you off?'

'No,' she assured him. 'He's already got one.'

He had known, vaguely, that there had been husbands in Kate's life, but not that she was still legally tied to one of them. For some reason the news affected him disagreeably.

There was yet another unpleasant shock awaiting him on Felixstowe docks. As he drew the Saab abreast of the Terson limousine, and got out, it was Marion Carter and not George Terson who emerged to greet him.

'Hallo Mrs Carter,' he said politely. 'I was expecting Mr Terson.'

'Yes I know you were,' she said affably. 'You've got me instead. Sorry.'

'Well Miss Laker sent me off the ship with a message for him.'

'I'll pass it on.'

'She just asked me to say "Thank you".' There was a moment's pause while he waited for Marion's answer, but she made none, just stood there looking at him. 'Thank you,' he repeated lamely. 'That's all. Do I take a message back?'

'If she can't be bothered to be here herself, no,' said Marion in a cold voice.

148

Matt at once began to move back to the Saab. He wasn't playing their games for them. 'All right Mrs Carter.'

'You're Matt Taylor,' she said suddenly. 'The swimmer.'

He grinned at her.

'And Chief Engineer,' she finished.

'That's right ma'am.'

'I do like your car. Mr Terson obviously pays his engineers more than I thought. Unless Miss Laker's supplementing your income in some way . . .' she left the implication hanging in the air. 'I do hope the work's not too hard.'

She returned to the back seat of her car and glided away. Matt had a feeling that if he touched his face he would feel the egg running down it.

'Well?' said Kate impatiently when he arrived back on the car deck.

'Surprise. Your Dad sent the girlfriend.'

'Marion!'

'Right. She thought the car was mine.'

'Did she?'

'And she had a couple of sharp things to say about money. Next time, love, say your own thank you's will you?'

Chapter 11

Matt Taylor's second meeting with Marion Carter in one afternoon took place in even stranger circumstances than the first. At least — the conversation was a good deal stranger, as he reflected afterwards.

On his return to the ship, he and Kate had taken the car out for a run to put it through its paces. When they arrived back they were met by a message that Marion Carter would like to see Matt Taylor — at once.

This time he joined her in the back of the car, and sat listening with his jaw dropping, as it became plain that Marion had come bearing gifts of a most unexpected nature.

'I've checked your record,' she told him, 'and a raise is the very least we can offer you. In fact what we are offering is promotion. It's a large company Mr Taylor.'

'I'm aware of that,' he said, while he frantically tried to collect his thoughts.

'And the choice is yours.'

'What choice?'

'We're offering you the post of engineering supervisor in charge of the entire fleet. You can be based in Florida, New York, the Bahamas or Singapore. That's your choice.'

'Well, that's quite an offer,' he murmured, stalling for time.

'Yes, we think so. Best of both worlds. Land-based. Twice your income and a personal guarantee that you can return to your job as Chief Engineer on any of our ships. Any questions?'

'Yes, Mrs Carter. I'd like to know why you're making the offer and not Mr Terson.'

Suddenly she was on edge, he was interested to note. 'Because Mr Taylor, I've had to assume temporary control of the company. Mr Terson is in hospital undergoing tests and although I'm sure it's not serious his doctors have insisted on total rest. From now on everyone reports to me. Perhaps you'd tell Miss Laker.'

That was exactly what he intended to do, he told himself as he headed back to the ship and towards Kate's cabin.

'Are you in?' he called, putting his head round the door.

The living area was empty, but a noise from the bedroom made him go in and look around. To his surprise the bedroom was also empty. He wondered if he had imagined the noise, but it had been very distinct — like a wardrobe door closing.

'Hello —' he called, wondering if Kate were playing games with him. It seemed unlike her to go hiding in wardrobes. She wasn't the type to leap out and call 'Peekaboo.'

'Come on Kate, I heard you,' he called.

'Did you?'

He spun round at the sound of her voice from the door that led to the living area.

'Boo!' he said, deciding that he must have imagined the whole thing.

'I forgot my keys,' she said, picking them up from beside her bed. 'What did Marion want?'

'I was on the receiving end this time,' he told her as they left the cabin. 'She offered me promotion.'

'*She* offered you —?'

'She says she's in charge for the moment. Your father's in hospital for tests and has to have complete rest.'

He studied her face as he said it, but it registered nothing — although he thought he saw it set slightly. Ah well, it was her business.

'Promotion,' she said at last. 'That figures.'

'Does it?'

'Purely on merit of course,' she added sardonically.

'Don't you think I merit promotion?' he demanded, slightly miffed.

'Of course. And off this ship naturally, since you're as high as you can go.'

'Yup.'

Just before they went their separate ways she gave him a wry smile. 'Aren't I going to rattle around in here by the time he's promoted everybody?'

For as long as he could Peter had avoided the inevitable discussion with Sandy. But it could not be postponed indefinitely, and while the ship lay in dock at Felixstowe he reluctantly agreed to meet her in the pub. The resulting scene was as bad as he'd feared.

'It wouldn't be the first time you'd asked Joe in,' he defended himself lamely. 'Would it?'

'Don't try twisting the facts to excuse your behaviour,' she told him furiously. 'You stood there and did nothing. You could see what was happening and you just stood there. I know the truth. But I want to hear it from you.'

For an alarmed moment he believed that she really did know the truth, but as she went on it became plain to him that her interpretation was way off the mark.

'Maybe I could accept it if you'd told me you didn't care for me any more — perhaps that you never did,' she raged in a whisper. 'But just because I'm not as — good as you are — a little beneath you in "class" — I'm damned if I'll let you treat me like dirt.'

'I've never lied about my feelings for you,' he mumbled. His head was down and he could not look her in the face.

'Then they obviously weren't enough. *I* wasn't enough. You're just like every other man on this ship. One woman's not enough for you — you've got to keep proving yourself. Well, I won't take it. I don't like being cheated on. But I'll tell you one thing, Peter. I'll find out who she is, even if you don't tell me, and by the time I've finished she won't want you either.'

She stormed off, leaving him there. She knew that some part of her rage was due to the thought of what she had to do now. She had no true regrets for the accusation she had made the previous night. Joe had asked for it. But now she had to sort it out for him, and she wasn't looking forward to it. She marched off to the Captain's cabin.

'I'd just rather you didn't take it any further Captain,' she said awkwardly.

'Why?' his face was grim.

'It wasn't quite the way I said.'

'Are you telling me you lied?' She looked down. '*Are* you?'

'He was drunk. He didn't know what he was doing.'

'That doesn't excuse it.'

'Maybe I encouraged him sir. Maybe he isn't the one to blame.' In the pain of what she saw as her rejection by Peter she was beginning to understand Joe's feelings more clearly. And the night when she had invited him and then shut him out now hung heavy on her conscience.

'You're the one to blame?' said John.

'Not altogether sir.'

'Then who is? What's this all about?'

Sandy looked hard at him. 'I wanted to show him up,' she gave a little sad laugh. 'It's funny — the only one it's showed up is me.' She rose from her seat with an air of finality. 'I wanted to clear things for Joe sir. That's all.'

'Do you realise the seriousness of the accusations you made?'

'Yes sir,' she looked him in the eye.

'Then why?'

'I'm not sure you'd understand.'

'Try me.'

Sandy shook her head. 'Men don't think being faithful matters. Maybe it only does when you're on the other end of it.'

'You'd better go,' said John quietly. She'd touched a raw nerve with that last remark, and he felt he'd had about as much of this conversation as he could stand. After a few moments to pull himself together he sent for Matt and told him about Sandy's visit.

'It doesn't sound like a good enough reason to me, John,' said Matt. 'Besides, it's a bit late for the truth now.'

'Well, there it is,' said John heavily. 'And that's an end to it.'

'For Joe too?' said Matt scandalised. 'He's supposed to forget it, just like that?' he snapped his fingers derisively.

'His behaviour is still inexcusable.'

'His behaviour can be cured by cutting the booze. What she's said about him — that's what Joe's got to live with.'

'He'll survive. We all have to,' said John harshly.

It was natural now for Peter to confide in Jo Bailey, who seemed to know so much about him without being told, and what was even better, did not condemn him. He called in at her cabin at the end of the evening.

'She didn't believe me,' he said dejectedly.

'Predictable,' said Jo.

'What now then?'

'It'll work itself out,' said Jo, conscious that she was evading the issue. 'Give it time.' She stretched out and took his hand, giving it a shake.

'I can't make her believe me,' he repeated.

'Nobody can,' Jo sighed heavily. 'She loves you.'

She gave him a drink, and talked to him some more like an aunty, and then got rid of him, because ultimately the problem was his own and no-one could help him with it. She hoped now she might be allowed to go to bed. She was as worn out as she could ever remember being. But when she had got into bed and stretched out her hand for the light there came another knock at her door.

This time her visitor was Linda, and as she listened to what Linda had to say Jo realised that her role as a shoulder for crying on had only just started. This was a crisis and a half.

'I just don't know what to do Jo. I just had to talk to somebody. It's not Larry's fault. He didn't do anything. It was my mother. She had him put away. But there's nothing wrong with him. All he needs is loving.'

'But you can't do it on this ship,' said Jo, incredulous. 'What on earth made you think you could get away with bringing him here?'

'He's my brother. I had to do something to help him. And I *have* got away with it till now.'

'But *how?*'

'I've kept him in my own cabin —'

'So that's —' Jo pulled herself up short. Suddenly Linda's sudden eccentricity was explained. The way no-one was ever allowed in her cabin, her inexplicable habit of 'talking' to it as she backed out of the door. The stories had gone round the ship, but no-one had thought too much of them because Linda was known to have a cockeyed sense of humour. Now it became plain — it had been Larry she had been talking to.

And now suddenly other things were coming back to Jo.

'Is that why you keep clearing the peanuts off the bar? I've seen you do it a few times.'

'That's right. I have to feed him somehow.'

'He's been living entirely on peanuts?'

'Na. I do other things. If food gets left out I nick it. I've had Miss Porter's lunch a few times — you should see her trying to work out where it's gone. And if I can't get anything I take him mine and then *I* live off peanuts. He doesn't stay in my cabin all the time. If one of the second-class is free I put him in there at night and take him back to my place during the day. That's where I put him that night Sandy wanted to stay with me — when she invited Joe and wanted to get out of it. But this trip there wasn't anything free in second-class so I had to keep him with me all the time. Trouble is — he gets bored. And when he's bored I can't always make him stay there, and he goes wandering. I've always managed to get him back before.'

'But not this time?'

'I can't *find* him.' Linda's voice became a wail. 'I've been looking for him all evening — everywhere.'

'I really do think you should tell Captain Anderson, Linda.'

'But I can't.' Tears were rolling down Linda's cheeks. 'They'd hand him back. They'd lock him up again. There's nothing wrong with him.'

Jo put her arm round the weeping girl. 'Just think about it. If you don't tell the Captain now, anything could happen.'

'But he's not dangerous. He wouldn't hurt anyone, I swear.'

'Wandering about this ship lost could be dangerous for him,' said Jo gently.

Linda looked at her pitifully. The armour of jokes that she wore against the world had been stripped away. Her face was haggard with love and worry.

She fumbled in her pocket and drew out a small photograph. To Jo it looked as if it had been taken in an institution. It showed a boy of about sixteen, with a blank pudgy face and vacant eyes.

'That's him,' said Linda. 'See how kind his eyes are. He wouldn't hurt a fly. If you could just help me look . . .'

'Okay love,' said Jo reluctantly. 'Give me a moment to get dressed.'

Kate was having a nightmare. Someone had shone a light in her eyes, a light she knew shouldn't have been there. And there was a figure looming over her menacingly . . .

Abruptly she opened her eyes to realise that it had not been a nightmare. The light over her bed had been switched on — and there was someone there —

'It's only me . . .'

The voice focused her attention. It had come from a boy who must have been in his middle teens, with a broad moon face. He was sitting on her bed, holding the picture of Emma in his hands, and smiling.

'What's her name?' he said.

Kate said nothing. Her throat had frozen. After a moment he tilted his head to one side and smiled at her. Something in that vacant smile made her want to scream.

'I'm called Larry,' he said. 'What's her name?'

'Emma,' said Kate in a dry whisper.

'Emma. Nice name,' he looked at Kate sadly. 'I was frightened.' He glanced over at the wardrobe. 'Don't like it in there — don't like being locked in.' He rose and looked at the wardrobe door as though expecting it to answer him back. 'Dark,' he said again. 'Like being dead.'

Dear God, had he been in there while she had been getting undressed? How long had he been in her cabin, watching her?

Kate had begun to ease herself out of bed, but without warning he whipped round to face her and she froze.

'I'm thirsty,' he said.

From somewhere she had found her voice. 'Then I'll get you a drink.'

His face lit up: 'Coca Cola?'

'If that's what you want.'

'To talk,' he said pathetically. 'Will you listen?'

'Of course I will,' she said, beginning to feel some of her fear evaporate. Now that she was properly awake and over her first shock she could see him for what he was, a scared child.

She moved to the fridge and took out a bottle of Coca Cola and poured it. Ater rummaging for a minute she found the ice-bucket and used the ice-pick to chip away a lump for him, which she plopped into the glass, and handed it to him.

As she did so the phone shrilled. Larry dropped the glass which smashed on the floor, and rammed both hands over his ears.

'Stop it,' he shouted. 'Stop that bell.'

Kate seized the receiver and spoke into it. 'Hello?'

But almost at once she nearly dropped the receiver, for out of the corner of her eye she had seen Larry take up the ice-pick and begin moving towards her with it. It was a small implement, but she knew that properly wielded it could smash her skull.

'It's a friend,' she said to Larry, trying desperately to keep her voice normal. He stopped in front of her, still holding the ice-pick. 'He wants to talk — like you do Larry.'

Her caller was Matt. Trying to keep up a flow of light chatter to him and watch the ice-pick nearly divided her brain in two. She was never afterwards able to recall what he had said to her or what she had said to him (although he said he'd called up for a goodnight chat) but as she could hear him preparing to ring off she had a sudden inspiration, and said hastily, 'But I thought you knew the answer to the key question Matt. *The lady sends for the engineer.*'

He had asked no key question. Her last remark had been apropos of absolutely nothing. But if her luck was in that very fact would alert him to the fact that something was seriously wrong with her.

'I'll get you another drink,' she said when she had put down the phone.

She filled another glass and held it out to him.

'You'll have to put that down if you want this,' she said, indicating the ice-pick.

He looked down at the object in his hand, and dropped it violently as if it had suddenly become red-hot.

'Sorry — I —' he stuttered.

'You don't like it?'

'No.'

'Nor do I.' Swiftly Kate bent down, picked the weapon up, and pointed it directly at him. He stepped back in fright. 'It's not nice, is it?' she said. He shook his head. 'Shall I get rid of it?'

He nodded and she backed till she reached the door that led into the corridor. She pulled back the catch, dropped the ice-pick outside and closed the door again. But this time she did not lock it.

'You said you wanted to talk,' she offered, moving over to the sofa. 'I'm listening.'

He began to talk disjointedly, spewing out a tale of bitterness and childish resentment, most of which seemed to be directed against Linda.

'She made them take me away — my sister,' he sulked. 'She brought me here.' He stared hard at Kate. 'You love Emma?'

'Yes.'

'You wouldn't let them lock her up — like she was dead?'

Kate felt a constriction of her throat, but after a moment she managed to shake her head and go on looking directly at Larry.

'My mother wouldn't have done it,' he said wretchedly. 'She loves me. It was *her*.' He seemed to mean Linda. 'She wants me dead, see. My sister does.'

At last there came the longed-for knock on the door, and Matt's blessedly normal voice calling, 'It's Matt, Kate. Can I come in?'

Larry started up but Kate said quickly, and in a voice loud enough to be heard outside, 'It'll be Matt. You'll like him.'

'No,' said Larry violently and began to back away.

In the corridor outside Matt and the Captain heard that rough voice and looked at each other. John was holding the ice-pick that they had found outside the door.

'If we bust in anything could happen,' John muttered worriedly.

'She's in trouble, for God's sake, John.'

They could just hear Kate's voice saying persuasively, 'I don't believe you want me to send him away Larry. I didn't tell you to go away, did I? Matt's a very special friend you see. Can I tell him to come in?'

'Captain Anderson —?'

John spun round at the unexpected sound of Linda Kennedy's voice. He wasted no time asking what had brought her here at just this moment, but seized her arm and moved her down the corridor until they had turned the corner, nodding to Matt as he went as a sign for him to go into Kate's cabin. He could just hear Kate calling, 'Come in Matt.'

As he stepped in Kate moved towards him with a too-bright smile and led him towards Larry.

'I want you to meet a friend of mine, Matt.'

'Hello,' said Matt guardedly.

'His name's Larry.'

Matt looked from Kate to Larry and back again, trying to assess the situation. Baffled, he followed Kate's lead.

'Shake hands with Larry, Matt,' she urged.

'Sure. Hi. Nice to meet you,' Matt made his tone jovial.

Kate took up the conversation, as desperately genial as a hostess who senses the party is falling flat.

'I don't know your second name Larry, but this is Matt Taylor. He's the Chief Engineer.'

'Second names don't matter.' Matt assured him. 'Nice to meet you.' He held out his hand again, but still Larry hung back.

'Come on.' Matt urged. 'If you're a friend of hers you're a friend of mine. Isn't that right Kate?'

'Yes,' she confirmed quickly.

'Then let's shake on it. Put it there friend.'

At last Larry smiled hesitantly and held out his hand. 'Hello,' he said.

The moment their hands touched Matt seemed to be made of steel all through, seizing Larry and yanking him into a half-nelson. From nowhere John reappeared in the doorway, bearing handcuffs. Larry began to kick and scream.

'Don't let them take me away again. Please don't let them take me . . . Help me — help me please . . .'

'*LARRY!*' Linda had followed John into the cabin just in time to see the handcuffs snapped onto her brother's wrists. At the sound of her voice he swung round and shrieked at her, '*You did it again . . .*'

The strength seemed to go out of him. Tears poured down his face and his eyes were filled with the bewilderment of betrayal as he fixed his eyes on Kate, then on his sister, then back to Kate.

'Where's Emma??' he said, weeping uncontrollably, 'Where's Emma . . .?'

Chapter 12

When there was no longer any way it could be avoided Peter Nuttall told Sandy the truth about himself. He had put it off till the last possible moment, dreading the scene that would follow, her tears, her incomprehension, her disgust. But he knew that after he had witnessed Joe Francis's attack on her he could never bear to make love to her again, and the time was coming when she would have to know why.

So he took her to his cabin, sat her down and, looking away from her as much as possible, told her what he had hoped no-one would have to know.

'Arguing about it isn't going to change anything,' he finished in a voice that lacked all emotion, he was relieved to note.

Sandy, sitting on the bed, was almost in tears, but still managing to fight them back. Anger and confusion were both written on her face.

'I just can't believe you're like that Peter.' She leaned forward till she was almost bent double in her anguish. 'I just can't.'

'It's the truth.' He was looking at himself in the mirror, with his back to her.

'Were you always?'

He turned to face her with a sigh. 'As long as I can remember. Yes.'

Slowly she sat up and leaned back against the wall, staring at him out of ravaged eyes.

'Did you ever love me?'

'No,' he said immediately. 'Well — yes — no, no I didn't.' Strain was beginning to distort his voice.

'Well which is it?'

'I don't know.'

'Yes or no?'

'It's not that simple. I'll try to explain.'

But she put her hands over her ears and squeezed her eyes shut, twisting away from him.

'I don't want to hear it again,' she almost screamed. *'I don't want to hear it.'*

'I'm gay Sandy,' he said relentlessly. 'A homosexual.'

Reluctantly she uncovered her ears and eyes. 'But you never acted like you were. You made love to me. How could you?'

'It's not impossible,' he muttered.

She regarded him in silent incomprehension for a long moment. 'Why didn't you tell me?' she said at last.

'But I did tell you. I just told you.'

A tear ran down one cheek. She wiped it away quickly. 'I mean before I fell in love with you.'

'Oh Sandy —' he floundered helplessly. 'Please — don't cry.'

He reached down to touch her but she flung out an arm to ward him off. She had closed her eyes tight shut again, but the tears rolled inexorably from them and down her cheeks. He stared at her, troubled, but having no idea what to do to help her, and trying for decency's sake to fight down a rising tide of disgust within him. Feminine tears, feminine hysterics, feminine scenes — how off-putting they all were. To cover his reaction he began to rant, 'Why don't you ask me how I feel about it? You think it's easy? I'm told it's a sin against God. Some people say it's a mental illness. You think I got up one morning and said "Hey, think I'll become a homosexual today"?'

'Oh please,' she said, coldly angry despite her grief.

'It certainly doesn't enhance my career potential.' He dropped down on the bed beside her, beginning to feel exhausted. 'Listen Sandy . . .' At once she turned away from him, but he continued regardless. 'Some people say it's just a matter of choosing a lifestyle. I wouldn't want to speak for everyone but in my case that's not true. The only choice I have is whether to be what I am or try to hide it.' He waited to see if she would turn her head back to him. 'Can't you even look at me?'

Without moving she said in a muffled voice, 'If I looked at you I'd want to strangle you.'

Tom Kelly wished the Captain would hurry up and arrive on the bridge. He disliked being alone there with Charles who seldom missed a chance to make some disparaging comment about John's absence or his work. The beginnings of a return to normality which Tom thought he had seen in Charles had been short-lived. If anything he'd grown worse. He'd even begun to make mysterious notes. Tom had jokingly asked him if he was keeping a diary, and Charles had answered non-committally, but the nasty suspicion had intruded that Charles was noting down the times of arrivals on the bridge — or something even more sinister.

Largely to see what kind of reaction he could produce, Tom now looked at his watch and asked innocently, 'Where's John?'

'Hard to say,' said Charles. 'The pub's not open.'

Tom gave him a hard look. It was worse than he'd feared. 'Probably in his office,' he said.

Charles shrugged. 'Could be. He does keep a good stock there.'

Tom took a deep breath. 'Stuff it Charles,' he said evenly.

'Eh?' Charles's look was bland and innocent.

'I don't want to hear it.'

'All right.' Charles shrugged a second time. 'I won't mention it again.'

There was a step on the stair and Susan Porter appeared bearing a tray on which stood a pitcher of orange juice.

'What a lovely day,' she said, looking out of the windows at the bright sea. 'Thought you men might like some freshly-squeezed orange juice.'

They both murmured their thanks, and she looked round the bridge.

'No Captain today?' she enquired.

Charles looked down at his feet and said nothing in a very pointed manner. Tom was forced to mutter, 'Not yet,' uncomfortably.

'Well, you boys seem to be steering a straight course without him,' she said cheerfully. 'I feel confident I'm in good hands.'

There was a sudden movement from Charles, as though someone had touched a reflex nerve. He looked up at Susan and a slight smile curved the corner of his mouth. He might have been seeing her for the first time.

'Hey,' said Tom, struck by a sudden thought, 'doesn't the triumvirate meet today?'

The triumvirate was John, Matt and Kate, who, as the top management on the ship had weekly meetings, one of which was due this morning.

'There's your answer,' said Tom to Charles.

'What was the question?' Susan looked from one man to the other.

'John's whereabouts,' said Charles, looking at Tom.

'Did I miss something?' she looked from one to the other again.

Tom ignored Susan and spoke directly to Charles . 'He'll be in his office getting ready.'

'Terribly responsible of him,' said Charles snidely.

'It is his job, isn't it?' Tom persisted.

After a moment Charles nodded very slightly, conceding defeat. Susan kept her eyes on Charles and said nothing.

In the Officers' Day Room the weekly management meeting was getting under way. John, Matt and Kate were seated together at one end of a conference table, each with a pile of papers in front of them. John switched on a small tape recorder and said, 'Weekly management meeting is now in session.' He consulted his agenda. 'First item: budgets.' He raised his eyebrows at Kate. 'Your report?'

Kate consulted a memo: 'I'm happy to be able to report that a change of suppliers and the arrival of a new Swedish chef have worked nicely together to produce a twelve per cent increase over last quarter in our restaurant revenues.'

'Twelve per cent?' said John, impressed. 'You're joking.'

'No,' she answered him simply. 'Item Number Two: Made bold by that success I'm filing a formal request for a reasonable increase in the entertainment budget. We'll hold a better night-club crowd — and sell more drinks — if we book a second act to fill between Jo Bailey's sets.' She paused and looked up. She had both men's full attention. 'I'd also like to propose introducing a limited but sophisticated menu in the club. Pâté, not peanuts. Funds can be shifted from freight contingencies to cover the start-up costs.'

'You want to spend the freight contingency money?' said Matt, not sure he'd heard right.

'It's just sitting there not doing anything.'

'What if we make a loss?' said John.

'We won't,' she told him calmly, handing him a sheet of paper. 'Those are my projections. The club has nowhere to go but up.' She saw they were both looking worried and added, 'I'm telling you gentlemen, sometimes you have to spend a little money to make money.'

The meeting proceeded. John deferred a decision about the freight contingency money, and Kate could tell she would have to do some work to convince him. She didn't want to press it now, because of something else that she knew was coming up on the agenda at the end of the meeting. She had already tried him out on this subject once this morning, and failed to persuade him to her way of thinking. This time it was vital that she succeed.

When it came to 'new business' John looked at her, knowing what she would say.

'Linda Kennedy's brother,' she said at once.

'I'm listening.'

'I've spoken to Linda and put through a call to her mother. These seem to be the facts,' she consulted her notes. 'Larry Kennedy is twenty years old. He is retarded, not insane. He was brought up at home, not in an institution. When he was fifteen he was employed at a restaurant as a washer-up. He held the job for four years without a single complaint being lodged against him. Last year, the restaurant closed. The employment situation being what it is, the family had no luck finding him another job. Since the mother is divorced and must work, and the other children are either away at school or working, Larry was left alone all day. Six months ago Mrs Kennedy found a mental home that would take him as a patient and give him a job in the kitchen. She thought he would be happier around other people and doing work he knew.

'In fact, he began to complain that he was being locked in his room at night, and was otherwise badly treated. The hospital denied his allegations. Mrs Kennedy hesitated to bring him home until she could get to the truth of the matter. On her last leave, Linda Kennedy went to visit her brother, with whom she is very close. She believed this story!

'She went home and had a violent argument with her mother, who couldn't be convinced that Larry really was being abused. Linda waited several days, then returned to the hospital and — without telling anyone and without being spotted — removed her brother and sneaked him onto this ship where she thought she could take care of him.' Kate put down her notes and looked up. 'That's more or less the whole story.'

Matt leaned back in his chair and spoke with asperity. 'All right, now give me some convincing reasons for letting him out of the brig. That is what you want, isn't it?'

'He hasn't any history of violence, and I don't believe he belongs in the brig.'

'He came after you with an ice-pick,' John protested.

'He was very frightened. I just wonder how much good's being done by keeping him in a place that's going to frighten him even more. He's terrified of being locked up.'

'Why don't we leave social work to the social workers?' said John.

'Decisions about crime control on the ship do fall into my area of responsibility,' she said mildly, so as not to antagonise him.

'And your area of responsibility falls under my authority,' he reminded her.

'Well I don't suppose I can argue with that, can I?'

She was not blind to the raised-eyebrow look that the two men exchanged at the 'new mild Miss Laker'. Well, let them have their smile at her if they wanted. The important thing was to get that scared boy out of the brig — as she had promised Linda she would.

It took another fifteen minutes' hard talking, but eventually she persuaded John that Larry should be allowed out of the brig on condition that Linda took full responsibility for him, and he was to be put off the ship at Felixstowe. John continued to be vaguely unhappy at the arrangement, but in the face of Kate's determination and her refusal to bring any kind of charge against the boy he allowed himself to be talked round.

Kate herself let Larry out of the brig, accompanied by Linda, who danced along beside her, getting under her feet. When the door was open brother and sister fell into each other's arms in a way that raised Kate's eyebrows slightly. Larry's hostility to Linda seemed to have faded somewhat, but perhaps that was the effect of long, lonely hours in the brig.

'I'm so glad to see you.' Linda cried. 'I'm so glad to see you.'

He towered over her, holding her clumsily in his arms, crying as much as she.

'Glad to see you too, Linda.'

'You can come out now,' she assured him. 'It's going to be all right.'

Kate said nothing. She had arranged for Linda to have ten days' compassionate leave to sort matters out, but she would not have bet money on its being all right. But there was nothing more she could do.

When the ship had docked in Gothenburg later that day Matt took her to lunch and allowed her to talk out her worry.

'The soft-hearted Kate,' he ribbed her, not unkindly.

But she was not in the mood for even the gentlest ribbing, and brushed his remark aside.

'Everyone has a flash of parental instinct now and then, don't you think?' she said.

Slightly to her surprise this seemed to make him uncomfortable, and he changed the subject.

'Tell me —' he said hesitantly, '— only if you like —' his voice made an unconvincing stab at being casual, '— who are you married to?'

'I don't mind telling you,' she said after a moment. Then she tried to match his light-hearted tone. 'Why don't I just give you a concise description of my matrimonial condition past and present?'

'You've got the floor,' he leaned back to listen.

She told her story precisely and in an emotionless voice, ticking off the stages of her life in much the same way that she had addressed the meeting that morning.

'I was married for the first time right out of university. It was a good marriage. I was very happy.' The tone of her voice did not change, he noted. It was as though she was ordering it not to. 'Bill, my husband, had been married before. Peter Nuttall is his son from the previous marriage. Bill was killed in an air accident, and I was single for some time. Peter lived with me. I remarried. Peter came to live with us.

'He was unhappy, and when he was old enough to leave — he left. By Alex — my second husband, I had a daughter, Emma, who died when she was three. The marriage didn't work out and we've separated. But I'm not divorced.'

'Why not?'

'It's complicated,' she said evasively. 'Why aren't you married?'

He smiled. 'It's complicated.'

'I'd like to know,' she persisted.

'But I wouldn't like to talk about it.' He was still smiling, but she could sense his determination and it nettled her.

'After I parted with all that revealing information?'

'That wasn't revealing,' said Matt. 'You told me what happened. You didn't tell me *why* any of it happened. *Why* things happen — as in "why aren't you married?" is a whole different kettle of fish. A lot more revealing.'

'You're a coward,' she told him.

He frowned across the table at her. 'You've got a little dirt on your ear,' he said, reaching across and rubbing her ear lobe between his thumb and forefinger. His touch was gentle and his eyes smiling.

'Yeah,' he told her, 'a sheep in wolf's clothing.'

She let the subject drop, and as they rose to leave she asked him, 'Are you going to accept my father's mistress's offer of promotion?'

'No. I've just arranged to meet her for lunch to talk about it a little further.'

She shook her head. 'You really are being sucked into the Terson family whirlwind.'

'Is that a bad thing?'

'I don't know.'

'Maybe I'd like to be sucked in a little further.'

She smiled at him. 'That's what *you* think.'

With fifteen minutes to go before the ship left Gothenburg, Susan Porter hurried out of her cabin and cannoned straight into Tony Grant.

'Christ!' he yelled in alarm as a gift-wrapped box flew out of his

165

arms and bounced on the floor. 'Why don't you look where you're going?'

She regarded him with disfavour. The ship had been so pleasant without him. Why couldn't his leave have gone on longer — like forever?

'Prince Charming,' she said grimly. 'Welcome back.'

He did not answer, but seized his suitcase in one hand and his package in the other and floundered down the corridor until he reached his own cabin.

Once safely inside he locked the door behind him and flung the suitcase onto the bed. He was still clutching the package tightly as he sat down on the bed and began to undo it. After a moment he had the gaudy wrapping off, revealing what looked like a shoe-box. He took a penknife from his pocket and very carefully began to slit the masking tape that fixed the lid to the base.

When he had finished, he lifted the lid off, then removed a layer of cotton wool that covered the box's contents. Underneath lay a dozen small boxes that looked as though they had been designed to take pills. Tony lifted one out and very cautiously peered inside it. It was filled with white powder. He replaced it and took out another box. This one was filled with brightly-coloured capsules.

When he had looked at them he replaced the little box and put the lid back on. So far everything was going just as he had expected. There was really no cause to be nervous. He just wished something would happen to silence the thumping of his heart.

Tom Kelly could never remember John being so late arriving on the bridge before, and he silently cursed the Captain for playing into Charles's hands. Charles was just standing there, saying nothing, his silence eloquent.

'Where's John?' Matt appeared at the top of the stairs, looking anxious.

'I don't know,' said Tom, when Charles had made it plain he was not going to reply.

'You don't know?' said Matt, irritated. 'We sail in five minutes.'

'Yeah,' said Tom uncomfortably. 'I know we do.'

Matt vanished, swearing, and at last Charles roused himself to speak.

'You know Tom,' he said placidly, 'I'm not going to be the one who hands John in. He's going to do it himself.'

Tom said nothing, but he hoped his disgust showed in his face.

'Two minutes,' said Charles looking at his watch.

There was a foot on the stair and John was beside them, buttoning his jacket.

'Sorry to be so late,' he said. He clapped Charles on the shoulder. 'Everything all right?'

'Yes sir,' said Charles heartily. 'Everything's fine.'

Tom said nothing. He had his attention fixed on a dial, and his eyes were very cold.

Kate, leaving her cabin in a hurry later that evening, had the feeling that Sandy had been lying in wait for her. At any rate Sandy loomed up very unexpectedly, and with an air of great determination. Kate was torn. On the one hand she was extremely busy. On the other hand Sandy's face bore signs of recent grief and strain, and she looked as though she was coming to the end of her tether.

'I have to ask you something,' she said, standing in front of Kate.

'I have a passenger complaint to attend to. Can we talk later?'

'Please — it'll only take a minute.' Sandy read Kate's refusal in her face and cut in desperately, *'Please.'*

'All right.'

Sandy took a deep breath. 'Did you know that Peter's gay?'

Kate stared at the girl, taken aback. Whatever she had expected it was not that this girl would know.

'Yes,' she said at last.

'Why didn't you tell me?' The question was an anguished wail.

'I thought about it. It's hard to draw the line between being helpful and interfering. I suppose I thought Peter should tell you himself.'

'He did. But it's too late. Somebody should have told me before . . .' her voice trailed off.

'I really have to go,' said Kate feeling guilty. 'Can we talk about it some other time?'

'Yes, sure,' Sandy turned away. 'Some other time.'

'I was trying to do the right thing.' Kate looked a moment at the forlorn figure. 'Please — come and talk to me later.'

Before she turned the corner Kate looked back at Sandy. The girl was still in the same position, leaning against the wall, her face averted. Kate had an impulse to rush back and comfort her, but she had an angry passenger who must not be kept waiting. Inwardly she cursed Peter who had twisted this girl's life for his own purposes. As she walked on Kate reflected that it probably wasn't coincidence that Peter had made a public announcement of his engagement only after Gary Rae had come on board — and actually in Gary Rae's presence. Gary had known Peter in the past, in circumstances Kate had not enquired into, but which she felt could probably be only too easily imagined. Whether Gary was gay or not himself, he knew the truth about Peter, and that made him a danger. Hence Peter's anxiety to get him off the ship — hence the loudly trumpeted engagement to Sandy. Had Peter ever, at any moment, given a thought to the way he was making use of that girl, Kate wondered?

Tom Kelly, coming into the corridor that led to the officers' quarters a few moments later, found Sandy still leaning against the wall, looking as though she might never move again.

'Is something the matter?' he asked kindly.

'No,' she said weakly.

'You sure?'

'Yes.'

He gave her a hard look, but only said, 'See you later then.'

'See you later,' she said, still in the same dead voice.

She moved off, as though to avoid further questioning, and Tom, after looking after her for a moment, went in the other direction. He was troubled, but there was nothing he could do at the moment. He was due back on the bridge, and doubtless that would bring its own problems.

He was right. As he climbed the stairs to the bridge Charles came out of the door at the top and stood waiting. Tom was beginning to feel that if he saw a lot less of Charles he'd never miss him.

'I want to show you something,' said Charles.

'Show me in there,' Tom indicated the bridge.

'I don't think you'd want me to.'

'What? Too sinister for the watch to clap eyes on?' Tom had a sickening feeling that he knew what was coming.

'Yes,' said Charles. He reached inside his jacket and took out half a bottle of whiskey. 'I found this right where the other one was.'

'What makes you think it belongs to John?'

'There was a different watch on this time.'

'I don't believe it.' Tom said flatly. 'John's not stupid enough to drink on the bridge. And even if he were he'd never be dumb enough to leave a bottle behind when he went.'

'He's not himself lately. I keep telling you.'

'He may not be himself, but I'll never believe he's crazy enough to booze on the bridge. Never.'

'I don't think it's possible to predict what a man will do when his personal life's falling apart.'

No, thought Tom grimly, it certainly isn't.

It took Matt half an hour to find Kate with the message that had come for her in the Radio Room, but eventually he ran her to earth in her office. She had just finished dealing with her complaining passenger and was feeling as though she'd been through the mill. But she smiled tiredly when she saw Matt.

'A telex for you,' he said. 'Your father's been moved to Intensive Care.'

A frown was her only reaction, but by now he knew her well enough to know that any deeper feeling about her father would be masked from him. She took the telex from him and studied it before saying, 'I'd like to make a call ashore.'

'Of course. Come along now and I'll have you put through.'

He sat by her in the Radio Room while she talked to Marion Carter. There was no tearfulness on Kate's side, but Matt gathered that there was a good deal on Marion's.

'Don't be hysterical,' Kate told her once. 'Listen — I'm going to get on a plane as soon as we dock. I'll be there tomorrow afternoon.' There was a pause during which Kate's brow contracted with anger. 'What do you mean his doctor doesn't want me there? What's the doctor's name?' She snatched at a piece of paper that Matt thrust towards her and began to write. There was another pause, then she said tightly, 'I think whether I see my father in hospital or not is my business, not yours.' Another pause. 'Fine. We don't agree. Goodbye Marion.' She slammed down the phone.

'Thought you didn't care about what happened to him,' said Matt curiously.

'We don't get on.' Kate snapped. 'That doesn't mean I want him to be seriously ill.'

'His doctor doesn't want you there?'

'His mistress doesn't more likely.'

'What are you going to do?'

'I'm going to call the doctor and see what's really going on.'

Matt shook his head, baffled. 'You and your old man certainly have a strange relationship.'

'Yes,' said Kate tensely. 'We do.'

Chapter 13

'You look a bit peaked dear.' Jo Bailey had just finished her morning's rehearsal, and she broke off, collecting up her music when she saw Kate approaching her.

'Mm,' said Kate. 'My father's ill. I was up till the wee hours talking to his doctors.'

'Oh luv — is it serious?'

Kate nodded. 'But not as serious as they thought at first.'

'I'm so sorry.' Jo's sympathy was genuine. She liked Kate a lot.

Kate sighed wearily. 'He'll be all right. He's a tough old bird.' She rubbed her eyes. 'And then I got hauled into the Captain's quarters to help him explain to a young couple why he couldn't marry them. It's a myth that a ship's Captain can marry people, but they wouldn't believe it.'

'What sort of man is our Captain?' said Jo curiously.

'You don't know him?' said Kate surprised.

'Never exchanged more than half a dozen words.'

Kate gave it a moment's thought. 'A very nice man really,' she said at last. 'Intelligent — attractive.'

Jo smiled. 'I can see that. Married?'

'His wife just left him.'

'Why?'

'I don't know really.' Kate hedged. She didn't feel she had the right to discuss John's private life, much as she liked Jo personally.

'The sailor's life?' Jo probed.

'Don't know.'

'Are there any children?'

'Two.'

'That's rough.' Jo shook her head.

'You fancy him?' Kate smiled.

'Darling, like I said, I don't even know the man,' Jo said hastily.

Kate left it at that. She had the feeling that Jo had reacted a little too fast, and there might be hidden emotions churning away there that no-one suspected. But she dismissed the thought. John's life was complicated enough already, and she, Kate Laker, wasn't setting up as a matchmaker.

John's mood that morning could best be described as morose. The previous day's events had upset him badly. First there had been his trip ashore at Gothenburg, his phone-call to the home of his Swedish mother-in-law where Maya was now living with the children, and his brief painful talk to Emily.

He still had a clear memory of himself, standing in the phone-box, clutching the toy horse that he had bought for Emily. He had promised her that he was coming round to give it to her right away. But then Emily had vanished from the phone and in her place there had been Maya — a furious tight-lipped Maya, who warned him that if he came anywhere near the house she would send for the police.

The shock had been appalling. He had known in theory that Maya wanted to take the children right away from him, because she had made no bones about telling him so. But this was the first time he had encountered the brute fact in practice, and the pain was like a blow in the stomach. He had spent the rest of the afternoon in a Gothenburg bar, drinking whiskey and staring at the toy horse. He knew that he had only just made it back to the ship in time to sober up under a freezing cold shower and get up onto the bridge.

If the afternoon had been bad the evening had been even worse. That fresh-faced young couple, determined to make him marry them, seizing the moment's impulse as the starting point for a life together. He had wanted to yell at them — 'I got married sixteen years ago to a woman I thought loved me — and this afternoon she threatened to call the police if I tried to see my children.'

But he hadn't of course. He had got rid of them with Kate's help and afterwards he had had another drink.

Now it was the following morning. Luckily he didn't have a hangover, because his head was strong. But he still felt thoroughly miserable, and in no mood to see Matt who was intent on bearding him in his lair.

Matt was not to be put off, and John forced himself to listen to his account of Charles's suspicious behaviour, culminating in the second whiskey bottle the previous day, which Matt had heard about from a worried Tom Kelly.

Within minutes their discussion had degenerated into a tense argument, because John, instead of being what Matt would have regarded as suitably shocked, seemed anxious to deflect his comments into more harmless channels.

'I said I'd talk to you,' Matt concluded in a slightly irritable voice, 'because drinking on the bridge is . . .'

'Well if I'd been doing it, it would have been an extreme case of driving under the influence, wouldn't it?' John interrupted.

'Well since you *weren't*, why the hell aren't you going to put the rein on Charles?'

'I think you should be more concerned about your own working relationship with him and let me tend to my own.'

'I'm concerned about the whole bloody thing,' said Matt, totally exasperated. 'I don't think you can afford to pretend Charles isn't a threat.'

John continued to straighten his tie in the mirror, pointedly ignoring Matt. Matt decided to plough on.

'I'm aware that this situation with Maya is getting the greater part of your attention. It's not as if I don't know what's bothering you.'

'You want to know what's bothering me right now?' said John coldly.

'Me?'

'Right.' John began to button his jacket.

'You're lucky anybody cares enough about you to watch out for you.' Matt snapped.

'I hardly think I need watching out for.'

'You might be surprised.'

John went over to his out door and opened it. 'No, I don't think anything would surprise me any more. If you want to talk to me you're going to have to do it *en route* to the bridge. I have work to do.'

Undaunted, Matt followed John out into the corridor keeping up the argument as they went. Their route lay through the staff quarters where, Matt was annoyed to notice, they encountered several members of the crew engaged in cleaning operations. He would have preferred not to be witnessed by the crew in the undignified chase.

Nevertheless he greeted them all politely, although it took a certain amount of effort to be polite to Sandy. He could not forget the damage she had nearly done to Joe. Still, she looked as though she were suffering for it now, poor little kid. She and Peter appeared to be having some kind of argument which made them blind to all approaching traffic, and both John and Matt had to step round them.

At the stairs leading up to the bridge John turned and faced Matt.

'I've heard you out. Now you hear me out. Your assumption that

I didn't know Charles was trying to do me in with a charge of drunkenness represents a kind of arrogance I don't care for. I've known about it for weeks.

'And I also know, better than you, that the loss of a wife can, in the short run, cause behaviour that's rather bizarre. If I choose to be compassionate that's my business. And if my experience and my instincts and my training all suggest to me that Charles isn't really going to do any real damage, *that's* my business. In other words, if I choose not to worry about what Charles is doing, *that's my business*. So why don't you just devote your energy to solving your own problems, and bloody well let me solve my own?'

Sandy waited till both John and Matt were out of hearing before turning on Peter again, speaking in a low voice, but with passionate intensity.

'But you *could* change if you wanted to. I read a big article about it in one of the magazines.'

'Which one?' he hissed. '*Science Fiction Digest?*'

'No. I don't remember. But there's a psychiatrist in London . . .'

'I've already been that route Sandy,' he interrupted her. 'I am what I am.'

'*What* are you?' She groped frantically for a comforting formula. 'You're just confused, that's all.'

Peter shook his head. His face was sad, although whether it was for himself or her it was impossible to tell.

'Iron hoof,' he said, very quietly. Then as she looked puzzled, he explained, 'Poof.'

'You don't have to be,' she said obstinately. Oblivious of the armful of towels in her hands she reached out trying to hug him. But he caught her arm and stopped her.

'Yes I do,' he said seriously.

They jumped apart violently as a door behind them opened and Tony Grant came out of his cabin. An unpleasant sneer took over his face as he saw them and thought he understood.

'Don't stop on account of me,' he begged.

'I was just going,' Peter snapped.

He looked briefly at Sandy, then turned and hurried off down the corridor.

'I'll do your room,' Sandy muttered.

'Thanks doll,' Tony stood back to let her enter. 'Would you change all the towels?' The door slammed shut with a loud bang. 'Please,' he said ironically.

Sandy felt she had just shut the door in time. She was almost in a state of collapse and would have started screaming if she'd had to go on talking to anyone. She leaned against the door with her eyes closed, fighting back the tears. She had cried so much already. She didn't want to cry any more. Crying was exhausting and she'd only just started her day's work. Somehow she had to keep going normally.

She plugged in the Hoover which she'd dragged in after her, and began to drag it across the floor in a listless manner. She performed all her movements mechanically, flinging up the bedspread so that she could vacuum underneath, and sighing with faint exasperation when the machine hit something.

She switched the Hoover off and got down on her hands and knees to reach under the bed and remove the obstacle. It seemed to be a shoe-box. When she had dumped it on the bed it was easy to get the machine under. She got up tiredly and went on with her work, hardly looking what she was doing. She knew she wasn't showing her usual care, but what did it matter? When she'd finished she pulled the plug impatiently out of the socket, yanking it with such force that she lost her balance and sat down hard on the bed. The impact dislodged the box that she had left perched precariously on the edge, and it fell to the floor, spilling its contents out.

With a deep angry sigh she got back down on her knees and began to clear the little boxes up and jam them back into the shoe-box. She barely looked at them as she did so, but the last box of all rattled in her hand and she stared at it suddenly. It took only a moment to rip off the lid, and reveal the brightly coloured shiny capsules that gleamed and winked in the light.

She stared at them, fascinated. Then she sat down on the bed and took out one capsule. It was a deep glowing red. She held it up between her thumb and forefinger and looked at it closely for a moment. Then she put it back in the box and replaced the lid. She continued to sit on the bed, turning the little box over and over between her nervous fingers.

It had been Charles's idea that Susan Porter join him for a drink at his table when he had finished his lunch. He did not miss the way something leapt in her eyes at his suggestion. He knew she was still interested in him. She had contrived to make that very plain since his return to the ship. But he observed this without feeling. His concern now was to ascertain to what extent Susan might be a useful ally.

174

He explained his 'worries' about the Captain in detail, and finished up, 'It's extremely difficult to make a charge of drunkenness stick.'

'I'd just feel so much more secure if you were the Captain of this ship, Charles,' she said wistfully.

'Thanks.' He spoke with no particular warmth. He was not even looking at her. But he calculated, correctly, that she would fill in any gaps in his manner to her. There was no estimating the extent to which a woman would be prepared to deceive herself, said the chilly little devil that seemed to be constantly whispering in his ears these days.

'I'll do whatever I can to help you,' she persisted.

'Thanks,' he said again. This time he turned to look at her, although there was no more warmth in his manner.

Each preoccupied with their own thoughts, neither of them noticed Tom Kelly who had opened a door a few feet behind them some five minutes earlier. He had remained where he was, rooted to the floor by what he was hearing. Now he slipped away, without either of them having realised he was ever there.

Tom had no doubts about his next move. He made his way straight to Matt, told his unwelcome news, and received some equally unwelcome news in return as Matt relayed his own conversation with John.

'I suppose if he already knew about Charles and he's decided not to worry it really isn't any of our business,' he said doubtfully. 'He didn't get to be Captain of this ship be being stupid, did he?'

'No.' Matt conceded. 'But what John figures to be Charles's potential to cause trouble, and what *I* figure are two different things.'

There was an awkward silence between them.

'You don't suppose,' said Tom at last, 'that there's the remotest possibility that the bottle really was John's.' Matt shook his head and Tom sighed, exasperated. 'God, what an ass Charles has turned out to be.'

'Hasn't he?' Matt agreed grimly.

'You think John should know what I just overheard between Charles and Susan?'

'No,' said Matt decisively. 'He doesn't want to hear it.' His eyes gleamed suddenly. 'But I've got an idea.'

'May I come in?' said Peter awkwardly when Sandy opened the door to him. He was already regretting having called at her cabin. He didn't know what he had hoped to achieve by it. Nothing would change the truth about himself, or her miserable incomprehension. But he felt a sense of responsibility for her that could only find ease in going back to see how she was.

Now he was here everything seemed to irritate him, from the rumpled patch on her bed which told him she had been lying there staring blankly at the ceiling, to the fact that her cassette recorder was playing the love duet from *Madame Butterfly* much too loudly.

'Would you take that off please?' he asked.

She switched it off at once. 'Certainly,' she said, surprised. 'You gave it to me. I thought you liked it.' She wasn't looking at him. 'I'd never even heard an opera till I met you.'

'Don't try to make me feel guilty, Sandy,' he snapped.

'I wasn't,' she said, taken aback. She had been speaking the simple truth without thought of its effects.

'Oh yes you were . . .' he persisted. Somehow his own guilt felt easier if he could blame her for making him feel it.

'No . . .' she tried to protest.

'Yes you were. But I'll tell you something —' they stared at each other. There was a scared look in her eyes as she tried to guess what might be coming next. 'I feel good about myself,' he insisted. 'It wasn't easy to tell you, but it was the right thing to do and I'm glad I did it.' He had begun to emphasise each word. 'I do feel good about myself. And I'm not going to let you take that away from me.'

'I never meant to make you feel guilty,' she said at last, when she could manage to get the words out.

He looked at her silently. In his heart he knew she was speaking the truth. More than ever he regretted having come here. The injury he had done her only made him feel angry, and then he injured her more.

'I've been thinking a lot Peter,' she went on. 'I love you very much . . . and I only want you to be happy . . .'

'Please . . .'

'I think you're right.' She took a deep breath, 'If this is what you are, then you should go ahead and just be it.' Suddenly she took a step towards him and put her arms round him, patting him gently on the back. She might have been a mother comforting a child. 'I'll do everything I can to make it easy for you.'

'You can't make it easy,' he said, knowing he was being ungracious but not knowing what else to say, confronted by her sudden generosity, so far beyond anything he could match. 'For either of us.'

'Just easier then,' she whispered sadly.

'What's the point? Why don't you just worry about yourself and let me worry about me?'

She stood back a little and looked at him. 'Because I can't be happy if you're unhappy. I can't just stop caring about you. I want to do whatever I can to make you happy. Then I'll be happy.'

'Then let's just drop this subject, all right? That will make me happy,' he said sullenly.

She smiled. 'Fine.'

At first Jo couldn't quite see who it was in the empty night-club, standing behind the bar, pouring himself a drink. Closer inspection revealed it to be the Captain.

'Care for some company?' she asked him cheerily.

John whipped round and tried to cover his start of surprise with a little laugh.

'This is rather embarrassing,' he admitted.

'Don't be silly,' she nodded towards the glass. 'I'm no stranger to that myself.'

'It's only mineral water,' he assured her, showing her the bottle he had just poured from.

'Then why embarrassing?'

'I'm the Captain, not the bar tender.'

'I'd favour a whiskey and water, myself,' she confessed. 'But I don't suppose either of us ought to drink in a public area.'

'You can. I can't.'

She perched herself on a stool and faced him. 'Whiskey's really not much good for singers.'

'I'm sure you don't overdo it,' he said politely.

'Not any more.'

'Used to.'

'Oh my dear, when my husband left me I jumped into the bottle and didn't come out again for nearly three years,' she said frankly.

'I'm sorry.' John kept his words cautious, although he felt a flicker of interest.

'Why do you think I'm working on this ship?' In answer to a shake of his head she went on, 'I drank to kill the pain, which I did, but I also killed my career in the process.' She gave a sudden sharp sigh as though blowing away her memories. 'Boring. It's all in the past.'

John felt his interest growing. How well he knew what she was talking about.

'Would you like to sit down?' he said, indicating a table.

'I'd love to.'

They fixed themselves drinks and sat down together. She talked to him, not about her sad past, but entertaining him with some of the funnier stories she could think of. There had been amusing incidents along the way, and with a little effort she managed to dredge them up, and had the reward of seeing him laugh. She could have killed Tony Grant when he came and interrupted.

'I want to talk to you,' he said to Jo. 'Privately please.' His tone was not pleasant.

She excused herself to John, promising to be right back, and followed Tony into a corner, out of earshot.

'Come on, where is it?' said Tony at once.

'Where's what?' she demanded.

'Don't play games with me. I want what you took out of my cabin. Did you think I wouldn't notice? Where is it?'

'Look Tony, I didn't take anything out of your room.'

He squeezed her arm tightly. 'Don't lie to me.'

'Take your hand off me,' she said, very deliberately, 'or I'll scream.'

With an uneasy look to where John sat, his eyes on them, Tony dropped his hand.

'I no longer have the key to your cabin,' Jo went on, 'and I don't know what's missing. It probably wasn't yours anyway,' she took a step away from him. 'Now just get out of my life. And stay out.'

She turned her back on him and walked back to the table, leaving Tony no option but to storm out in silent fury.

'Sorry,' she said when she got back to the table.

'What's going on with him?' John jerked his head towards the doors at the far end that Tony had left swinging violently behind him.

'You wouldn't want to know.'

'I would, actually.'

She gave him a wary look. 'It's not worth talking about.'

'Are you sure? Is he giving you trouble?'

'Tony's just trouble for whoever happens to be handy. It's nothing personal.'

'Would you tell me if it were trouble?' said John, thinking of Wally James, and also of Maya, who had concealed her feelings from him for a long time.

She threw him a saucy look. 'I'd much rather tell you about the time I played to a Shriners' convention.'

'What are Shriners?' he said, fascinated.

'It's an enormous club with members all over Australia. And all the men wear funny red hats about this high,' she indicated with her hands. 'With tassles on them.'

'Really?' he was eyeing her, grinning.

'Do you want to hear about it?'

'By all means.'

When Matt's plan had been explained to him Tom Kelly decided he approved of it. He was even able to offer a refinement of his own. When the details had been agreed he and Matt went their separate ways to put the thing into operation.

Matt ran Susan to ground in the sauna, where she was sitting in the bar, reading a magazine. The brief towel she was wearing allowed him an uninterrupted view of her long legs, which he enjoyed for a moment before saying warmly, 'Hello.'

'Hello,' she said politely.

He sat down and cleared his throat. 'Susan, do you mind if I ask you something ever so slightly personal?'

She shrugged. 'I don't suppose so.'

'Why are you letting yourself be drawn into Charles's sleazy scheme?'

His tone was so casual that at first she did not take in what he had said, and was caught completely off guard.

'I don't believe you just said that,' she managed at last.

'Why?'

'Because it's so —' she floundered.

'Direct,' he supplied kindly.

'Well . . .'

'I believe in that.'

'What?'

'Being direct.' He realised she was staring at him in stunned silence, and took advantage of it to go on, 'I mean, is it for professional reasons like he'll give you a promotion if he gets to be captain? Or is it more personal — like you want to be the next Mrs Charles Woodhouse?'

'You —' she struggled for words. 'What do you mean talking to me like this?'

He remained calm. 'I'm trying to give you the idea that very little goes on around this ship that somebody doesn't know about.'

'You rotten, interfering . . .'

'Just a minute, just a minute,' he soothed her. 'The significance of this will probably be lost on you, but I'm really a lover . . . not a fighter. This line of conversation doesn't actually interest me all that much.' He rose and headed for the door. 'Ta ta.'

He got out quickly, before she could recover herself sufficiently to retaliate. He wondered if he'd managed to do any good.

While Tom was putting Phase One of the plan into operation, Matt was occupying himself with the far more difficult Phase Two. It involved confronting Charles on the bridge.

'You're looking mighty like a captain these days,' Matt assured him, coming directly to the point.

'What do you mean?' said Charles in a hard, suspicious voice.

'I think you know what I mean,' and Matt proceeded to recount his morning's conversation with Tom Kelly.

'I didn't plant any bottles up here,' said Charles disdainfully.

'Kelly says you did.'

'He's lying. If that bottle belonged to anyone it belonged to John, and if John drinks too much that's John's problem.'

'Oh come off it, Charles. This is schoolboy stuff,' said Matt in disgust. 'What's happening to you?'

'I think a more apt question would be what's happening to John.'

'You know damned well what's happening to him. He's having a tough time. His wife's left him, he's a little distracted. He's hanging onto the gunwale in a storm, and you're trying to push him overboard.'

'It's a plea for compassion you're making then?' said Charles in the voice of a man who just wants to be sure he's got everything straight.

'Yeah, it is.'

'I have two reactions to that. First, I don't feel sorry for John because Maya left him. He created that situation himself.'

'Give me a break,' muttered Matt.

'You give me a break. Do you see *me* boozing morning, noon and night?'

'*What?*'

'Keeping bottles hidden in places I might need to take the odd nip?'

'Charles . . .'

'You know what happened to me?' said Charles quietly.

'Please, I don't want to . . .'

'You don't want to hear it. I know. But I'm going to tell you. My wife didn't leave me because I screwed up — *like John did*. My wife got in her car to drive to her mother's house. The brakes failed at some crossroads and she was hit broadside on by a lorry doing seventy. When they finally cut her out of the wreck Jenny was in so many pieces they couldn't even put her back together again.'

He regarded Matt's white face with some satisfaction. It was plain that Matt had got more than he bargained for.

'Just like Humpty Dumpty,' he continued remorselessly. 'You didn't know the details.'

'No,' said Matt quietly.

'Well, that's how it was. So I don't feel sorry for John. And second, on a less personal note, it's not just disgraceful, it's bloody dangerous to have a drunk commanding this ship.'

'You just won't quit will you?' said Matt wearily. He faced Charles. It was time to lay cards on the table. 'If it ever does become necessary for this ship to have a new Captain — I'll do everything I can to stop that appointment going to you.'

'And why's that?'

'Because you're one of the most devious people I've ever met. And you're not as competent as you think you are. And you don't give a damn about people — which I think is a big flaw for the Captain of a passenger liner.'

'Well — I know where not to go for a recommendation, don't I?'

'Right. I'd support your competition.'

Charles looked as though he could not believe what he was hearing. 'What do you mean?' he said with a puzzled frown.

'If it comes to that point, my friend, you'd better remember you don't hold the only Master's Ticket on this ship. Tom Kelly has one, and he'd make a terrific Captain.' Matt smiled a cold smile directly into Charles's face. 'And he's got as much experience — and more integrity — than you.' He chucked Charles on the arm. 'See ya,' he finished lightly.

And he departed, leaving Charles to his reflections.

It took all the courage he possessed for Joe Francis to knock at Sandy's door, and when she opened to him in evident surprise he nearly ran away.

'Hello,' he said, unable to look at her.

'What —?' her voice trailed away.

When the silence between them had become uncomfortable Joe managed to make a start.

'I want to apologise to you for what I did,' he stumbled. 'I don't know what was the matter with me. Sometimes I drink too much.'

'Oh Joe . . .' Sandy sighed. She was sad rather than angry. Joe would never know what, indirectly, he had done to her. For Sandy had understood by now that it was the sight of Joe and her together that had disgusted Peter into his confession.

'I'm really sorry Sandy. I'm so sorry. I wouldn't ever want to do anything to hurt you . . .'

'It's all right,' she said indifferently.

'I must have been crazy,' he persisted, desperate to get some kind of a response out of her.

'It's all right Joe. Really. I'm sorry I led you on.'

'That's no excuse. Well — an excuse for a kid.'

'We all act like kids sometimes.'

'It'll never happen again, I swear.'

'I'm glad. Look, I'm sort of busy right now.'

'Can we talk some other time?' he begged.

'Of course we can,' her voice was dead.

'All right then,' he said miserably. 'I'll see you later.'

She nodded, ''Bye.'

''Bye.'

She had shut the door before he finished speaking. Head down he trailed off along the corridor and bumped into Jo Bailey.

'Is something wrong?' she said, regarding him with a frown.

'No.'

'Come on, what is it then?'

He shrugged miserably, 'I just apologised to Sandy . . .'

'You did? That's wonderful.' He shrugged. 'What's the matter luv? You should be proud of yourself. And happy.'

'It didn't change anything.'

She maintained her cheerfulness resolutely. 'You never know. You've taken the first step.'

'I've got to get to work,' he said not convinced.

'Well I'm proud of you.'

'Thanks,' he moved past her, still with his head down.

'Keep up the good work,' she persisted.

He gave her a rueful smile before disappearing round the corner Jo sighed to herself.

A moment later Joe and his troubles were wiped from her mind as a cabin door opened and Tony Grant stepped out in front of her.

'Hey, wait a minute . . .' he said.

But she slipped past him and went on walking. He hurried after her, seizing her arm and spinning her round.

'I said *wait* a minute,' he snapped.

Without pausing Jo drew back her hand and slapped him across the face with all her strength. He fell back, stunned, less by the force of the blow than by the unexpectedness of it.

'Don't you ever touch me again,' she said in a low voice.

He rubbed his cheek. 'That took a lot of courage,' he said quietly.

'Not really.'

'You get that courage from being cosy with the Captain, I suppose.'

'Hardly.'

His voice became threatening. 'What were you talking to him about Jo? Me?'

She gave a short mirthless laugh.

'I don't think it's very funny,' he yelled.

'Why in God's name would we be talking about you?'

He stared at her blankly. 'Well,' he said lamely after a minute, 'just don't ever discuss me with him. Unless you want me to do some talking about you.'

'Do your worst darling. I can't go through life worrying about what you're going to say.'

'You'd better worry,' was all he could think of to say.

She began to walk away. 'Sorry Tony. Life's too short. I hope you find whatever it is you've lost.'

As she took a last glance back at his livid face she realised that she was really over him at last. It was a nice feeling.

Matt was with Kate in her office when the telex arrived.

'It's from Marion,' she said, baffled. 'Asking me to call someone named Alan Lansing in London.'

'Who's he?'

'No idea.'

Kate paled a little. 'Maybe my father's died. That's the only thing I can think of. And Marion doesn't want to tell me herself.'

'But who's Lansing?'

'I'm going to find out.'

He went with her to the Radio Office, and sat watching as she waited for the call to come through. She seemed calm but he noticed she couldn't help biting her lip. Suddenly she became alert.

'Yes — Mr Lansing. This is Kate Laker. I've received an urgent message from Marion Carter to telephone you . . . Mr Lansing, who *are* you?' As she listened to the answer something that might have been a cynical sneer crossed Kate's face. Matt kept his eyes on her.

'I see,' she said at last. 'Yes, of course I understand. We all need a friend at court,' she gave a sudden smile. 'I'm not without a sense of humour Mr Lansing. Yes — I'll meet you when we dock in Amsterdam. How about my office? You'll want to see where I work, won't you? . . . I look forward to it. Goodbye.'

'Who *is* he?' said Matt, whose curiosity was becoming more than he could stand.

'Come to my quarters.'

Once they were inside her cabin, he said, 'Your father hasn't died, obviously.'

'No.'

'What then?'

Kate put her hand to her head. 'Things are happening so fast. That man — Alan Lansing — no — you know my father has given power of attorney to Marion.'

'Yes.'

'Well Marion apparently doesn't feel entirely competent to run the whole show . . .'

'It is a big show . . .'

'Most of the company's legal matters are handled by a large international law firm. Marion has decided to turn her decision-making power — or a large part of it — over to one of that concern's lawyers.'

'Alan Lansing?'

'Right.'

'So your father gives Marion the rudder, and Marion passes it right on to . . .'

'Alan Lansing.'

'So until a few days ago your father ran this company, then for a minute or two Marion ran it, and now some lawyer you've never heard of is running it.'

'Right,' said Kate. 'Until my father gets out of hospital.'

He grinned. 'You do have to be fast to keep up with all the changes around here.'

'Indeed. Lansing's meeting me in the morning. He also wants to see you at lunchtime — instead of your seeing Marion — about her offer of promotion.'

'Whew. He's coming on like gangbusters, isn't he?' said Matt tersely.

'Feels that way to me.'

'So what else could you tell about him?'

Kate shrugged. 'He's intelligent. Somewhat witty. American. And he's running the whole company. At least for a while.'

'How do you feel about that?'

She paused a moment. 'Well I don't get on with my father. And I don't get on with Marion . . .'

'So you may as well not get on with Alan Lansing,' he supplied for her.

'Precisely.'

'Ah yes. The power of negative thinking.'

She refused to laugh at his little joke. 'I'm sorry. It's just a bit difficult to absorb. From Father to Marion to — Alan Lansing?'

'The only problem with strangers,' said Matt, 'is it's always so hard to predict what they're going to do.'

'It's hard to predict what anyone is going to do,' said Kate.

Matt reached over and caressed her knee. When she remained oblivious he snatched his hand away.

'It is, isn't it?' he said feelingly.

Chapter 14

'Miss Laker?'

Kate looked up at the man who had appeared in the doorway of her office, and repressed a slight start of surprise. Alan Lansing — if this were he — was almost exactly as she had pictured him on the telephone; somewhere in his late thirties and wearing clothes that were conservative, but well-cut and obviously expensive, and carrying a briefcase. What the telephone had not told her was that he was black.

'Mr Lansing —' she said in an even voice.

'Yes. Hello,' he stepped into her office and held out his hand as she came round the desk to greet him.

'It's good to meet you,' she said.

Somewhere deep in his eyes there was a faint gleam of appreciation for the way she had recovered herself. But all he said was, 'Are you sure?' When she raised an eyebrow he went on, 'I do represent Marion Carter who represents your father's interests, and I'm aware of the tone of your relationship with both of them.'

'You don't believe in wasting any time, do you?' she said.

'Do you?' he answered pleasantly. He had put his case down and begun to unbutton his coat.

'No, actually.' Kate took the coat and waved him to a seat.

'Good. Then we'll get along well. I don't mean to be rude.' While she was hanging the coat he said, 'You look quite comfortable in your uniform.'

'Thank you. I am.'

'Do you intend to keep wearing it?'

'Mr Lansing, may I sit down before we begin to talk about business?'

'Miss Laker,' he said with a smile. 'I was talking fashion. Please sit down.'

She did so, feeling crossly that he had managed to put her at a disadvantage.

'You're very young to be in a position of such authority,' she said, trying to recover some lost ground.

'I don't believe in wasting time.'

'You've said that twice. Now you're wasting *my* time.'

'That's not possible,' he said gently.

'Oh?'

'You're a Triangle employee. In effect you work for me. So any time that's wasted is mine, isn't it? Shall we get on with it?'

'Let's,' she said, tight-lipped.

'Marion and George — your father — have identical concerns. That means that while Marion has employed me, I effectively represent you father's interests.'

She gave a grim smile. 'I felt it the minute you walked through the door.'

'What's that?'

'My father's presence.'

Lansing paused to look at her steadily. 'Miss Laker, I don't have any personal quarrel with you.'

'Of course. Since you call George George, and Marion Marion — please call me Kate.'

'If you'll call me Alan,' he said charmingly.

'Certainly — Alan.'

'Thank you,' he opened his briefcase and took out some papers, but did not look at them. 'Kate, your father has two major concerns relating to you.'

'Only two?' she said satirically.

'First, he doesn't want you in this position. As Purser on this ship. Are you prepared to resign?'

'No.'

'All right,' he said calmly. 'Second, in the event that the issue of making Triangle Line a freight rather than passenger carrier comes before the stock-holders, your father is anxious to know how you'd vote.'

'My father's too ill to be anxious. You're anxious. Marion's anxious.'

'Can you tell me which way you'd vote?' he persisted.

'I'm afraid not.'

'Fine,' he smiled. 'That's essentially what I came to find out.'

'But surely you already knew my position on both counts.'

'I'd been told,' he said, still pleasant. 'But I tend to think of situations like this the same way I think about — oh — camping in the Rocky Mountains.'

Despite herself she was amused. He was likeable. There was no getting away from that.

'How's that?' she said.

'I'll read all the charts and maps available, but until I've actually hiked the trails myself I don't really feel I know the territory. I like to be sure the maps are right.'

'Are they?' she said quizzically.

'I'm afraid they are.' He rose to go. 'I'm glad we met.'

'I'm sorry we can't be friends,' she told him, adding rather sarcastically, 'I don't know many people who go hiking in the wilderness.'

'Friendship or lack of it doesn't come into the picture,' he told her seriously.

'Allies then,' she said, taking down his coat.

'I'm employed by Marion Carter. If that doesn't exactly put us on opposite sides of the fence it does suggest we're not likely to be allies. It's just business Kate. Nothing personal. Maybe it'll help you see things more clearly.'

'By that you mean what?' she said coldly.

'I mean that eliminating the personal element may improve your focus,' he had begun to move towards the door. 'It may help you see where you are.'

'At the moment I'm in my office. Seems perfectly clear.'

He gave a small shake of the head. 'No. Do you know the phrase "between a rock and a hard place"?'

'Haven't heard it.'

'Think about it. Because that's where you are. Goodbye.'

'And then,' said Kate, telling Jeremy Gates all about it over lunch in Amsterdam two hours later, 'he asked me if I knew the phrase "between a rock and a hard place" which I didn't. Then he said that was where I was.'

'Ominous, isn't it?' Jeremy frowned. 'I've only met him over cocktails myself. He was quite pleasant.'

'I don't want to think about him,' said Kate shortly. 'Tell me about this,' she tapped a long piece of folded paper beside her plate.

'Tony Grant's contract.' Jeremy confirmed. 'Don't strain your eyes. It doesn't require him to do anything of substance beyond running the roulette wheel.'

'What about booking entertainment?'

'He apparently made that arrangement informally with the last Purser.'

'To be perfectly honest,' said Kate, tackling her food with renewed enjoyment, 'I haven't been paying much attention to Tony lately.'

'You think he's stopped fiddling the table?'

'I really don't know what he's up to.'

She might have been more interested if she could have seen Tony at that moment, and overheard the conversation he was having in an Amsterdam phone-box.

'Yes Mr Collier-Brown,' he said when he got through after a nerve-racking wait, 'the reason I'm calling is to say there's been a little problem with the parcel. Yes — a problem — part of the parcel is missing. Not the whole thing — just two bottles . . . I don't know that Mr Collier-Brown. If I knew who had them I'd get them back, wouldn't I?'

He mopped his brow.

'Look Mr Collier-Brown, I don't think it's a very good idea for me to take that parcel all the way to England since somebody on the ship obviously knows I have it. I know what I said — but I know what *you* said but — well, I'm not convinced it's safe.'

As he listened to the angry voice on the other end Tony slumped slightly.

'Yes Mr Collier-Brown, I remember my gambling debts. It's not that I don't appreciate . . . I said it's not that I don't appreciate . . . yes, I understand. I'll deliver the parcel. Thank you Mr Collier-Brown. Goodbye.'

He rammed the receiver down onto its rest and leaned wearily against the side of the box.

Over the main course Kate and Jeremy got off the subject of the ship. He entertained her with the latest exploit of his secretary, a warm-hearted girl whose affectionate nature was always causing her trouble.

'The things some people will do for love,' said Kate when he had finished. 'Amazing isn't it?' She was laughing in genuine amusement.

'I really couldn't say,' Jeremy confessed. 'I never seem to be afflicted with the emotion.'

'Then why did you send me that car?' she said, seriously.

He paused between bites and stared at her. 'Car?'

'The one that matches my eyes.'

He put down his fork. 'Kate,' he said gravely, 'if I were going to send you something to match your eyes, it wouldn't be a car. It would be something uncompromising and very sharp. Like a dagger.'

'Thank you. You didn't send me a car?'

He shook his head. 'You must have a suitor you don't know about.' He studied her frowning face. 'That shouldn't surprise you.'

She shrugged and went on eating, and he let the matter drop. He felt the time had come for some serious business. Kate knew, none better, that his aim was to turn the ship over to freight, yet every time he looked at the figures she submitted it seemed to him that she was sabotaging his aims.

'It's management by objective Kate,' he said. 'You set a goal and then . . .'

'Jeremy, I know what management by objective is,' she broke in.

'Then why is profit increasing on the passenger side?' he said irritably. 'That's not the goal, is it?'

She shrugged. 'Maybe I'm the victim of my own efficiency.'

'Management by objective,' he repeated, angry but still in command of himself. 'The objective is to get rid of the passengers and turn this line over to freight.'

He stopped abruptly. Kate had sat up in her seat and was staring at something by the far wall.

'I wouldn't discuss your objectives too freely right now if I were you,' she said softly. She nodded across the room, 'Over there.'

Jeremy turned in time to see Alan Lansing and Matt Taylor sitting down together.

'I just lost any interest in having dessert,' he said. 'How about you?'

'Not me. I'm still hungry.' Kate smiled. 'I thought you were tough.' She rose to her feet. 'I'm going to go and say hello to the new kingpin.'

Gates also rose and indicated for the waiter to bring his bill: 'I cast my vote for trying to get out of here without being noticed,' he said.

'Nope. Confrontation.' Kate stretched her arms above her head like a fighter warming up. 'I feel like a wee confrontation,' she said whimsically. 'Just a little one.'

'Would you mind terribly if I missed it?'

'You can do whatever you like,' she told him.

'I'll meet you outside then.'

'Fine.' Kate headed away from them and towards Alan Lansing's table. Once there she dropped a hand on Lansing's shoulder in familiar fashion.

'Hallo Alan — Mr Taylor.'

Alan gave her a pleasant smile. 'Well Kate, have you taken to following me?'

'On the contrary. I was here first. I'm just leaving.'

The hint of a smile had brightened Matt's face. 'What a surprise,' he said.

'It shouldn't be.' Kate assured him. 'Mr Lansing and I have similar tastes in a lot of things.' She looked Matt over pointedly. 'Including restaurants,' she added, 'and shipping lines.' She took a step away from the table. 'Just wanted to say hello . . . and goodbye.' She turned and headed for the door.

Lansing cleared his throat. 'Where were we?'

Matt forced himself to be serious. Kate's style had delighted him. 'Your offer,' he said.

'Right,' said Lansing. 'So are you interested?'

Matt hesitated a long moment, 'If it's possible I'd like to think about it a while longer. I've been at sea since I was sixteen years old and regardless of the benefit, this job would mean changing my whole life and starting again on land. Is it a slot you could hold for — say — six months?'

'Yes,' said Lansing very slowly. 'It is. I like that in a man.'

'What's that? The ability to look a gift horse in the mouth?' Matt laughed ironically.

'The ability to think a situation through to some of its less obvious conclusions.'

'Thank you.'

'Business today is just like the old cowboy movies, there are good guys and bad guys.'

Matt smiled: 'Black hats and white hats?'

'Exactly. You learn quickly.' He looked hard at Matt. 'And I think I want you on the team. So I'm prepared to wait. You take all the time you need to think about the offer.'

It was inevitable, Matt supposed, that no sooner was he back on board than he headed for Kate's office to swap notes.

'So what did you and Lansing talk about over lunch?' she said when they were seated on opposite sides of her desk.

'What did you and Jeremy Gates talk about?' he batted the question back.

'How did you know I had lunch with Jeremy?' she fielded.

'Eyes like a hawk. I saw you when we came in.'

'Did Lansing see us?'

Matt shook his head. 'No. He was too busy looking me over. It's a good thing I wore my best suit.'

'Marion picked the right man.' Kate mused. 'He thinks just like my father. What did he say?' She leaned across the desk in a theatrically conspiratorial manner. 'And what did you say?'

In a movement that exactly matched hers he too leaned forward until their noses were almost touching, and dropped his voice to a dramatic husky whisper.

'He repeated Marion's offer. He wants me to become Engineering Manager. I asked him if he could wait six months. He said he could.'

Kate's voice was equally husky. 'I'm surprised. He doesn't seem like the sort of man to wait for anything.'

'He said he wanted me on his team,' he said, directly into her eyes.

'I don't blame him,' she murmured.

With a comic abruptness Matt pulled back and restored his voice to normal.

'Now what were you and Jeremy Gates talking about?'

Kate too pulled back and became her usual brisk self. 'I'm afraid what Jeremy Gates and I talk about will have to remain between Jeremy and me.'

'Is it fair to ask if what's between you is professional or personal?'

'You've asked that before. I told you it was professional.'

'I find that so hard to believe,' he said, half to himself.

'Why?'

'Well Kate, sometimes when a man and a woman look at each other in a certain way . . .'

She interrupted him with a laugh. 'Ha! You think Jeremy Gates and I were looking at each other "in a certain way"?'

He cleared his throat awkwardly. 'Sometimes Kate, when a man and a woman look at each other in a certain way it means something very special.' His eyes met hers unwaveringly. She looked right back, but a little smile was playing round her lips. It was a smile that could have meant anything. 'Of course sometimes,' he shrugged, 'it doesn't.'

Kate, he thought, could have sat for the Mona Lisa with that smile on her lips.

It was not entirely by arrangement that John Anderson and Jo Bailey met up in Amsterdam. But neither was it entirely by accident. She had happened to mention where she planned to do her shopping, and neither of them was very surprised when they bumped into each other there. John, who had found Jo both an entertaining talker and a good listener, found himself pouring out the story of his marriage.

'I don't know how long she'd been involved with this other fellow before she told me,' he said as they wandered beside a canal. 'A long time I think.' He thought for a moment. 'I can't be a very sensitive person.'

She shook her head. 'No. That's just part of life at sea. Strange things happen.'

He hesitated a moment. 'You weren't really involved with that croupier, were you?'

She chuckled. 'You mean — speaking of strange things?' He shrugged and smiled at her. 'Yes, I was.'

'He doesn't seem like your type. Not a bit like your type.'

They walked in silence for a moment before Jo said, 'He started out as my manager. I don't really know how, but for a while it got more personal.'

'Is it over?' he said quietly.

'Oh yes. I stay as far away from Tony as I can. He's a rotten egg, that one. Really went wrong somewhere.' She glanced at her watch. 'I suppose we should be getting back to the ship,' she said reluctantly.

'So soon?' he was surprised as he looked at his own watch and saw the time. 'My goodness. What a shame.'

'Don't you like your job?'

'I love my job,'

'You sounded a little disappointed.'.

'Not because I don't like my job.' He gave her a puzzled frown, 'Because I'm enjoying myself. For the first time in — a long time.'

'Me too,' she said.

Somehow a mutually understood disinclination for ending the afternoon made it natural for him to offer to show her the ship when they returned. It took an hour, and they finished up in his quarters, where Jo dropped with relief onto the couch. Her feet were hurting.

'I must say I envy you,' she said, looking round her. 'You get to work up there —' she pointed over her head. Above them was the bridge, which was the last place they had visited, '— and run everything. And you've got a regular home away from home down here.'

'Just plain home,' said John. 'There isn't any other home, remember?'

'I'm sorry,' she said, inwardly cursing herself for her blunder. 'That was the wrong turn of phrase.'

'No, I'm sorry,' he smiled. 'Let me get you a drink.'

While he was fixing it she stood up and began to look round. He watched her out of the corner of his eye.

'Do you remember the first time you were in love?' he said, lightly.

'Certainly.'

He handed her the glass. 'How old were you?'

'Twelve.'

'Not the boy next door?'

'Yes, he was,' she sat down again, beside him.

'What became of him?' he asked.

'I married him.'

'But he wasn't —?'

'Yes. The only husband I've ever had.'

'That really must have been rough.'

'I told you, I drank for three years.'

He felt it safer to change the subject. 'I remember the first time I was in love. Her name was Pamela Kendall and we were five. We tied our shoelaces together and vowed never to leave each other.'

'What happened?'

'Her mother called her home for tea.'

Jo laughed. 'A short relationship.'

'A harbinger of things to come,' he said, suddenly serious.

'Don't dwell on it John. It won't make getting over it any easier.'

He looked up at her and smiled. 'You're right. I'll have to find something else to dwell on.'

That night, with the ship four hours out of Amsterdam, ploughing through the dark sea, Kate realised that she had slipped unobtrusively across another bridge in her relationship with the rest of the crew. It was not merely that Matt and Tom Kelly included her in a game of poker in the Officers' Dayroom, but they also shared their worries about Charles.

'You get bloodthirsty up-and-comers like Charles in any business though, don't you?' said Kate as Matt prepared to deal.

'Yeah,' Tom conceded. 'But it's been incredible watching him go through this transformation. Right from Charles Jekyll into Charles Hyde.'

'And that little viper Susan . . .' said Matt, spraying cards round the table.

Tom gave a slight smile. 'Well now, Susan's just a bit confused.'

Kate gave Tom a shrewd glance, then smiled at Matt. 'I believe he fancies her, Matt.'

'No —' said Matt incredulously.

'Yes, I think he does.'

Tom shrugged: 'There's no accounting for taste.'

Kate's eyes met Matt's. Both had noted that Tom hadn't denied it.

'Miss Laker —?'

Kate looked up at the hesitant voice behind her, and saw Joe Francis standing in the doorway.

'I'm sorry to bother you —' he said hesitantly, '— but I think something's happened to Sandy McCormack.'

Something rang in Kate's mind. A couple of hours ago Peter had said something about Sandy not having reported for work while the ship was in port. Kate's private opinion was that Sandy was probably having a good cry in her cabin.

'I've knocked on her door plenty of times,' Joe went on. 'And I left a cassette tape outside it hours ago. It's still there.'

'All right, I'll get my key.' Kate rose and followed him out.

On the way to Sandy's cabin she said, 'Did you check with Peter?'

'No.'

'I know it's a sensitive area for you, but that's probably where she is.'

They had arrived at Sandy's door. The tape still lay on the floor, the brightly-coloured bow that Joe had tied round it looking both incongruous and pathetic.

'It never hurts to err on the side of caution,' said Kate, and knocked. When there was no answer she knocked again, harder.

'Sandy?' she called.

Still there was silence.

'It's been like this all day,' said Joe.

Kate took out her master key to Sandy's cabin.

'Stay out here,' she commanded, and vanished inside. A moment later Joe, pacing fretfully up and down the corridor, was rooted to the spot by the sound of Kate's voice calling sharply, *'Joe, get in here! Joe.'*

Joe only got as far as the door. Then the scene that met his eyes froze his blood. Kate was half kneeling, half sitting on the bed, trying to pull Sandy into an upright position. The girl showed no signs of life, and lolled frighteningly in Kate's arms.

'Get Tom Kelly,' said Kate tersely.

'Oh Jesus.' Joe whispered. He could feel his knees buckling under him from the horror of it.

'Go on.'

'Is she alive?'

Kate gave up the struggle to lift the girl. She let her drop back on the bed and slapped her hard across the face.

'Sandy,' she called.

'Is she alive?' said Joe in anguish.

'I don't know. I don't think so. *Would you go get Tom Kelly?'*

He fled the room.

Chapter 15

'*Why* did the girl want to kill herself?' demanded John furiously.

'Apparently because Peter Nuttall broke their engagement.' Kate offered.

'And people wonder why I take a dim view of involvement between members of the crew,' John muttered.

Kate was silent. She didn't want to get drawn into this subject and she could feel herself getting pulled out onto very thin ice indeed. She'd protect Peter's secret for as long as she could, but just how long that would be now that Sandy had caused a public crisis by trying to kill herself there was no way of knowing.

So far the affair had turned out less badly than she had feared. Sandy was not dead, and Tom Kelly's prompt action in making her violently sick had finally managed to bring her round. But that only meant that the very worst had been averted. Sandy's attempted suicide had raised questions that weren't simply going to go away, and John was busily going through those questions now.

'That's all there was then?' he persisted. 'A broken engagement?'

'Essentially, yes,' said Kate uncomfortable with the lie, but unable to see what else she could do but tell it.

'Where did she get the drugs?'

'I don't know. She wouldn't tell me. Does it matter?'

He stared at her as if she was mad. 'Quite a lot. If someone on this ship gave her the pills he — or she — is guilty of aiding and abetting. If she got the drugs from a member of our crew, then a member of our crew is guilty of attempted murder.'

John left matters there for the moment. It had been a hell of a night, and now that he knew Sandy was safe he wanted a breather before he pursued things any further. Something told him Kate had been less than frank with him, but also that he'd get nothing further out of her this morning. There was always later.

There had been no way of preventing the news going round the crew, and in one way or another it was occupying most people's thoughts. Charles Woodhouse expressed himself with brutal frankness.

'I'll tell you the truth. As far as I'm concerned they should have let her kill herself if that's what she wanted.'

He addressed this to Matt, who was standing with him on the bridge, and who turned and stared at him. Matt had thought himself beyond being surprised by anything Charles now said or did, but nonetheless he was appalled.

'Does that surprise you?' said Charles, catching his look.

'Unfortunately, no,' said Matt coldly.

'You think it's cruel.'

Matt shrugged. 'I think it's you.'

'You fancy you know a lot about me, don't you?'

'Not any more.'

'You never did.' He looked out over the sea for a moment before adding, 'Why don't you go back down to the engine room, where you belong?'

'Pardon me?' said Matt in total disbelief.

'I run this ship when John's not here.'

'I've never been ordered off a bridge in my life,' said Matt slowly. He still wasn't sure he'd heard right.

'Then it's about time you had that experience, isn't it?'

'Look Charles . . .'

'If you're unhappy with my decision why don't you take it up with John? If he's not too drunk.'

'You're crazy,' said Matt in a soft voice.

'Get *off* the bridge Matt.'

Matt took a step forward and faced him so that he could lower his voice even more. What he had to say was just for the two of them.

'I've got two things to say, and if I was you I'd listen,' he said. 'First, for eight hours out of every day you are the Officer of the Watch, and indeed you do outrank me. But for the other sixteen hours you serve at the pleasure of Captain Anderson, Miss Laker and *me*.'

'You're out of line . . .'

'Keep it in mind. And if I were you I'd also keep in mind that Tom Kelly outranks you when he has his Watch. It's just informaton Charles. Just information.'

'Are you through?' said Charles coldly.

'No. The second thing I want to bring to your attention is what will happen if you try to move John out by making a report upstairs. An enquiry will be held. If you have filed the complaint you will be looked at with some suspicion. I can't speak for Miss Laker but when they query the Senior Officers you know they aren't going to get anything but bad news about you out of me.'

'Are you through?' Charles repeated.

'Yes.'

'Then get the hell off this bridge.'

Matt turned and departed. But before going through the door he looked back and said softly, 'My friend, you are overplaying your hand.'

He wished he could be quite as certain of that as he had tried to sound. There was always the outside chance that Charles's monstrous plan would succeed, despite the efforts of himself and Tom Kelly to put a spoke in it. He felt a sudden urgent need for Kate's company. Just being with her would help lift the depression that was beginning to threaten him at the mere thought of Charles.

He found her in her cabin. She looked weary and rumpled after being up all night with Sandy, and there were dark shadows under her eyes. At her request he massaged the back of her neck, reflecting wryly that they could be aptly described as two old crocks together — which was not, to put it mildly, the kind of relationship he had had in mind.

'There?' he said, experimenting with his fingers.

'Oh yes,' she rotated her shoulders blissfully. 'That's it.'

He massaged for a while, then put his hands on either side of her face and turned her head towards him.

'Keep it like that for a minute,' he said, and kissed her.

'Does it occur to you,' he said as he turned his attention back to her neck, 'that we've been carrying on a flirtation for an awfully long time? For adults, I mean.'

She wriggled her shoulders again under his hands. Her eyes were closed.

'Yes it does. I've often wondered how you got to be such a tease.'

'You're accusing me of being all talk and no action?'

'I haven't heard that since I was a teenager,' she said with a little smile.

He stepped round the chair and crouched in front of her. 'That's my point,' he said quietly.

She opened her eyes. 'What?'

'We're acting like teenagers.' He put his hands on her knees. 'Sometimes I feel like we're trying to prove something to someone.'

'Who?' she said, frowning slightly.

'I don't know. Some great judge and jury in the sky.'

'What are we trying to prove?'

He took her by the arms. 'Stand up.' He rose to his feet, almost lifting her with him. 'We seem to be trying to prove that the inevitable can be postponed forever.'

'Why would we want to do that?'

'I don't know.'

He put his finger under her chin and tilted her head back. For a moment they stood looking at each other silently. Then, as he dropped his head, she moved towards him, and their kiss was as natural as the flight of an arrow finally reaching home at the end of its arc.

When they pulled apart he could sense that she was troubled about something. He spared a moment to laugh at himself. When had he last been able to read a woman's thoughts? When had he bothered? But he wanted to know all about Kate's thoughts, so he sat on her sofa and made her lie down stretched out with her head on his lap while he stroked her hair and they talked.

'What is it then?' he asked.

'There are real issues to be considered before you and I jump into an affair.'

'Jump?' he almost squawked. 'Just thinking about how long we've been leading up to it makes me tired. Here. You sit up and let me lie down for a while.' When he was lying with his head in her lap he sighed blissfully and murmured, 'Better. Much better. Now what are these issues we have to consider?'

She looked down at him and frowned. 'You've got a bit of dirt on your ear,' she said, rubbing his earlobe between her thumb and index finger.

'Mmmm,' he purred. 'I can't think seriously when you're doing that.'

She stopped at once and folded her hands in her lap.

'That's the first issue,' she said primly.

'What?'

'You and I represent two-thirds of top management on this ship. Don't you think if we were having an affair charges might be levelled that our thinking was being clouded by our personal judgement?'

'I should hope it would cloud my thinking, at the very least.'

She ignored the look of mischief in his eyes. 'Any professional agreements we reached would be suspect.' She also forced herself to ignore the way he looked up at her and sighed — like a dog that sees a juicy bone, that he had coveted but never really believed he'd have, moved just out of reach. 'Second, even though there's no formal policy against it, John discourages intimate relationships among crew.'

'We're different.'

'I don't think we are.'

'We'd just have to be sure no-one found out,' he said hopefully.

She bestowed a withering look on this naïvety. 'Somebody always finds out.'

He folded his arms across his chest. 'Has this line of patter done much for your social life?' he demanded fretfully.

'Hasn't hurt it,' she informed him.

He sighed in resignation. 'What's the next issue?'

'Credibility with crew.'

'Yes?'

'If you and I have an affair, your reputation with the crew is enhanced. You're macho. You scored. I, on the other hand, become a tart.' She shook her head. 'It's a shame about the double standard.'

'Next issue?'

'Alan Lansing. An affair with you might be just the thing he'd use to get me off this ship.'

'This is exhausting me,' he complained.

'I don't know why,' she said, looking at her watch and pushing him gently aside. 'All you've had to do is listen. I had to think it all through.'

'Where're you going?' he said, sounding injured.

'To work.'

'I don't believe it,' he pulled himself up straight.

'Pardon?' She looked back at the door.

'Never mind Kate,' he sighed. 'Never mind.'

Sandy lay in the Infirmary staring wretchedly up at the ceiling. She felt as if there was nothing left inside her, so many times had she vomited. Right now she hated everyone, from Joe who had sounded the alarm, to Kate who had got into her room in time, to Tom Kelly who had poured emetics down her all night, and held her head while she threw up the drugs.

Now he was there again, looming over her, his face kind and concerned.

'I'm going to get some breakfast,' he said. 'Want me to bring you anything?'

'No,' she said ungraciously.

'Stay put.'

'As if I have a choice. My legs are like soggy spaghetti.'

'I wouldn't leave you here alone if they weren't.'

'You make me sick,' she told him.

'Good,' he returned pleasantly. 'See if you can bring up some more of those tranquillisers.'

He ignored her furious look, and left her. At least without him there was peace — peace to sort out her miserable thoughts, and plan ways to try again.

But her peace was shortlived. She heard the door open again, and there was Joe Francis standing beside her. She went on staring at the ceiling, but it didn't make him go away.

'I just wanted to say I'm sorry — if — what I did — had anything to do with your wanting to —' he stammered to a halt, unable to bring himself to say 'kill yourself'. 'If there's anything you need, just give a whistle,' he offered.

She sighed. 'I need to be alone.'

He was gone, but almost at once it seemed she had another visitor. She turned agonised eyes towards the door.

'Can't I be alone for five minutes?' she said weakly.

It flitted across her mind that she had never before seen Tony Grant looking as he did now. He looked half-crazed, like a trapped animal, his eyes were wide with fear. Then the thought faded. It was too much effort.

'This won't take long doll,' he assured her

In her confused state she had to get him to explain three times why he'd come. Each time he grew more frantic to make her understand. At last she closed her eyes.

'I swear Tony, I'm not going to tell anybody where I got the pills.'

'If you do . . .'

She opened her eyes and managed a mirthless smile: 'What? You'll kill me? Good. I hope you're more successful than I was.' She turned her head away.

Baffled he looked at her, then changed his tone.

'I'll go to gaol if anyone finds out,' he cajoled. 'You don't hate me enough to send me to gaol, do you?'

She looked back at him with eyes that were dead. 'I don't hate you Tony. I don't care about you one way or the other.'

His terror grew. He wasn't getting through to her. No matter that she was giving him all the promises he asked for — she wasn't giving them for the right reasons. And that meant she could change her mind as soon as she was more herself.

'What can I do for you?' he gibbered. 'Anything. You name it. It's yours.'

For the first time a flicker of interest showed in her eyes. 'You can give me some more of what you've got in that box. Only more of it. And stronger.'

He was so frightened that he took a step backwards. 'I couldn't do that.' For a moment her desperation had touched him. 'A nice little doll like you shouldn't want to kill yourself.'

She turned her head away from him again. 'If you can't help me then just go away. Please. I won't tell.'

She heard the door close behind him, and she lay there with her own thoughts. She felt weak enough to fade away into nothing. If only she could just slip over the side into the sea. She knew she'd vanish beneath the waves without a struggle and it would all be over. All the pain, and anguish, and fear — all gone. There'd be none of the terror and indecision that had haunted her yesterday while she tried to make up her mind whether to take the tablets. She'd been strong then, and healthy, and that had given life some claim on her to pull against the misery that was tempting her in the other direction. But now she was too weak to feel the tug of the living world. All she wanted to do was close her eyes and slip away with the least resistance. There would never be a better moment than now.

Gingerly she edged herself off the side of the bed and tested her legs on the floor. They were feeble. They wouldn't hold out for long, but long enough perhaps for her purposes. Slowly she edged her way to the door.

She was heaving by the time she had made her way up to the deck, her enfeebled body frantically trying to cope with the demands she was putting on it. Sweat was running down her face and her legs had turned to jelly. But there wasn't much further now. She could see the rail, and the morning sun gleaming on the sea beyond.

'Sandy.'

The shout alerted her to the sight of Tom Kelly coming towards her, his hands full of a tray bearing tea and toast. In another moment the tray had crashed to the ground and he was holding her by the arms.

'What are you doing?' he demanded.

'Leave me alone,' she wept.

He shook her. 'Don't be a jackass.'

She began to scream hysterically. 'You leave me alone Tom Kelly. It's none of your bloody business what I do.'

He shook her again. 'Are you going to walk back into sick bay or am I going to have to put you over my shoulder and carry you?'

She seemed to shrink into herself. Her shoulders shook with

defeated sobs. After a moment he put his arms round her and she let him lead her back to the Infirmary.

'Well I'm sorry I don't agree with you. I think it would have been better if I hadn't come clean.'

Peter scowled at Jo as he said it. It was Jo, after all, who had urged him to tell Sandy the truth, and it was a relief to him now to blame her for the consequences. It gave some small ease to the churning of his own conscience that told him he should never have let an unsuspecting girl get involved with him.

Jo guessed, vaguely but accurately, at his motives, for she now said, 'Come on luv,' in a voice calculated to let him know she saw through him.

He leaned over the rail looking into the sea, unable to meet her shrewd eyes.

'Sandy bloody near killed herself because I told her I'm gay.'

'Would it have been any different if she'd found out later?' said Jo gently. Despite herself she was sorry for Peter, who was a nervous wreck. 'Or from somebody else?'

'I don't know,' he said distractedly. 'I never meant to hurt her.'

No, she thought silently, I don't suppose you did. You just never got around to thinking of it from her point of view. In fact, you're just bloody thoughtless.

His next words confirmed her unfavourable opinion.

'And I'll tell you something else. You know what this is going to mean in terms of my job? It's going to mean that I don't *have* a job. Because the word's going to get out all over this ship that Sandy McCormack tried to kill herself because of Peter Nuttall.'

'I don't think . . .'

'What?' he interrupted her sarcastically. 'You don't think the word's going to get around? Or you don't think I'm going to be in a world of trouble when it does? You're a dreamer Jo. A very nice person, but a dreamer.'

And if you could know what I'm thinking about you, she mused as he walked away from her, you wouldn't even think I was such a nice person.

Peter had barely been in his office a few minutes before there was a knock on the door and Joe Francis came in. When he saw that Peter was alone he dropped the deferential air he had prepared in readiness for Kate, and became belligerent.

'I want to talk to you.'

'Can it wait?' said Peter, hoping he was concealing his alarm.

'It won't take long.' Joe loomed over him. 'I just came to say that I know why Sandy tried to kill herself, and you know how I know. As long as you stay away from her from now on, you got no problems at all. *No problems at all,*' he repeated the last words loudly and slowly.

'Get out of here,' said Peter through lips that could hardly move.

He heard the door slam behind Joe, and he sat back in his chair, stunned. If Joe knew, everyone was going to know within a short time.

'What did Joe want?' Kate had come in and was looking at Peter strangely.

Peter tried to sound confident. 'Thinks he can order me not to see Sandy. I like his cheek.'

'Why, did you upset her when you saw her before?'

'Well —' he said awkwardly, 'I haven't actually . . .'

'You mean you haven't been to see Sandy at all since this happened?' she said, aghast.

'I thought I might make things worse,' he shrugged miserably. 'I don't know what to say.'

'Well I think you'd better work it out,' she said angrily.

By the look in her eyes he knew she meant now. Reluctantly he rose to his feet.

'I'll go and see her now then,' he muttered.

In the doorway he met John. They greeted each other briefly, and John waited till the door was shut before saying to Kate, 'You look fresher than the last time I saw you.'

'I've had a shower. It's not a substitute for sleep, but it does help.' She watched as he sat down. 'You don't often visit me in my office. Is something wrong?'

'I'm not sure,' he hesitated as though seeking courage to go on. 'I don't really think I've heard the whole story behind Sandy McCormack's suicide attempt,' he waited but she said nothing. 'I haven't, have I?'

'No,' she said reluctantly at last. 'There was more to it than a broken engagement.'

It was becoming plain to her that one way or another John was going to find out the truth.

'Then I think I ought to be told, don't you?' said John firmly.

'I'd have to betray a confidence — and I'm in the habit of keeping my word.'

'Was it anything to do with the incident with Joe Francis?'

'No.'

He stared at her, baffled and angry. 'I only want to know so I can do whatever's necessary to help her.'

204

'There's nothing you can do.'

'I could order you to tell me.'

Her eyes challenged him. 'You could.'

'But I don't want to do that.'

She thought for a moment. 'I'd be willing to tell you "off the record" if you swore to me — as a friend, not as a superior — that it would go no further.'

'But that would effectively stop me doing anything to help.'

'Believe me John, you *can't* help.'

He thought for a moment. 'All right then. Unofficially you have my word it'll go no further.'

She took a deep breath. 'Peter is a homosexual.'

He was completely taken aback. 'Peter Nuttall?' he said at last, more to prove to himself that he hadn't lost his voice than because he doubted who they were talking about.

'Yes.'

'I had no idea.' When she remained silent he looked up at her sharply. '*You've* known all along?' There was the ghost of reproach in his voice.

'Well — he is my stepson.'

'Didn't it occur to you to tell Sandy?'

'Please — don't make me feel more guilty than I do already. I was sworn to secrecy. It never occurred to me that she'd try to kill herself.'

'No, I don't think it would have occurred to me either,' he conceded after a moment. 'Did that incident in the engine room have anything to do with Peter being . . .' he made a gesture with his hand.

'Yes, I think so. But I can't be sure.'

'That means other members of the crew know about him?'

'A few. We tried to keep it quiet of course.'

'I didn't know,' he said, depressed.

'Well John, you're the Captain,' she meant it kindly, but saw at once it was the worst thing she could have said.

'All the more reason I ought to have known.'

It was as though somebody had said 'Wally James'. Kate hurried on, trying to say what would make him feel better.

'No it's not. Your crew tends to think of you in your professional capacity before they think of you as a person. That includes Peter. The consequences of his boss knowing about him could get quite serious, couldn't they?'

'Possibly. I don't really know. This isn't the Navy. I'm not aware of Triangle having any policy concerning homosexuality.'

'A great deal of policy is unwritten,' she pointed out.

'As long as it doesn't affect the quality of his work, I don't mind.'

'Yes, but how could he know that?'

'I'll tell him.'

'No you won't. I don't want him to know I've told you. He resents me enough already, and I don't want this to become a further source of irritation.'

'Then you tell him.'

'*No*. I won't admit breaking a confidence. I shouldn't have told you.'

'Yes you should,' he said heavily. 'You've put my mind at ease. At least this business makes more sense. Why does being Captain of this ship disqualify one from membership of the human race?'

'It doesn't.'

'It seems to. I think Peter might have trusted me.'

'You can't have it both ways. Most of the time you encourage the distance between yourself and your crew. I presume because it helps maintain discipline. You can't expect them to come running to you with their personal problems, can you?'

'I suppose not.'

'You won't breathe a word of this?'

'Not a word,' he promised.

He rose to go. 'Is there anything we should do for Sandy — other than having her observed in hospital for a few days?'

'I can't think of anything.'

At the door John met Peter coming back. He looked flustered and upset.

'I was just going,' said John hastily.

'That didn't take long,' said Kate when Peter had slammed the door.

'She got hysterical. Said she didn't want to live without me. Tom didn't think I ought to stay.'

'I'm sorry,' said Kate awkwardly.

'Maybe you should have talked to her.'

'Oh I don't think . . .'

'Woman to woman, you know?' his eyes begged her.

She was ashamed of her own reluctance, but the fact was she too did not want to face Sandy. In the face of that devastating, uncomprehending grief, there was nothing anyone could do or say. But she knew she must go through the ritual of trying. So she went along to the Infirmary, and it was as bad as she'd feared.

Sandy lay still, staring at the ceiling. Her face was ravaged, but worse still was the bleak look in her eyes.

'I once read an article about *Anna Karenina* by an American writer.' Kate said to her quietly. 'Have you read it?'

'Saw it on telly.' Sandy's voice sounded as though it was coming from a million miles off, but at least she was responding.

'Then you know the story. Remember how sad it was when Anna killed herself?'

Slowly Sandy nodded.

'This writer said she'd always thought it was a shame Anna didn't have a friend standing there in the station to say "Anna, don't throw yourself under a train over that man". I've been through this. There'll be other men.'

'She wouldn't have listened,' said Sandy in an old voice.

'Well we really don't know, since Tolstoy didn't give her that friend.' Sandy said nothing, but Kate ploughed on into the silence. 'She might have listened.' Kate reached out and touched Sandy's hand. It was as cold as if she were already dead. 'Don't kill yourself over this man, Sandy. I've been through it. I promise. There'll be another man.'

After a moment the girl turned her head and looked Kate in the eyes. Tears began to well out of her, falling without restraint as if they would never end.

'Oh Sandy,' Kate whispered. 'I'm so sorry.' She reached out and gathered the girl in her arms, and sat there holding her while Sandy cried and cried.

When the restaurant had closed after lunch it was Susan's habit to go along to her cabin and take a shower and have a lie-down. It kept her going through the long evening. And increasingly these days she felt she needed something to help her keep going. The hope that had soared in her when Charles's wife died had faded, soared and faded again. It was just simmering now, not quite extinguished but ready to die. There was no doubt that he had increasingly sought her company since he realised that she could be an ally in his fight against John Anderson, and she had made the most of this, her one advantage. But when they were together he seldom talked of anything but ship matters as they related to the Captain. All her efforts to get him onto something more personal had failed, and she would soon reach the point of despair.

Damn him! she thought as she brushed violently at her hair. Why had she had to fall in love with him? Why couldn't she simply get over him? But she knew the answer to both those questions. It was her way to fall for men she couldn't have — she'd learned that in the past. And once in love, she rapidly found her feelings turning into a sick obsession that made her willing to do anything for the man, however unreasonable, however much her common sense protested. There was always another Susan, who stood outside her, watching her 'daft carryings on' (as the other self insisted on calling them) and prophesying disaster. And in the end it was exactly that divided self that brought disaster. She'd learned that too — in a mental home.

She looked at her face in the mirror and though she looked older than her twenty-five years. More like thirty, without make-up, and with the lines of weariness and sadness already beginning to show. She leaned forward and the towelling robe fell open revealing her breasts. They were small and firm and attractive — only there was no-one who cared to see them.

A knock on the door made her clutch the edges of the robe together.

'Who is it?'

'Charles.'

Quickly she re-tied the robe securely around her. She had enough dignity left not to want Charles to think she was openly trying to seduce him. After all, she'd tried that once — and where had it got her?

'Hello,' she said, opening the door slightly.

'May I come in?' He sounded unsure of himself, which Susan could never remember his being with her before.

'I'm not dressed,' she said.

'Good,' he said. While she still doubted what she had heard he reached a hand inside the door and touched her on the cheek, very gently.

'May I come in?' he repeated.

Wonderingly she stood back to let him in. When he had closed the door he reached out and took her into his arms, and she went to him, wondering if she was dreaming.

When they had drawn apart he looked at her.

'You knew I'd be coming — some time?' he said tentatively.

She nodded, joyfully accepting his suggestion of an implicit understanding between them, although she had not known, only hoped with a hope that grew ever fainter.

He sat down on her bed and pulled her down beside him, holding her hands tightly.

'It's not easy for me —' he said, and broke off to draw a long breath. 'I was married for so long . . .'

She put a finger to his lips: 'Don't talk about it if it hurts,' she said.

'I made up my mind about you a long time ago, Susan. But — I guess —' he smiled ruefully, 'I'm out of practice.'

Slowly she leaned forward and put her arms right round him, drawing him close to her as if she would envelop him in her love.

She would never admit to herself that she was disappointed in what followed. He made love to her distantly, as if his mind was on something else, but that, she assured herself, was natural in the circumstances. Had he not told her that he was 'out of practice' and implicitly pleaded for her understanding? She was prepared to understand anything, if only she could have him.

Afterwards she curled up against him, her arm thrown across his chest. She could not see his face, but she could hear his voice coming from over her head. He told her that he loved her, and she thrust aside the thought that the words sounded like a prepared speech.

He drifted away onto other subjects — the ship, the Captain, and she followed him wherever his thoughts wanted to go. She would talk about anything he liked to keep him here.

She listened as he explained his dissatisfaction with Matt Taylor. The closer she could come to his thoughts the more necessary she could make herself to him.

'I can hardly believe what you're telling me,' she said in wonder.

'You mean you'll sleep with me, but you don't trust me?'

'I trust you,' she said at once, scared by a slight hardness that had come into his voice.

'Then take it on faith,' he kissed her ear. 'Matt is not a good Chief Engineer. If we did things by the book he'd still be endangering the passengers and crew long after you and I are wrinkled and grey.' She lay still, a little troubled by this sudden turning against a man she had always believed to like. As if sensing her doubt he tightened his arms round her and said, 'I love you Susan. And now we're a team. Will you help me get Matt off this ship?'

He waited for her to look up and say yes. When she did not he unwrapped his arms from about her, and clasped them behind his head.

'You don't care about me,' he said with a resigned sigh.

At once she hoisted herself to where she could look into his eyes.

'That's not true,' she said desperately.

'Then why won't you do the right thing and get rid of Matt?'

She put her arms urgently round him. 'I will Charles. *Do* you love me?'

He took her in his arms again and kissed her.

'You know how I feel about you,' he said.

At last Kate succeeded in quietening Sandy to the point where she could be left. She got out of the Infirmary, feeling as though she had been hauled through a wringer. After the dreadful sleepless night she had spent, the day's events were becoming too much for her. She was desperately glad when she saw Matt coming towards her down the corridor that led from the Radio Room. He stopped and turned back with her, and she told him everything that had happened, including her painful scene with Sandy.

'Don't worry,' he soothed her. 'She'll be fine in time. Everything's going to be all right.'

Meaningless words really, but it was such blessed comfort to have him there to say them.

'You're probably right,' she admitted. 'I'm just tired.'

'Right. What you need is a little sleep. Your place or mine?'

She laughed and shook her head. She'd miss it if Matt ever gave up trying at ludicrously inappropriate moments.

The Radio Officer came out and stood there, looking awkwardly from one to the other.

'May I have a word with you Matt?' he said at last.

The two men moved away, and Kate saw the Radio Officer thrust a telex into Matt's hands. He read it, stiffened slightly, muttered something to the Radio Officer, who disappeared, and returned to Kate.

'What is it?' she said, worried for him. 'Bad news?'

'Yes, but this isn't for me,' he said. 'It's for you.'

'What's happened?'

'Your father's dead,' Matt took a deep breath. 'And before he died he married Marion Carter.'

Chapter 16

Things were looking up for Arthur Parker. It was so long since he'd had anything to offer that could count against Miss Laker, and now here was this burly young man who'd stormed into his office saying that the ship had just docked at Felixstowe, and there was something suspicious going on on board, and what was going to be done about it? Through a welter of incoherence Parker managed to make out that the young man was concerned about Miss McCormack, the girl who'd tried to kill herself a fortnight back.

'She was not crying wolf Mr Parker,' Joe Francis insisted for the fifth time. 'Sandy McCormack tried to do herself in and I want to know what *you're* going to do about it.'

Parker checked a file. 'We've sent her to a nursing home — two weeks ago. It's more of a health farm really. Somewhere she can relax and get herself together again. A psychiatrist will be on hand of course.'

'A shrink?' Joe was horrified.

'A doctor,' Parker said smoothly. 'Someone who might be able to help her solve her problems.'

'Listen mate, she's not the one who's sick in the head. It's that Nuttall needs seeing to.'

Parker winced. He supposed that being called 'mate' was part of the price he had to pay if he hoped to get hard information.

'Of course,' said Joe when he came to the end of the story, 'Captain Anderson *knew* Peter had been beaten up in the engine room.'

'Then why wasn't it reported?'

'That doesn't matter any more,' said Joe impatiently.

Parker smiled. 'But it does matter Mr Francis. It appears there's been some kind of collusion on board to protect Peter Nuttall. And I can only conclude that Miss Laker instigated the cover-up.'

'What does that matter?' said Joe irritably. 'I'm here about Sandy.'

Parker leaned back in his chair. He was beginning to enjoy this. 'You're aware he's Katherine Laker's stepson?'

Joe stared at him: 'What are you getting at?'

'For obvious reasons we don't encourage relations working on the

211

same ship,' said Parker. 'It could be that Miss Laker made a grave error in protecting hers.'

'All I want to know is if Peter Nuttall's going to get what he deserves from you lot,' said Joe obstinately.

'Not my concern I'm afraid,' said Parker languidly.

Joe stared at him. Then the message seemed to get through.

'Have you ever thought of taking a short sea voyage with us?' he asked in a voice that was almost conversational.

Parker grinned as he shook his head. He knew what Joe was getting at. 'No.'

'Very wise.'

Joe left without another word, and Parker sat there pensively for a moment. So much had happened recently that sometimes he didn't know if he was coming or going. What with Alan Lansing (who was still an unknown quantity, which made Parker nervous) taking over the running of the company, and then Terson's death followed by the abrupt announcement of his marriage to Marion — nothing was the same any more.

And yet everything was the same. The messages he'd received from on high made that abundantly clear. The new powers-that-be wanted Kate Laker removed from that job just as much as the old ones. The game was still the same. The king was dead. Long live the queen and her prime minister!

After a while he stirred himself and shouted, 'Sophie, pack an overnight bag. We're flying to Amsterdam.'

Tony wished desperately that Mr Collier-Brown would just go away and leave him alone. Mr Collier-Brown had been giving him a hard time recently. He'd been *very* displeased about the pills that Sandy had taken, and when he was displeased he had ways of making himself unpleasant.

Today Tony had thought he'd got off without seeing him, but then suddenly Mr Collier-Brown had risen out of nowhere.

Tony took a nervous look over his shoulder, but the container truck behind which they were standing effectively screened them from the ship.

'Surprise you?' said his demon.

'Scared the hell out of me,' Tony snapped. 'That customs guy opened my bag, looked straight at the stuff, then closed it again as if he hadn't seen a thing.'

'Blind,' said Mr Collier-Brown tersely.

'Ordered by you?'

'My superiors.' He smiled a mirthless smile. 'I do have them.'

'Then I'll refuse any invitation to meet them,' said Tony at once. 'You're doing a good job as a frightener all on your own.'

'Good. That's healthy.'

'For you maybe. I'll tell you something. I've felt a lot safer on the wrong side of the law.'

Again that smile that didn't reach the demon's eyes. 'But you don't have much choice, do you?' He began to drift along, forcing Tony to follow him. 'Amsterdam, this trip, it's all arranged.'

'You mean you're moving in?' Tony demanded. When Mr Collier-Brown nodded he said, 'On the pick-up?'

'That's who we're after.'

'What about me?'

'You'll be okay,' said the big man in an indifferent voice.

'What's the guarantee?'

Mr Collier-Brown shrugged. 'In this game there aren't any.'

'What about what's left on board?'

'Forget it. I'll pick you up in Amsterdam for the final run down.'

He turned away to go, but Tony called him back, desperately.

'Hang about. I said what about me? How do I know you'll keep me in the clear?'

'You don't. Just thank God you're small fry. Hadn't you better deliver the couple of ounces you've got?' He gave a little jerk in the direction of the case Tony was clutching, and walked off.

Jo gave a smile of real pleasure when she saw Linda Kennedy come on board, suitcase in hand. The ship was a duller place without Linda, even when she was causing trouble.

'How's your brother?' she asked, falling into step as Linda headed for her cabin.

For answer Linda just shrugged.

'No matter how you feel, I'm sure it's the best thing that could have happened . . .' Jo went on.

'Wrong.'

'But he's where he can be properly looked after now, back with your mother.'

'So long as it suits her.'

'He *wanted* to be with her. You've got to face up to that.'

They had reached Linda's cabin door. The younger woman stopped and turned. 'Oh yes, it's what he wants. I'm talking about when what *she* wants gets to be more important than the moment of motherly conscience. Come on in.'

While Linda unpacked, Jo sat on the bed and brought her up to date with what had been happening while she'd been away. The news about Peter and Sandy brought a cross grunt from her.

'A load of junk, that's what men are,' she snapped.

'Not all of them, Linda.'

Linda gave her a curious look. 'Don't tell me you've found a real one?' Jo's only answer was a shrug that inflamed the girl's curiosity. 'I had a feeling all along there was something about Peter. But it never entered my head. Poor old Sandy's neither.'

'It was difficult for him too, Linda.'

'Come off it — if he knew what he was he should have kept away from Sandy.'

'He loved her,' Jo felt impelled to say. 'In his own way.'

Linda's only answer was a snort. In truth she was alive with curiosity, and it annoyed her somewhat that Sandy's absence meant that there was no-one to tell her the details. She tried to make up for it that night in the staff pub. Joe Francis, getting drunker and drunker, was prepared to confide the little he knew to anyone who would listen. Eventually, however, even Linda got tired of the same story, the same threats repeated over and over, and when, for the fourth time, Joe said, 'I'll kill him if he goes near Sandy again.'

She said in mild exasperation, 'Come on luv. Give it a rest. Go to bed and sober up. You'll catch it if anyone sees you like that.'

Before her words could take effect the door opened and Peter himself came in. Linda groaned, but couldn't resist shooting him a surreptitious look. It was not lost on her that Peter tried to keep well out of Joe's way — a vain hope as Joe was intent on catching his attention.

'I want to buy you a drink,' he yelled. 'Pour him one Linda. Crême de menthe isn't it?'

He put a world of scorn into the last words. Crême de menthe might have been invented as the essence of decadence.

'Take your hands off me,' said Peter frozenly as Joe threw an arm mockingly round his shoulder.

Joe's voice became falsetto. 'Oh sorry, not your type, am I?' He gave a drunken laugh as Peter lashed out, uselessly, then moved back beckoning Peter on. 'Come on then, come on. Swat the flies.'

'Forget it Joe,' Matt had walked in at tht moment, sized up the situation and intervened without hesitation.

'You forget it mate,' said Joe belligerently. 'Not me.' He turned his attention back to Peter.

'Joe —' Matt's voice was thunderous. 'Cut it out.'

'Not till I've finished with him.'

Intent on what was happening before their eyes, no-one saw Susan Porter appear at the door, and stand watching.

'He thought he'd got away with it, didn't he?' Joe went on. 'Well he hasn't. I saw it. *I saw that guy beat hell out of you and I stood by and watched.* But I figure he didn't knock the stuffing out of you enough, and now, by God, I'm going to finish the job off for him.'

Before he could move his heavy frame, Matt had slid swiftly in between them.

'After you've finished me off Joe,' he said quietly.

Joe looked at him blearily. 'It's got nothing to do with you, Matt. Keep out of it.'

'Me first,' Matt repeated.

Their eyes held for a long moment. It was Joe who broke first, moving away to the bar and muttering over his shoulder, 'You're not always going to be around.' He half-turned and yelled at Peter. 'You hear that? He's not always going to be there. Lots of dark corners on this ship.'

The tension relaxed. Mattt bought himself a drink at the bar and took it to a table, keeping his eyes on Joe, who slumped dejectedly. Peter had beat a hasty retreat. There was no sign of Susan.

Linda too kept an eye on Joe, and when the evening was ending and the pub was almost empty, she brought him a glass of milk.

'What do you want to go getting drunk for?' she chided him. 'Does you no good. Ruins your health and your pocket.'

'I know, I know.'

'And you shouldn't start fighting. There's never been a bust up yet between an officer and a rating where the rating hasn't been given the sack. Not that I know of anyway. And whatever else he bloomin' well is, Peter Nuttall is a junior officer.'

She brought him another glass of milk and pressed it on him remorselessly.

'Anyway, you'll be going on shore leave soon, won't you. Give you a break at least. Got any plans?'

'No.'

'Where do you live?'

'Nowhere — Ipswich — Felixstowe — you name it.'

'I don't get you.'

'Got no family you see.'

'Come off it. I do your cabin, remember. I've seen letters, photos . . . all from home.'

He sighed, too thoroughly drunk to control his tongue. In a few minutes it had all come out, the story he had spent years hiding.

'Can't go there,' he said.

'Why not?'

'I got into some bother — years ago. I was hooked you see.'

'Hooked? You mean — drugs?' she said, aghast.

'Started off in a small way. Doesn't everybody? Went onto bigger kicks.'

'I suppose the booze is a substitute for it then,' Linda mused. 'What happened?'

'I hadn't any dough so I started to push the stuff, didn't I?'

'And the bother?'

'Didn't pay for it, did I? I owe 'em thousands. If I go back to London they'll get me.'

'Hurt you, you mean?' she said blankly.

'Kill me.' He paused for a long time. 'So I went to sea. Nobody knows where I am.'

'Except your mum, eh?'

'Posted them letters myself,' he said, shaking his head. 'Didn't want it to look funny that I didn't get any mail.'

'Joe,' she said urgently, 'what are you going to do?'

'Sign on again. And again after that.'

She stared at him. She had never heard of the Flying Dutchman, but she was fully alive to the horror of a man who would spend his life signing on for the sea because he was afraid to land.

'Well you'd better keep out of fights, then,' she said lamely.

'I know,' he said wretchedly. Suddenly he put his face in his hands. 'Oh Sandy . . .'

'You'd better get off to bed, Joe. You'll feel better in the morning.'

'I'll go in a minute,' he promised. 'You won't breathe a word to anyone about this, will you?'

'No,' she said, meaning it. 'Honest I won't.'

''Cos if they ever found out, on board this ship, I mean, Matt or the Captain — and Sandy — well, I'd have to leave, wouldn't I? I don't want 'em to know I've nowhere to go. Specially Sandy . . . what have I got to offer her . . .?'

'I promise,' she said, her heart wrung for him. Impulsively she gave him a little kiss, then she went down the far end of the bar to busy herself with clearing up. The night was almost over.

Susan, returning to the bar, gave a small smile of satisfaction when she saw Joe still there. That suited her just splendidly. She had something to say to Joe.

216

He stared at her as he listened. He was just sufficiently sober to take in what she was saying to him, and just sufficiently drunk to accept it without question.

'When was all this?' he said at last.

'Just after it happened,' she told him. 'You know how things spread on this ship. Next thing I knew, everyone was saying *you'd* beaten Peter up in the engine room.'

Joe shook his head as though trying to clear it. A little snake of alarm was whispering in his ear that he'd deal with this better when sober.

'Wait a mintue — wait a minute — I never touched him.'

'But Matt said you did,' she insisted. 'It would never enter our heads that Matt would lie about you. We presumed that's why everyone was so hush-hush about it.'

'But I didn't do it! I didn't do it!' he muttered.

'Well of course I believe you Joe. I do really. And the only reason I'm telling you this is because I like you. And trust you. And I hope you trust me . . .'

'Yes — yes I do — but —'

'And after all, Peter is an officer. And you know what that means. It means the bullet — instantly.'

He peered at her out of vague eyes.

'All I want,' said John, 'is one good reason for your ordering Matt Taylor off the bridge.'

They were in the Captain's cabin. John had a relaxed air, but it was the relaxation of a man who was confident in his own authority rather than a man in a good mood. This, if Charles had the wit to perceive it, was the old John Anderson.

'As officer of the watch I had every right,' said Charles guardedly.

'The reason, Charles.'

'You need to ask me?' John nodded. 'Since you haven't been that interested in what the hell's been going on for more time than I can remember, why now?'

'I'm sure you càn remember Charles. It's your job to remember. Now — the reason,' said John relentlessly.

'Don't come the heavy hand with me John.'

John sighed. Charles wasn't going to be warned, was he? All right. 'I haven't begun,' he said quietly. 'The relationship on this ship between deck officers and engineering officers has until this moment been unusually healthy. And I choose to keep it that way.'

'Of course,' Charles smiled but said no more.

'I take it,' said John, 'from your refusal to answer my questions, that you're prepared for the matter to be taken to a higher level?'

'You're next to God. We're to take it higher than that?'

John nodded, 'To God.'

Charles considered this. 'One question would lead to another, and Head Office has a happy knack of getting to the bottom of everything.'

'Exactly.'

'That doesn't bother you?'

John shook his head. Then he rose and went to the door, opening it for Charles.

'You'll have time to decide whether or not you want this taken further before I see Lansing.'

'You're seeing Lansing?' said Charles, unable to contain his surprise. 'Could be a bit risky for you as well.'

'Yes,' said John impassively. He stopped Charles in the doorway. 'Just one more thing. Your time and energy could be better spent on this ship taking a little petrol and vaseline to the rust. If a ship's back breaks there's nothing anyone can do. The best way is to take care of the small things about which we can do something. Same goes for people. Goodnight again.'

John would probably have got a certain amount of satisfaction if he could have seen the temper in which Charles stormed back to his own cabin. The last words, with their implication that he was a lazy, careless officer, had flicked him on the raw, as had the open contempt with which they were uttered. For the first time Charles began to see how things might not go his way.

He had a bad night. He would have preferred to be alone. Instead there was Susan, whom he had invited, and for whose benefit he had to play the ardent lover. He made love to her with a cold savagery that startled her and left him feeling no better. But his worst moment was still to come when, in the morning, as he was dressing, she told him proudly what she had done for him the night before. For the first time the mask he assumed with her slipped right off, and he yelled at her to shut up.

'You *asked* me to help you make trouble for Matt.'

This crude way of putting it infuriated him even more. 'Forget it,' he snapped.

'But you *asked* me,' she wailed, unable to think of another line to take. 'All I did was to try to stir up a little trouble between him and Joe. And he believed Matt had spread it about that . . .'

'Susan please . . .' he closed his eyes. 'Things have changed.'

'What do you mean?'

'It's between John Anderson and myself now.'

'What happened?'

'We had words.'

'About what?'

'That's my business.'

'But I don't understand. One minute you ask me to help you . . .'

He clenched his hands. 'Just forget everything I ever said, will you?'

'Everything?' she asked in an odd voice.

'That's right,' he was buttoning his shirt and missed her implication.

'That includes what's happened between us too does it?'

'Get dressed,' he said abruptly.

'You didn't mean a word of it, did you?'

'Of what?'

She yelled at him, 'What you said in this bed when you made love to me.'

He moved to the door. 'I'd rather we talked about that when you've calmed down.' He left before she could speak.

Matt stared in irritation bordering on real anger at the sight of Joe Francis facing him across his desk. Joe looked hungover and sick as a dog, but Matt had no sympathy for this. For one thing it was entirely Joe's own fault. For another, what he had just said was almost beyond forgiveness.

'I've called you some things in my time Joe, but I'd never have guessed you were such an idiot you'd believe that Susan woman's gossip,' he said at last.

'Then I'm supposed to believe Susan Porter lied?'

'Right on.'

'Why? What's she got to gain by lying to me?'

'How the hell would I know?' Matt yelled. 'But if you're prepared to listen to her you'll damn well listen to me. I did not tell anybody, living or dead, that you beat up Peter in the engine room. I've got better things to do with my time.'

'Yeah. Miss Laker.'

Matt rose to his feet and leaned over the desk to Joe.

'Now you listen Joe, and you hear. If I've ever got anything to say about you I'll say it straight to your face like I always have. If you continue behaving in this picknose way — you're fired.'

'And I'll make damn sure you never get to use your chief's ticket on any damn vessel worth working on.'

Chapter 17

Despite an offer of indefinite leave, Kate was back at her job within a week of her father's death. It was Tom Kelly who remarked drily that she was obviously as hard as she needed to be, and Matt Taylor who slapped this down firmly.

'I think "courageous" is more like the word Tom,' he said, in a voice that warned Tom to keep off the subject in future.

Thinking about the conversation warned Matt how far he'd come in his relations with Kate, since at one time he'd have been the first to call her hard.

He did not press her for details of the funeral and her meeting with Marion, and she did not offer confidences. She was too confused with the shock of having her father snatched away from her without a word of farewell, and almost without warning, to speak of it. Too late now to wonder if they might have been reconciled in the shadow of his death. And probably a waste of time, since his last-minute marriage to Marion looked to Kate like a calculated slap in the face for herself. It was too soon to calculate its effects on the company, but there would certainly be some. And that must have been what her father had intended. Somehow he had meant to prevent his daughter taking complete control of Triangle Line, and that final rejection stood like a barrier between her and true grief.

In the meantime things went on as before. Alan Lansing ran the company while everyone waited for the will. And Kate sat at her desk and did her job on a day-to-day, minute-to-minute basis. She knew she was largely functioning on automatic, but for the moment that would have to do.

It was almost a relief to turn her attention to tiny problems — like the mystery of the car. Except that now she felt she had thought the mystery through to its solution, and one day, about three days after her return, she went to the Radio Room and put through a call.

She winked at Matt, who happened to be passing, and who stopped to listen, and as soon as she was connected to the London office of the car dealers that she had asked for, went into her prepared routine.

'Hello, my name is Katherine Laker. I wonder if I could have a word with your Sales Manager please. Yes, it's about a car I'd like to buy. I'll hold on.'

Matt looked at her wide-eyed, trying to work it out.

'You're buying the Saab?' he queried.

She smiled mischievously. 'How else could I sleep at night, now I've worked out who gave it to me?'

'You *know?*'

She nodded. But despite his pleas she refused to say more. After a moment the Sales Manager came on the line, and Matt listened, fascinated, while Kate made arrangements to pay out an amount of cash that made his eyes pop, in return for a car she already owned. When the conversation was ended Kate put down the phone and left with a satisfied smile on her face. Truly, Matt thought, the ways of the Terson family were hard to comprehend.

When they docked in Amsterdam she took the Saab out alone, refusing his hints that she should let him come with her.

'Just giving her a bit of exercise,' she said as she climbed in on the car deck.

'A quick streak round the docks?' he said, disbelieving.

'Why not? Arthur Parker would be very jealous.'

'So he's next on your lists of possible donors.'

'Not next. He's it.'

'He couldn't afford the bumpers,' said Matt sceptically.

'He didn't. But he could afford to fly here to Amsterdam.'

She drove off without further explanation. Had there been more time she might have let Matt in on some of her thought processes. It was some days now since her restlessly searching brain had lighted on a tiny incident that had made almost no impression on her at the time. Arthur Parker, making out a requisition for a company car for a valuable employee had asked Kate to call in at his Felixstowe office and add her signature to the request. It was not, he explained, an unusual procedure, given her shareholding in the company, and given the extreme importance of the man to Triangle. She had signed.

But she had also done some investigations. And she had discovered something about the 'valuable employee' that had made her eyebrows rise up almost into her hairline.

Now she was on her way to Triangle's office in Amsterdam, where she knew Arthur Parker would be waiting for her. She had arranged that in advance. She was looking forward to the next half hour.

She pulled up outside the office and dialled Arthur's number on the car telephone.

'Get this on tape,' said Parker to Sophie, as soon as he knew whom he had on the line.

'Are you sure?' she said. 'You can't edit these tapes.'

'I won't need to.'

She shrugged and switched on.

'Miss Laker,' he boomed heartily. 'Sorry about the delay, but I was held up with a problem concerning Peter Nuttall.'

If he had hoped to disconcert her he was on the wrong track.

'What problem Arthur?' she said cheerily into the phone. 'He's quite happy.'

He reeled off everything he'd heard from Joe, without naming his source.

'But what an embarrassment for you Miss Laker,' he said at last. 'Knowing is one thing, but that incident in the engine room is quite another. Pardon? — No, I'm sure you didn't overstep the mark by concealing it to preserve his status quo, as it were.'

'You've missed the point again Arthur,' she almost sang. 'I couldn't see why your valuable time should be wasted on such a minor incident. Your question answered? Good. Take a look out of the window.' She waited until she could see him appear at the window above. 'Now, haven't I kept it nice and clean? You do recognise it, don't you? Or shall I wave to you so as to identify it?'

Parker wheeled away from the window and made a movement to Sophie to switch off the tape.

'I'm sorry Miss Laker. I don't think I quite understand what you're referring to.'

'The car you ordered for the Amsterdam admin guy,' she spelled out. 'The man you were so desperate to keep working for the company that you asked me to sign for it as well. Just to add a little weight. You remember?'

'The only problem appears to be that the particular man you ordered the car for left the company anyway, and you, unfortunately, forgot to tell me. Are you there Arthur?'

'Anyway, I just want to say "thank you" Arthur. As I don't qualify for a company car — least of all this particular car — it was extremely kind of you to pass it on to me. Odd that our tastes should be so similar.'

She could hear him almost purring down the line. 'But as you say Miss Laker, you unfortunately don't qualify for a company car.'

She grinned. He thought he had her. If only he knew. 'That's why

I'm so touched Arthur,' she said. 'I realise how hard on your pocket it must be, since there's no way you can charge it to the company. I really am extremely moved by your generosity. I could say "why me?" But I was brought up to believe in accepting gifts as graciously as one gives them.

'Never again will I hear you called mean — devious or — dare I say it? — downright dishonest. Oh no. All I'll do is point to the car and say — "how many men give presents like that, and without strings?" Thanks again Arthur. 'Bye.'

She replaced the receiver.

Without a word Sophie took out the requisition for the car that bore Kate's signature and held it out to Parker. He stood looking at it for a long time.

'You could always eat it,' she said.

Without glancing at her Parker took out his lighter and set fire to the paper. He dropped it into the ashtray and watched it burn.

'Are you going to raid your piggy bank to pay for her car then?' she said.

'I shall just wait,' he said, 'for the bill for that car to hit my desk. I shall then query the bill. At that point the car manufacturers will demand the return of the car about which I know nothing at all. They'll turn this place upside down in order to repossess their car. Bastards — these bad debt collectors.

'Then they'll discover who is in possession of the said car, and finally — finally — her head will roll.'

Sophie looked puzzled. 'She'll just show them her copy of the order form she signed with Jeremy Gates and you.'

'But my signature isn't on their copies. There was no carbon paper, when I signed.'

Sophie looked at him with a twinkle in her eye. 'You were even smart enough to keep it out of the papers you sent to Head Office,' she said appreciatively. 'But you knew you'd won.'

'Of course.'

'And the top copy — the one with your signature — is that little pile of ashes.'

'Yes.'

She smiled at him: 'Wasn't it a good thing I took a photocopy?'

He turned pale. 'What did you say?'

'The way I see it, you're either going to be fired or promoted when the truth comes out. I just want to make sure I'm in the clear either way.'

'You have a price, I presume?'

'Wouldn't you?'

Parker leaned back in his chair. He seemed to be considering. 'I'd like you to take a memo. Don't date it yet.' She picked up her pad and pencil, and he began to dictate. 'To Head of Personnel, Amsterdam. I regret to inform you that my secretary does not conform to the conditions required by Triangle Line and has today been relieved of her position.'

He stared at her blankly amazed face.

'When you've typed that out, give me the top copy and keep the carbon in your file,' he smiled at her. 'Or photostat it, if you'd rather.'

In another office of the Triangle building in Amsterdam, Alan Lansing was confronting Jeremy Gates. There was already between the two men an instinctive mutual dislike and distrust.

'You are aware that Marion Carter and George Terson consulted my corporation when Mr Terson was in hospital,' Lansing was saying. 'We have done a certain amount of work for them in the past, and there exists a great deal of mutual trust, both on a personal and a business level. I represent that trust. On their marriage, and George's subsequent death, it was natural that Marion should turn to me.'

He paused to allow the implications of this to sink into Gates.

'Yes,' he said again. 'When you talk to me, in effect you are talking to Marion Terson *and* Triangle Line.'

'I was sorry to hear about George,' said Gates at last. Lansing guessed he was trying to collect his thoughts.

'I think you were sorry to hear about his marriage, not his death,' said Lansing, who saw no reason to wear kid gloves for dealing with Jeremy Gates.

'That too was a shock . . .' Gates conceded carefully.

'Exactly. Now, I am aware of your financial prowess, aware too of what you have done in the past on behalf of the company. That was amply rewarded by Terson giving you your present position. However, that is not what I want to say . . .'

'Could we get to the point?' Gates interrupted him.

'The point is I don't want to see your talent and time wasted in a futile attempt at a takeover.'

'Futile?' Gates looked up sharply.

'I said *I* was acting for Mrs Terson and Triangle Line.'

'Is this a declaration of war?'

'A declaration of intent . . .' Lansing said the words with emphasis.

'So what do you intend to do?'

'Initially I have decided it's high time we all met face to face.'

'All?'

'All necessary parties, that is. You, me and Katherine Laker. It's time you put your money where your mouth is. I want to know exactly what it is you want, how you intend to get it and who you have in mind as an accomplice.'

'Accomplices are hard to get.'

'Which is exactly why Kate will be at the meeting,' said Lansing.

Gates shrugged. 'Since you insist on Miss Laker being at the meeting, I can hardly see much point in any further discussion till then.'

'Good. You know where I'm staying. The meeting will be in my suite.'

'Do you think my office might be bugged?' said Gates, slightly nettled.

'I'd rather the meeting were held on my own ground, which definitely isn't bugged,' said Lansing patiently.

'When?'

'You will be informed. There are one or two matters I want to straighten out.'

'Kate?'

'Your backers.'

'My backers?'

'I'm aware,' said Lansing, 'that you have been buying shares in the company. Not openly of course. I'm also aware that your backer is Dutch.'

'In diamonds as a matter of fact,' Gates shrugged.

'That's a good business. Especially in Holland. I like a good business sense. What we both have to find out is how good Kate's business sense is. Right?'

'I think I know that,' said Gates. 'When does she dock?'

'Kate or the ship?'

'One and the same.'

'She's docked. But then, as Managing Director, you must have known that. Or are diamonds taking up too much of your time?'

'Of course I can guess what the meeting's about,' said Kate to Matt when they were sharing a drink in her cabin.

'Gates wants your new mother's permission to marry you,' he clowned.

'No.'

'After you're divorced, of course.' For some reason this was a sore point with him.

'Marion wants all the cards on the table,' said Kate.

'With hers up her sleeve?'

'Precisely where mine will stay.'

'Good for you,' he took a long swallow. 'Now are you going to tell me what fiendish plan you've dreamed up for Arthur Parker?'

'It's very simple and not at all fiendish. I've no doubt that Arthur thinks he's got me where he wants me now. He's just waiting for that bill to turn up — and then he's going to refuse to pay it. Then all he has to do is wait for the scandal to break. Only he'll have a long wait, because I'm making my own arrangements to pay for the car.'

'But how much —?'

She told him.

'It's all right,' she said, laughing as his eyes popped. 'I don't mind the cost. The only thing I regret is that I shan't be around to see Parker's face when he realises he's been done.'

It hadn't been hard for Jo to get herself an invitation to Tony Grant's cabin. All she had to do was drop a hint about how she'd watched him going through customs, and that obliging customs man she'd seen stare straight at something in his bag — and then pass it over. After that Tony couldn't wait to be nice to her, and she accepted his invitation because it might be useful to have a look round his cabin and see what he was up to these days.

When they'd finished the first bottle she held out her glass and smiled invitingly.

'More,' she said.

'Can you wait while I get another bottle?' He turned at the door. 'I'd never have believed it, but I actually miss you,' he said sentimentally.

Tony didn't change, she reflected as he went out. He went right on thinking everyone else was too brainless to see through him.

While he was gone she moved into the bathroom to freshen up. The harsh light over the mirror showed her a sight she didn't care for.

'Is that me?' she asked herself dismally, peering forward. 'Oh God, it is.'

She put her hand on the little ledge below the mirror to balance herself while she got closer still, and in taking it away she knocked something onto the floor. It was Tony's shaving bag. Sighing, she bent down to pick up. As she picked it up, it rattled.

She stared at it for a moment, shook it. Then, moving quickly she pulled back the zip and looked inside. Three small bottles fell out into her hands. They were all unlabelled, but she could see they contained pills. The sound of the door opening galvanised her into action. It took just a second to slip the bottles back into the shaving bag and replace it on the shelf.

'Jo? Where are you?' Tony appeared in the bathroom doorway, a bottle of wine clutched in his hand. Jo was busily applying fresh lipstick.

'Trying to turn the clock back twenty years,' she told him over her shoulder. Then, in a casual voice, she added, 'Is that what those drugs are for?'

She thought he would drop the bottle. In the mirror she could see his reflected face, white with shock.

'They could be "eternal youth" pills,' she went on, 'or they could be drugs. The kind Sandy tried to kill herself with. Why are you carrying them around with you?'

'Believe it or not, it's straight,' he said in a faint voice.

'Not if I can prove you gave those pills to Sandy. It's called aiding and abetting.'

'Come off it,' he gave a sick laugh.

She finished her work and turned to face him. Her voice was hard. 'Not this time Tony. Not now you've turned your grubby hands onto people's lives.'

She made for the door, but he moved to block her path.

'Is this what all the come-on was for?' he demanded. 'Just to try and get even with me?'

'To get even with you I'd have to grovel in the dirt, and that's not my scene.'

'Just teasing then?'

Jo smiled, but there was no warmth behind it. 'Who was teasing who, I wonder?' She pushed past him to get to the door. 'I have everything I need.'

'Captain Anderson you mean?' he sneered. She turned and looked at him sharply. 'You can't keep anything quiet on this ship, love.'

'Keep remembering that Tony. 'Cos I've got all I need on you now.'

John was not a fanciful man. Had he been, he would have said that the sword of Damocles had fallen in the shape of a message from Alan Lansing asking him for a meeting in his Amsterdam hotel room later that afternoon. Lansing had been unable to be precise about the time of the meeting, saying that he had another one first that might take any time. He'd be grateful if John would arrive early and hold himself in readiness. It was not a comforting message.

That meant he had quite a wait ahead of him and no way to fill up the time but worry. He desperately wanted a drink, and he desperately wanted the comfort of a chat with Jo Bailey, and he wasn't sure which of the two he wanted more.

Wandering restlessly on deck he encountered Tom Kelly. 'You been ashore?' he asked.

'Just a quick dash,' said Kelly. 'I wanted a plug for my radio and I thought — as it was made in Holland — I'd get one.'

'And did you?'

'No. They didn't know what I was talking about.'

It occurred to John that there was something about Tom Kelly that didn't ring true at the moment. It might just be an air of furtiveness that he carried with him, as though he was making up his excuses as he went along. Or it might be the fact that he was spruced up in full, smart uniform — an odd garb for a man making a quick dash ashore to buy a plug.

'How about you?' Tom said. 'Are you going ashore?'

'Mr Lansing has asked me to meet him. I think we both know why . . .'

Tom sighed. 'If there's anything I can do John . . .'

John shook his head. 'I get the feeling Charles has done it all.'

'Tony.'

Peter Nuttall's voice stopped Tony as he was halfway across the Reception Area. 'I need to talk to you.'

'Me?' Tony tried to gather his wits.

'Yes.'

'Not now.'

'Later then?' Peter persisted.

'I've got a tight schedule,' Tony hedged. He didn't want to get near Peter. Now he knew the truth about him he felt a physical repugnance. Besides, there was no way of knowing what Sandy might have said to him.

'Couldn't we meet up in Amsterdam for a drink?' Peter suggested.

Tony seized on this as a way of deferring the evil moment.

'Sure. Do you know that open-park space?'

'Not the one by the canal?'

'Yes — Vondelpark.'

'I know the one.'

'Good. I'll see you there around five?'

Peter nodded, 'Fine.'

'You'll be wearing that awful red coat?' said Tony suddenly.

'Never go ashore without it,' Peter said. 'But anyway it won't be that crowded will it?'

'I'll carry a rose,' Tony couldn't resist saying.

Peter suppressed an irritated sigh. 'It's like leprosy, isn't it?'

'What the —?' Tony backtracked hastily. 'Give over. What you are or what you do doesn't bother me.'

'But I bet you wouldn't swap places. See you later.'

Tony waited till he'd gone, and stood thinking for a minute. Then he went to his cabin for his coat, and slipped hurriedly ashore. There was a telephone kiosk on the docks that would do him nicely. This was one call that he didn't want to make from the ship.

He drummed his fingers while he waited to get through, but at last the voice he wanted was on the other end.

'Yes — the Vondelpark as usual,' he said. 'Five o'clock. I'll be wearing a red coat. Yes, it's all there.'

He was smiling as he put down the receiver.

Jo paced the Reception Area, looking for the third time at her watch. She was waiting for John, who had decided that he needed her more than a drink, and called her to ask her to go ashore with him. As she paced she was aware of Linda, fretfully staring out to sea.

'I don't half miss Sandy,' said Linda at last. 'All on my own with nowhere to go, and stuck here for who knows how long.'

This last remark was a reference to a minor piece of industrial action that threatened to hold the ship up at Amsterdam. Maddening as it was Jo reckoned that it might even be a blessing for John, as it would give him that much more time with Alan Lansing to state his case.

'I could meet you while John's in his meeting if you like,' she offered.

'John who?

'Captain John.'

Linda's eyebrows rose. 'You ain't half a dark horse. And I blamed Tony. Ah well. I reckon I'll do a bit of research in Amsterdam.'

'Into what? Cheese?'

'How to burn a bob for a trick.'

'Linda,' Jo hoped she sounded shocked.

The girl grinned. 'A monkey a turn they say. The red light bit. So long.' She stopped and turned back with a giggle. 'I'll probably find more of the blokes from this crew there than I ever saw on the ship.'

Not for the world would Kate have admitted that she was nervous about the coming meeting, but Matt *knew* without being told. That was obvious from the way he put his head round her door when it was time to go, and intoned, 'Five minutes, Christians.'

She gave a shaky laugh, and was surprised to realise how glad she was to have him there, glad that he had insisted on seeing her to the hotel, and kicking his heels for the whole afternoon till she came out. It was good to have Matt around.

As befitted Marion Carter's personal representative, Alan Lansing was staying at Amsterdam's most luxurious hotel, and the suite to which Kate was ushered was as palatial as a company boardroom. Lansing got the courtesies over with as quickly as possible. Alone of the three he gave no sign of being nervous. When they were all seated round a table he invited Gates to open up. Jeremy took a brief look at his notes and launched into a speech in which he presented the company's financial picture in a dark light, while taking care to lay the blame on outside forces. Kate had to admit that it was a masterly performance from a man on the tightrope who could hear the snapping of crocodiles' jaws in the pit beneath.

'Due to inflation the company is now under-capitalised,' said Jeremy with emphasis. 'The bank has a debenture over the entire assets and could well call in their loans.'

'I need hardly say that all that is required is a slump in world trade, a general recession, and *world* shipping will feel the pinch, not just Triangle Line.'

Lansing looked up quickly: 'In that case, with bankruptcy round the corner, I can hardly see the attraction in wanting to control the line. So what drives you on Jeremy? Is it like an ambition to be Prime Minister in a country that's not worth living in anyway?'

'I believe I have the solution,' said Gates. 'This line has been run on an almost feudal basis. The days of dynasty in big business are long gone.'

'And I represent that feudal system?' said Lansing when he was sure Kate wasn't going to speak.

'With Marion Terson,' Gates confirmed. 'Yes. The king is dead. Long live the queen. I don't find that very acceptable.'

'You can always resign . . .' said Lansing casually. He noted with satisfaction that he had succeeded in disconcerting Gates. 'But of course, your proposals for the line might not make that very acceptable. To us, I mean. Always assuming that we like your proposals.'

'My proposals are not for the line as it exists at present.'

'Then what changes do you have in mind? I'm prepared to listen Jeremy. Since it appears you intend to combine Kate's shares with those you and your backers have acquired, I think it would be wise. Are there any more interested parties?' He looked from one to the other. 'Your husband, Kate?'

If looks could kill, he realised, he'd be dead that minute. Kate's furious response made it plain he'd trodden on dangerous ground.

'We will leave my husband out of this,' she said through tight lips. 'Alex has no wish to be involved in business — of any kind.'

'So,' Lansing continued; 'it's your forty-nine against our forty-six. That figure is correct?'

'Correct,' said Kate, 'if we combine our votes.'

'Well, I'm listening,' he went on, 'but remember, I'm representing Marion Terson. In the end her decision will be to put her money where your mouths are. I do not intend to dispense that decision lightly. Shipping is not as predictable as the weather. I won't agree to throwing in Marion's lot with a fashion — a trend either. Trends come and go. Who remembers the seaplane any more? So the floor is yours, Jeremy. What is your golden key?'

'One moment,' said Kate quickly. They both looked at her. 'I'm not so sure that Jeremy's ideas and mine are quite the same.' She smiled at Jeremy to soften her words. 'I like to think that the line will basically remain unchanged. Let's say for sentimental reasons.'

In the pause that followed, Lansing's sensitive antenna divined the extent to which Jeremy Gates had been taken by surprise. Interesting, he thought.

'Well Jeremy?' he asked blandly.

He was unsure of his ground now. 'The idea is basically to turn the line over to freight,' he said. 'That is where the money is. Our three main ships, working to capacity, could more than double our turnover. Once we've moved in that direction we can build more purpose-built ships.'

'And meanwhile,' said Lansing, 'the cost of conversion?'

'Minimal.'

'How minimal?'

'It's a lot cheaper to rip out fittings than to refit,' Gates told him.

'Well Kate, let's hear what you have to say,' said Lansing.

Kate took a deep breath and looked straight at Jeremy Gates.

'I like passengers,' she said. 'My father's business, this whole thing, was built up on passenger-company good relations. I don't want that to be thrown away. Unlike Jeremy I can't get emotional about a crate. However, I too will listen to all proposals, but in the end it will be my money where *my* mouth is.' She leaned slightly towards Gates. 'Surely you have always known that?'

'I've always known how independent you are,' he said coldly.

Light was beginning to break over Alan Lansing.

'So it's not a *fait accompli?*' he said to them both.

'It never was,' Kate told him.

'Interesting,' he mused, half to himself. 'Please go on.'

'My shares belonged to my mother,' said Kate. 'In the end I shall do with them as I see fit. Equally, I have no reason to believe that my father has cut me out of his Will. We may not have seen eye to eye, but I cannot believe that he would have been so Victorian.'

'If that's so —' said Lancing, '— if by your father's Will you increase your shares — that, of course, would make your vote very powerful indeed.'

'True. And that's what I'm talking about. I'm not interested in money. I'm interested in the control of this company. None of you can deny that it's in my blood. Why, even the money my father started his business with came from my maternal grandparents. I have a duty to that money. I will not see it go to waste.'

'So are you voting with Jeremy,' Lansing asked her, 'or with Marion?'

'There's no love lost between Marion and me . . .' Kate said slowly. 'There was no love lost between my father and me. That doesn't mean that I have no interest in the Line.'

'This is a business meeting Kate,' said Lansing, not unkindly. 'Do we need to digress in this way?'

'This is not a digression,' she said. 'I don't care how many pieces of paper you have there. I knew my father's mind and he didn't keep a diary. On these matters you have to rely on me. I knew about his plans for his company — *his* company. And I knew about all the attempts to put him out of it,' she looked at Jeremy Gates. 'You needn't think you were the first. I don't for one moment expect you'll be the last.'

'Kate,' Jeremy said uneasily, 'we must resolve this meeting.'

'Because you have other interests,' she said, 'that are more pressing than mine?'

He fell silent under her gaze.

'My father never really forgave my mother for not providing him with a son and heir to carry on the name of Terson,' Kate went on.

'As a result of that she turned to drink and it killed her.' She whipped round on Lansing so suddenly that he blinked. 'Oh yes, I'm sure that you have the death certificate and all other relevant bits and pieces. What you do not understand is *me*, what it did to me. Nor do you understand the reasons for many of my actions.

'Many years ago, when I was a little girl, he gave me a ship in a bottle. He told me it wouldn't come out of that bottle. I wanted that ship. I didn't want it to be unobtainable, and I got it out of the bottle — undamaged. As perfect as it had been in its cocoon. He died never understanding why I did it.' She looked at them with a faint smile. 'I see at last I've got your attention.'

'Is this what we're here to discuss?' demanded Gates.

'It is precisely why we're here,' said Kate. 'I'm prepared to pick your brains Jeremy, because this company is my birthright, and I will not be denied it by my sex. And I'm prepared to hear what you and Marion have to say, Alan. And when I've heard it all, I'll decide what I'm going to do — and I'll decide all by myself.'

Lansing addressed Jeremy Gates: 'Were you aware of these reasons why Kate seemed to be so interested in your plans?'

'I'm still not convinced that what we're hearing has any relevancy . . .' Gates said.

'It is entirely relevant,' said Kate firmly. 'Everyone in this room is using the other, and all that matters is who wins. I don't suppose either of you has played all his card . . .'

Alan's lips twitched in appreciation of this hit, but he said nothing.

'The fact that my stepmother has seen fit to bring you in, is in itself interesting,' Kate told him.

'It was your father's wish also,' said Lansing.

'It's funny —' said Gates, '— thinking that Marion is now your stepmother.'

'Yes,' Kate conceded without amusement. 'The situation does have its hilarious side. It's particularly amusing that she isn't here.'

'That's what *I'm* paid for,' said Lansing.

'Dogsbody or bodyguard?' she challenged him.

'A bit of both. I'm not complaining.'

'There is one matter that I'd like to raise,' said Gates. 'If we can get back to business . . .'

'At present,' Lansing told him, 'with the power of attorney invested with me, Marion is part of the business. We were discussing, as it were, a silent partner . . .'

'Partner?' said Kate sharply.

233

'Well naturally. As Terson's widow she represents his interests. Until the Will is read and whatever redistribution is necessary takes place.' He turned to Gates. 'What was the matter that you wished to raise?'

'The five per cent voting shares you are obviously counting on to hold off my plans.'

'What about them?' said Lansing.

'Indeed,' Gates replied. '*What* about them? From what I've heard I'm not so sure you can count on them.'

'Do you conduct business on rumours Jeremy?' Lansing demanded coolly. 'Personally I don't pay any attention to them. In fact if, let's say, George Terson had acted on rumour, you would have been fired years ago. And in that case, where would we all be now?' He waited to see if Gates had any rejoinder. Then, satisfied that he hadn't, he said, 'So — shall we call this meeting to an end?'

'Just a minute —' Kate halted him. 'Who is the person holding the five per cent?'

'Didn't Jeremy tell you?' Lansing asked innocently. 'Not even when you planned to become partners?

Touché, she thought, not without a hint of admiration. She looked hard at Gates, who smiled back.

'A card I was keeping up my sleeve,' he told her.

'Then the meeting is over?' said Lansing.

Kate ignored him and spoke directly to Gates. 'I think you should tell me,' she said quietly. Gates only looked at Lansing. 'Alan?' said Kate. 'You both know?'

'Didn't your father tell you?' Gates asked her.

'We rarely discussed his private affairs.'

'Then I suggest you speak to Marion,' said Gates. 'She obviously meant much more to him than you did.'

Kate went white. 'How dare you?'

For a moment there was total silence. Gates stared at her, satisfied that he had revenged himself for the way she had cut the ground out from under him that afternoon.

Kate lifted her chin, gathered her things together and left the room without another word to either of them.

'Is it your move?' said Lansing. 'Or have we got a stalemate here?'

Chapter 18

'Killing us both won't help,' said Matt plaintively.

Far from slowing down it seemed to him that the Saab perceptively picked up speed. Kate's hands were steady on the wheel, but her face was white and set.

'What happened at that meeting?' Matt said. 'Did you lose?'

For answer she slammed on the brakes with a suddenness that had him clutching his seat. She pulled in to the side of a broad road in an Amsterdam suburb, and sat, her chin leaning on her elbows which were against the steering wheel, gazing directly ahead.

'I found something,' she said.

To Matt's amazement a tear fell slowly down her cheek. When she made no effort to brush it away he leaned over and did it himself.

'Hatred grows with the years,' she went on. 'And love fades. That things could get to this . . .' she kept her head turned away from him. 'But nothing will stop me. I can't stop now.'

'You can still cry,' he said gently. 'You still care. You can still love.'

She turned to look at him, brushing away another tear.

'With all you know about me?' she said.

'I don't know a thing,' he leaned over and kissed her and she slipped easily into his arms.

'I'd like to take you to the moon,' he said at last.

She leaned against his shoulder, smiling. 'I've been.'

'I keep forgetting what a well-travelled lady you are.'

'Gothenburg, Amsterdam and Felixstowe,' she said.

'The Garden of Eden then?'

'As Adam and Edna you mean?'

'Just try to remember how you felt when Gates mentioned Marion Carter.'

'I can. Too well.'

'And it changes nothing?'

'Just makes it more difficult.' She pulled back and looked at him. 'Are you sure you want to risk being involved with me?'

235

For answer he kissed her again.

'Until you accept that promotion that's still dangling in front of you,' she said.

He shook his head. 'Until you say "enough".'

It seemed to John that he spent an eternity wandering the streets of Amsterdam with Jo. Once they approached the hotel, only to discover that Alan Lansing was not ready for him yet, nor likely to be for some time. There was nothing for it but to resume walking. John tried to imagine what he'd be going through if he were alone at this minute, but gave up the attempt. Jo seemed to fit at his side at a moment like this in a way that he now realised Maya never had. He remembered that he hadn't even told Maya this was happening. Why bother? He had sent his own lawyers into combat with hers and things were getting more acrimonious every day. He was, as far as he could see, no further forward regarding his children, but it was wonderful what other things could be found to fight about in a divorce.

At last he slipped into a phone booth near the hotel and put through another call.

'He's ready to see me,' he told Jo when he came out.

At the hotel entrance they stopped, and after a moment's hesitation she kissed him quickly.

'It might help to know I care,' she said.

She walked away without giving him time to reply, which he was glad of, because his thoughts were too confused for an answer. And right now he didn't even want to think of Jo. He needed all his attention for what lay ahead.

As soon as he entered Lansing's suite he knew that nothing was going to be as he had imagined it. The mere fact that he had been asked to come here instead of to the office was something that he supposed might have given him the clue, but it hadn't occurred to him until he heard Lansing's cordial greeting and found himself sitting down with a drink in his hands.

Lansing did not seem anxious to come to the point. He talked in general terms about George Terson, Marion, the company, Terson's death. He spoke as though to an equal not an employee, and certainly not an employee who had been called to give an account of himself, and imperceptibly John found himself relaxing.

'It's a bad business,' Lansing said at last, referring to Terson's death.

'How's Marion taking it?'

'As you would expect. She hasn't been totally destroyed by it, so she'll bounce back.'

'She's a fine woman,' said John. 'I have enormous respect for her.'

'She has for you too. So much so that she asked me to handle your problem.'

'I can handle that myself,' said John, suddenly defensive.

Lansing shrugged slightly. 'Marion told me to give you as much help as I could.'

'You had reports?'

'From Gates.'

'Then why not pay attention to them?' said John with some sharpness.

'I did.'

'And?'

'Gates is no fool,' conceded Lansing. 'He insisted on having the report filed officially, in writing. So I made enquiries — through Marion.'

'Well come on man,' said John irritably. 'Don't keep up the suspense.'

'I know, obviously, who made the report — or should we say complaint?'

'So do I,' said John.

'And I have chosen, with Marion's complete approval, to ignore it,' said Lansing simply. He glanced into John's baffled face. 'That's what you want, isn't it?'

'I don't know . . .' said John slowly.

'At the very back of my mind I've been thinking lately of retiring. This would have been a good excuse. There comes a time when man needs all the peace he can get and leave the wars to someone else.' John sounded as though he might be talking to himself.

'But that would be no way to go out,' said Lansing. 'On trumped up charges . . .'

'A great old shipmate of mine, Wally James — he decided that way was the cleanest . . .'

'But you'd never be able to get your master's ticket back in a situation like that,' Lansing objected.

John sighed. 'I'm not so sure I want one. You see, you give up ocean ships to be near home. That's the beauty of a ferry. Then, when you have no home . . .'

'Marion told me,' said Lansing when John had trailed off. 'She also asked me to ask you if you remembered why the company was named "Triangle"?'

John creased his brow. 'There were several reasons. The main one was to do with George Terson's first three ships . . .'

'Your advice helped George to make quite a number of correct decisions. Can you take some advice from me?'

'I always listen, anyway,' John smiled.

'Don't you make the wrong decision now. You have many friends. Marion is only one of them. She took the trouble to get to the whole business personally.' Lansing paused as if trying to decide whether to say something. 'Do you know Tom Kelly?'

'Naturally,' said John, puzzled. 'He's First Mate.'

'So does Marion . . .' Lansing let his voice fade away. As the implication hung in the air John's eyes opened wider. For the first time it dawned on him that Tom might have had something to do with the incredible way things were turning out today. Tom had got him off the hook. The possibility had never occurred to him, but now John saw in his mind's eye Tom Kelly, standing there in full uniform, lamely explaining that he'd just dashed ashore to buy a plug. Where had he really been? This hotel? Talking to this man? John would have bet money on it.

Lansing looked up. 'And right now, Marion needs all the help *she* can get,' he said.

'Marion is no babe in the wood, you know,' said John. 'She's tough, but count on me.'

Lansing smiled. 'She told me you'd say that. In exactly those words.'

John grinned back. 'Apart from being the boss George Terson was an old shipmate. There's nothing I wouldn't do for him, or for Marion. He was a wily old salt.'

Lansing considered for a minute. 'Are you aware that the company is under threat of a takeover?' he asked at last.

'I've heard rumours. Who hasn't?'

'Then maybe you'll appreciate just how wily George Terson was.'

'I don't get your drift.'

'The insurance he took out years ago . . .'

'I don't know anything about insurance. The only way I could help is to back Marion with the shares he gave me as a token when they were practically worthless.'

Lansing gave him a long, slow look.

'Exactly,' he said softly. 'That little five per cent . . .'

John's eyebrows shot up. 'Is that what it's down to? Just five per cent?'

'That's what it's down to. You see, you are very important to the company. Not, as I understand it, that it wasn't always the case. It sure beats resigning.'

'You'll keep me informed of all developments?' said John.

'Absolutely.'

'There is just one thing . . .'

'And that is?'

'I can only use them as I see fit. If, amongst the various warring parties, there emerges a policy which I consider is the best, I'll go for it.'

'I don't think anyone could ask fairer than that,' said Lansing cautiously.

'But it might not suit you or Marion . . .'

'We'll have to wait and see . . .'

Peter gave a sigh and looked at his watch. It was just after five. He hoped Tony wasn't going to be long. He pulled his red coat a bit more closely round him, for the wind was chilly and seemed to blow more strongly in the open spaces of the park.

He was half aware of a man who walked slowly past him, and paused just long enough for a package to drop from his coat. The man stooped and picked it up, and then approached Peter.

I think you dropped this,' he said quietly.

Peter looked at the package which the man had thrust into his hands. 'No. This isn't mine.'

'It was here on the ground,' the man persisted, giving him a puzzled look.

'Well I can't help that,' said Peter irritably. 'It still isn't mine.'

He looked up as a familiar voice hailed him.

'Hello,' Jo called cheerily. 'Fancy meeting you. The one thing about stopping off in foreign cities is you can't miss the crew. You'd think there wasn't anybody else in the place except us.'

Peter smiled at her before giving his attention back to the man.

'Sorry, it's really not mine,' he said, attempting to hand the package back.

To his surprise the stranger seemed reluctant to take it. A moment later surprise was swamped in bewilderment and then in fury as the park around them seemed to become alive with policemen, who laid rough hands not only on the stranger but on Jo and himself. Within seconds they had all three been bundled into cars, their protests ignored, their anger laughed at.

From some way off Mr Collier-Brown watched the scene in satisfaction. That was just what he had hoped to see. He turned to Tony Grant, standing beside him.

'You've finally done it,' he said with approval. 'I didn't think you would.'

Tony watched the cars drive off with their reluctant occupants.

'It's going to take a lot of explaining,' he said.

He was smiling.

It was at Alan Lansing's request that Kate presented herself in the Amsterdam office of Triangle Lines the following morning. She was wearing her full, formal uniform, something which she hoped would serve to re-emphasise her position.

'Thank you for coming so early,' he said when she was seated in his office.

She shrugged, 'I'm a loyal employee. You seem to be the boss.'

'I just wanted to say goodbye before you sailed.'

'Goodbye,' she said politely. She was determined not to help him.

'And to sound out your feelings in the wake of yesterday's meeting.'

'That's more like it,' she said, and then stopped.

When the silence had grown uncomfortable Lansing said impatiently, 'Well?'

She shrugged again. 'I don't feel any differently than I did before we met. Nothing was resolved, was it?'

'We both know we're on the same side of the passenger/freight issue.'

'So?'

'Doesn't that count for something?'

'No.'

'Surely it ought to?'

'I thought I made myself clear yesterday.'

He suppressed a sigh of exasperation. 'I'm not very bright. Why don't you spell things out for me?'

'All right, I will. Regardless of my commitment to maintaining Triangle Line as a passenger carrier, I'm unable to align myself with you because, as my father had, you and Marion have effectively locked me out of the company management.'

'You have this job . . .'

'Mr Lansing, you still have Arthur Parker looking for my first miniscule mistake. And I certainly haven't heard talk of promoting me even though my area's showing a tidy little profit.'

'You'd throw your votes with Jeremy Gates, knowing he wants to turn Triangle over to freight,' Lansing said with slow, deliberate emphasis.

'If he offered me the opportunity to do the work I'm capable of — yes.'

He permitted himself a little sarcasm. 'I'm shocked.'

'Sorry?' she said.

'Your father devoted his life to building the best passenger line . . .'

'I don't want to hear all this breast-beating about my father's devotion to passengers,' she interrupted testily. 'It's a sham.'

'Oh is it?' Lansing smacked his hand against the side of the desk. 'This desk, these offices, that uniform you're wearing . . . these belong to a sham passenger line, do they?'

'Well the shipping line's real enough,' she agreed. 'But passengers are people. And every time my father talked to me he proved how little he cared about what people could do or wished to do. You and Marion are just the same.'

'You've lost me.'

'I'm a person,' Kate explained as if to an idiot.

'What has that got to do with Triangle Line's ships continuing to carry passengers?'

'Everything. All of you are fine with the concept of people, but when a real live one comes knocking on the door saying let me in, she's as welcome as yesterday's news.'

'No room at the inn, eh?' Lansing could barely repress a sneer.

'You said it, not me.'

They glared at each other till Kate broke the silence with a short laugh.

'You find this funny?' said Lansing furiously.

'That just reminded me that a lot of the men in this company referred to my father as God . . . so I guess that does make me the daughter of God, doesn't it?'

'A novel concept.'

'I'm sure someone else has thought of it.'

'I'm sure,' he was amused now.

She stood up and prepared to leave, 'I have work to do.'

'I don't think we've finished talking.'

'This conversation isn't going anywhere,' she replied shortly. 'Goodbye.'

He made no further attempt to stop her leaving. He was too angry, although on the whole he felt he'd kept his temper well. Besides which, he knew something she didn't. He'd read George Terson's Will, and the daughter of God was in for the shock of her life.

At about the time Kate Laker was leaving Alan Lansing's office, Mr Collier-Brown was having a few uncomfortable moments in a police station on the other side of Amsterdam.

'Apologising doesn't change the fact that Miss Bailey and I were arrested by the Dutch police and have just spent a night in custody because of your incompetence Mr Collier-Brown.' Peter stopped there because his fury was choking him.

Mr Collier-Brown took the chance to get a word in edgeways. 'Nevertheless I'm terribly sorry. It took all night to check your credentials. That becomes a necessary formality when arrests are made on suspicion of drug trafficking.'

Peter looked the burly man up and down with contempt. 'Don't you English police have to notify someone when you take a case across international borders? Like the other country's police?'

'I'm afraid we just had some crossed wires . . .'

'If I crossed my wires this badly, Inspector, I'd be out of a job.'

Inspector Collier-Brown looked at his hands. He supposed they were entitled to their fury, although he was inwardly impatient at the waste of his time.

Jo spoke in a quiet exhausted voice. 'Didn't you know the Dutch police were after the same fellows you were?'

'As I said Miss Bailey, this has been an unfortunate case of the right hand not knowing what the left was doing.'

'Your first mistake was using Tony Grant as a double agent,' Peter snapped.

'Courier,' Collier-Brown corrected automatically.

'Sorry.'

'A courier. We think of people like Mr Grant as friendly couriers.'

Jo gave a short mirthless laugh. 'The thought of Tony as a friendly anything just seems too funny.'

'Where is he?' Peter demanded.

'I don't know,' the Inspector told him.

'You mean you haven't arrested him?' Peter couldn't believe his ears.

'There are no charges against him . . .' said the Inspector, visibly embarrassed.

'You mean we spent a night in gaol because he left us sitting where *he* was supposed to make a drug pick-up for *you* . . . and *he* walked away.'

'I'm afraid so.'

Peter looked at Jo, 'Tony's going to be sorry he set us up like this.'

Before returning to the ship they dropped into a small restaurant for breakfast. Over his meal Peter continued to rage, while Jo listened in weary silence.

'I don't see how you can be so calm,' he said. 'Tony knew those drugs were going to be delivered and he let us take the drop for him.'

'I'm not calm,' she told him. 'I'm just tired. And embarrassed. I don't want to think about it right now.'

'Tony's the one who's going to be embarrassed,' he said through clenched teeth.

'Forget about it Peter.'

'Why?'

'If you get into a spitting match with him you're going to end up playing just as dirty as he does. I know.'

'That's fine with me.'

'Peter . . .'

'All right, all right,' he said, to shut her up.

'I mean it.'

He managed a smile that was meant to be reassuring. 'I said all right. I won't do anything.' He saw that she was still looking suspicious. 'Relax. Eat your breakfast.'

For one other person the bright Amsterdam morning had brought no joy. Arthur Parker was confronting (or being confronted by) Alan Lansing, who had gone straight to see him in another part of the Triangle building as soon as Kate had departed.

'You haven't really explained what you're doing in Amsterdam, have you?' said Lansing.

'I come fairly frequently,' Parker assured him. 'I like to stay on top of everything sir.'

Lansing gave a long hard look to Parker, then to Sophie, then back to Parker again.

'Really?' he said.

'Yes sir.'

'There's something you ought to know.'

'What's that sir?'

About two weeks ago I looked at every receipt, every bill, every voucher, and every cancelled cheque you've generated in the past year.' He did not miss the sick look that washed over Arthur's face. 'Your records indicate you haven't been in Amsterdam at all in the past twelve months. So what is it that brought you here?'

'Well . . .' Parker was floundering.

Lansing favoured Sophie with his most charming smile. 'Not very fast on his feet is he? Was it my meeting with Jeremy Gates and Kate Laker?'

'Oh no . . .' Parker tried to recover himself.

'But you knew about it?' Lansing said remorselessly.

'Yes but . . .'

'All right then. Just come out with it. I couldn't blame you for being curious.'

Parker heaved a sigh of relief. He was off the hook. 'Well, yes . . .'

'You were curious,' Lansing repeated.

'A little.'

'You came to Amsterdam to satisfy your curiosity?' Lansing seemed to want everything spelled out.

'In a manner of speaking.' Parker was unwilling to commit himself totally.

'And you brought your secretary with you. To satisfy her curiosity?'

Parker began to panic. 'No — it wasn't that at all.'

'Why is she here?'

'She — she asked to come.'

'That's not true,' said Sophie in a quiet venomous voice.

'I beg your pardon?' Lansing turned to her.

'That's not true,' she said more firmly. 'I didn't ask to come along.'

'You did,' Parker squeaked. 'She did. She distinctly asked . . .'

'Be quiet Arthur,' said Lansing.

'But . . .'

'*Arthur.*'

Parker sank into an uneasy silence.

'This is a waste of my time,' Lansing went on. 'Let me tell you what I'm thinking.'

'Of course sir,' Parker practically stood to attention.

Lansing turned to Sophie. 'How long have you been Mr Parker's secretary?'

'Four years.'

'And would you say you know the ins and outs of the General Manager's office in some detail?'

'Yes.'

Lansing turned back to Parker. 'I like Sophie's directness Arthur. You often leave her in charge when you're out of the office, don't you?'

'Yes sir.'

'You trust her . . . feel confident she'll be able to handle any crises that come up.'

'Yes.' There wasn't much else he could say.

'I thought so,' said Lansing. 'I have confidence in her too. So much, in fact that if you make one more mistake . . . just one . . . I'm going to give her your job. I've got a list of complaints about you down to here,' he indicated his fingertips. 'It starts with insufficient profits, and goes right through to junketing in Amsterdam at company expense . . .'

'Mr Lansing . . .' Parker tried to say from a dry throat.

Lansing ignored him, and turned to Sophie. 'Don't you agree?'

'Yes I do,' she said without hesitation.

'She's marvellous,' said Lansing to Parker. 'Did you hire her?'

Parker nodded, unable to speak.

'Well, that's one thing you did right, isn't it?'

Peter Nuttall and Tony Grant, encountering each other in the Reception Area, were equally startled.

'You — you —' words failed Peter.

'Don't say it,' Tony begged. 'Don't say it. I'm sorry. I'm sorry man.'

'Sorry?'

'How did I know they'd take you for me?' We don't even resemble each other?'

'My God,' Peter moaned.

'What can I do to make it up to you?' He put a hand on Peter's arm.

'Don't touch me,' Peter snapped, pushing the arm away. He began to walk away, throwing over his shoulder: 'And don't talk to me.'

Tony pottered after him. 'Come on Peter. It was a mistake.'

To his surprise Peter stopped and turned to face him. His anger had apparently drained away, and he was smiling.

'Wait a minute,' he said. 'You're right.'

'About what?' said Tony, feeling he'd lost the thread of the argument.

'It was a mistake. I shouldn't be so angry.'

'Right,' said Tony, grinning with relief. 'Look here's the way it happened . . .'

'Not now, I haven't time. Tell me over a drink.'

'Yeah. All right.'

'Good,' said Peter pleasantly. 'Give me a call.'

'Will do.'

Peter had begun to move away. 'See you soon,' he called over his shoulder.

He was glad Tony couldn't see his face with its expression of concentrated hatred.

Jo Bailey was wondering if she was famous after all. At any rate it was the first time a man had stopped her in the street with the words, 'It's Jo Bailey isn't it?'

To cap it all he'd got out of a big shiny Mercedes.

'I'm Jeremy Gates,' he said, 'one of Triangle's Managing Directors. May I drive you back to the ship?' He showed her a card to prove identity.

'Is there something you want to talk to me about?' she asked warily.

She really felt she'd had enough for one day. After her breakfast with Peter she'd elected to remain in the city to do some shopping while he returned to the ship. Now she was laden with parcels, and all she wanted to do was get back. She certainly didn't want a chat with anybody.

'Yes,' he said. 'I understand you've been seeing quite a lot of Captain Anderson lately.'

'What does that matter to you?'

'I may be able to make it matter to you,' he said charmingly. 'More than it does now.'

'I don't understand.'

'There's no law that says an affair of the heart can't be of benefit to the wallet is there?'

She froze, staring at him over her parcels. 'Excuse me?'

He began to realise that his approach had been wrong. 'I don't think I put that quite the right way.'

'What are you talking about? Some sort of blackmail.'

'Not at all. Please let me begin again.' He thought for a moment. 'Are you aware that Captain Anderson owns five per cent of Triangle Line's shares?'

'No. And I don't think I want to have this conversation with you.'

'It's for the Captain's good, Miss Bailey. As well as yours.'

She took a couple of steps back. 'Somehow I doubt that.'

'Why don't you let me drive you back to the ship?'

'No thank you.'

An edge crept into his voice. 'If only because you're an employee of the line and I'm a Managing Director.'

'Mr. Gates,' she said, quietly angry. 'I've had a difficult night and I'm exhausted.'

'Then a ride is just what you need,' he gestured towards the open door of the car. 'I've a proposal to make that could be very much to your advantage — and to John Anderson's.'

Disbelieving, she climbed into the back seat. Though she'd have died rather than admit it, it was a blessed relief to get the weight off her feet. On the trip back to the ship she listened while he outlined what he wanted and where John fitted in.

'This is all very interesting,' she said at last. 'But I don't see what turning Triangle Line over to freight has to do with me. Or with John.'

'I want Captain Anderson's shares. I'm going to offer him a very handsome price. Soon. In the next few days.' She sat obstinately silent. 'The only objections I can imagine he might have to selling out are emotional — spiritual if you will.' Jo raised a quizzical eyebrow. 'A fanciful devotion to the idea of carrying passengers.'

'But why are you talking to me about this?'

'Because you seem the person most likely to be able to influence him insofar as his emotions are concerned.'

'Why would I want to . . .?'

'I can think of two reasons. First, for his own good. If the Captain sells me those shares he'll become — overnight — a very wealthy man. He'd be able to stop working and be more than comfortable for the rest of his life. If, on the other hand, your own welfare concerns you more than the Captain's, I'd be happy to make it worth your while to influence his thinking. I've made it my business to know a thing or two about you, Miss Bailey. And it seems to me you'd be foolish to turn your back on a substantial infusion of cash.'

For the rest of the journey she did her best to ignore him. When she got out of the car she had the satisfaction of knowing that she had left him guessing, but it was small comfort, and as she went back on board she felt sick and depressed. All she wanted to do was hide herself away in her cabin.

She was leaning back in a chair, her eyes closed, enjoying the blessed relief of a cigarette, when there came a knock at the door. She opened her eyes and looked towards it, but made no move to get up. Perhaps whoever it was would go away.

He didn't. The knock came again, more insistent this time. Sighing she got up and opened the door.

'Good morning, John,' she said in a subdued voice.

There was something tentative in his manner. 'Hello. May I come in?'

She couldn't meet his eyes, 'No . . .'

'Want to lick your wounds alone do you?' he said. The news of her night in gaol had reached him several hours ago.

'I think it would be best.'

'Why?'

'It's hard to explain.'

He took a step nearer to her, forcing her to step back.

'Let me come in,' he said firmly.

She sighed and retreated. She had not the energy to fight him.

'I'm trouble, trouble, trouble,' she said wretchedly. 'Always have been.'

'This wasn't your fault.'

'Doesn't matter.'

'Jo . . .'

'You're the Captain of this ship,' she said desperately. 'You don't need to be worrying about the scrapes I get myself into.'

'But it wasn't your fault,' he said adamantly.

Jo had been pacing up and down, but now she stopped and faced him.

'Listen to me John, your wife was a lady. I know it. I know she never saw the inside of a police station under any circumstances. *Any circumstances*. Certainly not from the inside of a cell.'

'Don't be ridiculous. Maya was Maya —' he paused as he thought what all this meant, '— and you're you,' he finished quietly.

'Right. Guaranteed to bring bad news and no double your money back.' She reached over to her bedside table to pick up some sheet music, and turned towards the door with an air of finality.

'You're hurting both of us,' he said.

'No. I'm doing us both a favour,' she said sadly. 'We're not that involved. Better to break it off now than give me time to drag us both into the gutter.' She opened the door.

'Listen to me Jo,' he pleaded.

'I have to rehearse darling. Shut the door behind you when you go.'

Matt Taylor thought that Alan Lansing certainly knew how to ruin anyone's day. Having called Kate in to see him early that morning he had followed it up with a call to Matt, also summoning him to a meeting. With the ship still trapped in Amsterdam, Matt and Kate had counted on spending the day together, but at this rate there wasn't going to be much of it left.

Alan Lansing came straight to the point.

'I want you to use whatever influence you have to encourage Miss

Laker to commit her shares to maintaining Triangle Lines as a passenger carrier,' he said.

'She knows her own mind,' said Matt.

Lansing paused for a moment before saying deliberately, 'You're wondering if our offer to make you Engineering Manager still stands?'

'It had occurred to me to wonder.'

'Well, of course, it still stands.'

'That's good to hear.'

'If I were you, though, I'd be asking myself why no one had given it to me in writing,' his eyes held Matt's steadily. 'You know how I want Kate Laker to vote.'

'He's about as subtle as a sledgehammer,' said Matt, telling Kate of it half an hour later.

'Just like my father was,' she agreed. 'What do you think I've been trying to tell you?'

'Hearing about it's one thing. Experiencing it's another.'

'Now you know,' she said with a touch of smugness.

He gave a small rueful smile. 'I didn't really want to be Engineering Manager anyway.'

She patted his arm sympathetically. 'Poor thing. I'd vote with Marion if I could. I'm more concerned with passengers than she'll ever be.'

'Forget about it.'

'But how would you feel if *your* late father's mistress demanded your support for some pseudo-humanistic transport system that was going to exclude you?' she said. 'Would you give her your vote, knowing she'd never let you be a part of it?'

'No.'

'Or would you vote for the plan that *would* include you?'

'That's what I'd do,' he said, wishing she would drop the subject.

'I know it's boring,' she said, looking at him in exasperation. 'But this company's in my blood and I want a bigger part in it than just sitting at home clipping its coupons. Oh never mind, I can't explain.'

'Never mind explaining. We still have time to spend the day together.'

They made a hurried return to the ship to change out of their uniforms into casual clothes, and then sallied forth again. This time they left the car on board and took a taxi into the centre of town. For the first time, Kate felt like a tourist in this city and for a few hours she forgot her troubles in Matt's determination to make her enjoy herself. He bought her flowers in the flower-market, took her to the zoo as if she had been a little girl, and laughed at her when she wobbled on her bike.

Once inside the park, Kate leaned her bike against a tree. Matt took a few determined steps towards her, and when he was standing directly in front of her he fell on both knees.

'Matt?' she said, puzzled

He held up a hand for silence. He seemed to be preparing himself for something. 'Don't say anything,' he commanded.

'But . . .'

'Kate, I want to make mad passionate love to you,' he declared. 'I've tried to be smooth. I've been macho. But that hasn't worked, so now I'm begging.'

'My God, get up,' she said, trying to keep a straight face. 'You'll catch cold.'

'No,' he said firmly.

'Someone might see you.'

'I don't care.'

'I care,' she said, amused.

He flung out his arms ecstatically. 'I've been waiting for you to say that. Come to my place. Tonight. Please.'

'All right, yes.'

Instead of getting up he sat back on his heels and looked up at her with his head on one side.

'Yes?' he said.

'Yes.'

'What about all those issues? The objections you had?' he said suspiciously.

'I've decided I'm not going to worry so much about compromising myself professionally since the big fish in the Triangle pond do it so readily,' she told him. 'We'll still have to be discreet.'

This time he sat down properly.

'I can't,' he declared flatly.

'Why not?'

'You've knocked the wind out of me.'

Chapter 19

Jo Bailey was in a fine temper when she presented herself at John's quarters at about nine o'clock that night. The way he had coolly summoned her into his presence was bad enough, but to have done it over the public loud-speaking system was the limit.

'Ah,' he said when he opened the door to her. 'You decided to come,' he looked at his watch. 'But you're late.'

'I'm not accustomed to being given orders,' she said crossly.

'I'm not accustomed to being given the brush-off,' he replied smoothly. 'Come in won't you?'

She went past him and he waved her to a seat on the sofa.

'I wouldn't dream of asking you to meet me anywhere compromising, like the bedroom,' he assured her.

'You didn't ask, you ordered. And this does compromise me.'

'How?'

'I said I thought we ought to stop seeing each other.'

He sat down facing her. 'You know Jo, a captain develops a pretty good instinct for people when he's been in the business as long as I have. My instinct now tells me you don't really want to break off this relationship before it's even had a chance. I think you're lying about your reasons.'

She was on her feet in a flash. 'Don't insult me John. I've had enough insults in my days.'

He grabbed her wrist before she could get past him.

'I'm not insulting you. I'm trying to get you to tell me the truth. There's more to this than you're telling me.'

'You're not helping your case by twisting my arm.'

Shocked, he dropped her wrist like a hot potato. 'I'm sorry I . . .'

'It's all right,' she said miserably.

'I just didn't want you to go.'

'Oh John . . .' she was too confused and upset to do more than say his name. But looking at his face she saw a sadness that more than matched her own. It decided her. 'There is something I didn't tell

251

you,' she admitted. 'This morning Jeremy Gates stopped me in the street.'

Briefly she outlined the entire conversation with Gates. His lips tightened but he said, 'What Jeremy Gates does — or tries to do — has nothing to do with us.'

'It has,' she said urgently. 'I'm always liable to be seen as a — a chink in your armour. There are things in my past. Things that could be used against you.'

'Will you tell me about them?' he said gently.

'If you like.'

'Then we've nothing to worry about. I'm not the Prince of Wales you know. I don't have to choose my companions from the royal families of Europe,' she smiled and he stretched out his hand, drawing her closer. 'There was one time in my life I met a woman I knew was different from all the rest,' he said. 'It was like two pieces of a puzzle, you know? Fit them together and make the picture whole. No other piece of the puzzle would have worked with me. I spent sixteen years with Maya and I don't regret a day of it.'

'John . . .' She didn't want to hear any more.

He grasped her hands tightly and went on as though she hadn't spoken. 'I never thought I'd have that feeling again. But I do, Jo. I don't care about the past. I feel luckier right now than any man has a right to be.'

'Please . . .' despite the happiness that was beginning to creep over her, she suddenly felt she couldn't bear any more. But John interpreted her reluctance by the light of his own doubts. He realised that he had taken for granted that her feelings were the same.

'I'm sorry,' he said, drawing back in dismay. 'I'm embarrassing you.'

'It's not that,' she whispered.

'I've said too much. I'm sorry. I thought you felt the same way.'

He tried to withdraw his hand from hers, but her grip on him tightened painfully. He waited for her to be able to speak.

'I do,' she said at last, and let herself be drawn unresisting into his arms.

Kate, returning to her own cabin to collect something twenty minutes later, paused in the corridor at the sound of voices coming from John's cabin. She was not normally an eavesdropper, but once she had heard the name Jeremy Gates, nothing would have torn her away.

'Jeremy Gates is an extremely ambitious man,' she heard John's voice say faintly from behind his door. 'Also said to be very competent. But apparently desperate to put his own stamp on the company.'

Then Kate jumped slightly at the sound of Jo Bailey's voice replying, 'I don't see how he could be very competent, trying to use me to influence the way you use your vote in Triangle Line. It seems like an awfully crude tactic, don't you think?'

'George Terson wouldn't have done it,' said John. 'Come in.' These last words were in response to Kate's knock at the door. She had heard enough to decide her.

When she had refused John's offer of a drink he noticed the set expression on her face and said jovially, 'Surely you're not here on business.'

'It's a bit late in the day for business.'

For the first time Kate noticed Jo, whose hair was in slight disarray, and whose eyes were definitely shining. John had kept his composure slightly better, but there was a new air about him too, which told its own story. Good luck to them, Kate thought. But she was determind to keep her mind on other things now.

'Actually I just overheard something the two of you were talking about,' she said bluntly. 'I couldn't help it. The door was open.' She turned to Jo. 'I may be crazy, but you seemed to be saying that Jeremy Gates tried to get you to influence the way *you* —' she turned to John, 'use your shares in Triangle Line.'

'Yes luv, I'm afraid he did,' said Jo.

Kate frowned as she tried to concentrate. Wheels were spinning in her head.

'How much stock do you have in this company?' she asked John.

'Quite a lot.'

She asked the sixty-five thousand dollar question. 'Not as much as five per cent of the voting shares . . .?'

Very slowly John nodded. After staring at him for a moment Kate burst out laughing. The other two stared at her, baffled.

'I'm sorry,' she said when she'd got herself back under control.

'You think the future of this line's a laughing matter, do you?' said John, a trifle stiffly.

'Not at all.'

'You *are* laughing.'

'Not because I don't care about Triangle Line. I'm laughing because I've finally worked out why everyone's put so much effort into getting me off this ship. I'm living next door to the swing votes —*you*. They were afraid I'd influence you.'

It made sense, John had to admit. Reluctantly he allowed his attention to be diverted from Jo to company business and listened as Kate poured out the story of her meeting yesterday with Gates and Lansing. He was unwilling though to accept her version of Marion's character. He was fond of Marion from way back.

'I'm sorry to disillusion you, John,' said Kate impatiently. 'But Marion is just as devious as Jeremy Gates. Lansing tailors his work to her orders.'

John looked at her silently, but his silence was a rejection.

'I'd like to tell you,' Kate went on, 'who Alan Lansing tried to use to force *my* hand but . . .'

'You're entitled to some privacy,' said John, a jump ahead of her.

'And I hope you understand why I can't support Marion and Lansing with my vote.'

He did. 'I wouldn't support them either if it meant I was going to be put out of a job. Passengers or no passengers. A man — a woman — is entitled to work.'

Before she could answer, the harsh sound of the Tannoy filled the room.

'Jo Bailey — please come to the Radio Room.'

'This must be my day to be paged,' said Jo with a smile at John. 'It's probably Jeremy Gates calling to see if I've influenced you yet.'

But when she picked up the telex that had arrived for her it was not from Gates but something much more interesting and exciting. Jo, however, did not seem excited. She took it down to her cabin and stood there reading it over and over.

'Isn't that just the way!' she said bitterly before throwing it into the waste bin.

After the havoc wrought by Susan, Matt's relationship with Joe Francis had settled down into a more or less friendly truce. They had worked out the situation in a second row, in which Matt had spoken his mind frankly.

'If you want out Joe, just holler.'

'That's not what I want Mate. Just the truth from you.'

They were arguing in the workshop which made it vital for a discussion to be carried on with raised voices. Somehow that helped.

'You'll never believe it,' Matt yelled. 'Sow a seed of mistrust in any relationship and it's never the same again. And it's always a woman who does the sowing.'

'Please,' Joe glared.

'Right. I'll tell you Joe. I say you're a lousy drinker. You cheat at patience, you don't change your socks till your shoes refuse to let them in. But you're one of the best in the game, which is why I put up with you.' He turned and walked away but turned abruptly to toss a large spanner at Joe. 'Catch!'

The spanner hit the floor as Joe stood staring at Matt, not quite sure how to take all this.

'And you're a no good fielder,' Matt complained. 'Just a toothless lion.'

Nothing more had been said, and some of their old camaraderie seemed to have returned. Tonight all was well between them as Matt made his rounds of the Engine Room, before knocking off for the night. It was an effort for him to keep his mind on the job. Part of it kept veering off towards the coming night — and Kate.

'How are we doing?' Joe bellowed above the noise of the engines.

'If you'll clean up that oil next to Number Three top marks,' Matt roared back.

'Done.' Whey they had progressed a few paces Joe added casually, 'Did you hear Sandy's coming back at Felixstowe?'

Matt smiled kindly. 'Don't kill her with attention.'

'You shouldn't joke about it,' said Joe earnestly.

'Sorry. Didn't mean anything.'

Matt gave Joe a friendly punch on the arm and went on with his checks but his mind was racing ahead to ten o'clock, when Kate was due to appear in his cabin — clutching a bottle of champagne. In the circumstances he thought the champagne was probably superfluous, but it was a nice thought.

Linda's throat was dry and her hands were wet. Now that the moment had come her courage was deserting her. But she was going to do it anyway — for Larry.

She'd tried every method she knew to get Larry a job on board this ship. She'd appealed to Miss Laker and to Tom Kelly, and they'd both put her off with vague words about later. Later was no good to Linda. She wanted some practical help, now. And the only person who had offered it was Peter Nuttall. And he, in return, had made the incredible demand that she commit a theft and implicate Tony Grant.

He hadn't told her why he wanted this, merely that it was his price. But he'd added that if Linda co-operated, Larry was assured of a job on the ship, where she could watch over him.

So now here she was, in the Casino, looking for a likely wallet or handbag, The sooner it was done the better, she reckoned. So intent was she on her purpose that she didn't notice Tom Kelly leaning against a wall nearby, looking as if he was killing time.

She found what she wanted at last, a ladies' wallet resting in the top of a wide-open shoulder bag whose owner was intent on the roulette wheel. It was the work of a moment to lift the wallet out and slide it into a deep pocket in her dress. Then she gave a quick look round and headed for the exit. Now for Tony's cabin.

Once outside, however, things started to go wrong. Tom appeared out of nowhere and grasped her arm.

'Give me that wallet,' he demanded.

'What wallet?' she blustered. 'Get your own wallet.'

Without further argument he thrust his hand into her pocket.

'Get your hands out of there,' she shrieked. 'I'll scream.'

'That wouldn't be very clever. You don't want to draw attention to yourself.'

He found the wallet and held it up. 'They might throw you in the brig for larceny.'

'It's mine.'

'Linda, I saw you lift it off the lady in there.'

'She's a friend.'

'You're a liar and a thief.'

She subsided into a raging silence.

'That's better,' he said.

'What are you going to do?' she demanded.

'Something against my better judgement. I'm going back in there to give this to Tony. Tell him I found it and let him ask the people at the table if it belongs to any of them.'

'But Tom . . .' she wept.

'Are you crazy?' he demanded angrily. 'Do you need money that badly?'

'I need that wallet.'

'Stay here till I come out.'

'I won't.'

He shook his finger at her like a schoolteacher. 'You will, or the next person you'll be talking to will be a lawyer.'

He left her, and she waited, furious but scared, until he returned.

'Now,' he said, when he'd got her in his cabin and made her sit down. 'You have a pretty good job. Why turn to a life of crime? Linda —' he sat down beside her and put a hand on her arm. 'You are in trouble.'

'I'm not,' she said, half-sobbing.

'Don't lie to me. Tell me what's wrong.'

She turned her head away. 'There's nothing wrong with me. I was just trying to get my brother a job on the ship.'

'By stealing a wallet?' he said, confused.

'It's a long story,' she said wearily.

'Well tell me.' She said nothing, and he went on in a gentle voice, 'If you can't tell me, who are you ever going to tell? Do you want to carry this around all shut up inside — forever?'

It was impossible to resist that kindly tone. The story came out in fits and starts. But on one point she was adamant. No names.

'Come on,' he urged. 'Tell me who's trying to get Tony.'

'Sorry. I told you the rest. I just can't tell you that. Wouldn't be right.'

'It wasn't right for that person to involve you,' he said.

'No I can't.'

'Suit yourself,' he said, realising he wasn't going to get any further at the moment. 'Now will you do what I say, and stop feeling responsible for your whole family?'

'Yeah, all right,' she said listlessly.

'Good,' he opened the door ready to go. 'I've got to relieve Charles. Stay and finish your crisps. Shut the door when you go.'

'I will.'

He leaned down and gave her a peck on the cheek. 'You're a good girl Linda. Don't do anything like this again.'

'I won't.'

She sat rubbing her cheek for a long time after he had gone, a wistful look in her eyes. Tom Kelly hadn't solved her problem for her — but he'd unwittingly managed to give her a new one.

After the scene in the park Kate had assumed — perhaps naïvely — that the gremlins that had always managed to thwart her affair with Matt before it even got started had finally recognised the inevitable and given up. It wasn't until she presented herself at his cabin door at ten o'clock that night, champagne in hand, that she discovered her mistake.

The messenger from the gods came in the unlikely form of Joe Francis whom she met emerging from Matt's cabin, a look of deep gloom on his face.

'Is something wrong?' she asked.

'Yeah. I forgot to clean up some oil below. He slipped. Hit his head.'

'Is he all right?' she asked, alarmed.

'Oh yeah. We got a doctor off the passenger list. Says he just has to keep quiet in bed till tomorrow.'

'Thank goodness for that.'

'Yeah, but it was all my fault.'

'I wouldn't worry about that if I were you,' she said, trying to keep the champagne hidden. 'I think I'll pop in and say hello.'

'I can't help worrying,' Joe fretted. 'He told me to clean up the oil.'

'We all make mistakes,' said Kate, wishing he'd go away.

'All the same . . .' he started to move off.

'Don't worry,' she smiled brightly. 'Good night.'

'Good night.' At last he turned the corner, and she was free to go in, which she did without knocking.

The room was in semi-darkness. Matt lay in bed, a small piece of plaster decorating his forehead.

'He said no activity,' Matt said as soon as he saw her. 'Flat on my back.'

If she hadn't been so disappointed herself she would have laughed at his mournful voice.

'I know you feel awful,' she said. Then to cheer him up she added. 'How do you think I feel?'

'I only have to stay this way till tomorrow,' he said in a voice of deep gloom.

'It's really very funny,' she said, her lips beginning to twitch.

'Not to me,' he sulked.

After a moment he hauled himself part of the way up in bed and reached for her.

'To hell with it,' he said recklessly.

She took a step back. 'Don't be an ass. Do what the doctor said.'

Matt let his head fall back on the bed, and groaned miserably.

'I'll come back another time,' said Kate, forcing herself to move away. 'The champagne will keep.'

'I don't believe this is happening,' he moaned.

Kate stopped, hesitant. Her own sense of deprivation warred with her desire to comfort him. At last she moved over and dropped to her knees beside the bed.

'Wouldn't life be boring if things always happened the way we planned them?' she suggested.

'Not in this case,' he said firmly.

'We'll have other opportunities.'

'Wait,' he said, struck by sudden inspiration.

'What?'

'The doctor said no activity till tomorrow.'

'Right.'

'Who said tomorrow has to start at sunrise?'

'It usually does,' she said, not sure she caught his drift.

'Wrong. Midnight,' he gave her a gleeful smile.

'You're willing to risk your health?' she said, part disapproval, part admiration.

'What good is health without happiness?' he said impishly.

He was feeling better with every second that passed.

'It's a good offer, isn't it?' said John wretchedly.

'The best I've had in thirteen years,' said Jo. She gave a dejected sigh.

They were standing just inside John's quarters, arms round each other, trying vainly to dispel the gloom that had been caused by the arrival of the telex offering Jo a long engagement in London.

'You'll really get to play the West End?' said John. She nodded. 'Is the money good?'

'Very good.'

'Then I think you have to go, don't you?'

'How can you say that?'

'It seems fairly clear,' he said heavily.

'Clear?' she sounded indignant. 'It's anything but clear. I meant what I said John. I feel the same way about you that you say you feel about me.'

She brightened suddenly, 'I've had a wonderful idea.'

'Don't keep it to yourself,' he urged.

'I could take this job in London. And you could sell all your shares in Triangle Line and come with me.'

'It may bear thinking about,' he said slowly.

'And then I had a terrible thought.'

'What?'

'What if I decided to stay on the ship to be with you, and *then* you sold your shares — and left me.'

'Oh Jo.'

'I feel like we're not alone. As if those shares are so important that they're like another woman in your life. You could leave me for them.'

He laughed out loud. 'A classic — no, not so classic — triangle.'

'What do you mean?'

'I feel the same way about this job offer you've got. Like it's going to steal you from me.' He laughed again.

'I don't think it's very funny,' she said, displeased.

He gave her a squeeze. 'We'll sort it out. Don't worry. We'll sort it out.'

'What are you thinking about?' said Susan.

She and Charles were high up on Deck Eight, huddled against the wind, looking out over the dark sea. She had the frustrating feeling that he so often gave her — that he had slipped away into another world of which she was not a part. For some reason she often felt lonelier than ever these days. Charles took her out whenever they docked, came constantly to her cabin to make love to her, and generally behaved as she had once dreamed of. And yet she was tormented by the thought that she never really reached him.

He said now, as he so often said, 'Nothing really.' And the answer shut her out.

'You look so serious,' she tried again.

'Do you really want to know?' he said, turning and speaking with unusual gentleness.

'Of course.'

'We hardly ever talk about things that are very personal.'

'I know,' she said sadly.

'I was thinking about Jenny,' he looked at her. 'Do you want me to go on?'

'Yes if you want to,' she said bravely.

'I was thinking about our child.'

'I didn't know you had a child.'

'We didn't. But Jenny was pregnant when she was killed. I was wondering what the child would have been like. You know — a boy or a girl — what sort of mother Jenny would have been.'

'Oh Charles, I'm so sorry.' For a moment all other feeling was lost in compassion for him.

'Come on,' he said, 'don't look so sad.'

She was silent. There was no way she could tell him her thought — that if only she could get pregnant he might love her as much as he'd loved Jenny.

'What time is it?' said Kate for the twentieth time. She didn't want to move her head which was in a comfortable position. She had slid down till she was half lying in her chair, and her feet were propped on Matt's coverlet.

'Ten minutes to twelve?' said Matt looking at his wall clock.

'It's your turn to talk.'

'I've got a question.'

'All right.'

'What's your husband like?'

'He's a failure —' said Kate after a moment's thought. 'Personally and professionally. He's a drunk. He gambles. And when he gambles he loses. He's unpleasant in the morning because he can't wake up. He's unpleasant at night because he can't get to sleep . . .'

'Then why are you still married to him?'

'I suppose because I feel sorry for him.'

'Fine. But why stay *married* to him?'

'I support him.'

'*You support him?* Why?'

'Because I feel sorry for him.'

'That's ridiculous. Why don't you divorce him?'

'I told you . . .'

'And marry me.'

She was so thunderstruck that all she could think of to say was, 'Oh come on . . .'

'Really,' he said seriously. He saw her giving him a sceptical look and hurried on, 'Look, Kate, underneath all this sophisticated packaging I'm just a working-class boy with a basic set of working-class sensibilities. Marriage is part of the picture.'

She smiled. 'You're very funny.' She was still treading warily, uncertain how to take any of this.

'What time is it?' he said.

'Six minutes to twelve.'

He hauled himself upright. 'I can't take any more of this. Your watch is six minutes slow. It's midnight.'

She got up, smiling. 'I'll open the champagne.'

'Forget the champagne. Just come to bed.'

She looked at his narrow bed. 'Do you think there's room in there for all of us?'

'*All* of us?'

She began to tick off on her fingers, 'You, me, my former husband, my present husband, my job, your job, your future job . . . if Lansing gives it to you . . .'

'*Yes*,' he said firmly.

'You're not just saying that?'

'No, I mean it. Now would you please come to bed?'

He turned out the light.

Chapter 20

'Signed, witnessed, dated and all in order. If you have any questions . . .'

Nicholas Stevens allowed his voice to trail off as he came to the end of George Terson's Will. He knew for sure there'd be questions. Kate Laker was white with rage.

'Yes,' she said at once. 'A couple. You're doing Alan Lansing's job. Why? And who *are* you Mr Stevens?'

'Ask me,' said John.

'I'm asking him,' she stated.

Stevens gave her a slight bow. 'Do you want my full CV, Miss Laker?'

'I'll take anything I can get,' she said through suppressed fury. 'You've just read my father's will leaving damn near everything —' she flashed a look at Marion, '— what do I call you now? Mummy? And yes, I'd like to know which cupboard you've been kept in.'

'Leave it Kate,' said John.

'I'll look after myself, John,' said Stevens smoothly.

He was a dark, vividly good-looking man in his mid-thirties. Behind the slightly flashy features lurked a sharp brain. He was alive to all the tensions that were now pulsating round the great hall of the magnificent Elizabethan house that had once been George Terson's and now belonged to his widow. One thing that stood out a mile to him was that he, Marion and John Anderson were all on the same side. It was Kate Laker who was the outsider.

To her he turned his full attention.

'Alan Lansing is in Singapore, completing contracts on an hotel chain the company's buying. I'm nine months into a retainer which has been renewed yearly for the past nine years and designed to look after Mr Terson's personal affairs. The Law Society will furnish my credentials.'

'I bet they will,' Kate snapped.

'Check them,' he said easily. 'Then apologise.'

Her eyes blazed. I've been left a two up and two down shack in a

Felixstowe field, and my new stepmother gets the rest. All from a death-bed marriage. How will your Law Society see that?'

'Not their function . . .' he said with a shrug.

'My marriage to George had nothing to do with his Will,' said Marion. 'That was made years ago. George wanted — George just wanted — George . . .' she stopped, unable to go on. John gripped her hand.

'It's completely watertight, Miss Laker,' Stevens assured her. 'I drew it up. You can, of course, instruct your own solicitors. It's up to you. But I'm very good at my job and although it'll mean very little to you, your father gave a lot of thought to your bequest.'

'Well good,' she told him. 'Because it'll give me a lot of pleasure seeing it burn.'

Marion lifted her head and spoke through tears. 'Kate please, if you're serious — please don't do that.'

'Oh yes, I'm serious.'

John turned on her. 'All right, it's yours,' he said furiously. 'Burn it down. Why not? There's been a lot of destroying. Bit more won't do any harm — unless you know who you're harming and it might just be you. Two things, Kate. George loved Marion and he loved you. She wanted his love. You didn't. It was your choice, so stop kicking.'

Her eyes blazed back at him. 'Talk about things you understand or keep out of it John.'

He refused to be silenced. 'Someone should have got hold of you many years ago ago and belted the life out of you — now you wouldn't even feel it.'

He got up and left the room to stop himself saying any more. Marion forced herself to be calm.

'Nick — please —' she said.

At a nod from her Stevens followed John out of the hall and the two women were alone.

'I don't want that cottage destroyed Kate. Name your price.'

'You can't afford it,' said Kate shortly.

'George was born and grew up there. It was special to him.'

'And that's why he left it to me. *Okay Marion.* I know all that. Why do you think I'm destroying it?'

'You can't.'

'Watch me. It's my property and I'll do what I like with it.'

'And the company's mine,' said Marion, roused to fight back 'Don't take me on Kate.'

'I'm going to contest that Will.'

'Fine. But you're wasting your time.'

'Not if I win.'

'The Will is watertight,' said Marion wearily.

'What makes you so sure?'

'Common sense. And an ability to read small print. John told you to stop kicking. Listen to him. You've got your shares — what I've got I built up with your father. And the things I'll hold on to will be those that keep George alive for me. You sneered at our marriage. Well, he wanted it. Had wanted it for years — but we were married from the beginning in our minds and bodies, and that's all I needed — ever.'

'If I believe you Marion, I'd've wasted too many years hating you and him — and you know why.'

'Yes, I know why,' said Marion sadly. 'And I know that now we either find a way of understanding each other or destroying each other. I've had enough fighting.'

'Olive branch Marion?' Kate's voice was almost a sneer.

'Yes — I'm offering.'

'I don't trust it.'

In the grounds outside the two men sought masculine sanctuary from the primeval threat of two quarrelling women.

'I was asked to leave,' said Nick.

'Why do you think I got out?' said John. 'Apart from losing my temper, those two terrify me.'

'Put them in a circus,' Nick suggested. 'Let them scratch their eyes out for money.'

'Certain lack of respect Nick,' said John, unwilling to concede how much this idea appealed to him.

'No, I'm full of it. Just hope they don't tear the line apart. George was intuitive about trouble. He'd let it bubble away, then just turn the fire out. Kick it out,' he added with sudden emphasis.

'Gates?' said John, latching on to the final words.

'Eh? Oh, not my job. Marion, Lansing, and maybe Miss Laker — their problem.'

'And my five per cent?'

'Well then, it's up to you. I do know George was ready to move.'

'And Marion?' John asked.

'I'll check. Though if I had five per cent of this lot I wouldn't be asking questions.'

'It's not real old son,' said John easily.

'Real enough to buy your own ship.'

John stopped dead. 'That much?' he said in disbelief. 'Two thousand quid, twelve years ago.'

'Oh the company was one small freighter then. It's a conglomerate now. You're very wealthy John.'

John shrugged indifferently. 'You've got to like money to use it, and I've never been that bothered. It'll be there when I need it.'

'Read the papers.' Stevens advised him. 'Don't be too sure.'

When John and Kate had departed Stevens went up to Marion's room where he found her packing.

'Sorry we couldn't talk before the meeting,' he said. 'But I'm always running late these days.'

'It's going well, isn't it?'

'Better than I could have hoped for,' he told her. 'George's introductions were the key, and I've had to take on a couple of partners.'

'Big time lawyer,' she ribbed him affectionately.

'Growing,' he agreed cheerfully. 'Marion — are you all right?'

'Silly question,' she sighed.

'Silly question. But let me do whatever I can.'

'If I need, I'll ask.'

'Holiday?' he indicated the nearly full suitcase.

'I shouldn't think so. I'm going on the ship. I want my time full, and there's no point trying to run something if you don't understand it. I'm okay with the books, so now I'll learn how the money comes in.'

'What about Alan Lansing?'

'I'm meeting him in Amsterdam. He needs a lot of signatures.'

'You know about Gates?' Stevens said. 'George was ready to move him — out.'

'Yes, we talked.' As always at the mention of George her face tightened with pain.

'I think he was right,' Stevens went on. 'If it's a fight with Kate, don't forget John's five per cent.'

'Dear Nick — I've built this company up with George, and I know every piece of it. Please don't worry about me.'

'Shall I carry your bag then?'

'Now there's a good suggestion.'

'It's what little brothers are for.'

'She's got the lot,' said Kate furiously as she got into the Saab beside Matt. He had been waiting for her outside the house.

'The lot?' he said.

'Everything. The line's under new management. Hers.'

'You didn't get anything?' he said, aghast for her. 'I mean, your old man was loaded. He could've spread it about a bit more.'

'Oh yes — I inherit a mud hut in a Felixstowe field.'

'Maybe he had a sense of humour, your old man,' Matt mused.

'Well I'm not laughing,' her tone became warning. 'And I hope you're not.'

'Who me?' he said quickly. 'Wouldn't dare. That's that then.'

'Far from it,' she said with a set face. 'I'm a fighter — hadn't you noticed?'

'Sure I'd noticed. Along with a few other things about you.'

His warm gaze was an attempt to take her back to the ecstatic night they'd shared a week ago. There had been other nights since, and there would be others in the future, but that first one was special to both of them for the sense of joyful discovery that could never come again after the first time.

But Kate was too far gone in her private anger to respond to him now. After a while she said, 'Let's go home.'

'Home?'

'The ship you fool. Where else is there?'

When they were back on board she made him take a walk with her along the windy deck.

'Clears the cobwebs,' she said.

'What are you talking about?'

'You're thick Matt,' she told him pleasantly.

'Yeah, I know. But I got a kind face.'

'I'm talking about this ship — home.'

'We can get closer to home,' he said hopefully. 'Your cabin's closer.'

'I see.'

'It isn't bad though, is it?' he said, determined to bring her back to a level he could reach.

'What isn't?'

'You and me,' he said patiently. 'Us.'

She looked round her. 'Do you see me owning all this?' she said. 'What would you say?'

'Not much. Call you ma'am if you like,' he offered.

'Seriously Matt.'

'Okay, so Mrs Terson has got what you want . . .'

'It should have been mine Matt. I can't help it. I know how it seems, but I inherited ambition from him as well as a shack.'

'You'll give yourself ulcers lady.'

'What about you?' she challenged him. 'You've been made an offer. What are you doing about it?'

'Thinking.'

'Well done. Do you want to share?'

'Not until I know you better.'

'You know me pretty damn well now. What else do you want?'

'More,' he said promptly, and led her away to his cabin..

As soon as John heard that Marion was on board he invited her to his cabin.

'I didn't have a chance to say — well — how sorry I am — about George,' he said.

'Thank you John.'

'If there's anything I can do — anything at all - just say the word.'

'There are so many loose ends, but I think I'll manage.'

'I'm sure you will. Just remember I'm here. Would you like a drink?'

'I don't think so, thank you.'

John sat down facing her. 'He was a fine man.'

She sighed sadly. 'Sometimes I think I'm the only person who saw that in him.'

'He couldn't have managed without you. I know that for sure.'

'That steel front he presented to the world . . .'

'He had to Marion. He was a businessman. He had a job to do, and he did it well.'

'He was fond of you . . .' she said affectionately, and held up a hand to silence his protest. 'Yes, I mean it, he was. Even when things were bad, he'd come back sometimes and say, "Met Anderson — we had a drink," and that's all he ever said. But I could tell he was — pleased in your company. Thank you for that.'

For a moment he was embarrassed by her sadness. 'I just wish there was something I could do, something I could say . . .' he offered wretchedly.

'There isn't.'

'I'm sorry.'

'You take it for granted,' she mused, 'having a person round you for years — even if it's only a voice at the end of the phone, or a hurried dinner between voyages. But you know it's someone who'll always come back, always be there. Then, pow! Nothing. No more — ever.

'George is gone and I'm left *feeling* as though I've lost an arm and *knowing* I've lost my very best friend. We had this joke, George and I. I always told him he'd outlive me. "The best always go first," I said, and we laughed about it.'

The tears were streaming down her face.

'Funny isn't it? I was right. The best did go first . . .'

After a night spent planning what he'd say to Sandy the first time he saw her again, Joe Francis found that his mind had gone blank when he came across her in the crew pub. She looked thinner, and there was a wariness in her face that hadn't been there before. But to his eyes she was just as pretty.

In the end he settled for saying, 'It's good to have you back Sandy,' as he slipped onto a stool beside her.

'Thank you,' she gave him a pallid smile.

'I missed you.'

'Didn't receive a get-well card.'

'Didn't send one.'

'That explains it.'

'Are you better?' he asked, half scared to touch on the subject.

She slightly side-stepped the question. 'Wouldn't 've let me out otherwise, would they?'

'Suppose not. I was wondering . . .'

'Yes Joe . . .'

'I've never —' his courage was deserting him, 'you're the first girl I've ever felt anything for — seriously.'

'Am I Joe?' She looked him in the face.

'Thing is, I'm not too sure what I feel.'

'Sounds confusing . . .'

'It is — very. I don't see you — I want a drink. I do see you — I need a drink — for courage, like.'

'Seems you spend most of your time drinking then,' she said after a moment. 'My fault?'

'Don't be daft,' he said awkwardly.

After a moment she reached over and touched his arm.

'Could we try again?' she said softly. 'I didn't mean to hurt you. With Peter 'n' everything — I got confused.'

'Same as me,' he confessed. 'We're just a confused pair. Love, it's all right. Really it is.'

'Perhaps I can help you sort out those feelings,' she said, still in the same soft tone.

'Perhaps you can.'

'Well, don't just sit there —' she smiled at him. 'Get us some orange juice.'

'Orange juice?'

'For courage Joe. It'll make a change from booze.'

Charles was preparing to go on duty when Susan stepped into his cabin, and he said, 'I'm in a hurry.'

She tried not to flinch. Too often that was his greeting to her these days. They seemed a million miles from the moment of closeness they had achieved up on Number Eight deck when he had told her about the baby. Never mind, she reassured herself. In just a second all that would be changed.

'Charles, what would make you happy?' she asked. '*Really* happy?'

He looked startled, but not pleased. 'I hadn't thought about it. Nothing, I suppose.'

'Nothing?' she fought down a twinge of dismay.

'Since my wife and child were scraped off some road I don't give the idea of "happiness" too much attention,' he explained patiently.

'Charles I . . . something I *know*, I'm convinced will make you happy . . .'

'Okay, what is it?' he said impatiently. 'What have you dreamed up this time?'

She took a deep breath. 'I'm pregnant.'

'What?' he stared at her blankly.

'You and I — our own child —'

She knew at once that the gamble had failed. The deadness in his eyes was giving way to a rage that seemed to consume him.

'You stupid . . .' he choked.

'Charles.'

'Is this what you planned for? Force me into a corner with your emotions and your tears?'

'Charles, I thought . . .'

He was beside himself. 'Thought? You didn't think at all, you stupid female. So this is how it's done. Emotional blackmail. Have you got a father with a shot-gun?'

'Oh my God . . .' she wept.

'Yes sweetheart, it doesn't work,' he sneered. 'You made a mistake this time.'

'I thought you'd be pleased . . . what you wanted, after . . .'

'That was *her*,' he yelled. 'Jenny. You're not my wife, never could be. Go away woman — just *go away*.'

Blinded by her tears she stumbled to open the door, and fled.

The one person Tom Kelly had never expected to find when he opened his door that evening was Linda. Still less had he expected to find her done up to the nines. He had to admit that she looked stunning — but he was disconcerted none the less.

'I never thanked you for that advice — about my brother,' she offered by way of explanation.

'Think nothing of it Linda.'

'But I think about it all the time.'

He didn't know how to answer this, and decided not to try. 'You're looking a knock-out tonight. Got a date?' he asked.

'I hope so. You.'

'You're joking.'

'Strange as it may seem, no I'm not — for once.'

'Linda, love . . .'

'Don't use that word — unless you mean it,' she pleaded.

'Linda, I had no idea.'

'No, well I don't go blabbing it around. So have I got a date, or shall I be dining alone tonight?'

'Look, come inside.' He didn't want anyone coming down the corridor and seeing them like this. But once she was in he said firmly, 'Linda, I'm old enough to be your Dad.'

'What does that matter? I love you Tom. Them words don't come easy to me.'

'You're behaving like a silly infatuated schoolgirl . . .'

'Oh yeah, that's what you think.'

'What I *know*. You'll get over it.'

'Don't be too sure.'

'You're a very nice kid Linda . . .'

'Kid? Is that all I am to you? What do I have to do? Bleat like a nanny goat to get attention?'

'You've got your whole life in front of you . . .' he said lamely.

'The old story. Then I want to spend "my whole life" with you.'

'You're imagining it.'

'Do you really believe that?' she demanded indignantly. 'Look at me. I can't sleep at night for thinking about you. I can't eat. I can't concentrate on anything. All I want is to see you, be with you.'

'Then you're being foolish — and you're wasting my time.'

Defeated she opened the door, but she turned and looked at him again. She drew a long breath that might have been a sob.

'Then I don't know how I'm going to remain on this ship . . .'

When she had gone he remained sitting for a long time, feeling rotten. Then he got up and went along to the bar. He'd promised Marion to meet her there about now, but he also felt very much in need of a drink.

'I've just been propositioned,' he told Marion heavily. 'Linda, sitting in my cabin, looking very Piccadilly and doing the undying love number.'

'Be careful.'

'I will ma'am,' he grinned at her. 'I get the feeling I'm reporting to the headmistress.'

'Well you are love.'

'It must give you a great sense of power, owning all this.'

'You buttering me up Tom?'

'Would I do a thing like that?'

'It pays to know whose side people are on. Only a saint or a madman can do without friends.'

'And you're neither,' he said with a grin.

'I hope not. Still carrying a torch for Susan?'

'How did —?' taken by surprise by her sudden change of subject he betrayed himself. 'I'm wasting my time,' he sighed.

'I could've told you that.'

'I like to find things out for myself.'

'That's what I'd hoped you'd say. So *will* you — find things out?'

He shrugged. 'You're the chess master and we're the pawns.'

'How would you like to be a mole instead?'

At the far end of the bar Jo and John were also huddled over drinks, talking in low voices.

'This contract — it's a big opportunity, right?' he said.

'The biggest,' she sighed dejectedly.

'I'm not stopping you Jo.'

'Oh yes you are. I know you don't mean to. But I'm split right down the middle. If I decide to take it, please come with me.'

'You make your own decision,' he said obstinately.

'How can I? You make it difficult.'

'Sorry love — not my intention. But I know where I fit.'

'You want to get back on those long voyages, don't you?'

'With nothing to keep me around Gothenburg now, yes I do.'

'You're right,' she agreed reluctantly. 'I really can't see you with a house and a garden and washing the car every Sunday.'

'Right.'

'You're leaving it all to me, aren't you?'

'Yes well — it's your life.'

'John — it's got to be worth a try — you and me.'

'Under different circumstances — maybe. But I don't see myself wandering around dressing rooms, doing the stage door stuff. And for heaven's sake, shows finish. I'll still be here. We're not kids — you know — everything has to happen yesterday.'

'No, we're not kids and I think I know what I want. Suppose I tell them to stuff their contract — and stay here with you?'

'Oh no you don't — I'm not taking that one on. You've spent your life waiting for — what do you call it — the big chance?'

'Yes.'

'And you junk that for me? Oh no love — it's not on . . .'

Kate was dressing herself with extra care. She had promised to meet Matt in about fifteen minutes, and Matt was worth a little care. She was not pleased to be interrupted by a visit from Marion.

'It's business Kate. Do you have time?'

'I'm off duty and about to go out,' Kate retorted.

'I'm talking about shares Kate. And therefore talking about your money. Now — have you got time?'

Kate pulled a face. 'Persuasive argument. Come in.'

She went on dressing while Marion sat on her bed and talked.

'You've been playing games with Jeremy Gates, and his backer's about to move. Have you made up your mind about which way you're going?'

'That's surely my business,' said Kate. 'And what I do with the shares that I own does not concern you.'

'Not me personally, no. But it concerns the way this company's going to operate in the future. And it therefore concerns us. George always looked to the percentage. Me too.'

'I think the future profitability of the company's pretty clear cut on this one,' said Kate. 'I've pushed my part of it up by twelve per cent.'

'And in a very short time. Congratulations.'

'So I reckon Gates' backers are pushing in the wrong direction.'

'Agreed.'

'Fair to assume then that the business you're talking about is, what do we do with Mr Gates?'

'Yes. He's an entrepreneur — not a company man. And I only want staff who are working for *me*.'

'That makes sense.'

'A golden handshake then? Offer him contract work when he's needed and no opposition from you on that?'

'None at all.'

'Good. For once we're working together in the company's interest.'

'It's where the power lies Marion that bothers me most.'

'You turned down your father's offer. Can I try one?'

'You can try. But anything you offer is going to have an expensive price tag on it, which I don't think I can afford.'

'A partnership?' said Marion simply.

'What?'

'We run the company together — you and I. I think we might make a good team, don't you?'

Kate let out a long breath. 'I've really got to hand it to you.'

'Well.'

'You've got a hell of a nerve.'

'Think about it seriously, Kate. Like it or not, we're both working for the same thing.'

'But not the way you operate.'

'Results are what matter. Haven't you learned that yet?'

'Don't try to teach me lessons,' said Kate furiously. 'You failed at that a long time ago. Or have you forgotten?'

'I don't forget a thing. You're being very stupid Kate.'

'That's exactly what you said to me when I was climbing the tree in the garden and I remember thinking then, "I'm not going to fall. Just to spite her, I'm not going to fall." And I didn't.'

Marion left without another word.

Matt was just finishing his final checks in the Engine Room when he collided with Joe Francis just coming off duty. One glance was enough to show Matt that Joe was drunk — bad enough at any time, inexcusable on duty. A second glance revealed the greasy marks that Joe's hands had left on Matt's white shirt.

'Look at that,' he said in fury.

'Couldn't help it mate,' said Joe indifferently.

'Like hell you couldn't. You've been drinking again. Get out of here. I want you back on duty in one hour.'

For answer Joe spat very deliberately onto Matt's shirt. In another second he was lifted almost off his feet.

'Do that again,' Matt hissed, 'and I'll . . .'

'You'll what?' Joe managed. 'You're all mouth and trousers, you.'

Slowly Matt put him down. 'No son. I'll have you on the car deck in the morning before they're up. Got me? *Before they're up.*'

'Oh that's easy, isn't it? You and your mates, very likely. And slammed in the brig for me trouble.'

'Just you and me mate,' said Matt, with meaning.

Chapter 21

Kate could not say at precisely what point Jeremy Gates had lost her support. For so long now, it seemed, she had been planning to vote with him on condition that he allowed her a place on the management team. Yet in her conversation with Marion she had dismissed him within a few moments. Through the long sleepless night that followed she went back to her own words again and again — 'Gates' backers are pushing in the wrong direction'. In that one sentence she had turned her back on all her own plans.

Why? Was it really because she would never forgive him for his last remark to her in the meeting with Alan Lansing — that her father had loved Marion more than herself? Or did it go back further to her instinctive realisation that this was not a man to be trusted, and therefore not a man to throw in her lot with? Or was it simply the discovery that the five per cent shares belonged to John, who would almost certainly use them to vote with Marion, and therefore Gates was a loser? Or was it a combination of all three? She would never know now.

Whatever the reason, she was now totally dependent on Marion for her position with the company. Marion had offered her a partnership, and Kate, with splendid illogic, had thrown it back in her face. She groaned as she turned over again and again.

What stared her in the face was the necessity of going to Marion and telling her that she had changed her mind. She would get her chance the following morning when the ship docked at Amsterdam. Marion had called another meeting, to take place in a hotel suite that she had booked. It would be between John, Kate, Lansing and herself, and would concern itself with the running of the company generally, and John's ship in particular. At some point Kate knew she was going to have to admit to Marion that she'd made a hasty decision, and this was as good a time as any.

She groaned again.

'So we're agreed gentlemen,' Marion said briskly. 'The passenger side of the operation is working well and will be helped by heavier discounts on the advance block booking scheme.'

The meeting had been underway for half an hour, and Marion was chairing it as though she had been doing nothing else all her life. Kate had still not arrived, but she had not been invited to the early part, which concerned the running of the company generally. That was the price of having turned down a partnership.

John and Alan nodded their assent to Marion's conclusions about the passenger side, and she went on, 'That still leaves a fairly large question over the way we handle our freight.'

'It's a continuing problem Marion,' said John. 'With the sort of mixed loads that we shift, space is bound to be lost.'

'Even so, I feel we can do better John.'

'You're thinking of changing the type of freight?'

'You'd lose a lot of friends that way,' said Alan.

'Certainly would,' John agreed. 'And I don't fancy pigs and geese running amok on my car deck.'

She gave him a faint smile. 'Well we'll keep them on the bridge then John. But we certainly need to rationalise the freight side of the operation and offer strong inducements to the shippers whose cargo stacks most economically.'

'No problem Marion,' said Alan.

'That goes for the entire line,' she told him.

'I'll check through it.'

'Create a new department if necessary. If we want to keep the company's profit running at least alongside inflation, every square inch has got to earn its keep.' She looked round, 'Kate should surely be here by now.'

'You said half past Marion,' said John. 'It's not quite, but I'll go down and check.'

He met Kate just coming into the hotel reception.

'I hope you're on your toes Kate. I think our Marion is a morning person.'

'I'm glad to hear it. That means she's possibly at a disadvantage after three o'clock.'

'I wouldn't count on it. She's been going through the accounts all morning with a magnifying glass. You could do worse than consider that partnership.'

'She told you about it?' said Kate, annoyed.

'She mentioned it in passing.'

'And now you're expressing your opinion on the matter?' Her tone warned him not to.

'Not an opinion, Kate. Advice.'

'Your advice has been noted, Captain.'

'Noted and ignored I think,' he said crossly.

'It's my decision. We don't want to keep them waiting, do we?'

Upstairs the courtesies were performed as quickly as possible, coffee was dispensed, and then they were all sitting round the table.

'We've covered the freighting side of the operation,' said Marion, 'and Alan will be circulating copies, so you can catch up later. Alan?'

'On your ship in particular Kate,' Alan took up the theme, 'passenger profit is rising fast. That situation does not obtain on other vessels. So . . .' he made a gesture that indicated the credit was hers.

'I think it's simply a matter of a fresh eye,' said Kate, 'and I've summarised the sort of things I've done here.' She produced sheets of typed paper from her bag. These she handed to Alan, who distributed copies to Marion and John.

'And all this was going on under my nose,' said John admiringly when he had finished reading. 'I knew the food was better.'

'Very concise Kate,' said Marion. 'And very good.'

'Yes,' said Alan. 'Certainly shows how you've achieved that profit increase. May I use this as a briefing document for the rest of the line?'

The compliment was wasted. Kate merely said formally, 'I'm an employee. There's nothing to stop you.'

'Thank you,' said Marion. 'The only thing not shown here is proposals for future planning.'

'Then I misunderstood,' said Kate, still in the same formal tone. 'I thought you asked for a report, not plans.'

With difficulty Marion kept her temper. John barely repressed a grin.

'Absolutely right Kate,' said Alan hurriedly. 'But since you've an obvious grasp of your side of the operation, might we ask your advice?'

'Of course Alan,' Kate said with perfect politeness. 'But I didn't want to seem too pushy.'

'Yes Kate,' said John. 'That would be very unlike you.'

This time it was Kate's turn to grin.

It was Sandy who was the first to see Joe in his battered state, staggering towards his cabin.

'Joe, whatever's happened love?' She ran to him.

'Nothing girl,' he said through swollen lips. 'Just looking for a bit of a wash.'

'Who was it? Come on Joe. No games between you and me now. Tell me.'

'Matt Taylor.'

'Oh good God — he's twice your size.'

'Should've made it easier,' he mumbled. 'You can work with your head on the tall ones.'

'But you didn't?'

'No, he's too damn good.'

'How did it happen?'

'Look love, forget it will you? Just let me get cleaned up.'

He let her follow him into his cabin, and when he had showered she set to work repairing his face.

'Made a bit of a mess, didn't he?' he managed to say. 'Still, there'll be another time.'

'No there won't Joe. You leave him alone. What do you go and rile him for in the first place?'

'I didn't rile him girl,' he said indignantly.

'C'mon Joe. I didn't just come down from the trees. And I know you and your drink.'

He sat in silence for a moment, enjoying her attentions. After a while he said, 'I think I could have him for this. Well I mean . . . officer striking a rating . . . definitely out of order, and I've got proof.'

She stopped dabbing at his face and stared at him. 'Joe, are you being serious? It's a load of rubbish. You're lucky he didn't kill you.'

'Yeah, I suppose,' he said reluctantly. 'But I do think I know how to handle it next time.'

'Yes all right Joe. Now I know you're joking.'

'That's right, love,' he smiled at her painfully.

She smiled back. 'You're a lovely little feller when you're like this,' she said. 'It's just when . . .'

'Yes, I know,' he couldn't look at her any more.

'So what you — we — gonna do?' she said, turning his face gently towards her again.

'That's nice love,' he said.

'What?'

'"We".'

'We,' she confirmed.

'I've tried hard love, honest I have,' he said.

'It isn't good enough, is it?' she reproved him.

'I just can't leave the booze alone.'

'There's no such thing as "can't".'

'I dunno what gets into me.'

'Gremlins Joe, that's what. You know what I was thinking?'

'What?' he looked at her hopefully.

'You need a new interest in life.'

'I've got one, haven't I' he said, daring. 'You.'

'But if we were married . . . new responsibilities, new married quarters. A complete change for you. Take your mind off the bottle.'

He stared at her. 'Married?' he seemed to be trying the word for size.

'Yeah. The Captain could perform the ceremony.'

Suddenly he was scared. The reversal in his fortunes was too abrupt for him.

'I dunno love,' he floundered.

'You want to marry me, don't you?'

'Suppose.'

'You don't sound very enthusiastic.'

'I thought we'd have a little time to get used to each other . . .' he hedged.

'But I am used to you Joe.'

'Yeah, well, that's as maybe . . .'

'It's going to happen sooner or later, isn't it?' she urged.

'Suppose it is.'

'Then why not sooner? C'mon Joe — what do you say?'

Slowly he nodded, while she blinked back the tears, praying that he would not see them, and understand too well that she was rushing ahead to a place where regrets would be in vain.

'. . .and we'd do well to make a note of that one too,' Marion concluded.

The other three were all scribbling furiously, trying to keep up with the flow of her instructions. Marion had got into the administrator's seat with a vengeance.

'Sorry, I missed it,' said John, flexing his fingers painfully.

'Then ask Kate on the way back to the ship,' Marion told him 'She didn't.'

'Then this summarises all the ideas that are to be discussed at our next meeting?' said Alan Lansing.

'That's it,' said Marion. 'And remember, any final decisions are naturally mine.'

'Of course Marion,' said John hurriedly. 'No one's disputing that.'

'Aren't they?' Kate muttered just loud enough to be heard.

Marion ignored her. 'Well, we've covered a lot of ground this morning. I think the rest can wait till another time.'

'What rest?' said John in faint alarm. 'You mean there's more?'

'I don't think Marion's even started — have you?' said Kate with a touch of acid.

'We're a large organisation,' said Marion, 'and it's my intention to look into every corner of it — and that's going to take quite a time.'

'Hope the corners aren't too full of dust,' said Kate drily.

'Well if they are dear I haven't forgotten how to use a brush.'

The two men grinned faintly at each other, both enjoying this exchange. John rose to his feet.

'Well, it's been quite a morning,' he said. 'Anyone fancy a drink?'

'Yes please,' said Kate.

'Marion? Alan?'

'No thanks John,' said Marion. 'I've still got some personal stuff to go through with Alan.'

'Oh have you?' said Alan. 'Okay. Maybe I'll catch up with you two later.'

When John and Kate had gone, Alan looked hard at her.

'You took us all by surprise this morning, didn't you?' he said.

'Good. That's the advantage of attack.'

'You make it sound like a war campaign. I just hope there aren't too many casualties.'

'Alan, are you having doubts?'

'About you? Never.'

'Good. I'd hate to lose you.'

'You won't. It's far too interesting here. And —' he dropped into an exaggerated Uncle Tom accent, '— you're *mah* first Boss-lady.'

'Idiot,' she grinned at him.

'No, it's good news for me Marion. Fresh ground, new challanges, different attitudes — also I admired what your husband achieved . . .'

'. . . and what I intend to improve on.'

Marion would have been satisfied if she could have heard the first words between John and Kate in the hotel bar below.

'I feel like a sponge that's been wrung dry,' said John, exhausted.

'She certainly knows how to crack the whip,' Kate agreed.

'You must admire the energy.'

'Oh I wouldn't go as far as that. Early enthusiasm has a habit of fading.'

'Now Kate, you don't believe that. Marion knows her stuff.'

'Well if she continues to work at this pace she'll wear out in a week.'

'Wishful thinking?' he ribbed her.

'Common sense,' she said shortly.

'Is it so difficult to step down?'

'It isn't a question of that John. It should be *my* finger on the "go" button.'

'But it isn't.'

'Not yet,' she looked up to see Alan approaching. 'Ah, the last survivor.'

'Is Marion coming down?' asked John.

Alan did a double-take. 'Jeez, I didn't ask. I'll go back up.'

'No,' said John. 'Get yourself a drink. I'll go.'

When they were alone, Kate said, 'You're a long way from home, Alan.'

'Not so,' he insisted. 'I can close my eyes and I'm right back in Manhattan — but I don't need to close my eyes very often. I've got very used to making a home where I am. It suits me. How's it with you?'

'You need to ask?'

'You are contesting the Will?'

'It's in the pipeline.'

'Good.'

'You changing your spots already?' she asked, eyebrows raised.

'No ma'am. But my sympathies are another matter. And I'm sorry, but you're gonna lose.'

'Everyone seems so sure of that. Except my solicitor.'

He regarded her quizzically. 'Odd about solicitors. They're always very supportive — when cheques are being signed.'

'You got any better ideas?'

'If I had, I'm afraid they wouldn't be on offer.'

'Ah, the loyal retainer.'

'Yes Kate — that's exactly what I am.'

Upstairs John was having a difficult time with Marion.

'Just for a minute love,' he pleaded. 'I think it would be a good idea if you two could spend a bit of time together not snarling at each other — and an hotel bar might be the place to start.'

'I'm not good at lunchtime drinks John.'

'Well then, have a tonic water.'

'All right. If I can finish up here I'll come down.'

'Good. Try not to be too long, because I've got a few phone calls to catch up on before I go back on board.'

'Trouble?' she was sympathetic at once.

'Well you know, a few odds and ends to tie up. Usual divorce stuff. Who has what, who wants what.'

'I'm sorry.'

'Got to be done though. At first, I thought I'd give her.the lot. I didn't care. She'd taken the only things that meant anything to me. My kids. Then I began to feel, why the hell should she have everything?'

'That's normal.'

'So here I am, rowing over tea towels and garden furniture — sixteen years of marriage reduced to that. Not worth it, is it?'

Kate was alone in the bar when they went down together. John ordered a tonic water for Marion and looked at Kate's orange juice.

'Boozy pair you two,' he said with slightly forced geniality. 'You will excuse me, won't you? I've got to get a call through to Gothenburg. And that's not going to be easy. See you both back on the ship.'

When he had gone the two women looked at each other. Both knew roughly why they had been left alone in this heavy-handed manner.

'I'm reconsidering your offer,' said Kate at last.

'It isn't like you to change your mind.'

Kate shrugged. 'I'm told it's a woman's privilege — but I don't believe that.'

'Snap decisions should be adhered to,' said Marion quietly.

'Was it a snap decision?'

'You tell me Kate.'

'What?' Kate opened her eyes wide.

'You gave me your answer earlier. I took you at your word.'

Kate stared at her, thunderstruck. 'Do you enjoy trying to humiliate me? Does it give you some kind of thrill?'

'Don't be silly. I made you a perfectly reasonable offer which you declined in no uncertain fashion.'

'So you're determined to treat me like a child.'

'Certainly. If you continue to behave like one. It's up to you dear.'

Within a short time Marion had managed to make her influence felt throughout the company. There were those who appreciated it, and those who didn't. Sophie was one of the ones that did.

'I rather like this new broom,' she commented to Parker when he entered the Felixstowe head office that morning.

'What are you talking about and where's my coffee?' he growled.

'I've got a sense that things are going to be moving for me,' she mused.

'My coffee, love.'

'I've got a couple of ideas,' she offered. 'Shall we talk them through?'

'No. Will you please get my coffee, Sophie?'

'You don't want to discuss them?' she said very deliberately, as if she was trying to get something clear.

'That's right. If you've got ideas put 'em in the staff suggestion box . . . and get my coffee.'

'Certainly Arthur darling.'

It was perhaps as well for Parker that he did not see the look she gave him before she left.

'Why did you want to see me here of all places?' said Susan wretchedly. 'After last time . . .'

She looked round at Charles's cabin where he had insisted on bringing her. For her it was still alive with the memory of their last appalling meeting.

'Last time I'm afraid I behaved very badly towards you and . . .'

'Badly?' she interrupted him with scorn. 'That's one way of putting it. I could give you other expressions . . .'

'Let me finish,' he begged. 'I was angry, upset . . .'

'I only wanted to make you happy,' she said tearfully. 'I thought . . .'

'Susan, will you let me apologise in my own way?'

She stared. 'You're apologising?'

'If you'll let me get a blasted word out, yes, I'm apologising,' he snapped.

'Oh.'

'Your news caught me at a bad time, that's all. I'm delighted, really I am. It'll be all right, Susan. We'll sort something out between us, won't we?

He put his arms round her and gave her a gentle hug. Her head was bent, so he could not see that her face was still troubled.

Half an hour later, while going about his duties on the bridge, he took the chance to ask Tom Kelly.

'Any truth in these stories about the battle of the car deck?'

'Oh it's going round is it?' said Tom resignedly.

'Just that Matt sorted out Joe Francis in no uncertain fashion.'

'Yes it's true,' Tom admitted. 'And a bit dodgy. I dunno why Matt can't look after his temper.'

'It's one of those things we must not do,' said Charles piously. 'And he knows it. Is Francis making a fuss?'

'No I don't think so. I don't think he will. They're out of the same pod those two. Law of the cockney jungle. It's just like the nick — you don't blab.'

'Probably right. But I don't like this ship being equated with Wormwood Scrubs.'

'Agreed. But you try talking to Matt,' said Tom, who had tried just that an hour earlier, and been sorry for it. 'I got a wet towel slung in my face when I tried.'

It wasn't until Peter saw Linda sitting alone at the bar, with half a pint of Guinness in front of her, and a cleaners' trolley that she should have been wheeling standing nearby, that he realised just how difficult he'd made life for himself.

He'd been more relieved than sorry when she'd told him of the failure of the plan against Tony. In fact he'd regretted the mad idea as soon as the words were out, and if Linda hadn't dashed off and insisted on doing it that very night he'd have stopped her before she started. When he heard how she'd been thwarted he felt as though someone had stopped him falling down a manhole at the last minute. His gratitude was doubled when Linda made it plain that she'd kept his name a secret, and that she intended to keep on doing so.

He had no doubt that Linda meant every word of it. But just the same, he wished it wasn't his duty to reprimand her now. It could be awkward for him if she turned nasty.

'You're on duty aren't you?' he said, crossing over to her.

'So what?'

'Well, if you need me to remind you — you don't drink on duty and I've had four complaints from passengers about unserviced cabins. And we're only three hours out.'

She stared at him out of miserable eyes. 'Well that's tough mate. 'Cos I'm having me break. Union says fifteen minutes every four hours. So you get your clock out.'

Despite his fears his temper began to rise. 'Do you know what I am?'

'Oh yes mate — everybody knows that,' she jeered.

'All right — do you want a report made? Or shall I get Miss Laker?'

'You can make a report. You can get Miss Laker — and anyone else you like. I don't give a damn mate.'

She got up and moved out of the bar, leaving him there alone. He stared at the trolley, which someone had to move. Quite simply he lacked the courage to go after her and order her back.

'I'm looking for Matt,' said Kate. 'Any idea where he is?'

'Bathing his bruises I reckon,' Charles told her.

'What are you talking about?' said Kate, who had not heard about the fight on the car deck.

'Ask him. It's definitely not my business.'

'Oh Charles,' she stopped him as he was about to go. 'I've heard the news.'

'Sorry?'

'About Susan. It's wonderful.'

'Yes, isn't it?' he said, without enthusiasm.

'Congratulations then. Bit of a surprise though,' she continued, watching his face. 'She told me she couldn't have children. Must have found a smashing doctor. See you later.'

He stared after her, then wheeled abruptly and went in search of Susan. He was due on the bridge at any moment but this conversation wouldn't wait. He found her and took her to his cabin, where a few brief questions established that Kate had been right.

'So you were lying?' he said at last, torn between rage and disgust.

'Yes,' she said in a small voice.

'There's nothing more to be said, is there?'

'I did it for you — for us,' she pleaded.

He stared at her in blank amazement. What the hell did she think she was doing for him?

'You make me very angry Susan,' he said at last.

'I love you Charles.'

'Then you have a strange way of showing it. Now get out before I do something I'll regret.'

'Charles . . .'

'*Don't* make excuses,' he yelled. 'Just go before I lose my temper.'

'You won't understand, will you?'

'There is nothing to understand. You just lied to me.'

'I wanted to give you so much.'

'Go away Susan.'

She left, dejected, and he began very slowly and methodically to bang his head against the wall.

It was late and Parker was just packing up ready to go home when

Sophie entered bearing a bottle of champagne in one hand, and two glasses in the other.

'Celebrating?' he asked.

'Yes, and with good reason. It's all thanks to you darling.'

'What?' A little stab of alarm hit him.

'Well you did tell me what to do with my suggestions, didn't you? And now I've got an office upstairs.'

'Oh no you haven't,' he said at once. 'Nothing happens here unless I say so.'

'Mrs Terson said so. I've got my own department Arthur. Set up specially to investigate the way the company handles its freight.'

'You're in charge of it?' he said in disbelief.

'All by myself.'

He decided to play safe. 'All right love. Congratulations. Won't make any difference to us, will it?' He nibbled her ear to emphasise his meaning.

'Can't see why,' she assured him. 'Well, not yet.'

'Good. Do you fancy a bit of — er —?'

'Yes, I do.' She warded him off as he advanced. 'But not here my love. My office — it's much more comfortable. And much bigger.'

He wilted.

'What's wrong?' said Matt, when Kate had thrown the third crumpled piece of paper away from her in disgust. They were in her office.

'It's getting to me Matt. This ship, the line, everything. I'm no match for it any more.'

'Don't say that,' he said in alarm. 'Blimey, if *you* crumble, what happens to the rest of us?'

'Maybe I've just been blinkered for too long, I don't know. You know those kind of days — it just piles on top of you, memories, failures, missed opportunities . . . and now you.'

'Me?' he said, bewildered. 'Didn't think I was a missed opportunity.'

'Don't you see? All my relationships have failed. Something in me wants to destroy the best things in my life . . .' She had begun to cry, ' . . . and you're one of the best things.'

He moved round the desk and put his arms round her.

'Hey c'mon Kate, don't cry.'

'I'm sorry,' she sniffed.

'Tell you what, finish here and I'll take you for a stroll round the promenade, have a go on the dodgems, take in a few side-shows — what d'you say to that?'

'Okay.'

'Good girl.'

As they strolled on the deck she found herself telling him about the ship in the bottle. It was an image that recurred to her frequently these days.

'Did you ever get it out?' he asked.

'Yes, but it was never the same, there in my hand. I couldn't hold it as close as when the glass had been between my eye and it. I'd achieved what I wanted — but I ruined something in the process.'

'Sounds like me,' he reflected. 'Can't leave well enough alone. That's what Betty used to say.'

'Betty?'

'My ex-bird.'

'What happened to her?'

'Married someone else. Even though it was my kid she was carrying.'

'Matt — I didn't know.'

'Yeah well, never told anyone,' he was looking down into the water. 'She needed a nine-to-five man and I couldn't give her that. Not with all this,' he indicated the ship. 'So here we are — you and me.'

'Yes,' she said contentedly.

'And I'll tell you something else sweetheart,' he said, slipping his arm round her. 'This isn't bad.'

She snuggled against him. 'You're a lovely man, Matt Taylor.'

For Charles Woodhouse the day had one final nasty surprise — although surprise was perhaps hardly the word for it. John had returned from his meeting with Alan Lansing in a suspiciously cheerful mood, and since then there had been no sign of any move to displace him — and it was beginning to dawn on Charles that his plans had failed. He did not believe it as final, however, until tonight, when he stepped onto the bridge to start his watch.

'Everything okay?' he asked, routinely.

'Fine,' said John. 'Looking forward to a bit of shut-eye.'

'Then it's all yours,' said Charles. 'I'll take over here.'

'Just for a while,' said John.

'Pardon?'

'Your duty watch— *that's* all you'll take over.'

As their eyes met, Charles knew that he had lost.

'Point taken,' he said gruffly.

'Good,' said John. 'I'm not ready to step down — for anyone — younger man or not.'

'Yes, Captain.'

'Goodnight.'

'Goodnight — sir.'

There was nothing more to be said.

It had been a rough day, and the last thing Kate wanted was to return to her cabin and find Marion sitting there.

'Marion, like it or not, these quarters are private. I'm entitled to that at least.'

'I've come to make an apology.'

'Apology?'

'For deliberately making you angry the other day. It wasn't necessary — and I'm sorry.'

'Think nothing of it,' Kate said icily.

'You're your father's daughter all right. I've heard him say that in exactly the same tone.'

'You just succeeded in ruining my day.'

'Blood and water dear. That's a fact you can't run away from.'

'Who's running?' Kate dropped down wearily on the bed.

'You. Your feet haven't touched the ground since this business started.'

'And that champagne's going to bring me down to earth?' Kate had just seen the ice bucket next to Marion.

'I thought it worth a try. I think it's time for us both to sit down and start behaving like the civilised people I know we both are.'

'All right. What are we drinking to?'

'The one thing we've got totally in common.'

There was a knock on the door. It was John.

'Sorry to trouble you Kate. Fancied a spot of company. Can you spare five minutes?'

'If I can bring a friend,' said Kate, conscious of irony.

'Of course.'

'Come on Marion,' said Kate. 'The party's moving.'

While Marion was gathering up the ice bucket John was knocking on Matt's door.

'Fancy a jar, Matt?'

'You know me,' came the voice from inside.

In John's cabin they found another champagne bucket on the table.

'Snap,' said Marion when she saw it.

'Where did that come from?' said John, seeing hers.

'We were starting our own celebration,' said Kate. 'What's yours for?'

'Oh, a couple of things that I thought deserved a few bubbles.'

'It's your birthday,' said Marion at once.

'How d'you know?'

'I didn't. I was being silly. Is it?'

'Yes it is.' There was a chorus of happy birthdays. 'Thank you. The other celebration isn't quite so regular. My divorce papers are through.' There was an uncertain silence. 'Come on. I'm celebrating. You can too.'

'If you say so Captain,' said Matt.

'And I want to say thank you. It's been pretty rough for quite a while, and all of you have let me know what friends are about. Kate, Marion, Matt — thank you.'

As they all raised their glasses his mind went to Jo, whom he would have liked to have here this minute. Jo, who had told him firmly only half an hour ago, that she refused to make any decision without his help. Whether he liked it or not he would have to be part of it. He liked it.

What the decision they would make together would be, he did not yet know. But if she went to London, there was always afterwards for them both. Even at their age, there was time. In fact, sometimes it seemed that the older you got the more time there was.

He would have had Jo to join the party if she had not been singing in the night-club right this minute. But on second thoughts he was glad she was not here. Himself and Jo, Matt and Kate, that would have left Marion the odd one out, cruelly reminded of her loss just when everything was going well for everyone else. He met Marion's eyes and raised his glass to her. She gazed back at him. Her eyes glistened but her chin was lifted bravely.

Kate sipped at her champagne, and pulled a face. It was flat. Then she looked up and caught Matt's eye. He was smiling at her in a way that made her heart turn over, and almost imperceptibly he jerked his head towards the door. She shook her head, but her eyes said 'Later', and they exchanged the warm sweet glance of people who share a secret.

She had Matt, and it seemed she was to have her partnership in the company too. Perhaps the champagne wasn't so flat after all.